He leaned back against the squ___, ___ disconcerting eyes roving her person. "So, we are on the North Road. Let me guess, we are headed to Scotland? I am supposed to be whisking you off to Gretna Green."

"What a clever man you are. Who would have ever guessed it after your stupid behavior this past Season?"

His smile was one of utter unconcern.

"Don't worry, my lord, we won't actually get there. I have even less interest in marrying *you* than you do in marrying me."

"I doubt that."

Eva glowered at him. "If that is true, then you'd better do exactly as I say and don't draw attention to your predicament. If you behave sensibly, we can all get out of this without leg shackles of either the marital *or* legal sort."

Also by Minerva Spencer

Dangerous

Barbarous

Scandalous

Notorious

And read more Minerva Spencer in

The Arrangement

Outrageous

Minerva Spencer

KENSINGTON
PUBLISHING CORP.

www.kensingtonbooks.com

KENSINGTON BOOKS are published by

Kensington Publishing Corp.
119 West 40th Street
New York, NY 10018

ISBN-13: 978-1-4967-3286-6 (ebook)
ISBN-10: 1-4967-3286-3 (ebook)

ISBN-13: 978-1-4967-3285-9
ISBN-10: 1-4967-3285-5
First Kensington Trade Paperback Printing: July 2021

10 9 8 7 6 5 4 3 2 1

Printed in the United States of America

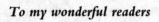

To my wonderful readers

Acknowledgments

Many thanks to my wonderful editor, Alicia Condon, who is lovely in every way. Also a huge thanks to all the folks at Kensington who work so amazingly hard to get my books out into the world. A special thanks to Susie Douglas, MLitt. QG. of Borders Ancestry, for her information about Coldstream, Scotland, and irregular border marriages.

Chapter 1

London, 1816

Godric Fleming, Earl of Visel, vowed to kill his cousin Rowland when he got his hands on him.

He strode down the alley, feeling like a fool as his ridiculous cape billowed out behind him as if he were some corsair. Which was, of course, exactly how he was dressed—or at least the English public's perception of a corsair.

When he reached the alley entrance he gaped. "Good God."

The street in front of the Duke of Richland's house was crammed with dozens, maybe even hundreds, of carriages. No wonder Rowland hadn't been waiting for Godric near the duke's garden gate as they'd planned.

Godric considered the mob of unmoving carriages, his mind as chaotic as the scene before him. Perhaps this mess was a sign he should call off his ill-advised plan? Perhaps there was still time to—

"Lord Visel?"

Godric spun around to find a huge boy dressed like a stable lad.

"Who the devil are you?"

"Mr. Rowland sent me to tell you the carriage is waitin' at the back entrance, my lord." The young giant hesitated. "Mr. Rowland said he needed to talk to you before taking the woman."

Godric clenched his jaws so tightly his head throbbed; trust that idiot Rowland to bring in even *more* conspirators. It was bad enough the two of them were planning to kidnap the woman—now this *boy* was part of the plan? Who else had the fool told? The bloody *Times*?

"No." He shook his head. No, he would not do it. He *could* not do it.

"My lord?" the boy asked, his brow furrowed in confusion.

"Come along," Godric said, ignoring the lad's question and marching toward the other end of the alley.

The oddest sensation filled his body as he walked, as if he were emerging from a dense fog, his head clearing with each step and his vision shifting slowly into focus. For the first time in months—hell, over a *year*—he could see. And what he saw was bloody terrifying.

Godric stumbled and the air whooshed out of his lungs at the enormity of what he had almost done.

Good God! What the devil have I been thinking?

You haven't been thinking, Godric old boy, his long-absent conscience pointed out.

No, he hadn't. Why the *hell* had it taken him so long to realize he was behaving like a bloody lunatic? And why had he only come to his senses *now*—after scheming and planning and preparing for weeks?

Does it matter why you've seen the disaster you've been courting, Godric? Just be grateful that you have—before it was too late.

Perhaps speaking to his prospective kidnap victim—Drusilla Marlington—earlier in the evening had begun to clear the madness from his mind? The young woman had done nothing to him—they hardly even knew each other—and yet he'd humiliated her and forced her into a marriage with a man who'd been courting another woman.

And when her unwanted marriage had—against all odds— showed signs of becoming a love match? Well, then Godric had decided to use her *again* to get to the man she'd married: Gabriel Marlington.

To be perfectly honest, her husband had done nothing to him, either. Yet all Godric had done since returning home to Britain was harass the man.

I've been telling you this for months, the dry voice in his head observed.

"Blast and damn," Godric cursed under his breath. Sod it all to hell; this was bloody lunacy.

He would get in the carriage, go home, and try to forget these past few months of insanity.

The relief that assailed him at the thought almost drove him to his knees.

No doubt he'd have a devil of a time with his cousin Rowland—a man so desperate for funds he'd ransom his own grandmother—but Godric did not doubt he could handle the little worm.

The hired carriage waited at the end of the alley, the interior darker than the night. Godric yanked open the door.

"We're going," he said to the figure sitting on the back-facing bench. "I won't—"

Something hard slammed into the back of his head. His vision exploded with red-hot pain and he staggered forward. "Wha—"

"Push him in, James!"

Big hands grabbed his shoulders and shoved.

Godric went headfirst into the carriage, turning his head just in time to avoid landing on his face and breaking his nose. Even so, the pain from the impact was so intense it was nauseating and his stomach cramped, preparing to void itself. He gritted his teeth to keep back the flood of bile.

His aggressor rolled him onto his back and then folded his legs up against his chest. A face lowered over Godric's: huge blue-violet eyes creased in a frown, red lips parted, a lock of silky black hair . . .

He blinked, "Y-you—"

"Hallo, Lord Visel."

Whoever was holding his ankles gave him a shove and his head struck the opposite door. The last thing he heard was, "He's out cold, James, but you'd best tie his hands."

* * *

Eva de Courtney, middle and least-favored daughter of the Marquess of Exley, worried her lip as she looked at the man who lay crumpled up on the carriage floor.

"Well, here he is. Now what do you want to do with him, my lady?" James had insisted on trading places with her and was jammed into the back-facing seat, his expression mulish, his huge arms crossed over his chest.

"You know what I want to do."

For such a large man, he could make the most piteous sounds. "Oh, Lady Eva. Are you sure you wouldn't—"

"I'm quite sure."

"But you don't know what I was going to say."

"I've been able to read your mind since we were both old enough to crawl, James Brewster. You were about to try and talk me out of my plan. Yet again."

Eva squinted down at the earl and used the toe of her boot to nudge the colorful turban off Lord Visel's head. "Would you look at that?" she said.

James bent to look. "What?"

"The bugger even dyed his hair." She cut her groom and oldest friend a quick look. "If that doesn't convince you he was up to dastardly deeds, then I don't know what will."

"I never said he wasn't up to something, my lady—I *know* he was. I just don't think this is the only way to handle it—certainly not the *best* way to handle it."

Eva made the dismissive hissing sound she'd picked up from her stepmamma, Lady Euphemia Exley. She thought the sound was a perfect response to most of the dunderheaded things men insisted on saying.

"Well, it's too late to argue about it or change our minds now. He saw me, so we can hardly just drop him at his lodgings as if nothing happened. He's sure to set the constables on us." *Or worse, my father.*

James chewed this over while the two of them gazed at Lord Visel's unconscious form.

"We could always cut his throat and dump him in a ditch."

"My *lady!*" His eyes were as round as saucers.

Eva laughed. "Lord, James—you've lost your sense of humor entirely. Of course I wouldn't actually *kill* him." *No matter how much he might deserve such a fate.*

"Perhaps we should sit him up, my lady? He's an earl, after all. I think we should get him off the—"

"No. He's fine where he is," Eva said. "I checked his breathing; he's alive." Visel's head would ache like the dickens when he woke up, but that was the least his wretched behavior merited.

James flung himself against the seat back, his abrupt movements causing the entire carriage to jostle. "Lord Exley will skin the hide right offa me."

"My father will never find out, James. We'll only be up north a week at the most—we can rent hacks for the ride back and make the journey in a fraction of the time."

"What if the marquess checks on you before we return?"

"Why would he? He believes I am going to join my sister at Lady Repton's country house, but Melissa and Lady Repton aren't expecting me to visit for at least two more weeks. It's perfect."

"A perfect disaster," James muttered.

"You worry too much. My father is so concerned with my stepmamma's delicate condition, he won't even recall my existence."

James made a skeptical noise but said nothing—probably because he knew it was true. Anyone with eyes in their head could see that her father worshipped his wife. Eva didn't blame him; she loved her stepmamma, too.

"We can still change our minds about this, my lady. We could—"

"Don't fret, we'll be finished with Visel and back before anyone finds out anything. Besides, my father assigned you to me as my groom. Strictly speaking, your hide is *mine*, so you can always claim you were just obeying my orders." The carriage passed a streetlight and illuminated his offended expression, and Eva laughed.

James didn't join her. Instead, he shivered. "My hide is more likely to find itself in Newgate after we get caught. Cor, my lady, he's a bleeding duke's heir."

"We won't get caught."

"Ha!"

"I'm telling you, my father shall never know. Melissa is an indifferent letter-writer and we should have at least two weeks, but probably longer. In the meantime, we will have plenty of opportunity to persuade his deranged lordship to leave my brother alone."

"What if he doesn't want to be persuaded?"

Eva had considered that, too. "Then you shall stay with him."

"And how will *you* get back to London?"

"I can hire a chaise and somebody to attend me if you are so concerned."

"What if Lord Visel says something to your father after we let him go? I don't see a man like him taking kidnapping without a fuss."

"Oh come, James. Do you think he would ever admit that a mere *girl*, and a crazy one to boot, kidnapped him? He'd be the laughingstock of all London. Trust me, he'll be far more interested in keeping this quiet than we are. You'll see."

"How the devil do you know he'll do what you want, my lady?"

"Why, James, are you saying I lack the ability to be persuasive?" Eva laughed when he groaned. "You let me worry about Lord Visel. I trust the chaise will be waiting for us at the Swan?"

"Aye, already paid for it."

"And did you engage it under his lordship's name?"

James looked pained. "Yes, my lady."

Eva grinned and sat back, resting one booted foot on the earl's motionless body. She had no qualms about using him as a footstool. He'd tormented Gabriel relentlessly since the day he'd returned to England. He'd also said extremely uncharitable things about *her*. All in all, he'd behaved like a coxcomb toward most members of the *ton*, even though all of Britain had been prepared to receive him with open arms. And why not? He was exceedingly handsome, he was the Duke of Tyndale's heir, and he had a reputation for military bravery that was unparalleled. But Godric Fleming had ignored the *ton*'s adulation and appeared only interested in persecuting Eva's brother. There was something wrong with him; something very wrong, indeed.

And Eva should know because she counted herself as something of a Visel expert—although not by choice. She'd been at her third wretched ball of the wretched Season when he strolled in looking like an angel cast down to Earth. She'd been sitting with all the other wallflowers, watching the activities from a safe distance. Drusilla, her best friend and now her brother's wife, had been sitting beside her.

Dru hadn't notice Visel's entrance because she had eyes only for Gabe.

Eva smirked to herself. Dru thought she'd hidden her infatuation, but Eva watched others so closely, sometimes she swore she could *hear* what they were thinking. She knew that her friend had fallen head-over-heels in love with Gabe the summer she'd first met him. Gabriel, of course, was a clueless clod-headed male who'd been too preoccupied with his mistresses and the beautiful Miss Lucinda Kittridge to pay poor Dru any mind. Well, except to taunt and tease her.

But they were married now, so all was well that ended well, in Eva's opinion. She had to give Visel credit for the marriage—if he'd not behaved like a buffoon, her brother never would have been forced to offer for Drusilla, which would have been a tragedy. Not that you could get Drusilla and Gabriel to admit that . . . yet. No, they were too stubborn to realize they were made for each other. Eva snorted at the foolishness of people in love.

They would sort out their problems in time. She gritted her teeth and prodded Visel's unconscious form with the heel of her boot. Yes, they would solve their problems if Lord Visel was not around to bother and meddle and interfere in their lives every ten minutes, which he couldn't seem to stop doing for some bizarre reason.

A low groan came from the floor.

"Er, Lady Eva . . ."

"Don't worry, James. You can hit him again if he comes around. He certainly deserves it."

It was James who groaned this time. "It don't matter how much he deserves hittin', my lady. It just don't do to be smacking earls over the head and—"

"Do you recall when Gabriel showed you how to shoot the pips out of a card?"

Silence met her question.

"Do you?"

"Well, yes."

"And how about the time Gabriel told your father you'd accompanied him to look at bloodstock rather than telling him the truth— that you'd gone to see a mill and became so ill on hard cider I had to pay two postilions to lift you into the carriage?" James's father was the stable master at her father's country estate and a man feared almost as much as his master, the marquess.

"But it was *you* that made me go to that mill, my lady. And it was *you* that kept buyin' me cider."

Details, details. "That isn't the point, James," she said in her best lady-of-the-manor tone. "The point is, Gabriel has been a good friend to you on many occasions. Now it is time we do something for *him*. If we don't get this man"—she gave Visel a hard shove— "away from Gabriel, Visel will end up either killing him or making Gabe kill *him*. And then my brother shall have to flee to the Continent and take up gambling to survive."

As they passed below a streetlamp she saw James scratch his head. "Now why would he have to become a Captain Sharp when he has plenty of money? And his new wife is bloody *rolling*—"

James was *so* literal. "Yes, yes, yes. All right, so he shan't have to become a card sharp. But that is beside the point. We are removing Visel from their vicinity so Drusilla and Gabriel can take his little boy into the country and start a life together." She didn't have to hide

Gabriel's illegitimate son from James because they'd discovered the boy's existence together, while spying on Visel—who had, in turn, been spying on Gabriel and Drusilla.

The hack shuddered as it rolled over the worn and rutted cobbles into the courtyard of the Swan with Two Necks. Eva pulled up the collar of her cloak and put on her hat, tucking up loose strands of her bothersome hair. She'd wanted to cut it short for the journey, but James had practically had a fit of the vapors when she'd suggested it. Sometimes he could be such a girl.

"You've a bit above your right ear." James motioned behind his own ear to demonstrate.

Eva caught the offending lock and tucked it in before looking at him, tilting her high-crowned beaver hat over her forehead. "There, do I look like a young gentleman escorting his drunken elder brother back to our parents?"

"You don't look like no boy I've ever seen," he muttered.

Eva ignored him and peered out the grimy window. "You go make sure everything is all set and tell them you've got a cupshot gent in here and want our chaise pulled alongside so we can easily load him."

James gave her one last, sad look and sighed before opening the door and hopping down, not bothering with the steps. After he shut the door, Eva bent to examine their captive. The light from the inn was shining through the window and slanted across his face.

He was wearing some stupid costume—she supposed it was a pirate outfit—and his turban had tumbled from his head, exposing hair that was normally an angelic pale blond but was now an inky black. He must have dyed it himself because there were smudges of black on his temple. In profile he looked just like many other aristocratic men of her acquaintance: a knife-straight nose, sharp cheekbones, and thin, supercilious lips. But somehow when you combined those features on Visel, they yielded something exceptional.

Eva did not believe it was just his shockingly good looks that distinguished him from the rest of his crowd, nor the fact that he was a womanizing, drinking, gambling fool, because those things, too, were usual aristocratic habits. No, there was something else. She thought it must be some expression in his eyes, or perhaps the way he held himself: aloof, confident, and coiled—just the way she imagined a dangerous jungle creature must behave.

She'd watched him like the proverbial hawk all Season long, and not because she found him attractive. She'd watched him because he never stopped watching her brother. Visel *hated* Gabriel with a ferocity that frightened her. He'd already managed to entangle him in one duel; a duel which he'd then stopped with a bizarre and very public apology. But his apology had not meant the end of his hostile behavior; quite the reverse. The few times she'd been close enough to see his face, she'd recognized the pent-up rage in his eyes. And that rage had been aimed at Gabe.

That was when Eva had decided to follow the man and see what the devil he was up to. When she'd found out *that*, it had been a logical step to kidnap him. Well, logical to her. Although she didn't like to admit it to James, her father would likely lock her in one of the towers at Exham Castle for the rest of her life if he ever learned about what she'd done.

She looked down at the earl's unconscious form and smiled grimly; she'd just have to make sure nobody ever learned about what she'd done—or what she was about to do.

Chapter 2

Godric hurt. Everywhere.

He opened his eyes and then quickly shut them again after his eyeballs caught fire, the bright, searing light sending agony arrowing directly to his brain.

"Ah, good morning, slugabed."

The voice clanged in his head like somebody pounding a mallet against a gong.

"I daresay your head is paining you a bit. I'm afraid there's nothing for it but to rise and shine. And I have this . . . ."

A delicious smell wafted beneath his nose, and his stomach gurgled with joy. "Guh. Coffee."

Low laughter echoed around him. "Sit up and I shall give you some." A small hand slid beneath his shoulder and pushed. "I can't lift you; you'll have to help."

"If I sit up will you stop talking?" His voice sounded as if he'd been gargling nails.

More laughter. "Look who wakes up grumpy."

Godric sucked in a breath, winced at the pain it caused, gritted his teeth, and pushed himself up.

Oh. God. His head sloshed, the sound remarkably like liquid in a ceramic jug.

"If you're going to vomit again, do it into the bucket next to your feet."

He shuddered, wrapped an arm around his midriff and reached blindly for the hand strap with the other. A small, gloved hand took his wrist and guided his fingers to the leather grip.

Godric clung to the strap like a child to its nanny and forced open his eyes. And saw *her*.

"*You*." Even to his own ears his voice pulsed with loathing.

She grinned, flashing perfect white teeth between her full, shapely lips. "Me."

"But . . . but—" Words were evading him.

"But . . . but . . ." She laughed. "You sound like a hen about to lay an egg." She then gave a credible demonstration of a cackling hen—noisily—and laughed some more.

Godric squeezed his temples with his free hand. "Please. I beg of you."

Another low chuckle.

"Why?" he said.

"Why did I kidnap you?"

He could only grunt, but it seemed to be enough.

"Why do you *think* I kidnapped you?" She didn't wait for an answer. "You were about to kidnap my dearest friend, who is also my brother's *wife*, Lord Visel. Two people, I will remind you, who married only because *you* forced them to. But that wasn't enough for you, was it?" She plowed onward, her ringing voice escalating. "No, you couldn't stand to see them happy with each other, could you? So you were going to take her, and what? Shame her? Shame him? Make him fight and kill you?" Her voice was like ice picks in his ears.

She leaned across the seat and the buckskin of her breeches stretched taut across her thighs. Which was when Godric's brain registered the fact she was dressed like a *man*.

"I took matters into my own hands and removed you from the picture entirely." She gave him a dirty look, the expression hard on her beautiful features.

"You are wearing b-breeches." It was not what he thought he'd say and her expression told him it wasn't what she'd wanted to hear, either.

She sat back in her seat and crossed her arms over her chest, her expression openly scathing. That was just as well, Godric decided, since her voice hurt his ears and he didn't seem to be thinking or speaking straight. Instead he let his aching, dry, burning eyes roam over her person.

In addition to skintight leather breeches, she wore scuffed black top boots—the smallest pair he'd ever seen—whose white tops were so filthy they would have made Brummell weep. Her clawhammer coat appeared to be a dark blue and the waistcoat beneath it gold and white striped. Her cravat was arranged in some hideous fashion that must be of her own devising, and on the seat beside her was a black beaver hat. Her hair was rudely bunched on top of her head and held in place with a great number of pins that glittered and glinted, catching the light from outside and flashing quite painfully.

"Coffee."

Her lips thinned but she reached into a leather satchel at her feet and pulled out the clay jug she must have waved beneath his nose.

"You'll have to drink it from the jug."

Godric let go of the strap, reached out a shaky hand, and began to slide off the seat.

"Well, bugger," she snapped, putting her free hand on his chest, as if her puny little arm could stop him from falling. Godric fumbled with the strap and caught himself, but not before he drove her to her knees in the small space between them.

"Bloody hell," she cursed, shaking the hand that had been holding the jug and sending glinting diamonds of coffee flying. She glared up at him while she sucked the skin between her thumb and forefinger. "You clumsy oaf, you made me spill."

Godric felt his mouth pulling into a smile.

"Think that's funny, do you?" She lifted the jug and took a noisy slurp. "Mmmm." She lowered the jug and wiped her mouth with the back of her hand. "Delicious." Then she slammed the bung into the jug with her fist and placed the coffee back in the bag before scrabbling up onto the seat, never removing her eyes from his.

His stomach growled loudly enough to be heard over the wheels of the carriage. His foggy brain snagged on the thought: a carriage.

He forgot all about coffee. "We're in a carriage."

"Can't slide much past you, can I?"

"Where are we going?"

"To Liverpool."

Godric squinted. He could not have heard her correctly. "What?"

"I've sold you to a cruel and brutal merchant captain." She paused, her mouth twisting oddly. "His name is Captain Blackclaw and his ship is called *The Torment*." She sucked her lower lip into her mouth, white teeth resting on pink softness. And then a snort broke out of her pretty mouth and she doubled over. "Oh, Lord! You should see your face, Visel." She rolled around on her seat, howling with delight.

The woman was, Godric decided, every bit as crazy as she was reported to be.

Eva knew she was behaving badly, but she couldn't help it. Mocking the haughty, handsome, and furious Lord Visel was simply too much fun to pass up.

"When you are finished amusing yourself, perhaps you might tell me where we are really going." His voice was like an arctic blast and he was glaring at her through eyes that were almost as pale as her father's. For one dreadful moment she experienced the same tightening in her chest she did when Lord Exley stared at her with such open disappointment. But then she recalled this man was in *her* power.

She crossed her arms. "I'll tell you where we are going when you need to know it."

His face darkened in a way that was decidedly satisfying.

"Right now the only thing you need to know is that you should behave yourself. Angering me would be ill-advised. In fact, it would be best if you kept me entertained—as you have been doing. Otherwise you shall find yourself tied up on the floor again." She smirked. "With a rag stuffed into your mouth."

He cut a glance down at his wrists and the red chafe marks on the tanned skin. Eva had not been happy about inflicting such pain on him. And of course James had almost suffered an apoplexy when he'd gone to loosen the bonds, insisting they remove them entirely rather than simply re-tie them. She'd let him have his way, but only after a very heated argument.

"That's it, my lady. When he wakes up it will be the end. And if we don't both swing for this—"

"Oh hush," she'd told him irritably, tired of his incessant naysaying. Probably because she knew he had a convincing argument for almost everything he said. "You can ride on the box if you're so terrified about what he will do when he wakes up."

"It would serve you right if I did," James snapped right back. "And what would you do when he woke up and found you all alone, I want to know?"

Eva had reached into the big leather satchel she'd taken from her brother Gabriel and produced one of her father's dueling pistols.

James had howled so loudly it was amazing he hadn't woken the dead, not to mention the dead-to-the-world peer tied up on the floor between them. "That is one of his lordship's dueling pistols, isn't it?"

"Well it certainly isn't one of her *ladyship*'s."

James had rapped on the roof.

"What are you doing?" Eva demanded.

"Riding on the box."

That had made her frown. "You can't. I forbid you."

"You just *told* me to."

Lord! But there was nothing she hated more than being proved wrong in the middle of an argument.

James opened the door when the chaise stopped.

"I order you to remain in here with me, James."

He gave a rude snort.

"I shall discharge you for insubordination," she threatened, waving the pistol.

James cut her a skeptical look and his calm brown gaze flickered to the pistol. "I hope that isn't loaded, the way you're waving it about."

"I'm a crack shot."

He rolled his eyes and hopped out.

"What am I supposed to do with him when he wakes up?" she asked.

"Hit him on the head—isn't that what you told me?" He slammed the door before she could answer.

"You are the worst henchman ever," she'd yelled after him.

That had been hours ago, just before dawn. Eva glanced from her captive to the window and realized they were passing some small cottages, a sure sign they were approaching civilization, which probably meant another inn. It was getting time for another change of horse.

Her hostage must have thought the same. "Where are we?"

"You needn't concern yourself with such matters. I've taken care of all your transportation needs. All you have to worry about is behaving like a gentleman while we change horses. If you are good, I will see that breakfast is delivered to the chaise."

His nostrils flared and he resembled a bull about to charge. "What's to stop me from grabbing you, my lady? I might not be up to snuff, but I'm certainly well enough to grab *you*."

"Hmmm." Eva reached down into the bag without taking her eyes from him. When she sat up, she held a pistol.

"What the bloody—"

"Tut tut, Lord Visel. What kind of language is that to employ around a lady?"

His red-rimmed eyes narrowed. "I recall dancing with you at the Pentwhistle ball—you have a mouth like a sailor."

His words pleased rather than insulted her, which, she suspected, had been his real intention. Eva recalled the night in question; she'd maneuvered him into asking her for the supper dance and he'd been surly and broody.

"I recall that evening, too, my lord. You weren't much of a supper companion."

He snorted.

"I believe you were hoping to eat your meal with The Kitten that night."

His eyes narrowed, but he remained silent.

It was just as well—even thinking about The Kitten irritated Eva. The Kitten—or Lucinda Kittridge—was the most sought-after debutante of the Season. She was perfect and beautiful and rich and sophisticated. And she always looked at Eva as if she were some type of grub worm.

The Kitten had sunk her claws into Eva's brother before Gabriel had been forced to marry Eva's closest friend.

Eva looked at her captive and made a *tsking* sound. "I know you were only *pretending* to pursue The Kitten because you believe it annoyed Gabriel."

The earl raised his eyebrows.

"You can look at me like that, but I know it's true. It was plain for all to see you didn't give two raps for The Kitten. Besides, even if you did, your grandfather would never countenance such a marriage." She snorted. "The Duke of Tyndale's heir marrying a butcher's daughter? I think not—no matter how downy she is."

His continued silence was beginning to irritate her, and she forced herself to hold the gun in a relaxed grip, pointing it away from him, just in case he annoyed her even more and her finger took action without consulting her brain.

"Is that loaded?" he asked.

"What do *you* think?"

"I think you really are as mad as everyone says, aren't you?"

Eva barely felt a twinge at his words. Barely. "And *I* think you really do have the death wish everyone says you do," she countered. "Why else would you taunt a person holding a loaded gun on you?"

The carriage slowed abruptly and they both looked out the window. A wooden sign proclaiming THE CROWN AND ANTLER passed by the window.

He turned incredulous eyes toward her. "Good God. We're on the bloody North Road."

Eva felt a flicker of worry at his disbelieving tone and forced herself to swallow it. She probably should have kept him blindfolded, or at least tied up. Not that it really mattered if he knew where they were, she supposed.

The carriage rolled to a stop and a moment later a shadow fell across them and James's face appeared in the window. His eyes went comically wide when they landed on the gun.

"Open the bloody door, James," she ordered.

He hesitated, but then opened it the merest crack. Visel began to lower his hand from the strap.

"I don't think so, my good man," she said, turning the barrel toward him and gesturing upward. "Keep your hands up."

James made a piteous noise. "Awww, Lady Eva, why'd you go and get out the gun?"

"Do you work for this woman?" Visel asked.

James's eyes became—unbelievably—even larger.

He opened his mouth to speak but Eva said, "That is hardly any of your concern, my lord. James, fetch us some food while they change the horses." She kept her gaze fixed on Visel.

"You are helping your mistress kidnap a peer, James. If you stop now, I might be able to put in a good word for you. But if you insist on—"

"Do as I say, James." Her voice was sharper than she would have liked, but it spurred the huge young man into action. The door shut with a click and Visel turned back to her.

Eva sneered at him. "Perhaps the next time you think to enlist his help, you might wait until my back is turned, you—you *bounder.*"

He appeared amused, rather than affronted, by her insult.

"You might not care about your own neck, my lady, but it is ill done of you to expose a loyal servant to such punishment."

Eva ignored the wave of guilt his words elicited. "Save your worry for your own neck, Visel. I shall take good care of James, don't you fret."

He leaned back against the squabs, his disconcerting eyes roving her person. "So, we are on the North Road. Let me guess, we are headed to Scotland? I am abducting you and whisking you off to Gretna Green."

"What a clever man you are. Who would have ever guessed it after your stupid behavior this past Season?"

His smile was one of utter unconcern.

"Don't worry, my lord, we won't actually get there. I have even less interest in marrying *you* than you do in marrying me."

"I doubt that."

Eva glowered at him. "If that is true, then you'd better do exactly as I say and don't draw attention to your predicament. If you behave sensibly, we can all get out of this without leg shackles of either the marital *or* legal sort."

"And what are you going to do if I don't behave? Are you going to stop somewhere along the way, knock me on the head, and get that big lummox to dig a hole for me?"

"You'd better mind your mouth, my lord. James may be a groom, but he is my friend and I value him far more highly than I do *you*. And you should also stop giving me good ideas—although I daresay I'd have *you* dig your own hole before I knocked you on the head."

His eyes widened and then he laughed, a great, big belly laugh that must have hurt his aching head because he winced. Eva didn't know what kind of response she'd expected to receive to her threat, but it had not been this.

"You should see your face," he said, his words a mocking echo of her earlier words.

She frowned. "Why. What's wrong with it?"

He leaned forward, his eyes suddenly hooded, his face slack and sensual. "Nothing, darling. Not a damned thing."

Eva was struck dumb—and not by his vulgar language—but by his hot eyes, which sent sparks of anticipation through her body. What did he mean? Did he—

His smile shifted into a sneer and he discarded his sensuality quicker than he could discard the snug-fitting coat he wore beneath his corsair robes. Of course his amorous look hadn't been real; he'd been taunting her—toying with her—just to see if he could.

Eva *hated* him. And all the other men like him, although none of them had ever been as bad as Visel. But she'd come across plenty of men during the Season who'd been similar. Arrogant men with their superior looks, their knowing smiles—men who thought she couldn't hear them whisper the words *mad* and *madness* behind her back. Except for Visel; he'd always *wanted* Eva to hear the things he said about her.

"What? Cat got your tongue?" he asked. The gleam in his eyes was one she'd seen more than a few times this Season, usually when he'd been taunting her brother. It was the same gleam that had forced her to the conclusion that Visel suffered from some form of male hysteria. After all, he'd been at war for over a decade. What must that do to a man?

But she would save that subject for later.

"Why did you leave the army and come back?" she asked. "I suppose you had to return home now that you're the duke's heir," she said before he could answer. "Still, you should have stayed in the country. Everyone can see you hate London—the Season, the balls, the empty, brainless entertainments. You make no effort to hide the fact you loathe society."

He shifted on his seat, grimacing at some ache or pain. "I could say the same thing about you, my lady. You sit in the corners of ballrooms with the wallflowers, you behave in ways that gain you the censure of *ton* matrons, your only associate is a woman from the merchant class with a clear disdain for the society she is trying so hard to enter. So, why do *you* do it?"

"I wouldn't expect such a stupid question—not even from you, my lord. I do it because my father makes me do it; because he believes it is a woman's duty and destiny to marry. If I were a man—" She bit her lip to keep from saying something he would only use against her.

His golden-blond brows lifted, exposing a thin white line that ran through the right one, and his cruel mouth pulled up in a smile that held no humor. "Go on, if you were a man, you would—?"

"Shut up." Even Eva could hear that her order lacked any heat. The man was irritating and exhausting and she would do best to ignore him. She turned away from him, looking out the window at the iron-gray sky. There would be rain soon.

"I never pegged you for a coward."

She whipped around and met his derisive gaze. "What is that supposed to mean?"

"You know exactly what I mean."

The carriage shifted as they stared at one another, the sounds of business outside the door unnaturally loud in the silence. His eyes seemed to have become a colder, icier shade of blue, although she knew that was impossible. She fought the urge to shiver but lost. His lips parted to show white but slightly uneven teeth. One of his front teeth was chipped, a tiny triangle missing from the inside edge where it met its partner. It jarred with the perfection of his features but did not make him any less attractive. Instead, it added a hint of danger to his otherwise too-angelic good looks.

"What is going to happen when the marquess catches us, I wonder?" he mused.

"He won't."

"Oh, my dear girl, if you think he will let a man abscond with his daughter without giving chase, you are sorely mistaken."

His smirky, know-it-all expression made Eva reckless. "He believes I'm at a country house party with my sister. If he even thinks to check on my whereabouts, it will not be for some time. I shall be back by then."

His brows arched. "Then why bother going all the way to the border? Why not let me out here and you can join your sister now?"

Eva was tempted. He was a treacherous man and she knew he would attempt to escape the moment he saw an opportunity. But it was too soon to release him; she wanted to give Gabe and Dru a couple of weeks if she could. By then they'd be in the country and there would be no opportunity for Visel to bother them, or at least not easily.

"I can see you find the idea appealing."

She flashed him a hard smile. "I find the idea of you shutting up even more appealing."

He chuckled, looking genuinely amused by her rudeness. The smooth, deep rumble of laughter hit her in the chest and slithered downward, settling low in her belly. Eva refused to let the effect he had on her body distract her from the business at hand. Men like him—sophisticated, confident, and sexually experienced men—had this effect on women like her, not through any effort of their own, but simply because of their life experience.

The things that took place between men and women were no longer a mystery to Visel. But when it came to bed sport, women of Eva's class were treated like mushrooms—kept in the dark and fed manure—until the night they were sacrificed to their husbands. Whereas a man like Visel had likely discarded his virginity at an early age, probably foisting himself upon some unfortunate domestic. And then he'd gone on to hone his sexual prowess with whores and widows.

Yes, that was all that separated Eva from Visel: experience. And he used his experience like a weapon that gave him the *illusion* of sophistication. Luckily for Eva, she had her stepmamma to advise her in such matters. Lady Mia made a concerted effort to inform all three of her stepdaughters about what went on between men and women.

Not that Eva had been completely ignorant before hearing her stepmamma's interesting information. After all, she'd seen animals coupling many times. She knew about the physical aspect of the act.

Of course her stepmamma had certainly expanded on that knowledge. Still, even the best information could not compete with actual experience, and she had none of that. At least not with anyone other than herself.

She'd contemplated, more than once, divesting herself of her bothersome maidenhood—just to see what all the fuss was about. The loss of her virginity would serve the dual purpose of making her unmarketable on the marriage mart; even more unmarketable than the threat of madness that clung to her.

The only reason she hadn't lain with a man was the possible repercussions of such an action: a child. The scandal of having a child out of wedlock would not bother her in the least. In fact, it would free her of ever having to marry. Also, her father had settled enough money on her that she could raise a child in more security and ease than the Regent's own bastards. But what she *couldn't* give a child was something money would not buy: a future.

She could never have children, either inside marriage or out of it.

"Tell me, what are you thinking, my lady?"

She looked up, having forgotten she wasn't alone.

"What are *you* thinking?" she countered.

He grinned. "I'm thinking that you might actually be more lovely dressed in snug breeches and that formfitting coat than you are in a ball gown." He leaned forward and Eva recoiled. "I'm thinking I'd love to see what your arse looks like in those tight leathers."

Eva gasped and heat crept up her neck, her body's treachery making her hate her appearance more than ever. Eva knew what he said was true: she *was* beautiful. Only a fool would try to deny it. All her life she'd hated what she saw in the mirror, not to mention the expectations that went with her appearance. Nobody would ever believe her—not that she cared—but she wished with all her heart that she was a big, lumbering, homely girl—like one of the kitchen maids at her father's castle, a girl named Em who had hair and eyes the color of mud—a girl she'd seen laughing and jesting with her father's grooms as if she were one of them. Everyone liked Em because of who she was—not because she looked like some sort of vapid, porcelain doll.

That was who Eva wanted to be.

The only man who'd ever ignored the way Eva looked was James. And there was a good reason for that, not that she'd ever tell. James had always behaved toward her the way he would with a younger son of the family: with respect but not with worshipful awe as other boys had always done. At least until they knew who she was; after that they looked at her with loathing and fear.

She loved James and respected him in return. She also wished she were like him. In fact, in her mind's eye she *was* like him: big and brawny and strapping. But in reality she was small, slight, dainty: the very image of her beautiful, mad, dead mother.

Thinking of her mother made her scowl. She looked at the man who'd made her remember the long dead Countess of Exley and fixed him with a narrow-eyed glare.

"You even look adorable when you scowl." His eyes wandered slowly from the toes of her boots, over her legs and torso, lingering on her face before settling on her unruly hair. "You can clothe your sweet little body in breeches and boots, but I'm afraid only a blind person would ever believe you are a man, darling."

She sucked in a breath at the shocking words *sweet* and *little* and *body* and *darling*, her heart thudding like a war drum in her chest, and her skin hot—*all over*.

He chuckled at whatever he saw on her face.

Hateful, *hateful* man. "You asked me what I was thinking, my lord earl?"

"Mmmm?"

"I'm thinking you'd better shut up or I'll gag you."

He patted the seat beside him. "You'll need two hands for that. Come on over here, sweetheart. I'll hold your pistol while you do it."

Eva was considering shooting him when the door opened a crack and James handed in another clay jug and a large oil-cloth wrapped package. "It's sandwiches and homebrew, my lady."

"Hand it to Lord Visel." She gave the smirking lord a tight smile. "He can put it to good use and stuff it in his mouth."

Godric hadn't thought he was starving until after the first bite. The sandwich wasn't anything special, just good dark bread with a slab of ham and a thick slice of Lincolnshire Red. The jug held a rich, sweet porter that soothed his aching head. By the time they were about an hour away from the posting inn, he was feeling almost human. With some very human needs.

"I need to use the necessary." The words sounded unnaturally loud in the post chaise, which had been utterly silent since rolling out of the innyard. Her full lips tightened and a fetching flush tinted her cheeks. So, the little hoyden had a vulgar mouth but she was not entirely cast away.

"I should hate for things to become unpleasant," he said when she continued to stare. "Well, any *more* unpleasant."

She huffed out a sigh and knocked on the roof with the hand not holding the pistol. The panel behind Visel's head slid open immediately.

"His lordship needs to make a stop."

"*Here*, my lady?" It was the voice of her earnest young henchman, a man who looked as if he desperately wished he'd told his mistress *no* back when he'd had the chance.

"Sooner rather than later, James."

"Er, yes, very good, my lady."

Godric and the girl glared at each other in silence as the carriage slowed a bit. He imagined the postilions were looking for a place a four-horse team could pull off the road.

"I can tell you are thinking you will escape, Lord Visel."

He looked from the window to her, unsurprised by her words. She was young but she was not silly. Of course she was also barking mad, but that seemed to add a low cunning to her thought processes.

Godric cocked his head. "Lady Eva, you have taken my money

and we are on a stretch of road with nothing for miles in any direction. What would I do out here on my own?"

"You seem an enterprising man; I daresay you'd contrive something."

"What I *will* contrive is a great degree of amusement when you are caught, my lady. Trust me: I'm hardly likely to wander off too soon and miss *that* show. You have my word as a gentleman that I will not try to escape."

She chewed her lip, something he was beginning to realize indicated cogitation. "Take off your boots."

Godric did not believe he'd heard her correctly. "I beg your pardon?"

She raised the pistol.

"Why?" he asked, crossing his arms over his chest.

"You'll hardly try something stupid in the middle of nowhere in stocking feet."

He looked out the window at the gathering clouds. "It is going to *rain*."

"Well, then I recommend you complete your, er, business without tarrying."

"I gave you my word as a gentleman."

"I don't care—I am *not* a gentleman."

The chaise shuddered to a halt and then rocked as somebody leapt off. When the door opened he was not surprised to see the boy, James.

He glanced from Godric to the girl and frowned, his pleasant face hardening. "Did he try something with you, my lady?"

"No, I'm merely waiting for him to take off his boots."

The boy's lips silently repeated what she'd said and he squinted at her. "But . . . *why?*"

"Good God, James, so he won't *run*. Look at him; that is exactly what he is thinking."

Godric smiled. "Actually, I was thinking how much I need a piss."

She flinched as if he'd struck her.

"Here then, your lordship," the boy said, his face flushed. "That kind of language isn't—"

"If you want your *piss*, you'd better take off your boots." Eva glanced at her watch, which hung from a plain leather fob. "You have one minute to take them off before we recommence our journey."

The boy shifted. "Um, my lady—"

"Hush," the little witch said, never taking her eyes from Godric.

He toed at the heel of one boot, giving the appearance of struggling. "My feet have swollen." He gave her a significant look. "I daresay because I've been wearing boots all night. I can't remove them."

She motioned with the pistol. "Help him, James."

Godric swiveled his legs toward the young giant. And when the boy reached for his boot, he kicked him right in the stomach.

Chapter 3

One minute Visel was moving like an old man with aches and pains, the next he'd kicked James faster than lightning and snatched the pistol right out of Eva's hand.

But not before her finger contracted in surprise and she discharged a shot through the roof of the carriage. Visel leapt from the chaise faster than a man in his condition should have been able. Eva launched herself at his back but her fingers slid off the slick satin of his colorful cape and she landed on the edge of the door, clipping her chin and biting her tongue hard enough to draw blood and cloud her vision with pain and stars.

"Not so fast, my good man."

She blinked her eyes clear in time to see Lord Visel take one of James's arms and twist it behind his back until the big groom grunted with pain.

"You leave him alone," Eva lisped, her tongue throbbing as she tried to turn her body in the narrow area between the seats, somehow managing to wedge herself more tightly in the process.

Visel didn't even waste a glance on her. "You there," he called to the postilions, both of whom had dismounted and were staring, eyes wide, mouths agape. "Come here and tie this man's hands. You'll find a length of rope inside the carriage."

The taller of the two boys—for that was really what they were, just boys—looked hesitantly between Lord Visel, James, and Eva.

She shook her head. "Don't do it."

Visel gave the postilions a withering glare and gestured with the gun. "Do as I say." He spoke with the confidence of one who expected to be obeyed: an officer, a peer, a *man*.

His commanding tone infuriated her.

"The pistol isn't loaded—he fired the only shot," she said, looking from the frowning earl to the wide-eyed young men. And then inspiration struck. "Please—you must help me. He is a pirate—a *French* pirate and I am Lady Eva de Courtney. He has kidnapped me and is taking me to his master, the pirate king Dirty Jean Ferrar."

Visel gave a half laugh, half snort.

"You see how he is dressed," she said, ignoring him and keeping her eyes on the postilions. "He is a vile minion of the pirate king, a villain, a man who aided Napoleon for years." She squirmed to sit up, scraping her head against the carriage doorframe and knocking several pins from her hair. "Please, you must help me." As if on cue, another pin *plinked* to the floor of the carriage and a thick rope of hair slid from its moorings and slowly unfurled until it curtained her shoulders. *There. Now I look like a girl.*

She fluttered her eyelashes for extra measure. "Please."

Visel threw his head back and laughed. "I'd clap if I didn't have this pistol in my hand. Your performance is a masterpiece."

One of the postilions had already begun moving toward the box when Visel turned from Eva to her small audience. "Here then, where are you going, boy?" he demanded imperiously as the postilion disappeared around the side of the carriage.

"*Please* don't let him sell me to pirates," Eva wailed.

Visel whipped around, no longer amused. "You hush or I shall be forced to gag you, my lady."

"'Ere then, you brute." The voice came from the back of the chaise. It was the smaller of the two boys, and he held a very old pistol with badly shaking hands. "You leave 'er alone."

Visel gaped. "Good God. You don't actually *believe* that cock-and-bull story, do you?" He went on before the boy could answer, his expression hardening. "Listen to me, you *pillock*, I am Godric Fleming—heir to the Duke of Tyndale. Do I *sound* like a bloody Frenchman to you?"

The boy blinked at this logic.

"That's why they sent him," Eva said hurriedly. "Because he is so clever at disguising his voice, he can sound like anyone."

Visel snorted. "I'm so clever I disguise my voice yet I failed to disguise my *person* as an Englishman?"

The boys took in his colorful cape.

There was a long pause, and then, "You toss that gun down and put your hands where we can see 'em." It was the *other* postilion who spoke—the one who'd stood near the horses. He'd managed to get his hands on a second gun, which he must have had close at hand because he never stepped away from the leader harness he was holding.

Eva gave Visel a quick wink and then turned to her rescuer. "Oh, *thank you,*" she said, making her voice higher and more girlish than normal as she squirmed onto her side so that she could get her legs free and hop out. She looked at Visel's furious face and held out her hand.

"Give me the gun, Captain Desjean. You will not be able to carry out your dastardly errand today."

Visel's nostrils flared and Eva had to bite her lip to keep from laughing. She waggled her fingers. "Come now, let's have it. We need no unnecessary violence."

"Go on then, Desjean," the postilion behind her ordered. "Hand it over nice and slow, like. We didn't whip the Frenchies so they could come onto English soil and steal our womenfolk."

Eva smothered her laugh with a cough. "That's right," she said in a voice rough with suppressed laughter as she chided one of England's most decorated war heroes. "Our brave men and boys fought to protect us from the likes of *you.*"

Visel shook his head minutely from side to side, his eyes never leaving her face as he flipped the pistol in his hand with the ease of a man comfortable with handling one, offering it to her, butt first.

She grinned. "Thank you for your cooperation."

His lips twisted into a smile that did not bode well for her if he ever got free.

She glanced down at James, who was still sprawled under Visel's boot. "James?" Her groom, whom she'd known all her life, was looking at her as if he'd never seen her before. "*James*, what is wrong with you?"

He shook his head, as if waking from a daze. Eva could see she would be in for another scold the moment they were alone together.

"Come, make haste, James. Tie Lor—er—tie Captain Desjean's hands."

Eva couldn't have said which of the two men looked more disgusted: the earl or her servant.

Well, she didn't care. "Put him in the carriage once you've secured him. I shall talk to our rescuers."

The two young men were together now, both guns trained on the earl as James tied his hands behind his back.

Eva slowed her walk and swayed her hips more. In her mind's eye she thought of The Kitten, a woman so beautiful and elegant and sought-after, it made Eva's teeth hurt. She willed herself to *be* The Kitten and lowered her lids, regarding the two gaping men from beneath her lashes.

"I cannot thank you enough for your bravery," she gushed in a breathy voice that was not her own. She stopped to the side of them, not wishing to insert herself between the armed young men and the earl—who'd turned toward them so she could see his derisive smile. Eva donned a smile of her own, thrusting out her chest the way The Kitten did. The men's eyes dropped to her bosom and their brows furrowed, making her recall her clothing.

"He dressed me this way to hide me," she explained, fluttering her eyelashes since a heaving bosom was no good for seduction if it was covered by a coat. She clasped her hands together, hoping to appear harmless, and leaned closer. "My father shall reward you both richly when we deliver this villain to him."

The two men looked at each other uncertainly. "Your father, my lady?"

"Why yes, that is where we are headed. He has a country house in—" She stuttered for a moment. Why would Visel have kidnapped her and now be taking her to her father's house?

"Taking you to your father's house, was I?" the earl taunted, fully facing them now.

"'Ere, you," the smaller of the two postilions said, waving his pistol in an anxiety-provoking manner. "When we needs to 'ear a peep out o' you, we'll tell you."

Eva smirked. "Yes, just so—no *peeping* until you are ordered to do so," she said to Visel before turning to the postilion, relieved to leave behind the subject of country houses. "Thank you, kind sir. What is your name?"

"Jemmy, my lady." He bowed and doffed his hat, forgetting there was a pistol in his hand and delivering a loud *clunk* to his forehead.

It was not easy to keep a straight face.

"I don't think we can do that, my lady," the other boy said, his expression much sharper than his compatriot's. Right now he'd fixed his gaze on Visel and his features had taken on a speculative cast. "He might be a Frenchie spy, but our employer tells us not to get mixed up in shenanigans." His intelligent gray gaze moved from Visel to Eva. "And this feels like shenanigans." His eyes swept her person and it was not only—or even largely—with appreciation. "We'll take you to the next town—there's a magistrate not far away. You can wait at the inn while word is sent."

"Bravo," Visel said, laughing. "That is a capital idea."

Eva shot him a narrow-eyed look and glared at James, who hastily turned the earl and assisted him into the carriage.

"Oh, I say, Ollie," Jemmy said before Eva could protest. "Can't we just drop 'im off and take her ladyship to her father?"

Ollie shook his head. "No, we'll let the magistrate sort this out, Jem, or it might be our jobs." Eva could see that was a compelling argument to the other boy, who had been three-quarters besotted and her slave before his companion had scuppered it.

As if she'd spoken out loud, Ollie looked at her again. This time there was naked suspicion in his gaze. "How come your man there didn't get you out of this?" he asked, gesturing toward James, who'd just put Visel inside and turned around.

James gave her an *I told you so* look.

Eva had been wondering from the beginning of her lie why James had docilely played along, so she was prepared with another lie.

"Captain Desjean has my younger sister, too. He said he would hurt her if we did not do as he said."

A hoot of laughter came from inside the carriage and Eva gritted her teeth.

Ollie's eyes flickered back and forth and he shook his head slowly from side to side. "We're bringing you to the magistrate—all three of you. This ain't for the likes of us to decide." He motioned toward the carriage. "You ride in there with them," he told James, pointing with the gun. Eva opened her mouth, but Ollie shook his head. "Please, my lady. I shouldn't want to tie the two of you up like the Frenchie. But there is just something about this whole thing that don't smell right. If everything you say is true, the magistrate will see that you get to your father."

Eva was impressed by Ollie's fortitude in the face of aristocratic displeasure but couldn't help wishing he was more like his friend.

"Very well," she said. "I'm sure the magistrate will see the truth of the matter."

Yes, and then she would be in the very deepest of trouble.

Godric shifted into the corner so his bound hands weren't pressing against the seat back.

"I don't know what you're smiling at," the little shrew snapped, giving him a look of pure loathing.

"I'm just imagining the tale you'll tell the local magistrate when we reach Doncaster. Sir Bertram Woodville is in charge of that area, and he and I were chums at Eton."

"How nice for you."

"His younger brother was in my regiment."

The young giant groaned and his head fell back with a *thunk*.

Lady Eva elbowed him hard in the side. "What is *wrong* with you, James?"

"It wasn't right, my lady."

"What wasn't right?"

"Making mock of a war hero."

Her eyes slid to Godric and he raised his eyebrows. She opened her mouth—no doubt to scold—but the boy wasn't done.

"They're going to clap me in leg irons and summon the marquess." His head rolled from side to side. "And there is probably some special crime I'm guilty of for abducting a war hero."

Lady Eva's jaw worked, the gears in her pretty head grinding away while she fixed her remarkable blue-violet eyes on Godric.

"This is all your fault," she said.

"Ha! I'm afraid I don't see how that can be."

"You *forced* me to do this because you wouldn't leave Gabriel be. Why do you hate my brother? What has he ever done to you?"

Godric felt the amusement drain from his face. "That is men's business and none of your affair, *little girl*."

"I beg to differ. He is my brother and I love him. Thanks to you, he is married to my best friend, whom I also love. While I might be happy they're married, their happiness was not your goal when you forced them to wed, was it? You only made sure they had to marry because you knew Gabriel had shown interest in The Kitten and you wanted to make him suffer."

Godric shrugged, hoping the mortification he felt at her apt assessment did not show on his face.

Her mouth tightened and her expression became speculative. "I don't think you even know what you are doing or why, do you? I think you're suffering from some form of madness—something brought on by the war: the male hysteria."

"*My lady!*" Her groom's voice was sharp and his eyes bulged, his chastisement making the girl's face flush.

Godric noticed all this through a red haze of fury and his hands shook and his heart pounded in his ears. "Well, you would know all about madness, wouldn't you?"

Lady Eva's nostrils flared and the boy's chin pulled down, his brown eyes blazing just as fiercely as his mistress's.

"That was ill done of you, my lord," the groom said.

Godric could face the girl's anger, but the boy's disappointed, accusing eyes were something else. They spoke more loudly than words and their expression was damning. It made him see himself plainly. He was being a bully; what he'd said was wrong and ungentlemanly and cruel.

"I apologize." He could barely grind out the words. "Your groom is correct: that *was* ill done of me."

She shrugged, but her full lips had tightened and there were bright spots of color on her cheeks. "It doesn't matter a whit to me what you say."

Godric knew that for a lie, but he kept his mouth shut.

"What matters is that you cannot hurt my brother from where you sit right now. *That*," she said, giving him a hard, chill look that should have been ludicrous on such a beautiful, youthful face but wasn't, "is what matters now."

Godric shifted in his seat, his arms aching and his shoulders sore. The physical discomfort added to his shame over his wretched behavior, making him even more irritable. Good God, but it was annoying to be wrong in front of such an *infant*. He seized on that annoyance, even though he knew he was only adding to the large pile of wrongs he'd already created. "I beg to differ, my lady. The issue of kidnapping is what will matter when we reach Doncaster and I speak to Sir Bertram."

"There are two of us—James and I. Why should he believe anything you say? In fact"—her hard expression shifted to one of sly amusement—"what if James and I tell him you were taking *me* to the border—that *you* kidnapped me with the intention of marriage? Hmm? We hired this chaise under your name, after all. What then, my lord?"

Godric looked at her groom, who would not meet his gaze. "And would you make your servant lie to a magistrate for you?"

The boy looked at her and her jaw seemed to become tighter by the second, her expression one of mute unhappiness. She looked . . . young. Which she was, of course. A good decade younger than he, at least.

He was behaving like a bully—again. "I will make you an offer, Lady Eva. If you untie my hands and apologize for your actions, I might have a different story to tell old Bertie." He didn't tell her that the story would have the same ending.

The boy's expression was one of fearful hope, until he saw her face, and then it fell.

"Never," she said, her eyes slits and her voice oddly menacing, like the hiss of a snake. "I will *never* apologize for kidnapping you. I only wish I really *had* knocked you on the head and dropped you in a hole, or sold you to some nasty band of sailors so you could spend the rest of your days chained to an oar."

The boy sucked in an audible gasp. "*My lady.*"

Godric chuckled, amused by her fire, which made her magnificent eyes flash and put color into her pale, sculpted cheeks. She was, without a doubt, one of the most beautiful women in England. It was a damned shame she was going to have to marry a man who'd never be able to love her, when she clearly had so much emotional need.

He turned to the groom. "Perhaps you and I might strike a deal—James, is it?"

That was the wrong thing to say.

The boy's face shut down as surely as the portcullis of a castle, and he turned to Lady Eva. "What do you want to do?" he asked his mistress.

Her expression, which had been as dark as a thundercloud, began to clear. She reached down into her leather bag of tricks and pulled out a grubby neckcloth. "I have an idea."

Eva could not wait to get away from Lord Visel. He was as cunning as a snake.

She held up the dirty neckcloth. "We gag him with this and then jump from the carriage. When they open the door at Doncaster, all they will find is *him*."

James's eyes became as round as guineas. "*That* is your idea?"

"What is wrong with it?" she demanded, more than a little affronted by his tone.

"Jumping from a moving carriage will *hurt*, my lady. It is possible one or both of us will be too injured to walk. What then?"

Eva saw she would have to resort to goading or shaming, both of which usually worked. "What a poor creature you are, James. Have you no spirit of adventure? I've fallen from my horse at far greater speeds and in more dangerous conditions. Recall that hunt two years ago when the—"

"Yes, yes, of course I do—and I also recall you almost *died*."

Eva ground her teeth, wishing she'd chosen another example to illustrate her indestructibility. "What about the time when—"

"What will we do once we jump?"

She was glad to leave the other subject behind. "We can get a ride with some farmer if necessary. We only need to get as far as a posting house. You must still have that money I gave you?"

"I believe some of that money is *mine*," Visel said.

Eva shot the earl a glare but otherwise ignored him. "James?" she said.

"Aye, I've got it."

"There is enough there to purchase seats for us on a mail coach five times over. We could even engage our own chaise at an inn."

He chewed his lip.

"I think you must know this is a dreadful idea," Lord Visel said.

She whirled on him. "Why don't you mind your own business, you—you interfering *cad*. This is none of your affair. You can get out of the carriage a free man in Doncaster and you and your dreadful school chum can do what you do best."

His lips curved into a grin that made Eva wish she'd shot him when she'd had the chance. "Oh, and what would that be, my lady?"

"Drinking, gaming, cocking, and whoring, just like any other degenerate fop."

He laughed. "How well you know me. It is almost as if we are man and wife already." He turned to James and his smile drained away. "You must know how this will all end, boy—even if you refuse to admit it to your mistress."

Eva was so angry her eyeballs were hot. "Stop. Talking."

"If you jump out of the carriage and make it back to Exley, his lordship will only have to bring her back to me. She will have to marry me and all three of us know that." He paused and then added, "And what do you think the marquess will say when he learns you helped his daughter kidnap a peer and then leap out of a moving carriage?"

"Don't listen to him, James. He is demented. He doesn't know anything about me or us or my family or my father and what he will do." She caught one of James's huge hands, which was clenched into a fist on his knee. "*Please*," she said when he turned to her, his brown eyes agonized. "Please."

James pursed his mouth in a deeply disappointed frown but nodded: he would do it. Eva acted swiftly, before he had a chance to change his mind.

She leaned toward him and whispered in his ear, "You grab and hold him and I'll stuff this in his mouth. All right?"

James hesitated for a million years before nodding.

They both turned to look at Visel. His expression was unreadable, his body tense and coiled. "Why do you need to gag me? I won't shout."

"I wouldn't trust you any farther than I could throw you."

Visel sighed. "Well?" he said, speaking to James. "Go ahead, I won't struggle. Trust me, I'll just sit back and enjoy the ride while your mistress breaks her legs, or worse, jumping out of this carriage. I'll be glad to be rid of the two of you; I only ask that the gag not be uncomfortably tight."

Eva looked at James. "He's wily, James, and this is probably a trick. But you grab his hands and hold him, and I shall tie on the gag."

Lord Visel chuckled, but he was as good as his word. He did not struggle even when Eva crouched in front of him, hunched over and her feet spread wide to keep some balance in the cramped confines of the moving carriage.

He watched her with a glint in his eyes she could not like as she tied the neckcloth around his head. But his looks hardly mattered anymore because she wouldn't have to look at his face in a matter of moments.

Once the gag was secure she scooted back to her bench, breathing heavily, as if she'd done something strenuous. Eva was surprised and maybe even a little disappointed that Visel had given in without a struggle. Not that she wished to be around him any longer than need be, of course, but she would have enjoyed giving him a good cuffing.

"I'll go first, my lady, and I'll take the satchel with me," James said, pulling her attention away from Visel. "I'm going to make sure these knots on his wrists will hold. Perhaps you might sort through the bag and remove anything that won't make the jump."

"Good thinking, James." Eva bent down and opened the heavy leather satchel. It took her a few minutes to sort through the accumulated debris: a half-full jug of coffee, an empty jug of beer, cutlery,

a heavily thumbed copy of *Gulliver's Travels*—her favorite book—
extra rope, a small bag of ammunition for the gun she'd borrowed,
and more. She removed everything except the cleverly folded map of
the North of England, two clean if slightly rumpled neckcloths, a
small folding penknife, her book, and a packet of hard candies that
James adored.

"All right," she said, sitting up and bringing the bag with her,
handing it to James, who was looking even more worried than usual.
She smiled. "It will be fine," she reassured him.

James smiled sickly and nodded.

Visel was watching her, his eyes hooded, but his lips curved into
a smile around his gag.

"I don't know what you're so happy about," she said, giving him
a dirty look. But that only made him smile more. He was a horrid man.

James's face was an alarming red as he slung the satchel over his
body crosswise.

"James?" she asked, squinting up at him. "Is aught amiss?"

His jaw tightened, he hesitated, but then he shook his head before peering out the window. "It's drizzling. This will be a mess, my
lady. Are you sure you—"

"Yes, let's get on with it."

"Neither side looks any better than the other." He frowned,
snatched off his cloth cap and stuffed it in the satchel, took a deep
breath, and cracked open the door on her right. He glanced ahead
and then pulled his head back inside. "Just make sure you jump as far
away from the wheels as you can. Push off from the—"

"Good Lord, James. I think I will know how to fling myself from
a carriage." But she was scared and her body had begun to sweat as
she stared out the window at the rapidly passing countryside; the carriage was moving *fast*. She swallowed down the lump of fear. "Go
on. Get on with it."

He cracked open the door, wedged his huge body in the gap, and
then sprang out. It all happened in the blink of an eye. The door

flapped free and she quickly grabbed it before it could spook the horses. She gave Visel one last look and a jaunty smirk that she did not feel.

"I hope you have a pleasant journey, my lord." She turned from him and crouched on her haunches, preparing to jump. She heard a muffled sound behind her just before a pair of legs wrapped around her middle.

Eva squawked and instantly began to struggle, thrashing and pounding on his legs, which were like bands of iron. "Let me go, you brute, you're squeezing me. *Let me go!*" She punctuated her words by hammering her fists on his shins.

"I don't think so, darling." The voice was distinct, certainly not that of a man who was gagged.

What?

Powerful legs drew her inexorably away from the flapping door, until he caught her with his hands and pulled her tight against his body. His arms replaced his legs and she found herself held in a vise-like grip.

"Now, now. Quit thrashing or you'll hurt yourself. And you don't want me to have to tie you up, do you?"

Eva bit her lip to keep from yelling. "Let. Me. Go."

He laughed, his big, hard body vibrating against her back. "I think not."

"Just let me go and this can be over and you can crawl back under whatever rock you came from."

"That's hardly a thing to say to your husband-to-be."

His words sent a thrill of fear through her. And something else.

"Please," she said, trying to remain calm—to sound rational. "James will be lying back there wondering what happened."

"I doubt that."

"He will—and he'll come for me if I don't join him. He knows where we are going and has plenty of money to pay to get to Doncaster."

"I don't think so, darling."

She squirmed in his unbreakable hold. "What the devil do you mean? Of course he—"

His face dropped close to hers, his hot breath on her temple. "James won't be expecting you. Who do you think untied my hands so I could grab you, sweetheart?"

Chapter 4

"I hate you."

"You've already said that. Several times, in fact."

Lady Eva was sitting across from him, hugging herself tightly, her face a mask of fury.

"My father will kill you when he finds you."

"You've said that, too."

"He will shoot you *and* run you through with his sword."

Godric chuckled. "A thorough, man, is he?"

She cut him a narrow-eyed look that pulsed with loathing. "He is one of the finest hands with a pistol or a sword in all of Britain. He will make short work of you."

"I have no doubt he could vanquish me with either weapon. However, if he kills me, I can hardly take you off his hands, can I?" he asked sweetly.

Her delicate nostrils flared. "I shall *never* marry you. *Never.*"

"Oh come, my lady. How could you think this would end any other way? You've spent the last twenty-four hours or so with me— much of it alone together in this carriage. If you think Lord Exley wouldn't hold a gun to my head if I *didn't* marry you, then you are deluding yourself." He shook his head, giving her his own hate-filled stare. "You've done for us both quite nicely: we are both firmly trussed up—*together*—just like a Christmas goose."

Godric could see the truth of his words penetrating the thick wall of fury that surrounded her. And his words were most certainly true: she'd bound them together when she concocted this asinine caper. He shook his head, all but choked by angry despair as he contemplated the future she'd forced on both of them. He might have the war hysteria, as she'd accused, and now he would have a mad wife to keep him company. And if she wasn't mad, she certainly behaved as if she was.

As if reading his mind she said, "Your grandfather will never allow you to marry me."

"I am a grown man, my lady," Godric said, putting enough cold disdain in his tone to freeze a small body of water. "The duke does not direct my actions."

"But you are his heir. And if you marry me, then—" For once the little harridan could not give voice to her thoughts.

"I am his heir but there is an abundance of second and third cousins. I have plenty of male relations to inherit without making a copy of myself for the dukedom." He cut her a cold look. "You may take comfort in the fact that I will never put a child inside you."

Her beautiful ivory cheeks flared and she blinked rapidly. "You mean—"

"Yes, you shan't have to do your wifely duty and produce an heir." Godric saw no reason to tell her the *real* reason he'd not be begetting any children on her—or any other woman—because he didn't *have* to tell her. The fact that a strain of madness ran in her family was a convenient—if cruel—excuse. Was it shameless and despicable of Godric to allow her to believe it was fear of her tainted blood that would keep him from breeding her? Yes, it most certainly was. If he had a heart—or a conscience—he might have been bothered by his lie.

For all that her face was usually an open book, Godric could not see what she thought of his words. Perhaps because she didn't know, herself. She was, after all, an innocent girl, no matter how outrageously she behaved.

"How old are you?" he asked, even though he wasn't sure that he wanted to know the answer.

"That is an impertinent question."

"Eighteen?" He grimaced when she did not answer. "Good Lord. Seventeen?"

"I am nineteen," she snapped. "Not that it is any of your concern."

He didn't bother telling her that his future wife's age was very much his concern. Godric wouldn't be surprised to learn she was lying. She seemed younger than nineteen, but perhaps that was her behavior. He had to admit he'd not come across a girl quite like her before, not that schoolroom chits were an area where he could claim any vast experience.

He pulled his gaze away and looked out the window. His sister Louisa would have been nineteen this year. She was as different from the firebrand across from him as two girls could be. She'd shared Godric's fair coloring but her temperament had been gentle and sweet. Louisa was like a dove to Eva de Courtney's hawk. Or perhaps his wife-to-be resembled a more clever bird like a raven or magpie; clever and mischievous and difficult to control.

"I can't believe James would leave me in your clutches," she groused.

Godric did not turn away from the rain-spattered window. "He did so for your own good."

"How do you know that? You didn't even talk to him."

"I didn't need to; he heard what I had to say and knew it was the truth—just as you would know if you'd take a moment to consider matters. The boy is no fool—for all that you have twisted him around your finger. He knew how this must end. Besides," he added just because he could not resist poking her, "if you think he fancied the notion of tramping about the countryside playing nursemaid to a gently bred lady in—"

"I do *not* need anyone to play nursemaid for me," she said through clenched teeth.

Godric watched as she struggled with her fury, all but glowing with rage at his words. How interesting: a girl who didn't mind being called mad but became furious when you questioned her self-sufficiency? It demonstrated an unattractive and unfeminine tendency toward independence. But worse than that, it showed she was opinionated and tenacious and committed to getting her way.

Well, so was he: what a marriage they would have.

"Why are we having this argument, Lady Eva? What purpose does it serve? He is gone and you are with me. By tonight we will be in Doncaster. When we arrive I shall summon Sir Bertram. I will put you in a room, find you suitable clothing, and we shall continue our journey toward the border on the morrow."

She bared her teeth and leaned forward. "You shall have to drag me to Scotland in chains."

"It is all the same to me," he said coolly. He'd be damned if he'd let the chit goad him into a shouting match.

Her face fell when she saw he could not be drawn. "Why? Why are you doing this?" she begged, her full lower lip quivering in a way that gave him wicked and highly inappropriate thoughts. "If you let me go now, nobody will ever know. You can go on with your life—I have seen you with The Kitten, I know you fancy her, you could marry her if you release me."

Godric didn't tell her that up until this morning—when he'd woken up in this bloody carriage—he'd had no intention of marrying anyone, ever. But what would be the point?

"I find this topic tedious, my lady." He cut her a repressive look. "If you cannot come up with something more interesting to say, perhaps you might have done and give us both some desperately needed peace and quiet."

He might as well have saved his breath.

"I shall be the worst wife ever."

Godric did not doubt it for a moment.

"I shall run away at the first opportunity and I shall—"

His hands shot out and he grabbed her upper arms, pulling her close until their noses were almost touching. "What you *shall* do is take yourself and your emotions in hand. You are nineteen, not nine. If you think I will tolerate bad behavior—threats, wildness, vulgar language, or disrespect—you are sorely mistaken. You will begin behaving like a lady from this moment on or I will find inventive and uncomfortable methods to encourage you to do so. And if you should have occasion to feel sorry for yourself and your predicament, let me remind you that *you* are the one who began all this by kidnapping me. It is time you learned your actions have consequences."

Her jaw hung open, her remarkable eyes went wide, and tangled masses of blue-black hair surrounded her heart-shaped face. Godric had the maddest urge to suck her plump lower lip into his mouth, pull her into his lap, and let his hands roam her small but exceedingly curvaceous and touchable body. She looked bloody delicious in her tight buckskins and miniature top boots. He could have her out of her breeches in the blink of an eye. His cock throbbed and he wondered if she liked to ride; he would certainly enjoy teaching her to ride *him*.

Godric flinched from his own thoughts in horror: What the hell was wrong with him? Good Lord, the last thing he needed to do was bed this hellion in a fit of anger. He thrust her back onto her seat. That was the last thing *either* of them needed. He would bed her when the time came, to make sure the marriage was legal, but that would be an end to it. He'd not been speaking in jest when he said he would not put a child in her.

Godric turned to stare out the window, forcing his thoughts to stop moving, breathing deeply and evenly, tricks he'd learned during the long years he fought in the war. Most people believed he'd led an active and exciting life. The truth was that war was boredom punctuated by unexpected moments of chaos and merciless violence. A person could go mad in such an environment unless they developed a method of coping.

Madness. He cut her a swift look. But she was gazing out the other window, her hands clasped tightly in her lap, her features taut. Was she mad? Was *he*? He'd certainly felt a certain type of madness when he'd heard the news about his family in his hospital bed in Portugal.

"I am sorry, Colonel," the King's guardsman had said, "but I have some rather bad news."

Yes, *rather* bad. Even now Godric couldn't help his bitter smile: how like an Englishman to call losing most of one's family *rather* bad news.

One moment he'd been pitying himself because his injury would not allow him to walk for longer than ten minutes at a time. The next, he was utterly without a family.

Yes, *rather* bad news, indeed.

Godric had learned one very, very, very important lesson that day. No matter how bad one's life was, it could always become worse.

The King's Arms was the busiest posting inn Eva had ever seen. Postilions appeared to be lurking in the hedges that bordered the road, awaiting incoming carriages and coaches. Another inn sat on the opposite side of the road and some sort of competition was raging between them. The scene was chaotic as the chaise rolled up to the crowded courtyard and stopped behind several others.

"We will wait in here," Lord Visel said, his commanding tone making her bristle. "And if you have any thoughts of weaving creative tales of pirate kings or kidnappings or any other drivel, I advise you to forget it. The innkeeper knows me quite well, as I've ridden this way many times." He gave her a mocking smile. "You see, this inn is on the way to *my* family's country seat, Cross Hall."

She ignored him.

They waited less than two minutes before the door opened.

A portly man dressed in the clothing of an innkeeper stood in the doorway, beaming as he lowered the steps himself.

"Ah, it *is* you, my Lord Visel. What a pleasure it is to see you again, sir." His eyes flickered briefly to the earl's unusual hair color, but of course the simpering sycophant made no mention of *that*.

"Thank you for your warm welcome, Mr. Johnson." Visel's pale, amused eyes landed on Eva. "I'm afraid I have a rather delicate situation."

Mr. Johnson's head bobbed up and down like an amorous pigeon's. "Oh, yes, my lord. Young Oliver explained it all to me."

Visel cut her an openly diverted look. "Oh, he did, did he?"

Eva narrowed her eyes at him.

"Yes," the innkeeper said, "he told me you were engaged on a mission of, er, some delicacy."

The earl laughed. "I suspected he was a wise boy. Did he mention summoning Sir Bertram?"

The innkeeper's servile face flushed a dull red. "Well, as a matter of fact, sir, he did. But that was before I saw you with my own two eyes. Of course now that I know it is really you, I wouldn't—"

"Please, do send for him. Tell him it is a matter of some importance. But, in the meantime, I would have your two best chambers and a private parlor." His cold gaze flickered over Eva. "I believe we shall use your side entrance just now."

Mr. Johnson had not stopped nodding. "Of course, my lord, right away." His small eyes slid toward Eva and he recoiled at whatever he saw on her face, darting away without waiting for a response.

"You frightened him, my dear," Visel said mildly.

Eva tried to catch Jemmy's eye, but he flipped up the steps and closed the door with a quick snap, clearly too ashamed by his traitorous behavior to look her in the eye.

She tried to find something in Visel's plan to complain about, but couldn't. She was every bit as eager as he was to avoid notice. It would make everything easier after she escaped him and made her way to Lady Repton's.

Once the carriage stopped, he exited first and offered her his hand. Eva ignored it and hopped down without any help from him.

The side door opened as they approached it. "Ah, yes, right in here my lord, my . . . er . . ." The rotund innkeeper blinked down at Eva, his round face shiny and red. "I beg your pardon, but if you'll take these back stairs, you'll be more private."

Visel took her elbow in a firm, unbreakable grip as the innkeeper led them to the second floor.

"This is our nicest room, my lord."

"This is yours," Visel told her, before turning to the innkeeper. "Have a bath brought up for her ladyship, and I'd also like to engage a maid for her and—"

"I don't need a maid. I can take care of myself. And I don't want—"

"Would you excuse us a moment, Mr. Johnson?" the earl asked, not waiting for an answer before pulling her inside the room and shutting the door in the stunned innkeeper's face.

Eva yanked her arm, but he would not release her.

"Listen to me." It was an iron tone of command Eva recognized: Lord Visel sounded remarkably like her father. But he was *not* her father and she was under no obligation to obey him.

She glared up at him. "Let go of my arm." She infused the words with all the venom she could muster, but his grip didn't loosen.

"Do not argue with me every step of the way or it will become tedious for both of us."

"Let me go and you won't have to worry about me and my tedium."

He walked her backward, until she was pressed against the wall, his tall, hard body not stopping until they were touching from shoulders to hips. He took her chin in strong, warm fingers and tilted her face to his, holding her immobile when she tried to pull away. This close to him she could see his irises were a dozen shades of blue intermixed with shards of white, the iris rimmed with pale, pale gold. The lines that fanned out from his eyes were myriad and distinct, and the grooves between his nose and mouth were etched deeply. Bits of gold glinted under the light of the wall sconce: his night beard. Something about seeing the tiny hairs scattered across his angular jaw and determined chin made her aware of her body, especially the region south of her belly and north of her knees: this was the face of a man, not a boy.

As Eva looked into his penetrating blue eyes, she knew manipulating him would not be easy; he was not the sort of man to bend to her will.

"If you behave like a child, I'll treat you as one." His body pressed against hers and the words rumbled like the threat of approaching thunder.

"How *dare* you speak to me this way? I am not your wife and have no intention of assuming that position, no matter what you say."

His lips twitched. "Trust me, darling, you will assume any position I say when the time comes." His smile disappeared. "You kidnapped me, hit me on the head, and dragged me halfway across the country. I dare a good deal at this point. I will not fight you every step of the way to Scotland. I will not argue in front of others. I will not be made a fool of. Do you understand me? I will punish you in private. I will put you over my knee and paddle you like the willful, wild, undisciplined, spoiled child you are."

She gasped. "You *wouldn't*."

One side of his mouth pulled up, the action unveiling a dimple in his tanned cheek. "Oh, but I *would*. And I daresay my hand would enjoy meeting your bottom." His eyes dropped to her mouth and his nostrils flared and for one dreadful moment she thought he was going to kiss her.

For one dreadful moment Eva wanted him to.

Instead, he thrust her away, strode to the door, flung it open and closed it ungently behind him, leaving her alone.

"Good Lord, Godric—this is remarkable."

"So you've said, Bertie—at least a half dozen times already." Godric topped up his friend's glass and his own while he was about it.

The other man, shorter, plumper, and with considerably less hair than the last time Godric had seen him, took a deep pull and shook his head yet again. "I've never heard anything like it—a chit kidnapping a man right from a *ton* party. If you told her father this story, you could not rightly be expected to marry her."

"If this story got out I would be the laughing stock of all England, Bertie. The great war hero Godric Fleming kidnapped by a girl barely out of the schoolroom? I think not. Besides, the chit would be ruined."

"But isn't she already ruined? I mean she is—"

Godric lifted his eyebrows at the other man and Bertie froze. "Have a care, Bertie. She is to be my wife."

Bertie took a big swig from his glass before answering. "Yes, yes, of course, old chap."

Godric forced himself to relax. "How are Amelia and the children?"

Bertie perked up. "She's blooming. We've got seven now."

"*Seven!* Good lord, Bertie—don't you ever let the poor woman have a night's rest?"

Bertie's homely face flushed with pride. "Four boys and three girls. All strapping, fine youngsters who take after their mother in their looks."

"That is worth raising a glass to."

They toasted Bertie's fine-looking children.

After that they drank several more toasts, becoming increasingly loose as the evening wore on. Godric had ordered a separate dinner for his betrothed and had not seen her since leaving her room. He'd been wise enough to lock her door but wouldn't have been surprised to catch her crawling out the window, falling, and cracking her head open on the cobbles below. So he'd told Johnson to pay a man to stand in the back courtyard all night. The innkeeper had looked at him as if he were unhinged, but it was better than hieing across the country searching for her tomorrow morning.

The woman was bloody exhausting.

And you will get to spend the rest of your life with her. Mocking laughter echoed in his head.

Christ.

Bertie maundered on about some hunt or other while Godric tried to impose order on his mental chaos. He hadn't been lying when he'd told the girl he'd not planned to marry The Kitten. What she didn't know was that he'd not planned to remarry at *all*. It had been an enormous bone of contention between himself and his grandfather, the Duke of Tyndale.

From the moment Godric's uncle—the present duke's eldest surviving son—had been killed in a carriage accident, his grandfather had come after Godric with a singlemindedness that was dizzying, even going so far as to make a journey to the Continent to apply pressure on him to sell out and come home. When Godric had refused, the duke had pressured the Beau to speak to him.

When Wellington had summoned Godric to dinner, he'd been fairly certain why he was being honored. "You've done your duty to your country for fifteen years, Lord Visel." The duke's use of Godric's courtesy title told him what was coming next. "Now it is time you do your duty to your family." Wellington was one of the most powerful men in the world; he was also Godric's commander. He could not disobey the Iron Duke, even if the man had only been making a suggestion.

So he'd sold out and come home. Tyndale had wanted to install him in the country estate that had always been occupied by the ducal heir, a rambling nightmare of a place where Godric would rattle around like a pea in a dried-out pod.

That had been the first of his grandfather's orders that he'd ignored. He would live at Cross Hall, he told the duke. What he hadn't told the other man—one of his few remaining relatives—was that he *needed* to live there. The death of his father, mother, two brothers and their wives and children, *and* his young sister, had only become real to him when he'd set foot in his childhood home. Never could he have imagined it so empty—so silent. Even with all the servants still occupying it, the house was like a tomb. A tomb without bodies. Because none of the bodies of his family had been recovered after their ship had been sunk by pirates.

"Godric?"

He looked up at the sound of his name and saw that Bertie was staring at him.

"Sorry, Bertie, I'm afraid I'm knackered and drifted a bit."

"Quite so, quite so, old chap. Here I am rattling on." Luckily Bertie was too good-natured to take offense at Godric's inattention. "I was just saying I could send word to Samuel Porter, the local tailor. It's late, but I know he'd work through the night if it meant kitting out a duke's heir."

"Yes, that would be excellent. I've only got this to wear." He gestured to the rather battered clawhammer and buckskins he'd had on beneath his costume. "And I managed to lose my purse somewhere along the way, I'm afraid," he said, not wanting to tell his friend that his bride-to-be had stolen his money and given it to her accomplice. "I shall need to dun you."

"Of course, don't give it another thought." Bertie grinned, his eyes flickering to the top of Godric's head. "I'm guessing you'll want to wash that out as well."

Godric squinted and then recalled what he'd done for the masquerade ball.

"What do you think, Bertie?" he jested tiredly. "Does it suit me?"

"I think that shade of black is not for you, old man. Besides, you wouldn't want to hide your gold curls from your adoring flocks of women." He stopped abruptly, his pudgy cheeks coloring. "Although I suppose those days might be behind you now that you're getting shackled."

Godric thought of his female companion stewing away a few doors down: his wife-to-be. He snorted and pushed away any questions of women, adoring or otherwise, and smiled at his friend.

"I suppose you'd better send a message to a dressmaker as well as a tailor."

Chapter 5

Eva was awake even before first light.

She paced the two rooms, telling herself to be calm. Nothing was ever gained by becoming angry with a man. No, *they* were allowed to be angry but women were merely supposed to smile, bow their heads, and meekly obey.

Well, if Visel was expecting her to be *that* kind of wife, he was in for an unpleasant surprise. *Lots* of unpleasant surprises.

What had he said? That she would not be required to do her wifely duty? So, he found her so revolting, he did not even wish to bed her. She squeezed her hands together so hard the bones ground against each other. Good. She was *glad* he didn't wish to touch her. The only way she wanted to touch him was with a shovel.

The door opened and she swung around: it was the earl. He swept her from head to toe to head, his eyes even paler in the bright light of day, his hard mouth pulled down at the corners.

"Why are you not dressed?"

"Somebody has taken my clothing."

His eyes flickered to the garments the maid had laid across her bed. "What are those?"

"That is an excellent question," she shot back.

His mouth tightened. "That is a dress and undergarments I had brought over for you at great inconvenience."

"I want *my* clothing—what I was wearing yesterday."

He took a step into the room and closed the door before leaning back against it and crossing his arms. "I believe it is time we came to some agreement."

Eva crossed her own arms and returned his cool, haughty look. At least as well as she could when she was dressed in a borrowed dressing gown while he was clean and pressed and kitted out in clothing that fit his big body as snugly as a glove. His hat and overcoat looked new but his other toggery was so well-tailored that she assumed this must have been what he was wearing beneath his ridiculous corsair robes.

"I do not wish to engage in arguments every day. Or even every other day. What can I do to accustom you to the idea that we will shortly be man and wife?"

Eva thumbed her chin and gazed upward in a gesture of exaggerated contemplation. "Let's see . . . that would be, um . . . *Let. Me. Go.*" She dropped her clenched fists to her sides and strode toward him, brimming with fury. "Why can't you leave me here? I can send a message to my father to come fetch me. I daresay James is already halfway back to London. My parents are not leaving for another few days—it will not take them long to come up here and—"

"No."

She couldn't help the frustrated noise that slipped from her. "*Why* are you doing this? I don't care if my reputation *is* ruined. I don't. You must have guessed I never intended to marry, so this makes no odds to me. You can go your happy way and never have to see me again."

Impossibly, his expression hardened even more and his arms dropped to his sides. He took a step toward her. When she would have stepped backward, his hands shot out and closed on her upper arms like vises.

"I am going to say this again and it will be the last time I repeat myself. You will become my wife. I do not care if you have no regard for your own reputation or name; I have plenty for my own and for the few family members that remain to me. I do not care to live out my life known as a man low enough to destroy a woman's reputation and make no amends. If you are harboring the bizarre belief that *anyone* in Britain would believe you abducted me, you are—" He hesitated, his eyes narrowing slightly as he realized what he was about to say. "Nobody would give any credence to such a story. Even if they did, that still does not change the fact you have been *alone* with me for two nights. And really, that is the crux of it all: you have been compromised. You have just seen your brother's response to compromising Miss Drusilla Clare—do you expect anything less from me?" She opened her mouth and he lifted one hand, his index finger raised in a cautionary gesture. "Do not say anything you will regret, my lady."

Eva ground her teeth, keeping her jaws clenched.

"If you cannot voluntarily bring yourself to get dressed and get into the carriage, then I will carry you into it, dressed as you are. If you cannot bring yourself to speak your vows in front of a member of the clergy, I will find one who is not so fussy about the, er, finer points of the ceremony."

She gasped. "You would marry me against my will?"

"I thought I'd made that patently clear. Yes. Yes, I would. Because I know you will end up marrying me in any event. If I were to let you go home, as you have requested, the Marquess of Exley would hunt me down like the vermin I would be if I released a young, unmarried gentlewoman to the vagaries of the road. And when he caught me—after he administered sufficient chastisement— he would make us wed. If I refused him, he would put a period to my existence, and there isn't a magistrate in the land who wouldn't applaud such an action. So, yes," he said in a low, menacing voice. "I will force you to do the sensible thing now and save us both a great deal of bother later."

Eva could feel the *mood* come over her; it had been toeing the edges of her consciousness like a willful goat testing its tether. Her temper was what her father and everyone else thought of as a sign of madness. Well, everyone but one person: her stepmother.

"You have a dreadful temper, Eva. That is all that ails you." Her beautiful, loving stepmother had taken her aside years ago—after one of the confrontations with her father that had left everyone in the house miserable and tiptoeing on eggshells.

"How do you know?" Eva demanded. "How do you know it is not m–madness?"

It had been difficult to say the word, but not to accept the truth. Her father had told them about their mother when Eva was not yet fifteen. She did not know why he'd waited so long, but she suspected it was because he'd not wanted to face the truth himself. No, only his new wife, Mia, had been brave enough.

"I have a terrible, terrible temper," Mia confessed that day. "My head becomes hot and my hands shake. My mind is like a trapped animal running around and around inside my head, looking for an exit."

Eva had been stunned. "Yes! Yes, that is exactly how it is with me. But—"

"You are not mad, my beautiful daughter. You are only angry—and you are not good at managing your anger." She had shrugged her delicate shoulders, as if such a thing—a thing that had plagued Eva all her life—was a mere inconvenience, a bagatelle. "You will need to *learn* to manage it. And I am proof it can be done." Her mouth had curved into an ironic smile. "Not always, perhaps, but often enough. When you feel these things happening to you, it is time to breathe deeply and clear your mind. It is not time to argue or discuss—you will not be able to do so rationally." Her pretty face had become hard. "Raising your voice, becoming hysterical? These are things that make *men* feel they can ignore us—that we are merely emotional females. I am not saying you must not *be* emotional, I am saying you should save your emotions for a time when you can examine them in private. *Never* let anger rule your behavior—or your anger *will* rule you."

Eva clutched at the memory of those words now, her eyes held by Visel's. A vein in his temple pulsed and she realized he, too, was struggling to manage his anger. Why? Because everything he said was true. She *would* have to marry him—whether he insisted on it or not. It was not just about her; it was about her family. What would happen if the truth about what she'd done got out? Rumors of such behavior would not only hurt her, they would hurt the rest of her family—especially Melissa. Sweet, gentle, and quiet, her seventeen-year-old sister would have even less chance of marrying than she did now. No, Eva had to marry him.

And then there is the fact that you want *him.* The thought rang in her mind with the sharp decisiveness of a judge's gavel, and she wondered if she'd said the words out loud. But he was still looking at her with haughty inscrutability.

A wave of exhaustion hit her, leaving her feeling shaky and worn down. "I will get dressed, my lord."

His eyebrows lowered and she realized her capitulation had put him off balance; Eva tucked that tactic away for future use. "You are not planning an escape?"

"No, I'm not," she said, realizing only as she spoke the words, they were the truth. She gave him a look as haughty as his own. "You can take my word of honor."

His jaw worked from side to side as he raked her with a pitiless blue stare. Finally, he nodded. "I shall send a maid up and will wait for you in the parlor."

Eva watched him leave before slumping into the chair.

Did she want him—was that true? She had to admit she was . . . *fascinated* by him. But it was more anger and hatred she felt toward him, for his persecution of her brother. If she *did* want him, it was only to punish him and *certainly* not to marry him. But if that was all she wanted from him, then why had she felt so hurt when he'd said he would not exercise his husbandly prerogative once they married? Why was it painful to acknowledge he had no interest in bedding her? Was that what she'd wanted, to be bedded by him?

You know it is.

Eva groaned. But there was no point in denying her body's reaction to him: her skin became hot when he looked at her and her innards churned in a not entirely unpleasant fashion when he gave her that heavy-eyed look. That was probably the effect he had on most women—after all, he was very handsome, virile, and he'd been praised often for his bravery. It wouldn't be abnormal to find such a man attractive. To want such a man.

Was that why she'd kidnapped him? Had she really done all this for herself? Had she lied to herself that she was doing it for Gabe and Dru? If she had, she had condemned herself to a certain kind of hell: she wanted him, or at least her body did, and he had made it clear he had no interest in touching her.

There was a soft knock on the door.

"Enter," she said. The door opened and the maid came into the room.

Eva sighed, stood, and prepared to face the coming day.

They didn't have the same postilions as before. In fact, Godric had paid both boys an obscene amount of money and asked the innkeeper to separate them and send them to opposite ends of the country. They would talk eventually, but Godric and Eva's elopement would be old news by the time any word of what had happened made its way to London.

He studied his betrothed, who sat across from him swathed in a plain gray cloak, with a pretty periwinkle-blue bonnet on the seat beside her. Her dress, he knew—even though he could not see it—was the same shade of blue. Godric knew that because he'd been the one to choose her clothing from the small dress shop. He'd chosen three gowns based on the recommendations of the seamstress. They all had loose bodices that could be adjusted with a drawstring below the bosom to fit almost any shape. All they'd required was hemming as his wife-to-be was exceptionally small in stature.

Godric studied her as she stared out the window, her profile perfect, sharp, and wintry. Good God, but she was a beauty. She had the sort of coloring he loved—dark, inky hair and navy-blue eyes with pale, pale skin. His own golden fairness was a disappointment when he looked in the mirror. There was something vapid about looking as though one should be sitting on a cloud plucking a harp— a comparison he'd heard times beyond counting from the women he'd bedded.

Lady Eva de Courtney looked like a character from some Greek fable. An untamable nymph or headstrong goddess.

Or a mad daughter of the moon.

"Why are you staring at me?" she demanded.

Godric smiled at her waspish tone. "You are soon to be my wife. It is my right to look at you. Don't you wish to look at me?"

"No." But her face flushed wildly, giving the lie to her words.

Godric chuckled, genuinely amused by her lack of guile; she might be nineteen but she behaved as though she were much younger. And she made him feel ancient. He supposed he *was* ancient by her standards: almost seventeen years older. Lord. He'd already been in the army for years by the time he was her age.

He eyed the young woman across from him. No doubt her father had spoiled her—such a clever, lively, beautiful daughter would be the apple of any father's eye—and parental indulgence certainly went a long way to explaining her unorthodox, willful behavior. Godric had met the marquess and his wife at several functions this Season. They did not like him. Well, that was an understatement—they actively disliked him. Godric could not blame them. He'd conducted himself badly this past Season, his behavior culminating in a challenge to the marchioness's eldest son, Gabriel Marlington. The only reason the duel had not occurred was because Godric had apologized to the younger man—very publicly.

His face heated at the memory of that apology. As mortifying as it had felt at the time, it had been the right and honorable thing to do. Not for himself, but for his grandfather. The duke was old— ancient, in fact. At eighty-six he had not many more years left, a piece of information he had wielded with all the subtlety of a cudgel to pressure Godric to do his bidding.

"Give up this foolish duel, Godric. You know you are in the wrong. If you should die—or kill him—who will take the burden from my shoulders? It will not only be me you have forsaken; it will be the hundreds who rely on the Duke of Tyndale."

Godric hadn't been lying when he'd told Lady Eva that an heir of his body was not necessary to the continuation of the dukedom. He *did* have several male heirs, but the next one in line—his cousin Charles—was far too young to take over the dukedom.

So Godric had apologized. In White's. In front of everyone who was anyone in *ton* circles.

"I shall make a terrible duchess."

He glanced up. "Hmm?"

"I *said*, I shall make a terrible duchess."

He suspected she was correct, but even he was not so impolitic to say such a thing. "How do you know that?"

The question gave her pause, but she was quick to recover. "You've seen me this Season—you know what I mean."

Godric could have told her he'd paid very little attention to her this Season, and it would have been the truth. It also would have insulted her. He was not yet, he hoped, reduced to being cruel to infants.

"You needn't worry about entertaining," he told her. "I plan on doing very little of it."

"I don't like living in the city."

He shrugged. "You may live where you please."

She brightened. "Truly?"

"Within reason." He studied her stunning face, suddenly curious. "Why? Where do you wish to live?"

"I wish to live in the country." She bit her cushiony lip. "On a stud farm."

A surprised laugh broke out of him and she glowered. "Why is that funny?"

"It is just . . . unexpected. So, you like horses, do you?"

"Better than most people." The look she gave him told Godric which category *he* occupied.

"A stud farm, eh? Fancy yourself an equine specialist?"

She snorted.

"What type of horses would you raise?" he asked.

"Racehorses," she said, her tone clearly implying there was no other kind.

"If you want to breed racehorses, you must know a bit about them—not to mention a great deal about racing."

"I'm a bruising rider and could have been a jockey if I'd been born a man." She hesitated and then added, "And I've been to more than a few races."

Godric heard the bitterness in her tone and knew the subject was not one he should tease her about, so he remained silent.

She gave him a cool, heavy-lidded look of scorn. "I could ride you into the dirt."

Her taunt surprised a laugh out of him. "Is that so?"

"It is."

"I don't suppose it has occurred to you I was a cavalry officer for over a decade and a half."

She shrugged. "It doesn't matter."

His eyebrows shot up.

"I don't care if you were a cavalry officer for a hundred years—I would still best you in the saddle."

"The only way a chit like you could best me is if I *had* been in the cavalry for a hundred and thirty-six years." Only after he issued the asinine taunt did he realize how childish it sounded. She didn't appear to notice, her attention snagged by a different fact.

"You're *thirty-six*?"

Godric bristled at her tone. "What of it?" he asked, not caring that he sounded testy.

She merely shook her head and turned to look out the window, her quiet acquiescence taking the wind from his sails more quickly than a taunt would have done.

"Why do we have to stop for the night?" Eva asked.

Visel smirked at her—yes, he smirked. "In a hurry to get up to Scotland and jump over the broomstick, my love?"

She gave him a scathing look. "The sooner we can get married, the sooner we can go our separate ways," she reminded him.

He cocked one eyebrow, a condescending action that made her want to slap him. "What's that?"

"You said I could live wherever I wanted," she reminded him.

"I never said that."

Her jaw dropped. "You *did*."

"Didn't."

"It was only about six hours ago. I know you're old, but are you so senile you could forget such a thing already?" Eva knew her voice had risen and she was sweaty all over, even though it was a bit chilly. She told herself to stay calm, but she already knew she wasn't in the mood to listen. To anyone—not even herself.

He gave her a patient, knowing smile that made her head throb. "We are stopping tonight because there is very little moon and I see no need to take any chances racketing straight through." He examined the nails on his hand, turning it this way and that. Eva noticed, not for the first time, he had attractive hands. Not soft and white and almost feminine like so many men of their class, but broad across the palm and tanned on top. Gold hair glinted on the back and the veins were ropy and blue beneath the thin skin. They were quite the nicest—

Eva blinked at the thought and at the physical sensations just looking at his hand evoked. This was bad. Very bad. She looked up to find him watching her, his head cocked, his expression inquiring. She dragged her attention back to the point she'd been pursuing. What was it again? Oh, yes, living arrangements.

"I want to talk about what you said earlier. I want—"

The carriage shuddered to a sudden halt, the wheels sliding sideways so that they both grabbed for a strap. The earl leaned forward to look out the window. It had rained constantly since this morning and had begun bucketing down after they'd left the last inn around two o'clock. It looked like dusk rather than only six o'clock.

"What is it?" she asked, even though she was looking out the same window he was.

"I don't know," he muttered before turning to her, his expression changing from thoughtful to stern. "I'm going to see what is going on. You. Stay. Here."

Eva bristled. "How dare you talk to me as if I were a dog?"

"Do I need to tie you up?"

She gasped.

He pointed an index finger at her. "Stay put."

Before she could tell him what he could do with both his order and his finger, he opened the door and hopped out, shutting the door and disappearing from view.

"You pillock," she said to the empty carriage and then pressed her face to the cool glass. She couldn't see anything but rain and dreary clouds and trees that seemed to press in upon the road.

She was about to open the window and poke her head out when the door on the other side opened. She spun around. "I wasn't doing anything," she blurted.

He climbed in without bothering to lower the steps. Eva wished she could do that—it was dreadful to be as runty as she.

"What is it?" she asked as he shook the rain from his hat and the carriage started to move.

He gave her a grim look. "A tree has fallen across the road and we must go back."

Hope surged in her breast. She tried not to let her excitement show, but he noticed it anyway.

"Not all the way to London, darling. Only as far as the last turnoff. We shall go to a town just off the main road. There are two inns; one of them should suffice for the night." His eyes narrowed as he wiped the excess water from his face with a snowy square of linen. "Don't get any ideas."

"What ideas might those be? Shooting you? I no longer have a gun. Running away from you? Ha! Where would I run with no money? In this." She plucked at the dreadful dress he'd purchased— a namby-pamby girly thing in a putrid shade of blue. "Not to mention up here at the back of beyond in the dark and rain?"

"Yes, to all of those ideas and also the ones you *didn't* mention."

"I told you I wouldn't run—I resent what you are implying."

He snorted. "Please. Quit behaving as if your mind has never been violated by such thoughts. I know you wouldn't give a toss about any of that if you believed you could get away from me."

"You sound familiar with the concept of women wanting to get away from you."

His mouth pulled into a smile that was not nice but sent odd curls of heat spiraling through her chest and into her belly. He leaned forward, resting his forearms on his powerful, leather-clad thighs. "Darling, you may imagine what you like about me and women in that fertile imagination of yours. But if you make a fool of me—or try—you'll become familiar with the *concept* of my hand on your bottom."

Eva recoiled. "This is the second time you've threatened me with physical violence. I am not a child to be spanked."

"Then quit behaving like one. We both know what we must do—marry each other—and you are only making our lives more miserable than need be with your incessant backbiting and complaining. If you are looking for somebody to blame, I'm sure there will be a mirror in your room at the inn."

His tone and words stung, all the more because she knew he was probably right. "Who do you think you *are*?" she retorted, for lack of anything better to say.

He gave a bitter laugh. "I'm the man you're going to spend the rest of your life with, sweetheart."

*   *   *

She fell into a moody silence and Godric had hopes that would be the end of any discussion until he could park her in a room, order dinner sent to her, and drink himself blind in the taproom.

Alas, it was not to be.

"I hate you." If looks could kill, Godric would be a rapidly cooling corpse on the carriage floor.

"So you've said," he answered in the most bored tone he could contrive.

"Where are my other clothes? I hate this dress."

"There are two others in the valise I purchased for you."

"I hate those, too."

"You haven't even *seen* them."

"That doesn't matter—you have putrid taste."

"You shall have to suffer with my taste until we can get you to a dressmaker and you can choose your own."

"Did you throw my other clothes away? Because they are *mine*; I paid for them."

He sighed and turned back to her. "Eva—"

"I never gave you leave to use my Christian name."

"Eva," he repeated, his jaw tight, "your other clothes are in my bag and—"

Her magnificent eyes widened in horror. "What are *you* doing with them?"

Godric briefly wondered what she imagined he was doing with them to give her such a look of revulsion. "I'm keeping them from your hands. You may wear that getup once we are safely on my estate and there is nobody else to shock."

"What do you care about whom I shock and how I do it? All you've done since returning to England is shock people. Over and over again."

She certainly had a point. How could Godric tell her he regretted his behavior these past months without sounding like a lunatic as well as an ass? The answer to that was easy: he couldn't.

"Stop arguing. None of this will change my mind."

"I want my clothes back and—"

"So you can get dressed in them and bugger off at the first opportunity?"

Her eyes widened at his vulgar language, reminding him, once again, that she was just a girl. He took a deep breath, counted to ten, and asked coolly, "Does your father allow you to dress in men's clothing?"

"Yes."

He thought for a moment, and then added, "In public?"

She blinked her huge violet eyes, her smooth forehead wrinkling. She opened her mouth, but then closed it.

"I thought not," Godric said.

"I never said anything."

"Yes, you did—just not with your mouth."

She sat in silence, her jaw working from side to side. Godric was almost curious about what she would come up with next. He really did plan to give back her suit of men's clothing when they were at Cross Hall. He had to admit he'd thought more than once of how fetching she would look wearing those top boots and nothing else while she rode the hell out of him.

"Why do you have that stupid smile on your face?"

He glanced up from his lascivious thoughts. "Do I?"

"I hate you."

He opened his mouth to taunt her further but saw she was looking tired, unhappy, angry, and even a little scared. And also very, very young. Godric experienced a pang of shame for teasing her; she was a young woman barely out of the schoolroom and he was a man in his thirties. It was time he behaved like one.

He sat forward and took her hand—she jumped and tried to pull away but he held her fingers firmly in his grasp. "I shouldn't have threatened to spank you. I would never lay a hand on you and I do not hold with beatings of any kind—not for anyone, child or adult." Godric had loathed watching soldiers being whipped in the army and had never utilized that form of punishment for his own men. Physical violence was repugnant to him, as it should be to any decent man.

Her hand had gone limp in his and she swallowed audibly before giving a jerky nod.

"I think you understand this marriage is a foregone conclusion."

Again he paused and again she nodded.

"The only decision we have to make now is how we shall go on with each other. When I said earlier that you may live where you choose, I meant we would spend the bulk of our time in the country. You will live with me at Cross Hall until such time as I come into the dukedom. At that point you will move to Tyndale Park and we shall spend as much time as we are able in the country. But my grandfather will not live forever, my lady. And when I assume the dukedom, I will have to shoulder the responsibilities that go with it. Your father is an important man in government and you must know a duke cannot secret himself in the country. I will have to go to London at least for the sessions. I don't plan to entertain in town and shan't need you with me." He paused. "As for now, I do not have a large stable at Cross Hall because I have not been back long enough to acquire bloodstock. But when I do, I would be pleased to consult with you about my cattle if that is an area of interest. I have a great-aunt on my mother's side—Lady Lavinia Price—who is rather well-known for her skill with horses, and even bred them some years ago. You might enjoy meeting her. She is an old lady now and not as active as she once was, but she still maintains an impressive stable." He gave her hand a gentle squeeze. "What say you—will we be able to get along without fighting every day?"

She frowned, her eyes wary and the set of her jaw pugnacious. "If I say I'll go along with you—and promise not to give you the bag—will you leave my brother alone?"

At the mention of her brother his hand tightened and she winced.

He immediately released her. "Did I hurt you?"

She shook her head, but her eyes were dark with suspicion.

"You will be my wife; your family will be my family." It was all Godric could do to force the next words out. "I will not threaten or harm your brother. You have my word."

Her shoulders sagged. "Very well. I shall try not to argue." She cut him a sideways look he would have suspected of being flirtation from any other woman. "Although my father says I argue more than— er, well, probably most—other people."

Godric could well believe it.

Chapter 6

It was true the town of Cocklesham had two inns. But it was also true they were both very small and neither one was entirely appropriate for a woman of his betrothed's status.

Godric chose the better of the two options—although not better by much—but it was not the sort of place where he could leave her unattended in her room and spend his evening in the taproom.

He registered them as plain Mr. and Mrs. Fleming, and was able to convey to the rather slovenly innkeeper that he would not be easy to deal with should any of the louts who were loitering around the premises find their way to the third floor of the inn, where he and Eva had taken the only two adjoining rooms, but no private parlor.

Godric had briefly thought to ask for a local lass to act as Eva's maid, as he'd done the night before, but he could see there was little chance of finding anyone respectable in the establishment. Instead, he waited until the innkeeper led them to their rooms, pressed a coin in his none-too-clean hand, and closed the door firmly after ordering hot wash water and two covers to be laid for them on the table in the larger of the two rooms. Once the man was gone, Godric checked the door and found the lock was broken. When he went to investigate the other chamber, he found the same condition there.

"This is not what I would have liked," Godric began when he came back to find Eva standing exactly where he'd left her. "I'd planned to give you privacy, but I fear I must keep the door open between us tonight. I will, of course, close it when you wash, but it would be unsafe to sleep in here without—"

"I understand," she said, her easy capitulation surprising him. He could see by the smudges beneath her eyes that she was more tired than she let on. "I'm not sure I can stay awake until the meal arrives."

They both glanced at the bed and Godric strode toward it and flicked back the sheet, grimacing. There were no vermin that he could see, but the bedding was stained and felt damp to the touch. He went to his room and took the well-worn blanket from the bed. It was faded but it smelled clean enough and was not musty.

He returned to her. "Why don't you lie down on top of the blanket and I'll cover you with this—it is dry and clean."

She complied, as docile as a child in her exhaustion. Godric covered her with the blanket as she regarded him through sleepy eyes. "Now you don't have a blanket." A huge yawn distorted the last word.

"You needn't worry about that. Get some rest. I shall be in the next room."

Her eyes drifted shut before he even finished. Though it wasn't cold, precisely, the room was excessively damp, which created a chill. So he fed more coal into her fire and stoked it into a blaze and then left the door between their rooms slightly ajar. He regarded his reflection in the fly-specked mirror that hung above the dresser. The man who peered back at him was as exhausted as Eva but looked at least four decades older. He almost felt as if he might be able to fall asleep, damp sheets or no. But he had a letter to write—one he'd avoided writing last night when he'd written to Eva's father.

When the servant came with cans of hot water, Godric asked for a quill and paper, already mentally composing the painful missive he would have to send the duke.

*   *   *

Eva woke with a start. The room was strange, and the only light came from the other side of the door, which was partially open. It took her a moment to recall where she was. Yes, at the inn in Cocklesham. Lord Visel had given her his blanket and she'd fallen immediately asleep.

Her eyes strayed to the door and she recalled what he'd said: that he would keep the door between them open. A soft light glowed from the cracked door; so, he was awake. She turned onto her back and stared into the gloom above her head as sleep slowly dissipated. And then she remembered what he'd said in the carriage, about wanting to stop arguing.

She'd been surprised by his kind words; he'd looked almost friendly when he'd said he wanted to make their marriage less contentious. And that he would see to it she did not have to live in London. He was, she knew, simply exhibiting common sense. They must marry. When her father learned what she'd done, which he would, now that James had gone . . .

James.

Eva chewed her lip to keep from scowling; she tried not to be angry with him, but she was furious. If he'd just done as they'd planned—but, no, Visel never would have let that stand, and James must have known it.

It had all turned into a mess, and it wasn't James's fault. It was *her* fault. She told herself she'd bought Gabriel's safety, even if the cost had been far higher than she'd expected. Still, Visel had told her she could live in the country—*and* choose her own cattle, *and* wear whatever she wanted. And he claimed to have an aunt who knew her way around a horse, so perhaps he wouldn't be all stodgy about a wife who shared the same interest.

Eva felt a twinge of anticipation at the thought of never having to go to a *ton* party or wear a dratted ball gown for the rest of her life. She realized she was smiling and shoved back the blanket. Her gown was a wrinkled mess, but that hardly signified—she always made a mess of her dresses, which was one of the reasons she preferred breeches. The other was—

"Ah, you are awake."

She started at the sound of his voice and turned.

Lord Visel was standing in the doorway between the rooms. He'd removed his drab overcoat and looked as fresh as a daisy in the clothing he'd been wearing all day—just as long as she'd been wearing *her* clothing. It never ceased to amaze her how she managed to stain, rip, lose—

He came into her room. "Are you hungry?"

She nodded.

His mouth curved into a genuine smile—not the mean, smirky look he'd given her all Season. "Has the cat got your tongue?"

Eva felt her face heat. "No, I'm still half asleep." She gave him a squinty look. "As I recall from yesterday morning, you weren't exactly chipper and cheerful when *you* just woke." Good Lord—was that only yesterday?

"Ah, but then you don't have a goose egg on the back of your head," he pointed out, gingerly feeling the back of his skull and wincing.

Eva grunted.

"Come," he said, extending one of the hands she'd been mentally rhapsodizing about earlier. "I've ordered some bread, ham, and cheese. We can serve ourselves."

She stared at his hand until his expression became strained, and then took it, allowing him to help her to her feet. Which was when she realized he'd removed her shoes. She looked up quickly to find him watching. Always watching.

"I thought you might sleep more comfortably without your shoes. Are you cold, or do you want me to take your cloak?"

Eva hadn't even noticed that she was still wearing it.

"I must have been tired," she said, looking up at him as her fingers picked at the knot she'd managed to make.

"Here, let me." His hands, warm and dry, moved hers aside and he looked down as he worked. "You've made quite a job of it," he muttered.

Eva took the opportunity to study him. The candlelight softened the lines that proclaimed his age, making him golden. His lips were slightly parted as he focused his attention on the knot. They were fuller when he wasn't sneering.

He glanced up suddenly and their gazes locked, his hands going still. Looking into a person's eyes at such close range was a rare intimacy; looking into *his* eyes made the blood roar in her ears.

His pupils grew large and his nostrils flared. His breathing, she noticed from a long way away, sounded labored. She swayed toward him, feeling a pull that emanated from her chest, as if he'd sunk a hook into her and was reeling it in, reeling *her* in.

He shuddered, like something had struck him, and his hands came around her upper arms and held her steady—then moved her slightly away. From him.

They were both breathing hard, their eyes locked, Eva searching for an explanation for what had just happened.

An emotion she didn't recognize spasmed across his face and he stepped back. "You should be able to untie the rest. There is a table set in my room," he said, gesturing vaguely in that direction. "I've forgotten something. I'll be right back." He strode toward her door, opened it, and then closed it so softly behind him that she didn't even hear the latch click.

Eva remained in the same place, frozen, the *thud thud thud* of her heart loud in her ears, every nerve in her body poised on the brink of . . . something.

She stared unseeingly at the door: What had all that been about?

What the devil had all that been about?

Godric glared at the door he'd just closed, as if it were to blame for the cockstand in his breeches.

Well done, Colonel Fleming, his inner critic mocked.

Oh, shut up.

He pressed the heel of his hand against an erection that was hard enough to break rocks and groaned at the pain/pleasure sensation.

Turn around, go back in, and take her. Why not? You'll be married in twenty-four hours—unless you get lucky and trees fall across every road to Scotland.

Godric knew that was true, and yet . . .

He paced the length of the dim hall and then back, thinking grim thoughts to combat his lust.

Why combat it? Why behave like a guilty parson dipping into the church coffers? What difference does a matter of hours make?

He paused and leaned against the wall, considering his behavior. Only a few days ago he'd been willing to kidnap a married woman and complete the job of ruining her reputation. And now he'd become all noble about bedding a woman he'd be stuck with for the rest of his days. Really, what *did* it matter when he bedded her? Before the ring was on her finger—metaphorically speaking, since he had no ring—or after?

There's a lad! Besides, it's been a long time since you've had a woman— weeks. Mounting her would calm you and clear your head.

Godric chewed the inside of his cheek; he wished he could head down to the taproom and continue drinking. Of course the four whiskeys he'd consumed while struggling to compose his damned letter were probably a large part of why he was currently as hard as granite and unable to control his rampant thoughts.

He absently noticed the wretched condition of his boots. He'd given his valet of almost twenty years—a man with the unfortunate name of Darling—the entire month to spend with his family. Mainly because he'd not wanted him frowning at Godric the whole time he'd plotted to kidnap and humiliate another man's wife. Godric could only imagine how Darling's face would look if he heard a chit fresh from the schoolroom had kidnapped *him* instead.

He groaned. What a bloody muddle this was.

That's the first sensible thought you've had in ten minutes. It is a muddle—one of her creation. You might as well get something out of it: like satiated.

No, he told the lustful, nagging presence driving him. *I know we shall be man and wife soon, and I'd much rather she doesn't associate the loss of her maidenhood with dirty linen in a filthy inn.*

What a romantic you've turned out to be.

Godric pushed off the wall; he'd already wasted enough time dithering in the corridor. He strode down the narrow, dingy hall toward the third door and yanked it open.

Eva was seated facing the door and looked up, pausing in the act of lifting a small piece of cheese to her mouth with her fingers.

His cock, which had begun to deflate, flared back to life at the sight of her plump, parted lips. Smug laughter echoed in his head.

She lowered the untouched food back to her plate as he eased into the chair across from her. "I'm sorry, I would have waited for you but—"

"No, I'm glad you didn't." He forced his mind away from his groin and looked across at her beautiful face, which currently wore a puzzled, questioning and *innocent* expression. "I needed to have a word with the innkeeper," he lied, lifting the bottle of wine he'd ordered and sniffing its contents. It wasn't as bad as he'd feared, but it wasn't good, either.

"Wine?" he asked.

She hesitated and then nodded, pushing her glass toward him.

Her hesitation made him wonder how often she drank.

"I am soon to be married—surely I am old enough to merit a glass of wine." Her wry tone sounded far older than her years, and her words made him realize she spoke the truth. So he poured her a glass.

"Thank you, my lord."

"You'd better use my name. It's Godric," he supplied, when she looked puzzled.

"Godric."

Hearing his name come out of that beautiful mouth did nothing for the situation in his breeches.

He swallowed down his lust and forced himself to assemble a

sandwich of the thick bread, country ham, and crumbly white cheese. Perhaps some food would help clear his mind of lustful thoughts.

"I don't think I've ever known a Godric," she said.

"Yes, well, there aren't too many of us about, thank God." He took a bite of his sandwich, grimacing at the dry, stale bread.

She put a small piece of food into her mouth, her actions dainty and precise, like those of a cat. "You don't like your name?"

He took a deep swallow of wine to wash down the food. "No," he said when he'd finished masticating the tough bread.

"Hmmm. I think it suits you."

Well, what could he say to that?

"Do you think we shall have to stay here long?" she asked, and then took a drink, her lips twisting into a tight pucker.

Dear God. She is just an infant—she isn't even old enough to drink wine.

"Godric?"

He looked up from her wine-reddened lips. "Hmm?"

"I asked how long you thought we'd be here?"

"Not past tomorrow morning, I'm sure."

She glanced at the window, even though it was dark and shrouded with hideous green drapes. "It's still raining."

He took another bite, not bothering to dispute her observation.

"We could always go back to the main road."

Godric gave up on the sandwich and tossed aside the dry, stale bread. He took a bite of ham, chewing while he considered her suggestion, which was one he'd thought of as well.

"If you're worried about anyone seeing me, I promise I'll stay hidden."

Godric looked at her as he swallowed and washed down his food with more wine. He'd taken the side road for precisely that purpose, to keep her from view.

"Let's wait and see what the weather is like in the morning," he said mildly, not wishing to disturb the tenuous peace between them by shooting down her idea.

"You said your family seat is in this area?"

Godric pulled his gaze away from her mouth; he could not recall a time when he'd found the way a woman *ate* arousing.

He saw she was waiting for a response. "I'm sorry, what's that?"

She frowned. "I asked if your family seat is in this area?"

"We passed the road to Cross Hall a mile or so out of Doncaster, so it is southwest of here." Godric experienced the same bittersweet burn in his chest he always did when he thought about his now empty family home.

She finished the last drops in her glass and took one of the over-ripe strawberries from the small bowl and popped it into her mouth, sucking her thumb and index finger to clean off the juices.

He'd had some of the most skilled courtesans in the major cities of Europe perform for his pleasure, but none of them could hold a candle to this mere scrap of a schoolgirl. And what was worse? She wasn't doing this to tempt him—she appeared to have no interest in flirtation at all. And certainly not with him, a man she openly loathed. She plucked up another berry and he could only stare, his cock pulsing with frustration beneath the table.

She saw his look and, thankfully, misinterpreted it. "Sorry," she said, her cheeks coloring in a way that would make portrait painters fight to the death to capture her likeness. "Gabe says my table manners are savage."

He flinched at the sound of the other man's name and her strawberry-reddened mouth turned down at the corners.

"You aren't going to get that look on your face every time I mention his name, are you?"

"I don't know—what look is that?"

The muscles in her face seemed to shift and rearrange themselves. Her eyelids became heavy, her lips thinner, and he would have bet a pony her nose got longer, her delicate jaw suddenly squared.

Godric couldn't help it, he laughed. "You're remarkably good at that."

Her face resumed its natural appearance in less than the blink of an eye and she put another berry in her mouth, chewing stolidly while fixing him with an unblinking glare.

Godric sighed. "No, I won't give you *that* look whenever you mention your brother." He hesitated and then said, "Whenever you mention *Gabriel*." The name was like ashes in his mouth but he pushed past the juvenile urge to show it. "Nor will I demonstrate anything but respect for his wife, Drusilla, soon to be my sister-in-law." He moved aside his unfinished plate and brushed his hands to clear any crumbs.

She held her empty glass toward him.

Godric frowned. "That does not seem like a wise idea."

Her face took on the mulish expression he already knew presaged her digging in her heels.

"Very well," he said, picking up the bottle and pouring. "Don't get that look on your face," he said, his words a mocking echo of hers.

To his surprise, she laughed. "What look?"

"No," he said, setting down the bottle. "I'm not the aspiring thespian you are. I could not mimic your expression and do it justice. The only reason I said anything about the wine is because I can see you are not accustomed to drinking it."

She took a deep gulp before setting down her glass. "I don't usually drink *wine*," she admitted, turning the glass round and round on the wooden table. "But that doesn't mean I haven't had spirits plenty of times."

Godric bit back a smile at her boastful tone. "Such as?"

She held up a hand and ticked off her fingers. "Brandy, Irish whiskey—"

"Who the devil would give a young girl hard spirits?"

"Nobody *gave* them to me. I took them." She cut him a disarming grin. "I can tell you this because now my father won't be able to punish me. But the inns in our part of Devon are no mystery to me." She took a noisy slurp.

"You go drinking at your local inns."

It was not a question, but she nodded.

"Why?"

"That's where mills usually are—although sometimes they're in barns and such."

"*Mills?*"

She preened under his surprised glare and took another—too large—swig from her glass. One more mouthful would empty it. At this rate she would be under the table within the hour. She wiped her lips with the back of her hand and smirked at him, reveling in her unladylike behavior. Godric suspected she believed such actions made her appear daring, sophisticated, and devil-may-care. In truth, they made her appear even younger than her nineteen years.

And also adorable.

He flinched away from that unwanted thought and said, "Let me guess, my brother-in-law-to-be takes you to such places?"

"Yes, Gabe's not stodgy like my father, grandfather, or my uncle Cian or . . . or"—her eyes raked him as if he were an untidy lawn—"like every other man—like *you* for example."

"Well, if you count not taking a woman to a fight as stodgy behavior, then you are correct: I am *extremely* stodgy. Pugilism is not a proper activity for any woman—especially not for an impressionable girl."

She growled—actually *growled* at him. "I'm not a *girl*, my lord. Nor am I any more impressionable than any man my age. And what is so bad about watching two men box one another? How can you say it's improper?"

"It's improper for females because it is a male activity." He gave her the smirk he'd learned annoyed her. "Or have finishing schools suddenly put pugilism on their list of accomplishments? Perhaps somewhere between needlework and watercolors?" Godric gave a genuine laugh at that.

Her eyes glinted dangerously and he knew he should stop teasing her.

"All jesting aside," he said, banning the smirk from his mouth.

"Mills and the places they occur are simply not safe for young ladies like yourself—or even for unworldly or unprepared males."

"I cannot believe that *you* truly believe that. *You*, who have been on the Continent and at war? I know there are many women—even women of my class—who follow the drum. Surely a country at war is far more dangerous than a country inn during a mill?"

Unbidden, Lucia flashed through his mind, her hands covered in the blood of their child. Godric snuffed all thoughts of her—of *them*—quicker than a candle.

"That is hardly an apt comparison; that was war, not play." He could barely force the hard, angry words through his lips. "Nor is it play for innocent young ladies to carouse at inns and mills. Do you even know what kind of men frequent such functions?" He hoped to God she didn't know about some of the behaviors he'd witnessed while attending his share of raucous country mills.

"I am no *innocent young lady* to be coddled and suffocated," she retorted.

Godric gave an ugly laugh. "Oh, what are you then, pray?"

Her nostrils flared like a lathered horse. "I am a woman—a woman with experience and knowledge of the w-world." He snorted at the ludicrous claim and she made a noise like an infuriated hen. "You are an odious pig who knows nothing about me!"

"I know you are the last female in Britain who should be allowed to roam untethered through inns and mills. I can just see you hopping into the ring if the urge struck you. I am astounded your *bro*—"

"Don't."

Godric's temper flared at her tone, but he left the issue of her idiotic brother alone. For now. "You'd better husband your memories of such reckless behavior because I forbid you to jeopardize your safety merely on a whim."

She put down her glass with a thump. "I can see how things will be already."

"Good, then I shan't have to explain to you how *things* shall be, shall I?"

She leapt up and Godric followed as closely as her shadow. "You are going to be a tyrant—like—like *Bluebeard* or—or some other ogreish husband."

Godric knew that now would be a bad time to laugh. Instead he fixed her with a calm, level gaze while she fidgeted, angry and frightened and ill at ease in her own skin. "You needn't worry about locked rooms with all the bodies of my other wives, Eva. I've not lived at Cross Hall for almost two decades, and my parents would have taken issue with a room full of dead women."

She stamped her foot, clearly unaware of how young it made her look. "You know what I mean. You will hem and hedge and control me until I am nothing but a colorless, simpering—" She stopped, her eyes wide and angry. Her jaw worked and her lips were parted but no words came out. Instead, she stared in mute misery, her breaths coming in shallow, sharp bursts. "I knew it would be the same—I knew marriage would be no different. I am always to be subject to another's will, like some—some *slave.*"

Godric felt an odd tightening in the region of his heart—a powerful, and surprising, combination of sympathy, empathy, and raw lust. And not a little alcohol. She was so very young and untried by life, yet she had brought herself to a place from which there was no return. She would, without a doubt, become his wife. *His wife.* The picture those words evoked was not the woman in front of him, and he flinched away from the ghostly image of Lucia that was never too far from his mind.

"This marriage means I will only trade one master for another."

Godric's head whipped up at her mournful words and he closed the distance between them in two long strides, as if he could outrun his own relentless thoughts.

She had to crane her head back to look up at him, her eyes burning and her cheeks flushed. His hand moved of its own volition and cupped the sweet curve of her jaw, his body thrilling at the warm and unspeakable smoothness of her skin.

"I don't wish to be your master, Eva," he said, not entirely telling the truth: her body, he decided, was something he wished to master very much indeed. He stroked her cheek with his thumb, mesmerized by the deep blue of her eyes.

Her lids fluttered at his soft caress and the slightest tremor rippled through her body.

"Shhh," Godric murmured, lowering his head and sliding his hand beneath her heavy mink-colored hair, cradling her fragile neck. He dropped a light kiss on her lips, which were even softer than he'd imagined. Her eyes had gone black and he recognized desire when he saw it.

Do it; take her. She will be your wife.

Godric started at the word *wife*, Lucia's dark brown eyes and sweet smile coasting across his vision. His hand slid limply from behind her neck and he took a step back, her body swaying toward him.

"If you are finished eating, you should get to sleep," he said gruffly. "We'll be leaving at first light."

She blinked up at him as she had earlier, when he'd woken her. But this time, when her eyes widened, the expression in them wasn't confused or sleepy, but hurt.

Her perfect features shifted into a mask of loathing. "I hate you."

Ah, so they were back to that.

Good. It was better that she hated him; there was less chance of his bending her over the table and fucking them both to ecstasy if she wanted to brain him with a poker.

Godric forced himself to give her a superior smile of amusement—the sort of expression guaranteed to turn any residual desire she might feel for him into detestation. "So you've said, sweetheart. Why don't you do your hating in your own room, so that I might get some sleep?"

For a moment he thought she would snatch up the nearest weapon—a plate, a butter knife, even a wine goblet, and attack him. Instead she drew herself up with the dignity of a duchess and dropped an icy curtsy.

"Good evening, my lord. I wish you pleasant dreams." She exited the room with a back as stiff as a plank, only spoiling her cold exit when she slammed the door hard enough to knock a piece of damp plaster off the stained wall beside it.

Godric inhaled until his lungs felt as if they might explode and then held the breath for a long moment before noisily expelling it.

Well done, my lord. Weren't you the one who said just this morning that you'd prefer not to fight and scuffle every day?

"Oh, get stuffed," he muttered to himself, filling his still half-full glass of wine until the liquid touched the brim.

It was going to be a long bloody night.

It was full dark when Eva woke up, and she had no idea where she was—at Exham? In London? Her eyes flickered to the small window covered with thin, ragged curtains; no, this was somewhere else. This was—

Godric.

It all flooded back to her: abducting him, arguing with him, and then, tonight, *throwing* herself at him.

Ugh. Eva shuddered at the memory of earlier this evening. She reached toward the nightstand for her pocket watch, which Godric, no, Visel, had allowed her to keep when he'd taken the rest of her things. She checked the time: amazingly, she'd been asleep for only a few hours and it was not yet two.

Eva sat up, which was when she noticed the soft candlelight flickering beyond the cracked door. He must have opened the door because she'd slammed it shut upon leaving him. Something about the thought of him spying on her as she slept gave her a tight feeling in her stomach. She pushed back the blankets and winced as her feet hit the cool, clammy wooden floor. The fire in the grate was glowing hotly, so he must have come in to stoke the fire.

That was considerate of him.

Eva's eyebrows slammed together at the unwanted thought. Godric Fleming was a *toad* without a considerate bone in his body. If he opened the door, he'd have his own reasons for doing so. Besides, she hadn't asked him to take care of such things—she could take care of herself; she refused to be grateful. Especially to such a bossy, superior, odious—

She ground her teeth together to stop the buildup of anger inside her. She really needed to gain control of her emotions or he would continue to prod and poke and manipulate her as easily as a child.

She tiptoed toward the door, which was open enough for her to make out that he wasn't in his bed. He was sitting in the same chair he'd occupied earlier, but he'd shifted it slightly until it almost faced her, as if he might have been watching the door, although he was not doing so right now.

No, he was most certainly not watching her right now.

Eva swallowed so noisily she was astounded he didn't hear it—but it was clear that his current thoughts were elsewhere. His head was tipped against the back of the chair, allowing her an uninterrupted view of the powerful column of his throat and the broad V of golden, muscular chest that was exposed by the open neck of his shirt.

That alone would have been enough to make her bones turn to water, but then there was his hand. A hand that was stroking softly over the front of his buckskins.

Eva pivoted sharply away from the door and sagged against the wall, fighting to catch her breath. She knew what he was doing because she'd done the same thing to herself time and again. Oh, not *exactly* the same thing, of course, but it was the same, really—only their bodies were different. Eva swallowed convulsively, her heart pounding like war drums in her chest. What he was doing was *private*. Perhaps the most private thing a person could do. To watch him would be wrong—despicable.

It would also be delicious.

She bit her lip at the hard throb between her thighs, pushed her hair off her face so that none of it would interrupt her view, and turned back to the cracked door.

The view had become even more entrancing while she'd been

wasting precious moments dithering. Now he was lazily rubbing his chest with the hand not busy on his breeches. His movements were smooth and sensual, his fingers splayed as he stroked in large circles, slipping beneath the edge of the fine linen, pushing it open to expose a small, dark pink nipple.

Eva had to swallow almost constantly to keep from drooling. Of course she knew men had nipples, but she'd never really given any thought to that fact before.

The tips of his fingers brushed the small disc of flesh and he gave a low groan, his body tensing and his hips arching off the chair.

Eva didn't know which shocked her more, his body's reaction to the slight touch, or hers. Her own breasts had tightened in response, seeming heavier, the soft cotton of her nightgown feeling like rough burlap against the hard points of her nipples.

Each stroke of his hand and his body's concomitant response made the part between her thighs—her *sex*, Mia had unabashedly called it—swell and ache.

Her eyes had been so riveted to his chest and her own body's response that she'd failed to notice he'd flicked open his fall.

Dear Lord.

Her chest froze as he lifted his hips and nudged the supple buckskin down just far enough to expose—

Steam clouded her vision as she saw his erect male organ. It emerged from the bunched-up linen like some sort of sleek, dangerous sea monster emerging from beneath the waves.

Eva breathed through her mouth, as if she couldn't get enough air through her nose, as his hand—that beautiful masculine hand she'd been admiring—slid around the thick, ruddy shaft and gave it a firm stroke.

A hiss of pleasure broke from his clenched teeth and his hips thrust up, his expression almost one of pain as he held himself still, arched, and impossibly erect.

The edges of Eva's vision blackened, reminding her to breathe, and her eyes burned, reminding her to blink.

He made a guttural noise somewhere between a grunt and a sigh and then lowered his hips back to the chair, his hand sweeping back up the silken shaft until he reached the top, which was glistening with moisture. He casually rolled his palm over the fat, bell-shaped crown before stroking back down to his root.

The gesture was the most erotic sight Eva had ever seen. She distantly realized that her thighs were sticky. When she clenched the muscles in her legs, her eyes crossed at the sensations that cascaded outward from her sex. She grabbed her mound over her nightdress and squeezed hard, as if that might stop the unraveling sensation that had begun inside her. But it only made it worse.

So did the way his hand moved over his organ, with confident strokes that were all the more arousing for their businesslike efficiency. Godric was supremely comfortable in his skin and his actions proved it. He took pleasure from his body like a man who knew what he wanted and how he wanted it.

Eva prayed for it to go on forever: the thrusting, the flexing of his muscles that occurred with each stroke, the mottling of his skin, the roughness of his breathing, and especially the fascinating transformation taking place in his breeding organ. His shaft seemed to have become thicker, longer, and the flared crown glistened wetly beneath the flickering light cast by two candles.

He began to grunt with each thrust, louder and louder, his motions jerky and the muscles in his forearms bulging beneath the skin. And then, suddenly, he froze, hips thrust, buttocks tight, his organ—his *cock*—moving even though Godric's hand was motionless. The shaft convulsed as he ejaculated, which was what her stepmother had called it: *ejaculation*. The word was dirty and mysterious, but the actual act was so much more erotic.

His body shuddered and the jerks became less intense, the small geyser erupting more weakly with each wave that rocked his body, until Godric's hips sank down in the chair and his head began to lift.

Eva squeaked and launched herself across the room, tripping on the hem of her too long nightgown and landing headfirst in the musty-smelling bedding. She flipped onto her side, her face away from the door, and focused every particle of her being on breathing in and out, slowly, and evenly.

There were slight sounds of movement from the other room and then a shadow appeared in the shaft of pale light that shone against the wall in front of her: a man-shaped shadow. He seemed to stay there for a hundred years, but it was probably only a few seconds. Only when he moved away did she realize she'd been holding her breath and expelled it slowly from between pursed lips.

She shivered at the thought of what he would have done if he'd opened his eyes and caught her staring and panting. If she lived to be one hundred years old, she'd never forget it.

It had been beyond foolish!

It had, there was no denying that. But Eva couldn't be sorry for what she'd seen.

Not even if it meant she wouldn't get a wink of sleep tonight.

Not even if facing him tomorrow was going to be impossible.

Chapter 7

"You're very quiet this morning, my lady. Did you get enough rest last night?"

Lord Visel's voice was so low that Eva almost didn't hear him over the rumble of the carriage wheels; she decided to ignore him.

"Sorry to wake you so early," he said when she didn't respond, not sounding sorry at all.

Eva forced herself to look up at the sound of his richly amused voice, inch by inch, until she met his eyes.

He grinned at her and in that instant she *knew* that he knew she'd watched him last night; she *knew* it. How could he look at her so proudly? Wasn't he *ashamed* at being caught at such a prurient act?

He chuckled at whatever he saw on her face.

Clearly not.

Oh, he was a wicked, wicked man.

Of course he'd had lots of practice, hadn't he? Plenty of lovers—just thinking the word *lover* made her body tighten—so it was understandable that such wicked behavior failed to even register with him. So here he was, acting normal: which was to say, being his usual irritating, smug, arrogant, and gorgeous self.

"We're not going to go back to being hostile to one another, are we?" He cocked his head, his tone gently cajoling.

She scowled at him and crossed her arms over her chest.

"I take it that's a *yes*." He smirked, as if her hostility *amused* him.

Men will use your anger to control you.

Eva stiffened at the memory of Mia's words.

Visel was watching her with detached interest, the way he might study an ant that had picked up a crumb too large for it to carry, wondering what would happen next.

"Of course not." Eva forced her body to relax, lowered her arms, and smiled: it was the hardest thing she'd ever done. But the look of surprise on his handsome face was worth it.

Consummate rake that he was, his recovery was swift; his eyelids lowered and his lips pulled up on one side. "I'm pleased to hear it. Since we have all this enforced intimacy, we might as well put it to good use." He smiled at whatever expression—probably shock—he saw on her face. "Not that way, darling. Not yet."

Eva whipped her head away from him, furious at her face, which she knew would be flaming. Instead, she stared out the window at the morning—which looked more like dusk, but at least the leaden sky hadn't yet opened up. That was too bad—a clear sky meant the border grew closer and closer with each hour. Eva forcibly shoved the thought from her mind.

A huge yawn distorted her face; she was *so* tired.

"Didn't you sleep well last night? Were you up late . . . reading?"

She could hear the humor in his voice but refused to take the bait. Besides, she was just too tired to think of a suitably crushing setdown. She could hardly keep her eyes open. Maybe she would close them. Just for a minute.

Eva was falling, falling, falling—

"Oof! Wha—"

"I've got you." Warm, strong arms closed around her and lifted her.

Eva scrambled to sit upright on the carriage seat, blinking rapidly to clear her eyes.

"Where—"

"Only about five miles from the last inn."

He sounded disgusted and Eva peered out the window—at first she'd thought it was night, but now saw it was torrents of rain that had blocked out the light.

"My goodness—what time is it?"

"Almost ten. You slept for over three hours. I don't think I've ever seen anyone sleep so soundly in a carriage."

Eva heard the amusement in his voice. "I can sleep anywhere. When do you think we will get there? To the border," she clarified, as if she could mean anywhere else.

"Not in this lifetime at our current pace," he muttered, as if to himself. "I don't know. I told the postboys we would keep going until the usual hour." He waved a hand toward the window. "And now this."

Which was when Eva realized the carriage was moving so slowly it might as well have been standing still. "I think I just saw a snail pass us," she said, and then yawned.

He snorted, unamused. "It wouldn't surprise me."

"Does this road go all the way to Gretna Green?"

"We aren't going to Gretna."

Eva frowned. "Where *are* we going?"

"Coldstream, where there's a place called the Bridge Inn," he said shortly, turning toward the window and giving her his sharp, achingly perfect profile.

"Why not Gretna Green?"

"Because Coldstream is well-known for laxity when it comes to particulars. They'll marry people at any time of the day or night."

"So they'd marry us if we showed up at three o'clock in the morning?"

"For the right amount of money," he said grimly.

"You sound like a man marching to the gallows," Eva said, unable to keep her irritation in check.

"Hmmmph."

Sudden anger coursed through her. "If you're so miserable about it, then why don't you just drop me off at the nearest inn? I'll send a letter to my father—I can tell him I ran away. I can tell him—" She stopped, beyond annoyed that her imagination was failing her at this particular moment. "I can tell him anything but the truth, and you'll be footloose and fancy-free."

He gave her a scathing look, but then turned back to the window without bothering to respond.

"*You're* the one who wanted to do this," she reminded him.

His head whipped around. "*Wanted?*"

"Fine. You're the one who ordered *me* to accept what had to be, without arguing. So why are you behaving like a vaporous schoolroom chit about it *now?*"

Every line of his body screamed amazement. "I beg your pardon," he said ominously. "Did you just call me a *chit?*"

"If the shoe fits. Besides, it was *vaporous schoolroom* chit."

He shook his head slowly from side to side and gave a helpless-sounding laugh. "You are quite the most antagonistic woman—scratch that—the most antagonistic *person* I've ever met."

Eva shrugged. "So I've been told." In fact, that seemed to be *all* she'd been told for as long as she could remember. The only person who'd *not* told her that was her stepmamma.

"You are strong, Eva, and the world is cruel to strong women. Sometimes a strong woman needs to hide her strength and wield it in more subtle ways. Sometimes a strong woman will even need to pretend weakness to get what she wants."

Eva knew she was being the very opposite of subtle, which was foolish because she was showing the man across from her all her cards. And she'd heard about Visel's much vaunted gaming acumen.

"So then," she said, moving on, "we will speak our vows, turn around, and get right back in the carriage and go where?"

"We shall take a room at the inn after the ceremony and stay one night."

"Good God, why?"

He leaned toward her with the same unnerving suddenness he'd displayed on more than one occasion. "Because *they'll* want us to stay a night to consummate our union, darling."

Eva's face flamed at the thick, sensual innuendo in his voice.

"You're joking."

He snorted and sat back, turning once more toward the window. "I wish I were."

"I've never even heard of such a thing," she said.

"Just because you've not heard of something doesn't mean it doesn't exist." He paused and then added in a tone heavy with irony, "I'm guessing that the things you *don't* know far outnumber those you *do*."

His insult—a prime facer of a setdown—surprised a bark of laughter out of her.

He stared at her with a dark, unsmiling look.

"What?" she asked rudely.

"Nothing."

He could make even that single word sound superior and conde-scending. Eva wanted to hit him, but that was nothing new. "Tell me, my lord, how do they know people actually *consummate* their unions? Do they send a witness into the room with them?"

"Yes."

Eva gasped, her eyes bulging. "But that's—that's—"

Low laughter rippled through the carriage, wrapping around her like a warm blanket, and heating her body so quickly that her palms were suddenly damp.

"You're a toad."

His teeth flashed a startling white in the grim gray of the carriage.

"Why do they care if people c-consummate their marriages or not?" Eva wanted to slap herself for stammering over that word like a green girl, but at least the horrid beast didn't laugh.

"I daresay they *don't* really care what people do—they just want to sell a room," he admitted after a moment of silence, his voice weary.

"You sound tired," she said, and then wanted to bite off her tongue for broaching the potentially dangerous topic. But perhaps he wouldn't—

But of course he did. His lips twitched into a smirk. "I didn't sleep a wink last night."

"Oh." That was all she was saying about *that* particular subject. She stared out the window at nothing, starting slightly when he spoke a long moment later.

"I have a difficult time sleeping under the best of conditions, and this situation is hardly the best."

Eva looked at him from beneath her lashes; he seemed sincere enough, the suggestive smirk nowhere to be seen. Perhaps he just wanted to make conversation? Eva dithered for a moment, and then asked, "Why do you have difficulty sleeping?"

He sighed audibly.

Good Lord! Just what did he want from her? "I'm sorry," she snapped. "Am I not supposed to ask about that, either? In addition to not asking you about your family or the war? Tell me, what *am* I allowed to talk about?"

"Why don't we talk about you?" His expression was hard and unreadable, but his voice was silky and dangerous.

Eva crossed her arms and hugged herself tightly, as if that might keep her from flying apart. But the thoughts had begun to whirl and multiply in her brain. Why did he have to behave in such a high-handed and confusing manner? And why did her body have such a powerful attraction to him, when her mind hated and loathed and wanted to get away from him? What was *wrong* with her to want to touch him so badly? Why did she want to make him like her? It was so pathetic. Why was he such a—a *cad*? A smug, hateful cad.

She inhaled shakily as the questions careened and crowded her mind.

"Well?" he said.

"Well what?" she repeated, genuinely confused.

"You were going to tell me a bit about yourself—your family."

Eva looked at his expressionless face, his opaque eyes, and wanted to make him *feel* something—and to show those feelings—for a change.

"Fine. Let me guess," she said in a tone dripping with sarcasm. "You'd like to talk about my mad mother—whom you've certainly mentioned more than once over the past few months. Am I right?" Before he could answer, her anger catapulted her onward. "I can't tell you much about her because I was only five when she threw herself off the roof at Exham Castle. I've heard—from some of the lovely people I've rubbed shoulders with these past months—that she was something of a tart who *fucked* her way through half the *ton*. There is living, breathing proof of that in the form of my younger sister Melissa—who one kindly dowager referred to as a cuckoo in Exley's nest. Within my *hearing*." She leaned toward him, mirroring his earlier action. "But what you're *really* curious about is whether my mother's madness runs through me. You want to know if you'll have to lock me in an attic at some point and hire a gaoler to keep me from mounting a stable lad or setting the house on fire or flinging myself from the roof of—what's the name of my new home?" she asked with exaggerated courtesy. "Horrid House? Conceited Court? Arrogant Abbey?"

His lips twitched. "Cross Hall."

The tinge of amusement in his voice only made her more furious. "I can see you've not got the nerve to spell out what you wish to know." Eva let all the loathing she felt at this moment saturate her tone. "But I'd like to settle the issue once and for all," she said, her words an echo of his earlier command. "So I'll answer your unspoken question: I don't know if I'll go mad, *my lord*. I don't currently *feel* any desire to leap off rooftops or eat the sitting room carpet, but I cannot give my word those compulsions will not one day seize me. I daresay you think that is an unsatisfactory answer. As it happens—so do I. While I have to live with such irksome uncertainty every day of my life, I'd rather not have to discuss it ad nauseam."

The very air rang with her sharp, cold words and Eva could sense the shock emanating from him. Whether at the pronouncement itself or her vulgar language, she couldn't have said, nor did she particularly care.

Eva had begun to hope he was done talking to her—hopefully for the rest of both their lives—when he said, "I apologize for any pain I've caused you these past months."

His words left her temporarily breathless. When she finally spoke, her voice was gruff. "Nothing you said caused me any pain," she lied.

"Even so, my behavior shames me." He hesitated and then added, "I imagine living with such uncertainty is a crushing burden."

To her horror, tears pricked her eyes. Blast and damn. A hateful, sarcastic Visel she could manage. Even an amorous, lustful Visel. But an apologetic, understanding Visel? No, that was something she'd not prepared herself for. She clamped her jaws shut and swallowed hard to rid herself of the dry lump that had lodged itself in her throat.

"It must have been very difficult to handle such knowledge as a child."

Eva studied him closely for a long, uncomfortable moment. "I've only known a few years," she said when she was sure he wasn't taunting her. "My father didn't tell us about her until I was almost fifteen." Eva chewed the inside of her cheek, wondering why she was telling *him* these things.

Because he will learn all about your family when he becomes your husband.

Husband.

She swallowed yet again. "My father thought he was protecting us," she volunteered, even though he'd said nothing.

"I can see that."

"Well, I can't," she retorted. "If I'd known for longer, I could have prepared for when he decided to ship me off to school—because *those* girls knew *all* about me before they even met me. My sisters and I had *no* idea what my mother had been like during her last years, but every member of the *ton* knew at least one sordid tale about the beautiful, mad Marchioness of Exley. And they were so eager to share it all with us."

Eva wasn't sure she could ever forgive her father for keeping them in the dark for so long, even though he'd apologized and admitted his mistake. If her stepmamma hadn't come along, it was likely Eva would still be living at Exham in ignorance. Which wouldn't be so bad, come to think of it. Except it would mean she would never have known Mia or Gabriel, who were two of her favorite people in the world.

"Do both your sisters live at home?" he asked.

Eva considered saying something rude—just because she was *feeling* rude—but decided she was too tired to come up with anything suitably cutting. Besides, she had the rest of her life to be rude to him.

"No, just Mel—Melissa. My older sister, Catherine, is married." A thought struck her. "Her husband was a captain—Baron Salford. Do you know him?"

"I know *of* him." He paused, his expression thoughtful, as if he were combing his memory. "I may have met him once at an officer's dance a few years ago."

"Well, his dancing days are behind him now, as he's confined to a chair." Eva didn't know her new brother-in-law very well, but what she did know did not give her much hope for her sister Catherine's happiness. Salford had been struck in the back with shrapnel, which left him unable to move his lower body. He was reclusive and quiet and Catherine had only met him because she'd been visiting Salford's sister. Eva was fairly sure the reason Cat had married him was because he couldn't have children and already had a son and heir from his prior marriage.

Eva's stepmamma had had plenty to say about her sister's choice, which was obviously motivated by Cat's concerns about having a child. But Cat had, for once, stood by her decision. The newlyweds lived only about two hours from Exham Castle, but Eva had only seen them twice in the six months since they'd married. Both times Cat and her husband had looked strained and unhappy, not exactly endorsements for the married state.

Eva realized the carriage had been silent for a while. Good. She didn't want to talk about her family. In spite of his apology—and the fact he would soon become her husband—Eva didn't feel like he deserved to know the inner workings and personal details of the people she loved. Not after the way he'd harried Gabriel. He'd need to *earn* the right to know any more than she'd just told him. The thought of him wanting anything from her enough to work for it gave her a bitter smile.

She closed her eyes and leaned back into the corner, resting her head on the squabs, already feeling the pull of sleep. The less time they spent together awake, the better it would be for both of them.

Chapter 8

Godric glanced around the dimly lighted, greasy smelling room; he was a bloody idiot. If anything, this ramshackle inn was worse than the one last night. Not only that, but they'd hardly covered much more than ten miles today; they were still miles from the border.

Around two o'clock, several hours after his uncomfortable interlude with Eva, the carriage became stuck in a bloody bog. He'd actually been grateful to get out of the cold, hostile environment of the carriage, even if it had meant he'd spent the next few hours in the pouring rain and ankle-deep mud.

He looked down at his muddy boots and breeches—hell, even his coat had muddy spatters—and grimaced. He doubted the filthy innkeeper—whom he'd discovered unconscious and slumped behind the bar in the taproom—employed a boots to clean his clothing and footwear. Well, he'd done for himself times beyond counting while on campaign; he'd do for himself again, it seemed.

A loud knock came from the adjoining room, and Godric opened the door that connected the two bedchambers. Eva was sitting right where he'd left her: fully clothed on the bed, rubbing her eyes with the still-gloved knuckles of one hand.

"Oy!" The shout came from outside the door, reminding Godric that he'd locked it.

He opened the door to find two surly-looking bruisers with a hip bath and a pint-sized lad carrying a steaming bucket that was almost as big as he was.

"Set it up in front of the fire," he instructed them.

"A bath?" The tired voice came from behind him.

Godric looked over to find Eva staring at the tub as if it were a miracle of biblical proportions. It had steam rising out of it but wouldn't for long if they didn't employ more than one spindly boy to fill it.

"I'll stay here until it is full," he told her when the three servants left. She didn't argue. Eva, he'd learned, was blessedly tractable when she was tired.

Godric glanced around the room as she finally untied her cloak and bonnet. The walls were yellowed and the paint was peeling. It looked as if it hadn't been given a thorough cleaning since the reign of the first George. Although the place was worse than last night's inn, at least both rooms locked. If this weather persisted or, God forbid, worsened, they just might be staying here awhile.

"I'm hungry."

Her words pulled him from his grim musing. "I'll make sure there is something waiting for you after you're finished in here."

She yawned hugely in response.

"Are you sure you don't want another nap between your bath and supper?" he jested. She was like a bloody cat and had slept on and off for most of the wretched day; he didn't understand how she could be tired.

"No, I am famished." The door opened and the two huge men entered, each bearing two large metal buckets.

"Enough, sir?" one of them said, his eyes sliding between Eva and Godric.

"Is that enough, Eva?"

"Yes," she said without even looking.

Godric gave the two men coins large enough to get their attention and then locked the door behind them.

"Don't fall asleep," he said, meeting her heavy eyes. "I doubt that water will be hot for long."

"I won't; I want this bath. I feel as if I'm coated in slime."

Godric knew the feeling. "Knock on the door when you're dressed. I'll need to use the bath water."

She frowned. "But it will be cold."

"It's not for me, it's for my clothes."

"Oh." She seemed to notice his mud-encrusted clothing for the first time.

Godric closed the door and left her to her bathing, ringing for two basins of hot water, which came quickly now that word was out about the money to be had.

He stripped and gave himself a thorough sponge bath before washing his hair in the water and rinsing it with the second basin. He dressed in the clothing he'd worn yesterday. When he'd purchased garments two days ago—*God, had it only been two days?*—he'd not imagined he would actually need more to get himself to the bloody border.

There was a tentative knock on the door.

"It's unlocked," he called out, finishing tying his cravat before turning to find Eva hesitating in the doorway. She was wearing her last clean gown, the pinky-rose color flattering to her ivory skin and dark hair. Godric doubted there was a color that *didn't* suit her. He frowned when he saw her wet hair. "You'll catch your death if you don't dry that. Use my hearth while we wait for our food. I'm going to go play washerwoman."

"Quit ordering me about," she said, but her voice lacked heat. "I'll dry my hair in my room so I can watch while you display your domestic talents."

Godric snorted but carried the pile of dirty clothing to the next room in his stocking feet as he didn't have a second pair of footwear.

She leaned sideways in front of the fire, her hair a heavy black curtain that she combed with her fingers. "I've never seen a man wash clothing before," she said with a sly curve to her lips that roused his slumbering cock.

"Have *you* ever done washing?" he asked, already guessing the answer. He dipped the corner of one of the tatty towels into the cool bathwater and commenced to clean his boots.

She wrinkled her nose. "Thankfully, no. I'd rather muck out a dozen stalls than faff about with clothing."

Godric wasn't surprised—not by the first part, nor the part about her mucking stalls.

"Did you have to do this sort of thing often, when you were, er, on the Continent?"

He cut her a glance, fully aware she'd avoided using words like *war* and *soldier* because he'd behaved like a vaporous chit whenever she'd done so.

"Sometimes, but not often," he admitted. "My batman kept excellent care of me." And Godric wished like hell Darling were here now. Although he'd have to suffer a bloody bin full of amused abuse from the laconic bastard. He held out the boot once he'd wiped off all the mud, eyeing it critically. Well, it would do for tomorrow, but it was undoubtedly ruined.

"I think those are done for," she said, echoing his thoughts.

He picked up the second boot. "There is steam coming from your hair," he observed. "You'd better be careful or you'll set it on fire."

She shrugged, but did move fractionally farther away. "If it caught fire, then I could cut it all off."

"That seems like a rather drastic way to go about getting a haircut. Why don't you just employ a pair of scissors rather than risking your life?"

She blinked at that. "You think I should cut my hair?"

"No, but you said you wanted to cut it."

"You wouldn't care if I cut it?"

"It's your hair."

She appeared to ponder that while he finished the second boot and then moved on to the breeches.

"My father doesn't care for short hair."

"Well, I'm not your father."

Although I'm certainly old enough. Godric frowned at the unwanted thought.

"What kind of hair do you like—on a woman, that is?"

Godric looked up from the breeches he was wiping with the cloth, having judged it unwise to get the leather too wet. She swallowed hard but met his eyes, her cheeks flushed. Was that from the fire or because she wanted to know what he liked? Why did that stir him? Somehow, he knew the answer to this seemingly innocuous question would mean the difference between a quiet evening and dodging sour looks or even actual projectiles.

"You'd look good no matter what you did with your hair. If you want it short, cut it short."

She looked so surprised, he thought he'd said the wrong thing, but then she smiled.

Bloody hell. He quickly turned his attention, and his eyes, back to the ruined clothing in his hands, which he noticed weren't at all steady. Well, he'd not slept for over twenty-four hours—he was tired.

Yes, that's it—you're tired.

Thankfully the arrival of dinner spared him from having to spend one more second on the subject.

Godric banked his fire, preparing for a long, tedious, sleepless night when there was a soft knock on the connecting door.

He opened it to find Eva holding a straight-edged razor; ragged chunks were missing from her shiny black hair. "Good God! I didn't mean you should cut it now."

Her face was the shade of a ripe cherry. "Don't make it worse— I already feel like an idiot." Her voice sounded a bit wobbly, almost as if she might cry.

Christ!

Godric sighed. "All right, I won't. Er, did you want something?" he asked when she just stood there.

She held up the razor. "Will you help me?"

"*Me?*" He would have been mortified at sounding like a castrated mouse if the prospect of cutting her hair hadn't terrified him even more. "I've never even cut my *own* hair."

Her shoulders sagged. "Please? I've done the parts I can see, I just need help with, well, the rest."

Godric didn't tell her what he thought of her work so far.

"*Please.*" Her lips twitched and almost made it to a smile. "You can't do worse."

"I wouldn't count on that," he said, but reached out for the razor anyhow. He held it up to the light, frowning. "Where did you get this?"

She shrugged, her expression evasive, and Godric decided he didn't want to know.

Instead, he thumbed the edge, which wasn't even sharp enough to scrape his skin. "No wonder you ended up hacking so horribly. This wouldn't cut warm butter. I'd sharpen it for you, but I didn't buy a strop in Doncaster. Here—" He closed it and handed it back to her. "We'll use mine, which is almost new."

He fetched his razor, which was still lying out to dry, and turned to follow her back into her room. There was a substantial pile of hair where the carnage had taken place, and Godric gestured to it. "You might as well stand there."

Once she was standing a few feet away from the mirror, Godric stood behind her, chewing the inside of his mouth while he considered the best place to start. He'd seen short hair on women plenty of times as it had been all the rage on the Continent. Some women even wore it shorter than his. He'd not been engaging in flattery when he'd told her she'd look good with any style of haircut, but he didn't want to make it shorter than she wanted.

He looked up and met her eyes in the mirror. "How long do you want it?"

She hesitated and then held her hand at the level of her jaw. She'd already cut the fringe—just a bit above her elegant black brows— so all he had to do was cut the sides and back. And also fix some of the jagged areas.

Godric got to work.

* * *

Eva realized two things as Godric cut her hair. First, she loved having his hands on her body, even if it was just to absently reposition her while he cut.

Second, she loved having short hair already. It was so liberating to watch the heavy strands fall to the floor, as if she was casting off weights that had held her down.

As she'd suspected, Godric did a better job than she had. Indeed, he was working with meticulous care and she could see the finished result was remarkably even. That wasn't as easy as it looked, given the amount of wave in her hair. And the shorter he cut it, the more the hair appeared to curl. But he worked without speaking, occasionally making satisfied grunts or soft noises of displeasure, biting his lower lip with his strong white teeth, and even sticking the tip of his tongue between his lips once. He was attractive all the time but became transcendent when he wasn't scowling or wearing that irritating superior smirk.

When he got around to the right side, where she'd done her hacking, he made a soft *clucking* sound and met her eyes in the mirror.

"It's a good thing you called me in when you did."

Eva couldn't help smiling. "You are doing a lovely job. I would have come to you sooner if I'd known you possessed such skills."

"Hmmph." He returned to his trimming, but she could see he was pleased.

A few moments later he stepped back and straightened his back with a groan. "I should have had you stand on something," he groused.

Eva shook her head and when the hair settled it looked like a curly black cap. Because the cut had removed so much of the weight, the hair fell just slightly above her jawline, but it looked good. She met his pensive stare in the mirror and grinned. "I like it a great deal. What do you think?"

His pale blue gaze seemed to darken as his eyes flickered over her reflection, and Eva felt her breathing hitch.

"It looks well on you," he said, his voice somewhat harsh, his

pupils most certainly dilated. Eva could not look away from their reflection in the mirror. They made, she knew, a remarkably handsome
couple. He so tall and muscular and fair and she so feminine looking—an admission that did not, for once, bother her. She watched his
hands settle on her shoulders, the span of his palms dwarfing her.

His eyelids became heavy and his smile was odd—sensual but . . .
resigned? He turned her easily and then took her chin and tilted her
to face him.

She thought she'd be ready when his mouth covered hers, but
the shock of his warm, soft lips was as great as it had been the first
time. His free arm slid around her body, pulling her closer while he
held her steady for his exploration. He pressed his hips against her and
a low groan escaped his lips when his erection pressed against the
stiffness of her stays. He kissed her less gently this time, almost chal-
lengingly, his tongue teasing as if he was waiting for some response
from her body or mouth, but she didn't know what.

Eva looked into eyes heavy with desire and knew this wasn't the
mocking man in the carriage. His touch was so light—his mouth, his
body, his hand . . . she fought the urge to mash herself against him,
the tension inside her spiraling in ever larger circles.

He traced her lips with the tip of his tongue, the touch unlike
any she'd ever experienced: soft, wet, insistent. When he began to
insinuate himself between her lips she instinctively opened to him.
The sound he made, one of animal need, cut the tenuous restraints
on her self-control and she thrust herself against him, earning an even
deeper growl.

She knew what the stiff ridge between them was; his hardened
state was the physical manifestation of his desire—for *her*—and she
opened her mouth wider to him, wanting to encourage his confusing
but arousing plundering. He delved and explored, caressing and
stroking her tongue, teeth, and even the top of her mouth. When he
began to move away, she closed her lips around him, sucking him
back in.

This time the noise he made was needy and desperate and he

pulled her tight, flexing his hips and grinding his hardness against her midriff. He pulled away from her mouth, his body stooped to accommodate the difference in height as he held her in a tight embrace, his breathing ragged.

"We need to stop this," he said, the words hot and damp against her temple. But he made no move to pull away.

"I don't want to stop."

He inhaled sharply at her harsh voice or immodest declaration, or both. "Eva—"

Eva turned her head slightly and encountered his exposed neck. He smelled of salt and skin and heat. She flicked him with her tongue before she knew what she was doing, tasting him. He shuddered and held her so tightly she couldn't breathe. It didn't matter; she licked him again, this time lowering her mouth over the pulsing vein and sucking him, the way one sucked the ripe flesh of a plum or peach, as if she did not want to lose a drop.

He made a guttural noise that sounded like surrender, his hands moving up and down over her hips, back, shoulders, finally settling on her bottom, which he grabbed with both hands and squeezed, holding her tight as he flexed his hips in suggestive thrusting motions. Eva knew exactly what he wanted. Mia had seen to her education in that area when she'd told Eva and her sisters about the sexual act and how it could bring just as much pleasure to a woman as a man, but far more often.

As a result of her knowledge, Eva knew why she was swelling, becoming wet, more sensitive, wanting. The feeling was similar to the one she experienced in her bed, alone. But it was *so* much more overpowering to experience it with another person. With him.

She savored her body's responses while she sucked and licked, moving her mouth lower, pushing her face into the folds of his neckcloth, nosing him like a cat or dog learning a new scent.

"Eva—"

He was going to talk, and his talking would stop all the lovely sensations, just as he'd done last night before throwing her out of his room.

Well, she wouldn't have it; she wouldn't let him stop. She pushed against him, not quite straddling his leg, but trapping it between her knees. She bit her lip to hold in the cry of pleasure as she rubbed her aching sex against his thigh.

He released her and stared down with dark, unblinking eyes, his mouth hanging open. She liked the feel of his muscular thigh against her fragile flesh, but she liked his stunned expression even better.

"I am no ignorant schoolgirl," she said in breathy voice, only partly lying. "I want—" She had no words handy for what she wanted, so she rubbed herself wantonly against him in demonstration.

An explosive noise of frustration burst from his parted lips, his nostrils flaring as he breathed in loud, soughing rasps. He pulled back slightly and she reached out to stop him. But instead of leaving her, he lifted his thigh ever so slightly. Eva whimpered and sucked in a harsh breath. Godric's mouth closed with a snap, his lips compressing into a cruel, thin line as he pinned her with pupils so huge she felt as if she were teetering on the brink of a bottomless well.

His leg moved again and Eva made a guttural noise, her eyes struggling to stay open.

So good. It felt so very, very good.

But it's him! a voice somewhere in the recesses of her mind shrieked. *You hate him.*

She did. She hated him, but she loved *this*.

The next time he thrust up she let her knees fall open and they both made raw, animalistic sounds. And then her impulsive, reckless nature took over and her body's needs overcame her weak will. The pulsing and throbbing itch drove her to recklessness and she lowered her hand to the juncture of her legs and rubbed the outer folds that protected her sensitive nub. She caught her lower lip between her teeth, her breathing heavy. She knew how to finish this—to make this stop, to give herself the most intense pleasure she'd ever known. It would only take—

"Good God."

Her eyes flew open as he backed her up so swiftly her head spun, not stopping until she was against the wall. He dropped to his knees and lifted her skirts and then froze, the hem just at her knees. When he looked up, the heat in his eyes and his taut face made her stomach twist and churn, made her sex pulse with exquisite sensations that rippled outward.

"Eva?" Gone was the sneering, distant aristocrat.

She glared down at him through heavy-lidded eyes. "What?" She didn't care if she sounded petulant.

"Do you want me to stop? This is not—" His already flushed cheeks darkened even more, and his inability to articulate what exactly was going to happen made her braver; he was not as composed as he looked, not nearly so much in control.

His body was tense with the effort it took to restrain his eager limbs and he hummed with want. For her.

"Have I—" He bit out a vulgar curse. "Are you afraid, Eva?"

She was afraid, but not in the way he thought. "No."

His mouth pulled into an odd, lopsided smile, and amusement joined lust on his devil-angel face. "No, you wouldn't be—would you?"

She pushed her hips against him in answer and his pupils dilated almost to the edge of his irises.

His gaze dropped. "Hold your skirts up," he ordered in a raspy voice that made her hands shake as she obeyed him.

"Higher." His haughty lips thinned and tightened in a way that made her legs weak. She felt his hands lightly drifting over her exposed knees, thighs, and then cool air on that most private of places.

Again, thanks to the precious information Mia had shared, Eva knew what he was going to do—and her body wanted it with a ferocity that dazed her.

He looked up at her, his expression smug, knowing, and . . . arousing. "Spread your legs for me, Eva."

She held his gaze, torn between the desire to disobey his arrogant command and the much stronger desire to feel what he wanted to do. So she moved her feet slightly and he lifted his eyebrows. Not until she'd spread her feet to the width of her shoulders was he satisfied.

"That's a girl," he muttered, the low, harsh desperation in his voice sending actual shivers through her. Eva bit her lower lip hard as he traced the seam of her sensitive lips, his finger grazing her swollen peak, which had grown larger and more sensitive.

Each stroke elicited a shudder and she tightened her inner muscles, prolonging the pleasure. His actions were skilled and confident, as though he'd done this same thing countless times before. Which he likely had.

Eva thrust away the stab of jealousy that pierced her chest at the thought—what did she care for such things? All she wanted from him was—

His thumbs parted her lips, opening the most private part of her to his view. He sucked in a harsh breath, looking awestruck. "So very, very beautiful," he whispered, entranced.

Eva knew what he was seeing because her stepmother had urged her to learn the secrets of her own body—not to wait for some man to teach her about them. So she'd eagerly looked at herself in her dressing room mirror, examining the part of her that could be so demanding of attention, and could give such joy when obeyed. While it delivered unparalleled pleasure, she'd certainly not thought it was pretty. Nor had she been as dumbstruck by her sex that she'd stared the way Visel was currently staring.

He leaned forward and took her bud between his lips and her knees buckled, a strangled cry escaping her tightly clenched jaws.

He steadied her hips with his hands but his lips did not release her. Instead, he engulfed her with the soft wet heat of his mouth. And then he began sucking and massaging her with his tongue.

Eva's vision doubled and she was making a gasping sound as she struggled to breathe. Her eyelids were heavy but she pushed them open: she needed to see him—to see his mouth on her. When she pulled her skirts higher, his eyes looked up into hers, his mouth bathing her in slick heat.

Her body slipped her control and shook hard; she was close to climaxing, but this time, unlike the others, she tried to keep the feeling in check, to savor the sight and feel of him. She tightened her muscles, as if that would hold back the flood. He released her swollen peak, his lips red and slick, his chin glistening. When she pushed her hips toward his mouth like a wanton begging for more, his mouth pulled into a smile that caused her muscles to flutter madly. And then his hand slid into the wet heat between her thighs and pressed at the entrance to her body. He circled the sensitive opening, around and around.

Eva spread her feet more and his eyes kindled as he inserted a finger inside her. She bucked against him and babbled something even she couldn't understand. And then he leaned down and sucked her into his mouth again and began to pump her with strong, rhythmic thrusts. She could hold back the flood no longer.

Godric watched her come apart under his hands and mouth, her lithe, young body shaking beneath him, her orgasm explosive in its intensity. He didn't know what he'd expected of a maiden, but it hadn't been such calm acceptance of an action that would send most married women of their class screaming in fear or outrage. But she'd not only enjoyed his oral attentions, she'd watched him and had done what she could to intensify her orgasm, welcoming him into her body. He tried to ignore the stab of angry jealousy when he considered where she must have learned about such pleasures: inns and pubs and mills, likely.

Well, he was no vestal virgin himself.

Godric waited until she was limp, boneless, and utterly his. And then he made her come again, just because he could. He drank in the sight of her pleasure until his engorged cock soaked the front placket of his breeches and he ached with want.

As the last of her contractions died away, he kept his two middle fingers buried deep inside her, loath to leave her snug heat, wanting to see her come apart again. And again. But enough was enough.

When he removed his hand he saw no blood. So, she'd not been lying: she wasn't a maiden, which went a long way to explaining her lack of inhibition. Godric felt an odd sense of relief mingled with disappointment: relief that he'd not just debauched her with the kind of activity one usually only practiced with one's mistress or a whore; disappointment that he'd not been the one to initiate her into this particular pleasure.

He shoved away both thoughts and pulled down her skirts before standing.

She gazed up at him from beneath heavy lids, her mouth slack. He slipped his arm beneath her knees and lifted her with ease. She was small, but she had a woman's flared hips, and the swell of her breasts looked generous for her narrow ribcage. He regretted not exposing her body to his view, but there would be plenty of time for that later.

"Mmmmm, so tired now," she mumbled into his coat.

Godric wasn't surprised: she'd just had more orgasms in the last thirty minutes than he'd enjoyed in the past thirty days.

When he laid her out on the bed, her eyelids lifted slightly as she struggled to stay awake.

"Do you want me to play lady's maid and remove your dress and stays?"

She nodded and yawned noisily, her heavily lidded eyes looking into his. "Please do, I can't believe I'm so tired, yet again."

If he'd had as many orgasms as she'd just experienced, he'd likely sleep for a month.

"I hate stays. Need I wear them?"

He had to swallow hard to answer her question, as if his cock had leapt into his throat. His brain was crammed full of images of her breasts free and unrestrained. "You needn't wear them for me," he said gruffly, his groin throbbing madly. He turned her on her side and located the tape that kept her bodice cinched beneath her breasts. He slid an arm under her and lifted her off the bed as he pulled her loosened dress to her waist. She moved pliably in his grasp, anticipating his instructions before he made them, clearly at ease with being undressed after a lifetime spent with a body servant.

Beneath the simple gown, she wore white muslin stays and a chemise. Her breasts were high and lush with large nipples that were dark pink and hard against the thin fabric. Godric's hands shook as he turned her again on her side and loosened the laces. She gave a soft, sensual sigh as he released her body from its bondage and he almost ejaculated in his breeches.

Good Lord. It had been far too long when unlacing a woman's plain cotton corset could make him this hard.

Once he'd loosened the garment he gently rolled her onto her back.

Astoundingly, she was asleep, her plump lips parted, the pearly skin over her collar bones stained with the vestiges of her passion. Her curly mop of hair contrasted starkly with the pale linen. He'd had a difficult time completing the bloody cut, his cock hard almost constantly, his brain trying to distract him with images of bending her over the chair back and hilting himself inside what he now knew was a sweet, tight sheath that would feel like heaven wrapped around him.

He groaned as his sensitive crown rubbed against his clothing. He needed to take care of the situation before he sullied his remaining breeches. He draped her cloak over her before putting the blanket on top. The bed linens looked clean enough, but they were damp and musty smelling.

He leaned over without realizing what he was doing and kissed her smooth temple, the action burying his nose in her short, ticklish hair. He inhaled her like a wine whose merits he struggled to identify, filling his lungs to capacity before expelling air in one noisy breath. He took another whiff, holding her scent in his lungs.

As he exhaled slowly, it hit him: sugar. She smelled like sugar, which he'd not even realized *had* a smell until that moment.

Godric pulled the blanket up to her shoulders as he looked down at her. She resembled a storybook princess and the image was far more potent than he'd ever have expected: skin like cream, lips like cherries, and hair as soft and black as a raven's wing. She was achingly beautiful and unlike any woman he could remember. She was part antagonist, part hoyden, part siren, part child.

Like any man, Godric enjoyed beautiful women, but his sexual desires had not always—or even mostly—been ruled by a woman's beauty. He'd not loved Lucia because of her physical appearance, but because of the lively spark in her dark, flashing eyes, and the joyous smiles she summoned so easily. In truth, Godric knew his dead wife had been pretty at best—until you knew her.

But Eva de Courtney? Hers was the rare beauty of a priceless object in a museum, and he felt an odd compulsion to collect her and put her on a shelf behind glass, to lock her away. He wondered if that impulse in others was what had made her the way she was—suspicious of men who wanted her only as a beautiful object.

She was not a piece of porcelain to be kept under lock and key. She was a living, breathing woman with wants and needs. Wants and needs he was ill equipped to satisfy.

Godric realized he was smiling. But it was a sad smile. He would try not to crush her spirit—to hem and hedge and control her as she'd accused him of attempting several times. But he didn't think that would be the problem. As much of a hoyden as she was, she'd proven tonight that she had the body and desires of a woman: a very, very sensual woman.

But she was also a girl, and he could see the way her eyes softened whenever he was kind to her. Girls, even hoydens, had romantic fantasies, and they would be fantasies he could not possibly satisfy, no matter that he knew his outward appearance might be that of an angel or storybook hero. Once upon a time he'd even been a bit like that hero, but not anymore.

He stood and gave her one last look before snuffing the candle and returning to his own room, leaving the door between them open.

He pulled off his boots and removed his coats and ruined cravat, keeping on his buckskins, stockings, and shirt. Not only did he not wish to lie naked on this disgusting bed, but he didn't want to shock her in the morning—in the extremely unlikely event he might get some sleep. She might be more comfortable with her own body than most of her countrywomen, but that didn't mean she would be comfortable with his.

After banking the fire, he lay on top of the blankets, one arm behind his head as a pillow. With the other, he opened his fall and wrapped his hand around an erection so hard it had become painful. As he stroked his slickened shaft he thought about how she'd looked standing exposed and open before him; how she'd tasted; how she'd sounded when she covered his hand and mouth with her sweetness.

It didn't take him long to bring himself to climax, his orgasm intense but far too brief, the mind-numbing pleasure dissipating too quickly and turning into the feelings of loss that always followed.

He would not sleep tonight, just as he had not last night. The fact he'd slept that first night could only have been a result of the whack on the head. He reached back and felt the lump, which was still sensitive but had lost some of its swelling.

His insomnia was not new. He'd been this way for a long time—even before what happened to Lucia and Carl, although it had been worse since they died. It was a somewhat predictable routine: three or four nights without sleep would pass and then he'd sleep like the dead for ten, sixteen, or, once, thirty hours at a stretch. Godric hadn't given in to insomnia without a struggle. He'd tried drinking himself to sleep, working himself to sleep, and, with Lucia, well . . . there had been many nights she hadn't slept, either.

Thinking about Lucia brought the inevitable guilt in its wake. Guilt that he'd not been there when she needed him, guilt that he'd not simply sent her to England after Carl was born—that he'd kept her with him because he was selfish. Guilt that he was about to forsake her memory and take a new wife—and that he was looking forward to the marriage in at least one way: he wanted Eva physically. And—after tonight—he wanted her badly.

Godric hadn't been a monk since the death of his wife. Quite the reverse—he'd fucked his way through his remaining time in the army and then fucked his way through London when he'd decided to extract his revenge. But always when he'd bedded women, he'd known it was to satisfy a physical need, not because he had any intention of forgetting his past and beginning a new life. As if he *deserved* to start over again after what he'd done.

Godric turned his head until he could look through the open door toward the bed where she slept. He could make out only a vague outline of her form, but he imagined he could see the rise and fall of her chest. He didn't love her—hell, he didn't even *like* her a good bit of the time—but he liked her body and, he realized after tonight, he'd not be able to deny himself the pleasure of it.

He was glad he could at least give her sexual pleasure—and a stud farm. The irony of the combination was not lost on him, and he smiled. But his smile drained away when he thought about the truth of their future together.

Godric only hoped physical pleasure and horses would be enough when she found out that was all he had to give.

Chapter 9

For the second morning in a row Eva could hardly look him in the eye. In fact, she hadn't; ever since they'd entered the carriage, she'd been staring at his chin, mouth, and nose. His mouth, she noticed, was flexed into a curve of tolerant amusement that made her yearn to hit him. But even that wasn't enough to make her look up.

Eva wished her stepmamma had told her how mortifying it could be to face a person *after* one engaged in shocking sexual relations with them.

She'd woken this morning to find he'd already dressed and gone. He'd had hot water brought up to her and then sent up a meal of coffee, bread, butter, plum preserves, ham, and boiled eggs. She ate alone, dreading his arrival but not worried enough to keep her from eating. She was far hungrier than she would have expected in her anxious state.

When he *had* finally shown up, it had been to tell her the carriage would be ready in a quarter of an hour and she should be, too. He spoke to her in a level, civil fashion, but she could hear the humor in his voice. No doubt because she was bright red and couldn't make eye contact.

The morning started off dry, if not clear. The sky was still the same dull gray it had been for days. It suited her mood.

Although he didn't speak, but just looked out the window, she could see the slight curve to his lips. Eva knew that he was thinking about last night. And that he knew she was thinking about last night. And she knew that he knew—

"Shhh," he said, leaning toward her, the sudden movement making her flinch.

The sound made her remember last night, when he'd soothed her like a skittish colt and then—

"I'm sorry if I shocked you last night, but we have done nothing to be ashamed of, Eva. I know I should have waited until we are wed—"

"You didn't shock me," she lied, her heart thudding. "I knew about—about, er—" What had her stepmother called it? Oral pleasure? She could not bring herself to say those words. She looked up and realized he was still waiting. "I know about *that*. And I know about plenty of other things, too," she added for good measure.

He sat back and nodded, his nostrils flaring, his mouth pursed tight. She had no idea what *that* particular expression was supposed to mean. And no intention of asking, either. She was just glad he'd stopped talking—especially about last night.

If Godric laughed right now—after her inability to articulate the word *cunnilingus* and her solemn pronouncement of her extensive sexual knowledge and expertise—she would probably kill him in his sleep tonight.

So instead he sat back. "If we continue at this pace, we should reach the border by noon tomorrow."

She nodded, swallowing hard enough that he could see the muscles of her throat moving. The action plucked at heartstrings he'd forgotten he even possessed. The girl was certainly an enigma: last night she'd participated in an act that was so erotic and *earthy*, most Englishwomen married fifty years had never even heard of it. She hadn't just participated, she'd watched him with hungry eyes, encouraged him with spread legs and thrusting hips, and reveled in the sensations he'd given her.

Yet today she was back to being a naïve nineteen-year-old.

He had to admit it: he was . . . intrigued. "How many Seasons have you had?"

She frowned and for a moment he thought she wouldn't answer his rather abrupt question. "This was my first."

"Isn't that a bit late?" Hell. Why didn't he just shut up? What did he know about young ladies and their come outs? Until five months ago he'd not set foot in a London ballroom in his life.

She looked out the window, her mouth turned down at the corners. "Yes, I should have come out at seventeen, or eighteen at the latest. But I became ill and was allowed to stay home."

"It must have been a serious illness."

She said nothing.

Godric wanted to break down this new barrier between them before it had time to grow, thicken, and obstruct the little bit of ease they'd begun to share. Christ. The last thing he needed on a daily basis was conflict with the woman he'd be tied to for the rest of his life.

"Yesterday you mentioned your younger sister—Melissa, was it?"

Her head turned slowly in his direction and he could see she was suspicious.

"What?" he asked. "Surely it is not unheard of to wish to know about one's future relatives?"

Her eyes narrowed and her lips thinned. "How many do *you* have? Why don't we talk about *you* if you are so eager to be sociable and chat?"

His first impulse was to repay her aggression with a punishing setdown. But then he looked at her—really looked, beyond the pugnacious expression and beyond her extraordinary beauty, seeing the scared young woman hiding behind those façades. Why *wouldn't* she be wary of kind or friendly overtures from him? From her point of view, he'd been an ass ever since the first moment they'd met. Hell, he'd been an ass from anyone's point of view, truth be told.

He'd been a cruel, taunting ass; until last night, when he'd knelt and worshipped her in a way that was entirely inappropriate for a man with his young bride-to-be. No wonder she was confused and angry.

He sighed. "Very well. Let me tell you about my family."

Eva was surprised by his calm capitulation. She'd been expecting one of his cutting setdowns delivered with his characteristic sneer— hoping for that, actually. She couldn't say why, but she wanted to goad him into another argument.

But she looked at him now, yet another version of the man who'd knelt in front of her last night and done such shocking—yes, she *had* been shocked, in spite of what she said—and pleasurable things. This new, friendly, interested man bore no resemblance to the one who'd either ignored or taunted her for half a year.

"I am a third son, with only one younger sister. I was encouraged to purchase a commission and serve king and country. I joined when I was sixteen."

"Why so young?"

"I was an indifferent pupil at school and had no interest in going to university. I'd been army mad since I was a boy, so it seemed like the best decision. Besides, sixteen is not so young. There are plenty who are younger."

"But those aren't usually officers." He gave her a look of surprise and she shrugged. "What? I may only be *nineteen* but I'm not utterly ignorant of matters beyond balls and Venetian breakfasts. I know two boys in the village who signed on at thirteen and fourteen. But they did menial labor."

He sat back, as if she'd poked him with a stick. "How the devil is it that you know village boys and what they did in the army?"

The anger that surged through Eva surprised even her. "It's hardly any of your affair who I know and how I know them, is it?"

He made a noise of frustration. "What is it?"

Eva frowned. "What is what?"

"What is this compulsion of yours to turn every conversation into an argument?"

She opened her mouth to refute the accusation, but then decided to tell the truth. Why not? He'd find out soon enough in any case. She shrugged. "I like to argue."

He gaped, his expression priceless.

"My father says I'm a contrarian, but I disagree."

It took him only a few seconds to catch on. His smile was grudging, but he laughed—a deep, rich laugh that curled through her body and concentrated low in her belly.

His amusement made her relent and answer his question. "My sisters and I grew up running with the children from the village that sits on my father's land. My mother died when I was not quite five, and then my grandmother and aunt raised us. But my grandmother fell ill soon after and my aunt simply couldn't manage Catherine and me as well as tend to my grandmother and my youngest sister—who is two years younger than I." She pleated the printed cotton of yet another of the putrid dresses he'd ordered for her—this one a dusty rose—recalling those carefree days with pleasure.

"What about your father?"

She looked up from the creased fabric of her dress. "My father rarely came home. He was—well, he had responsibilities elsewhere." There was no point in telling the man across from her that her father had learned by then that his dead wife had been barking mad—the insane daughter of a mother who ended her days in an institution—and feared seeing that same madness in his own daughters so much that it had turned him bitter and cold. So the marquess had stayed away, only coming home to manage estate business or for their birthdays and holidays. At least he'd thought to come home for those.

Godric was looking at her as if he wanted to ask something; something she probably wouldn't want to answer, so she said, "I know about your family, about how they died. Lord Byer told me."

That was a lie; her brother's best friend had actually told Gabriel, but Eva had overheard.

His eyes frosted over like an alpine lake and his mouth tightened. "I am relieved to hear that, my lady. It means we do not need to speak of the subject ever again."

"But don't—"

"This is not a matter up for debate. You will learn just how *stodgy* I can be if you decide to pursue this topic."

His profile was harsh and wintry so she let the matter lie. Besides, Eva knew that tone well. She couldn't help marveling how much Lord Visel sometimes sounded like her father. It was the tone that said a line had been drawn in the dirt and crossing it would be at one's peril.

It shouldn't surprise her that he had an aura of command; he'd been in the military almost half his life and was accustomed to giving men orders and having them obeyed. And now she would be just another one of his soldiers.

Eva looked away from him to the other window, a heaviness in her chest. He could bring her physical pleasure, and it appeared, after last night, that he wished to do so—at least when it suited him. But as for any kind of parity? That seemed unlikely. He would become her lord and master and she would be his chattel. Once again, she would belong to a man who believed she was mad; a man who would never know her or like her. And she couldn't even hate him for it because it was *all* her fault they were in this situation.

Yes, Eva was the person who'd done this to both of them, and now they would both have to live with it.

The carriage gave a worrisome shudder and slid to the side before the postilions regained control.

Across from her, Godric stirred from the silent, brooding funk he'd settled into after their aborted conversation and turned his disturbing gaze on the scene outside the window.

The rain, which had begun to sprinkle less than an hour after their departure, was now falling so heavily it was like looking through a gray curtain.

He shook his head, his expression one of disgust. "We should have stayed at the inn," he said, cutting her a brief glance. "I apologize for dragging you out in such weather."

The shocks just kept coming: Visel admitting he was wrong? Visel apologizing? To *her*? Although she did not taunt him out loud, he must have read it on her face.

"Yes," he said as he sat back against the cracked brown leather squabs. "I do apologize, especially when I've done something foolish."

"That must keep you busy."

He gave a short bark of laughter at her insult.

What an odd, odd man.

"I, for one, am relieved we left that inn," she said, squirming under his considering look. "My hair stinks of mold, my clothes are damp, and the food was appalling."

"I'm afraid we probably won't encounter anything better on our current path. I'd hoped to make the main road today and spend a night in relative comfort. But it looks as if things might get even worse."

They both turned to look out the window.

Eva hadn't been surprised to learn the road north was still blocked this morning; who would want to work in this weather? Godric had told the postilions to keep working northward, even if it meant having to go farther west to do it. As a result, the road they were on was so ragged and narrow that the soaked branches of trees often dragged over the roof of the carriage.

He pulled his gaze away from the window. "Tell me why you fancy yourself a horse breeder," he ordered in a direct manner that set her teeth on edge.

"Why? So you can insult and belittle me?"

"Perhaps. Does that frighten you?"

She bristled. "You couldn't frighten me if you tried."

His smile said he believed otherwise.

Goaded, even though she realized exactly what he was doing, she said, "James's father, the marquess's stable master, worked for the Duke of Langham before my father lured him into his service many years ago—before James was born."

"Ah, Langham—he's had some champions, hasn't he?"

She nodded. "And he keeps several breeding establishments. Our family visited his and I saw his main stables. He's considered one of the finest judges of horseflesh in the country."

"Does your father engage in breeding?"

"Only my stepmamma."

Visel's jaw sagged so low it was a wonder it didn't come unhinged. Her face burned at what she'd said, but she couldn't regret it.

He gave a disbelieving laugh. "You really are incorrigible."

Eva tried not to preen, even though it wasn't her own shocking comment but one she'd heard while engaging in the despicable act of eavesdropping—or *Evasdropping*, as Gabe called it. No matter how hard she tried, she simply couldn't help herself, even though she felt dirty and ashamed every time she did it.

She'd heard the breeding comment while hiding in the library window seat while Gabriel engaged in one of his frequent arguments with his mother. Her stepbrother had muttered the comment not quite under his breath after Mia had, once again, nagged him on the subjects of his scandalous affairs (Gabe had employed *two* mistresses and kept them in the same house), and his lack of interest in marriage and offspring.

Mia's answer to Gabe's outrageous comment had been swift, sharp, and in Arabic. Eva had always marveled at the way Gabe and his mother bickered with each other, and then embraced afterward. That was *not* the way she and her sisters interacted with their father.

When she'd asked Mia about their frequent arguments, she blamed them on Gabe's years in Oran.

"Gabriel was raised to believe his word is law."

"That doesn't sound much different from Papa," Eva had countered.

Mia's lips had curved into one of the secretive smiles she wore whenever the subject of her husband was raised; it was a smile that made Eva's stomach flutter.

"You are correct, my dear, men the world over believe they are kings to be obeyed without question." She'd shrugged. "Whomever he marries will have to have a strong but subtle hand to control him."

And that was another thing—the way Mia *did* control Eva's terrifying father without even looking as if she was trying.

Eva cut the equally terrifying man across from her a glance under her lashes, wondering if she could employ similar methods on Visel once they were married. Right now he was looking at her as if Eva were an unpredictable forest creature that had just wandered into his midst. She decided she could use that uncertainty to her advantage.

"My father has no interest in breeding racehorses," she said, as if she'd never uttered the incendiary comment—keeping a man off balance was a tactic she'd watched Mia employ often. Based on the way Visel's forehead furrowed, it had worked. "But James's father still has a hankering for it and Papa allows Mr. Brewster to do a bit of breeding. They've sold a goodly number of pleasure horses, but none to race."

He nodded, but said nothing, just studied her with an inscrutable, brooding look that made her feel as if she were ten years old.

Why did she even bother talking to him as if he might care?

Eva clamped her jaws shut, determined not to say another word. Not. One. More. Word.

Godric watched the kaleidoscope of feelings play over her face, her emotions as evident as white, fluffy clouds dancing across a clear blue sky. Eva was far from stupid, but she had as much guile as a kitten. Oddly, that knowledge made him feel tender and protective toward her—a reaction that alarmed the *hell* out of him.

You can pity or feel protective of her all you like, his constant critic observed, *but don't try to fool yourself—or her—by pretending you are anything other than hollow inside.*

Godric noticed she'd gone quiet while he'd been engaging in his private turmoil. Her lips were pressed into a grim line that said he'd neglected his part of the conversation—and offended her in the process.

See? You can't even engage in a simple conversation without disappointing her.

"I had six mounts during my time on the Continent."

Her head whipped around.

If his words surprised her, they stunned him. He'd never volunteered information of any kind to anyone since returning home. Not even harmless information about his horses.

She opened her mouth, but then closed it.

"Go ahead, you can ask," he said.

Well. The surprises just kept coming.

"Did you—were they—"

Good God, why had he opened this can of worms?

"Two of them were retired."

She nodded, her expression somber, so he knew she'd put the pieces together.

"Did you prefer a particular breed?"

Godric laughed rather bitterly and she sat back as if he'd struck her. "I'm not laughing at you," he said. "I'm laughing because the issue of horse breeds and quality was a major bone of contention for cavalry units. As a regimental colonel I was in charge of purchasing mounts for my men." And given a pitiful stipend to do so. "You might be aware—as an aspiring breeder—that there is no government stud or formal remount system in place."

She nodded. "Yes, Papa said the current system was shameful and left soldiers at the mercy of unscrupulous dealers, who often sent broken-down draft horses."

Perhaps Godric would not dislike his new father-in-law, after all.

"That was true, unless one employed more devious tactics." Her expression was nearly rapt—and all because he was talking about horse trading. What man could resist a pretty woman regarding him with such a look?

"I frequently found suitable mounts from local sources." He wondered if she would know what he meant.

She frowned for a moment and then her brow cleared. "Ah." Her lips pulled up slightly at the corners. "Didn't that prove difficult at times?"

"Difficult?"

"They would have Portuguese horses—didn't you have to teach them English?"

Godric grinned at her teasing. "I'm afraid they learned English far more quickly than I learned Portuguese."

"And did you favor any particular breed?"

"Thoroughbred cross, sturdy—somewhere between fifteen hands to fifteen-three, if it was coming from home." Wellington had, in fact, tried to insist on no mounts below fifteen hands, but beggars couldn't be choosers and shipments continued to contain horses much smaller.

"I preferred Hanoverians or Trakehner if I had a choice," he added.

"Prussian warmbloods."

Godric nodded. "That was the second to last horse I had—a gelding who was smarter than several generals I could name." He muttered this last part under his breath, but she heard it and laughed, her expression one of delighted surprise. "What?" he asked rather rudely, and then added, "Why are you looking at me that way?" He left no doubt whom he was mimicking.

"My voice isn't high and squeaky like that!" she said. Godric laughed and she gave him an amused look. "What way am I looking at you?" she demanded with a smirk he would have called coy on any other woman.

Godric snorted. "It's not going to happen. I've already told you I lack your thespian skills. You never answered my question about why you laughed."

She shrugged. "I was surprised you would say something so irreverent about the military."

"It's not irreverent to state the truth."

She smiled. "I shall remember that for later."

This time Godric laughed outright. "Now why am I not—"

The carriage made an awful screeching noise and pitched to one side as the sound of screaming horses drowned out the deafening crack of something striking the carriage.

Chapter 10

Something hard and hot slammed against Eva, and strong arms closed around her middle, which was when she realized she was no longer in her seat.

"Eva? Are you hurt?" Godric asked.

She shook her head, her heart lodged in the vicinity of her throat, and he shifted her until she was sitting sideways in his lap. The angle was odd because the carriage was so tilted it was almost on its side. The window had cracked from the impact, and rain was dripping on his hatless head, his golden hair mussed and wet, his brow furrowed with concern as he squinted down at her. "Does anything hurt?"

"No." Her voice was hoarse, as if she'd been screaming.

"I'm going to open the door and see what is going on." He lifted her with an ease that left her mouth dry. His body, she knew from last night, was corded with muscles and now she'd felt their power.

He picked his overcoat up from the floor. "I'm going to cover you with this so you don't get broken glass on you."

Eva nodded and was engulfed in darkness.

"I'll not be long," he promised, and she felt the carriage shift and heard the sound of tinkling glass. She waited a moment and then carefully lifted the coat. The rain fell so heavily it was as if a bucket had been upended over her head. She burrowed back under the wool barrier and tried to steady her pounding heart.

As inconceivable as it was, she was more shaken by her brief physical contact with Godric than her brush with death. Although that might be exaggerating matters, it was possible she might have been injured.

"Eva?"

She moved the coat aside slightly and looked up. He'd opened the door and was leaning through, holding out a hand. "Shake the glass off the coat and then hand it to me." When she had, he tossed it over one shoulder and held out both hands. "Take my hands."

Eva reached out, realizing only when she felt the warm damp leather of his gloves that she'd taken off her own earlier.

He lifted her with ease, the rain pelting down on her as he raised her from the confines of the carriage and then set her carefully on the ground before holding the coat over her, sheltering her.

She was staring up into his darkened eyes, and he down into hers, when somebody cleared his throat. They both turned to find one of the postilions. "We're ready, sir."

Godric nodded and then explained to her, "One of the wheels broke just before the carriage hit the ditch."

"The horses—"

"Are fine." His lips curved into a smile—different from his usual smirk. "The lads are going to ride them to the next village and bring back help."

Eva wanted to say she could ride one of the leaders but knew that wasn't true. The postilions wore special wooden boots to avoid having their legs crushed; it would be foolish to ride the horses without such protection.

"What are we going to do?"

He leaned closer and said, "Once they've gone we'll get out your other clothes and you can put them on—you'll need top boots to walk in all this muck," he said in response to her look of surprise.

"When you're dressed, we might as well follow them as the carriage offers no protection in its present condition."

Eva nodded.

"You can go," Godric said to the waiting men, who wore oiled slickers that made them look just like seals.

"Aye, my lord. We'll be quick about it."

Godric waited until they'd cantered off before turning to her. "I'll fetch the bag from the boot."

When he returned, he balanced the new leather bag—which he must have bought in Doncaster along with their clothing—on the side of the carriage and handed Eva her breeches first.

She held them a moment, staring at her hands.

"I won't look."

Eva heard the amusement in his voice and it prodded her just as she suspected he knew it would.

It was an arduous, damp, miserable process, but at the end of it Eva was wearing breeches, warm boots, three coats—her waistcoat, clawhammer, and drab benjamin—a shirt, stiff new York tan gloves, and a neckcloth tied sloppily around her throat.

"Here." Godric handed over her tall beaver hat while he held up his now-soaked cloak with the other arm.

Her short hair was far easier to tuck under her hat than it had been before, and she was soon ready. She looked up to find him examining her with a bemused expression. "What?"

He shook his head. "Nothing."

"Your cloak is soaked"

"Yes," he agreed, lowering the heavy garment and exposing them both to the weather. "Luckily it's not terribly cold."

Eva begged to differ, but kept her mouth shut. It wasn't as cold as last year—which people had taken to calling the Year Without a Summer—but it was still well below average.

Godric tossed the sodden garment inside the carriage, shut the door, and then picked up both of their bags.

"I can carry mine," she said.

He just looked at her. "Come, let's—"

"Drop those bags and turn around *very* slowly."

Godric's first thought was, *You've* got *to be bloody joking!* It was as if the universe was conspiring to keep them from the Scottish border. Perhaps that should tell him something? Perhaps—

"This is no jest," a youthful male voice said, the tone unnaturally high. "Turn around."

"Don't say anything," Godric muttered to Eva, who gave him her usual glare.

When they turned, Godric couldn't see their assailant at first. He began to lift his hand to shield his eyes.

"Don't move!" This was practically a shriek.

It also helped him locate the voice's owner. Godric squinted, not sure he could believe what he was seeing.

"Good Lord, are you wearing a *dress*?" Eva's voice dripped with amusement and disbelief.

Godric bit back a groan.

"That's none of your affair," their captor snapped at her, coming out from under the foliage that hung close to the road. Yes, it was a young man and he was indeed wearing a dress, as well as spectacles that appeared to be missing one lens and were perched unevenly on his nose. He was also carrying a long, odd-looking rifle.

He shifted the gun so that he could hold it with one hand, propping it none too steadily on his hip. "I'll take your money and—and the bag with your clothes." He gestured to Godric with something that bore a striking resemblance to—

This time it was Godric who couldn't keep his mouth shut. "Is that a blunderbuss?"

"It's an arquebus, actually." The young man sounded pleased. "One of the oldest on record. There is quite detailed scrolling on the bronze work near the hammer. It is possible it once belonged to Donatello Visconti, a Viennese lord."

Godric could only stare.

Eva, predictably, laughed. "You sound like my old governess. You don't need that arky-whatever; you could just bore your victims to death."

Godric briefly closed his eyes.

"You'd better shut up," the gun expert shouted. "I'm not afraid to use it."

Godric opened his eyes. "Now, there's no—"

"Why don't you make me shut up?" Eva demanded. "I'll bet that thing isn't actually loaded. Even if it is, you don't look as if you've ever fired a weapon in your life. I could probably hurl a stone with more accuracy. I could—"

Godric slid one hand around her shoulder, covered her mouth with the other, and pulled her close to his body.

"Here, take the bag." He jerked his chin toward the bag that contained his clothing. "And if you allow me to reach into my coat, I can give you my purse."

Their captor was red-faced and glaring at Eva, the bodice of his rather revealing gown rising and falling quickly. "You'd better keep him quiet," he warned as he gathered up his sodden gown with one hand and stumbled through the mud toward them.

Eva's jaw began to move and Godric tightened his hand slightly, not surprised when she bit his finger.

Godric yanked his hand away. "God*dammit*, that hurt," he muttered through clenched jaws.

"Keep your hand off my mouth," she growled, sounding remarkably like a badger.

"Then keep it *shut*."

"I *will*."

Godric would believe that when it happened. He casually lowered both his hands to his sides.

"Stay still," the boy's voice quavered as he came close enough for Godric to see that he was not a boy, but probably Eva's age. He was small, only a few inches taller than Eva and almost as slender. Godric could tell by the way he was shaking that he was more than a little nervous. One long, elegant finger was poised on the ancient firing mechanism—or at least Godric assumed it was the firing mechanism. What he knew about arquebusses—arquebussi?—could fit in a thimble, with room to spare.

The boy snatched the bag and staggered back. And then realized he hadn't gotten the money yet. His jaw worked so that Godric could see the tendons moving below his pale skin. "You needn't give me all your money, just—just half."

Godric's eyebrow shot up at that, but he hardly wanted to argue. Once the boy had taken half the money—a decent sum since Bertie had advanced him a pony at Doncaster—he took a wobbly step back, his expression suddenly uncertain.

"I'm—I'm sorry about—"

Eva snorted.

The boy's eyes swiveled from Godric to Eva, and Godric instinctively took a step toward her, preparing himself to thrust his body between her and the gun, if necessary.

Their robber's eyes widened comically. "Why, you're a *girl!*"

She opened her mouth.

"*Eva.*"

She cut Godric a sharp look and then, to his eternal surprise, shut her mouth with a snap.

He turned back to their robber. "You've got what you want. Why don't you be on your way." It wasn't a question.

The boy stiffened at his tone, his face flushing at whatever he saw in Godric's eyes. He lowered the gun slowly, careful to keep it from touching the mud, and then shook his head, lifting the bag at the same time. "I-I can't do this," he said, almost to himself. "Here." He shook the bag. "Take it back." His jaw trembled. "I'm sorry," he said again.

Godric took the bag, embarrassed for the boy, who he was sure was crying. If Eva noticed, she would—

"Are you blubbering?" she demanded in open disbelief.

The boy's mouth tightened and he began to raise the gun.

Fortunately, the sound of horses distracted all three of them and they turned toward the bend in the road where the postilions had ridden off a scant quarter of an hour earlier, although Godric had to admit it felt like a thousand years.

A team of horses rounded the corner at a trot and Godric frowned when he saw they weren't connected to a carriage.

"What in the—"

"Good afternoon, lady and gents," a lazy voice drawled behind him. "Nobody make any sudden movements. You'll want to lower that firearm young, er, lady."

It was the most exciting day of Eva's entire life. A near-death carriage wreck and being robbed *twice*—and there was still half the day remaining.

Their first robber reluctantly handed his blunderbuss or whatever it was to the gaudily dressed highwayman who'd come up behind them. A handful of men spread out around them and Eva realized these were not of the same caliber as the first robber: these were hard, desperate-looking criminals.

"Keep your mouth shut," Godric murmured beside her.

Eva swallowed as she saw one of the robbers—a man wearing a battered top hat with a large emerald pin fastened to the crown—staring at her. He was grinning, exposing a mixture of brown and black teeth along with several empty sockets.

"Now what manner o' gun is this?" the head robber said musingly as he turned the gun this way and that.

"It's an arquebus. One of the oldest on record, dated—" Robber One paused, his Adam's apple bobbing. "Er, it is possible it once belonged to Donatello Visconti, a Viennese lord."

The robber's eyes opened comically wide, and he turned to his crew, who were all grinning broadly at him. Except the man with the hat, who was staring at Eva.

"Is that so," the main robber said. "Now 'oo would 'e be when 'e's out and about—this Donatello Vis—Vis—"

"Er, Visconti, sir. Well, um, he's actually, that is, he *wouldn't* be out and about. He's dead, you see."

"Ah," the robber said after a long, uncomfortable pause, his gaze moving from the boy in the dress to Godric and Eva. He squinted and then frowned. Eva couldn't blame him; what a trio they must make. He appeared to have been rendered temporarily speechless. And then he turned to his men, scowling. "'Ere then, what are you lot doing lazing around when there's work to be done? Get that carriage hooked up!"

The men surged toward the tipped carriage like a single organism, the two riding the leaders—*not* their postilions—joining the others.

"Where are the postilions?" Godric asked.

"Don'tchu worry, lad, we don't 'arm honest working men," the leader said, his grin back in place. "We trussed 'em up, but the boys'll check on 'em later and cut 'em loose."

Eva glanced up at Godric, to see if he believed the other man, but he didn't meet her gaze.

While they'd been talking, the other thieves had surrounded the carriage and now began to set it upright, the action involving lots of grunting and cursing as the men slipped in the mud and lost their footing.

It was better than a pantomime.

The carriage had just slid back into the ditch for a third time when the most decrepit wagon Eva had ever seen rumbled toward them. The man in the driver's seat wore a soldier's coat and pulled the wagon to a halt not far from the carriage before leaning awkwardly on the side of the wagon and then hopping down on one leg.

"Why, he's a—"

"Shhh," Godric whispered.

The one-legged man studied the post chaise for a long moment before slipping a cane from beneath the board he used as a seat and limping to the back of the wagon, which she saw was heaped with all manner of rubbish.

Meanwhile, the men had pushed the post chaise upright. One of their number, the smallest, crawled beneath and shoved something— a block of wood that appeared to have come from nowhere— beneath the axle of the broken wheel. When the men released their hold, the carriage shuddered but stayed in place.

The one-legged man limped toward the coach with a carriage wheel slung over one shoulder and a wooden toolbox hanging from the hand not employing the cane.

They *all* appeared oblivious to the pounding rain.

The leader of the band of thieves ambled toward them. "That's Donny," he said in a confiding tone. "'E's forgotten more about carriages than most men will ever know."

Indeed, Donny did seem to be quite handy and set about attaching the new wheel—slightly smaller and wider than the original—in a matter of moments.

While they'd been watching Donny, the two men riding the leaders had hooked the horses to the carriage.

Donny stood and then limped a few feet away before calling out, "She's good."

The chaise began to roll. The too-small wheel gave it a rather drunken gait as it rumbled down the narrow, rutted road, but it didn't seem to slow it down too much and soon the chaise had disappeared around the bend.

"So, that's that," the leader said with a huge grin, coming close enough that Eva could see he wore something that might have once been a soldier's coat.

"Now, let's have what's in your pockets without any fuss, eh?" He looked from Godric to Eva. "You too, girlie."

Eva scowled up at him as she detached her watch and chain and handed it to him. "That's all I have."

The man with the hat, who had been hovering in the corner of her eye, came closer at her words.

"She's a girl, Flynn," he said to the older thief—Flynn, it seemed.

"Aye, Matthew, that she is." Flynn pulled out the most disgusting handkerchief Eva had ever seen and brushed the rain off his face before leaning toward her, as if to get a better look. His eyes crinkled at the corners but Eva saw no amusement in them. "And she's a beauty at that."

Eva felt Godric's body move closer. "She also happens to be my wife."

Flynn turned at the sound of Godric's voice, which was soft but carried all the menace of a cracking whip.

Flynn's eyebrows jumped up in mock surprise. "Is she now?"

One of the men who'd been loitering with the others—a tall, hulking blond man—spoke up. "Don't you recognize him, Flynn? It's Fleming—*Colonel* Fleming." The man's cold, flat stare made it clear that the memory was not a pleasant one.

Flynn's eyes widened. "Is that right? Why, I'll be, Paul, I believe you're right. Colonel Fleming hisself—a real live war hero, lads."

The men behind him chuckled and Eva chanced a look at Godric; she'd thought he'd looked hard when he'd gone after her brother, but clearly she'd been mistaken. Right now he looked like the grim reaper come to collect his latest victim.

"And you must be Gentleman Flynn." Godric's eyes seemed paler, his pupils mere specks, their color the glinting gray of a freshly sharpened axe.

Flynn put his splayed hand across his chest. "Why, I'm flattered you've 'eard of me."

Again his men laughed.

Eva was surprised she'd not guessed the man's identity sooner. Gentleman Flynn and his band of deserters had been in the paper for months as they ransacked the countryside. She knew robberies as far south as London and as far north as Leeds had been attributed to them.

Her mind spun to recall all she'd read, but there was likely a healthy amount of rumor blended with fact. Had his band of merry men ever killed anyone?

"Here." Godric's voice pulled her from her thoughts. He'd drawn his heavy gold signet ring off his pinky. "I'm going to get my purse." Flynn nodded and held out a hand. Godric slapped both money and ring in his palm. Hard. "Take this and be on your way."

Something in Flynn's eyes kindled and he took a step forward, pushing his face into Godric's. "*Your* sort no longer gets to order me around, *my lord*." He made a hawking sound in his throat and then spat at the ground near Godric's feet.

Eva flinched back at the disgusting gesture, even though the phlegm had come nowhere near her boots. When she looked up from the muddy road she saw Godric holding a cocked pistol to Flynn's temple.

She gasped, her jaw hanging open. *Where in the world had that come from?*

Of course her surprise was nothing to Flynn's.

"Now then," Godric said coolly, "tell your men to lower their weapons or I'll blow a hole through your head bigger than a twelve-pound shot."

The small hairs on the back of Eva's neck stood up at the barely leashed violence in Godric's tone.

A muscle in Flynn's jaw flexed and his eyes flared with hatred. But the look was gone in an instant, tucked back behind his jovial mask. "You 'eard 'im, boys."

Most of the men hadn't been holding weapons as they'd been too busy working on the carriage. Only two of them had guns: the one called Matthew and another man.

Flynn chuckled. "It was a mistake not friskin' ye, I see that now." His eyes slid to the side, assessing the pistol poised a few inches away from his brain. "That's a right pretty piece. Why di'n'cha use it when the boy was robbin' ye?"

Eva was startled; Flynn had watched that? How long had he been in the trees? There was only one reason he would have been there: he must have sabotaged the carriage and been waiting.

Godric ignored Flynn's question. "You, gun expert," he called over his shoulder without taking his eyes from Flynn.

The young man in the dress had been gaping like a fish. "Me?" he squeaked.

"Take the guns from the other two and then hold the pistol on Flynn and keep it on Flynn until I tell you otherwise."

"Aww, Colonel," Flynn whined. "The boy is shakin' like a leaf! 'E's like to blow a hole through me if I so much as twitch."

"I recommend you don't twitch," Godric said. "Eva, take the arquebus."

Eva sidled around Godric and took the big gun from Flynn's unresisting hand. She staggered a bit under its weight.

"You know it don't matter if you take all our guns—even if you shoot each and every one of us. The rest o' my men'll wonder when we ain't behind 'em. They'll come back." Flynn smiled in a way that made Eva's skin crawl so badly she thought it might crawl right off her body. "And when they do, it won't go well for you." His eyes slid toward Eva and she took a step back. "Especially the girl."

"Is that so?" Godric cocked his head, sounding amused. "Because I can't help feeling that if I cut off the head of the snake, the tail will just twitch a bit before going still. How about that, Flynn? How about I just kill you?" He knocked Flynn's hat off with the point of the gun and pressed the muzzle against his temple.

Flynn swallowed noisily. "You could do that or you could stay here and I'll let your wife go."

Godric laughed. "Because I would take your word for anything." His lips twisted into a jeering, almost feral grin. "The word of a thief, a liar, deserter, and a *rapist*."

Flynn's body stiffened. "I *never* raped a woman. That's a bloody lie."

"Then why do you want my wife—why did you say it would go bad for her?"

Flynn looked poleaxed. "Not to rape—to ransom, man! I just meant she'd be livin' rough with us while we waited. Yer the bloody Duke of Tyndale's heir! Even an ignorant criminal like myself 'as 'eard of 'im—richer than Croesus. I don't need the both a ye—just one'll do."

"You want to ransom me to my grandfather," Godric said flatly.

"Aye," Flynn said, his tone indicating any idiot should have known that. "I'm a thief, a liar, a deserter, a grave-robber, a forger, and 'alf o' dozen other things besides. But I ain't no killer or raper. And I don't allow it among my men, neither. You must o' read about me in the papers—ever 'eard o' me killin' and rapin'?"

His men grumbled behind him, but the one in the hat was still looking at Eva. "What about him?" she blurted, jabbing the arquebus in the starer's direction. "He hasn't stopped staring at me since he got here."

Flynn's eyes widened in a look of genuine confusion. "Who, *Matthew?*"

"He's not stopped smiling at me—leering."

Flynn gave a genuine laugh. "'E's simple, my lady—but 'e likes pretty things."

"I'm not a *thing*."

Flynn grimaced. "Awright, awright, don't get in a twist. But you know what I mean—beauty, that's what our lad Matthew likes. Why, 'e'd never 'urt a fly."

Eva looked at the man in question. Who was still smiling his blank, eerie smile.

"Why don't you fight?"

Everyone turned to the sound of the voice. It was the same man who'd recognized Godric first. "Isn't that how it goes with a *gentle-man?*" he sneered, his accent far more refined than all the others. "Have a duel? We've not got fancy swords, but we've got these." He held up two fists the size of Christmas hams.

"That's not going to get you your ransom, is it?" Godric sneered right back.

"No, but it'll allow one of us to hit *you* in the face."

The murmuring among the men rose above the rain, which seemed to have lessened suddenly, as if even the heavens were interested in hearing where this was going.

"Vote," somebody muttered. "Vote," another said more loudly. And then another, and another, the word echoing under the gunmetal-gray sky.

"A vote it is," Flynn said. "All in favor of settlin' this like gentlemen?"

"*Aye!*"

"All opposed?"

Only the rain could be heard.

Flynn grinned up at Godric. "A fight it is. If 'is lordship fights and wins, we let 'im and 'is wife—"

"And the boy," Godric added.

Flynn's eyebrows rose, but he nodded. "Awright, we'll let all three of 'em go. If 'e fights and loses, then 'e comes with us, we let the other two go, and 'is lordship writes a pretty beggin' letter to 'is granfer."

The men roared their approval.

"So, my lord," Flynn said with a hard glint in his eyes. "It's all up to you."

Chapter 11

"Agreed." Godric stepped back from Flynn but didn't lower the pistol.

"Don't do it," Eva shouted.

Godric glanced down at her, surprised. "I thought you enjoyed a good mill?"

Her jaw sagged and she stared up at him, her eyes wide as she shook her head. "I am not jesting, Godric. He's a liar—he'll never keep his word. Please, don't do it. We've got three guns—"

"Four," their first robber—the frock-wearing arquebus expert—chimed in.

"Four guns," she corrected. "We can take our chances."

Godric grinned, amused in spite of the situation. "Don't you have any faith in me, Eva?" Without waiting for an answer, he glanced at their new ally. "What's your name?"

"Andrew," the boy blurted, and then swallowed loudly, the gun he was holding on Flynn wavering. "Um, Andrew Lowell, sir," he amended.

Godric turned back to Eva and said in a low voice. "I want you to go with Andrew. Keep to the road. Get rid of that damned arquebus and move as fast as you can. One of the postilions told me the nearest village is only three or so miles down the road. If you—"

"No."

Godric blinked. "I'm sorry, *what?*"

"No, and don't use your colonel voice on me, either." Her words were pure bravado because he could hear the terror in her tone.

"Eva, now is not the time to argue. Now is the time to—"

"Would you leave *me* behind?"

"That's hardly the same—"

"It's *exactly* the same. I'm not leaving you." She crossed her arms, the mulish look he'd come to dread shifting her features.

"Er, Colonel Fleming? Are we planning to do this before we all float away like leaves in a stream?" Godric flicked Flynn an irritable look and the other man held up his hands and shrugged. "I'm just sayin' the rain ain't slowin' none."

Indeed, it seemed to have picked up yet again.

"Eva—"

"No."

"Blast and damn and bloody hell!"

She flinched at his vulgar tirade but didn't budge. Godric wondered why his head hadn't exploded yet—his eyes were hot and dry, even though he felt as if he were treading water.

"Goddammit, Eva," he ground out, glaring at her stubborn, beautiful face.

"No." She was as unbudgeable as a boulder.

"Fine," he snapped. "Take this." He offered her the gun, butt first. "I want you to go stand by Andrew and I want one promise from you."

"I'm not leaving."

He ground his teeth. "Not yet—but if things look bad—" He gave her a hard look. "You've boasted that you've been to mills— promise you'll leave if it looks bad for me. Promise. If you really want to help me, then go."

She swallowed convulsively, her jaw quivering as though she was fighting tears.

"If I lose I can't protect you, Eva—but you will be able to help me if you can get to a constable."

She gave a rough jerk of her head and snatched the gun. "I promise."

Godric smiled. "Good girl. Now, keep an eye on Flynn and his men—I'm sure they have knives and such hidden on their persons, although this lot likely wouldn't have a gun small enough to hide."

Eva nodded.

"I don't trust Flynn any farther than I can throw him." Both their eyes slid to the Falstaffian highwayman.

"Me either," Eva said.

Godric grinned and gave her a quick, hard kiss before nudging her shocked person toward Andrew, who had a gun in each hand and was visibly shaking.

"Keep an eye on Andrew—make sure he doesn't blow off his own head."

A tiny smile played around her lips, but her eyes told a different story.

"Go on," Godric urged. He waited until she was beside the boy before turning to Flynn's men. "So, which of you would like to beat on a peer?"

It didn't surprise him when the strapping blond man with fury in his eyes stepped forward.

Godric smirked around at the silent men as he unbuttoned his sodden coat, his fingers moving slowly from the cold. "What? No vote, first?"

His opponent glared. "You think that's funny, don't you—the likes of us thinking we have the right to have a say in how things run—to vote."

Godric snorted as he handed his coat to Eva, who took it without ever lowering the gun from Flynn. "Yes. I think it's funny that a band of thieves and deserters think they deserve the vote."

The other man scowled as he threw his oil-slicked coat to one of his companions and began working on his regimental coat, which had been overdyed an unattractive gray-brown.

Godric didn't blame the man for making use of what was probably the best-made garment he'd ever owned. He knew most soldiers who'd fought in the war had come out of it with little more than the clothing on their backs, and some, like Donny, the wizard with the coach wheel, had come out with far less. But he *did* blame the men for their desertion.

"Your sort has always viewed ours as if we've no more brains than a draught horse. Cannon fodder, that's all we are to you."

"Actually," Godric said casually, removing his waistcoat, "I support the expansion of the franchise—although I draw the line at including criminals."

The man took a step toward him, his expression murderous. "You're nothing but a—"

"Steady on, Paul," Flynn said, stepping between them and putting the flat of his hand on his furious minion's chest.

Paul scowled but stayed where he was. They both pulled their shirts over their heads at the same time and Godric had to admit the other man stripped to considerable advantage. He was an inch shorter than Godric, but a good stone heavier, his thick muscles obviously honed by years of work.

When Godric turned to give Eva his shirt, he couldn't resist smiling at the way her eyes caressed his torso; what man—closer to forty than thirty—wouldn't be gratified to have a beautiful woman look at him like that?

"All right, then—the rules," Flynn bellowed, clearly getting into his role as master of ceremonies.

Godric ignored Flynn's self-important babbling, his eyes on Eva as he stretched his body to warm up his cold muscles. He flexed his torso and twisted at the waist, grimacing at the pops that rippled down his spine. He knew he was showing off for her, like a cock for a hen, but the look on her face—mute desire—warmed him far more than the few exercises.

Her pupils flared and he knew she was thinking of last night. Remembering how she'd looked while he knelt before her sent blood rushing south. For the first time since he'd woken up with that knot on his head, Godric actually looked forward to marrying her. Not just to warm his bed, but because he liked her spirit and the way she made him feel alive. Who knew? Maybe they'd find a way to rub along. If they didn't kill each other first.

"Ready, my lord?" Flynn yelled behind him.

Godric gave her one last look and then turned away; he was as ready as he'd ever be.

Eva's heart was pounding and sweat was mingling with the relentless rain. She backed closer to Andrew, keeping her eyes and gun on Flynn, although he and the rest of his men appeared enrapt at the sight of a disgraced soldier stepping up against a national hero.

"Godric said to keep an eye on them," Eva told Andrew when she reached his side. "Can you hold the gun straight while cradling that bloody blunderbuss?" she snapped when he didn't immediately respond.

"It's a—"

"I know what it is!" she hissed. "What I want to know is whether you can shoot to kill if you need to."

"*Kill*. He never said anything about killing." His eyes widened, the one behind the glass hidden by rain and fog, the empty frame showing a hazel eye that threatened to pop out of his skull.

Eva snorted, turning enough that she could keep an eye on the combatants, who'd commenced to moving carefully around each other, clearly struggling to find their footing in the deep mud that hid a multitude of ruts and potholes. "What do you think they will do if he loses?" she demanded. "Do you actually believe they'll let us go?"

"Flynn promised. He said—"

"I heard him," she snapped, wincing when the bigger man—Paul—jabbed faster than her eye could track, clipping Godric's jaw when he didn't move out of range quickly enough. Paul was stocky, but he was *fast*.

Godric's left hand shot straight out from its guard position, which was the first time she noticed he was sinister. Her lips curled; how appropriate.

Paul bobbed and dodged his fist by only a hair. Eva chewed her lip as she weighed both men's strengths and deficits: Godric had a better reach, but Paul was undoubtedly quicker—younger—perhaps as much as a decade younger. He also had pure rage on his side.

Paul threw a couple more jabs, probing Godric's defenses, his style quickly readjusting to fight a left-handed opponent. He had good enough technique, but Eva couldn't help noticing that he sometimes overreached, almost enough to allow his elbow to lock.

Godric's style was, wisely, defensive and she admired his form as he danced just out of range of yet another jab. She'd known his body was magnificent from what she'd seen of it a few nights ago, but he looked even more virile stripped. His body was somewhere between lean and stocky. While his muscles were developed and defined, they were also compact and graceful. It was an aristocrat's body—but an aristocrat who'd used his body *hard*. There wasn't an ounce of fat on him, and Eva could see the muscles of his ridged stomach and narrow waist flexing and stretching as he loosened and became more limber. She knew by watching his eyes that he was slowly becoming a purely physical creature.

She loved mills—loved to watch two strong male bodies pitted against each other, loved the sheer physicality of the fighting itself. Of course she also enjoyed looking at naked male torsos. Eva never told Gabe how often she'd dragged James with her to some country inn or farmer's barn to watch fights. James tried to act like he didn't want to go, but she'd recognized the look on his face when he watched. He was just as dangerously stimulated as Eva.

"I saw you box twice," Paul said, his tone almost conversational, although anger pulsed just below the surface.

"Oh?" Godric easily dodged a rapid jab followed by a right cross, and then smiled as he flicked his head to toss his hair off his brow, sending a spray of water flying.

"Yeah," Paul said, "MacNamara and Olsen."

Godric grinned at some memory.

"You tore them both up," Paul said, his jab missing Godric's jaw and connecting with his shoulder.

Godric grunted at the hit but didn't stumble.

The two were well matched for all that their strengths were so different. Godric made up the disadvantage of his years with superior science. What Paul lacked in skill he made up for with rage, bulk, and youth.

They traded punches, neither scoring a solid hit. Paul continued talking, his voice breathier as time went on.

"My brother was under your command," he said after finally delivering a hit that connected soundly with Godric's jaw and sent his head back with an almost audible snap.

Eva realized she'd bitten her lip so hard she'd drawn blood.

Godric staggered and leaned into a crouch, as if off balance, but then he came up under Paul's guard with two furious uppercuts, the second slamming Paul's jaws together so hard, Eva felt it in her own teeth. Godric then danced out of reach, easily avoiding Paul's sloppy counterpunch.

Both men circled, catching their breath, and the muttering of Flynn's men grew louder, their actions more restless—dogs scenting blood.

"Was your brother a cowardly deserter like—"

Paul threw a right hook that knocked Godric back at least three feet. Flynn's men surged up behind him to box him in.

"Get back!" Eva yelled, taking several steps toward Flynn, the pistol aimed at his chest.

Flynn raised his hands in a staying gesture. "You 'eard 'er, boys. Back—step back from 'is lordship."

The men grumbled but shuffled away from the brutally dancing couple.

When Eva turned, Godric had blood running from the corner of his grinning mouth as he gave her a quick wink.

She shook her head in disgust. *Men.*

"Barry wasn't a deserter—more's the pity for the poor bastard." Paul spat a bloody mouthful into the mud between them. "He'd probably still be alive if he'd deserted. But he had some cracked belief that you'd keep your men safe." He barked out a laugh while throwing a clumsy jab, which Godric avoided with ease, repulsing Paul with a left cross that made him grunt and stagger back.

"He believed that drivel until the day he died. Hell, he probably still believed it as he waited for you." Paul went after Godric with a flurry of jabs, driving him back. "But you never came."

Godric's chest was rising and falling more rapidly, his breathing audible even over the rain. A Season spent drinking and carousing had not been good for his wind.

Luckily, Paul couldn't seem to stop talking and was almost as breathless. "Orthez, do you recall that, *Colonel?* Do you know the day I'm talking about, you bastard?" Eva saw it before it happened: Godric losing focus, paying attention to his opponent's words rather than his actions.

Paul saw it, too. "You were supposed to bring support—but you split your men!" He flung himself at Godric and latched on, clutching him like a fatal lover while he delivered a series of punishing jabs to his side.

"Flynn—break them apart!" Eva yelled, but he was frozen, his expression avid: Paul was exacting revenge for every common man who'd suffered at the hands of an officer.

Eva lunged forward, but Andrew grabbed her upper arm, his slender hand remarkably strong. "Don't," he said, his voice sharp over the sound of fists hitting wet flesh. "You'll only distract him."

Eva jerked her arm away but knew he was right. What was wrong with Godric? He was standing limply in Paul's brutal embrace—all but offering himself up for punishment.

"You left him to die!" Paul's hoarse scream rang out like a war cry. "And you did it all so you could save your *whore!*"

His words were like spurs to the flank of a horse, and Godric, who'd been swaying limply under the onslaught only an instant earlier, exploded. "*She was no whore!*" he roared, his left arm a blur, the uppercut connecting solidly with the underside of Paul's jaw and lifting him off his feet.

Paul stumbled, weaving, and Godric drove him back with a flurry of blows, which the other man absorbed with increasingly staggering steps, until his feet slipped in the mud and he went down on his back. And still Godric didn't let up.

He dove on top of the prone man, his fists relentless hammers. "She was no whore—*she was my wife!*"

The words were so garbled and slurred together, it took a moment for Eva to recognize them, her brain slow to put meaning to the words.

His wife?

Chapter 12

It took all Flynn's men except the corpulent man himself, to pull Godric off the now motionless Paul.

"You stay right here," Eva ordered coolly, the point of the pistol aimed at Flynn's substantial middle when he began slipping through the mud toward his wounded minion.

"But, Paul—he needs—"

Eva cut a quick glance at the men still trying to stop Godric's punishing fists, more than one of them getting clipped in the process. "Paul will be fine," she said.

Flynn goggled in justified disbelief.

There was no denying that Godric had lost track of himself and given in to his rage. Eva knew the feeling. Of course, she'd never had the option of pummeling a foe to pieces. It looked cathartic.

"Christ, woman—he's going to kill him!"

"You were happy enough to leave Godric in his clutches a few minutes ago," she reminded him.

Flynn shifted from foot to foot. "Dammit! He's my brother-in-law."

Ah, so that explained the emotional attachment.

"My wife will bloody kill me if something happens to him."

Eva snorted. "You're a bit late for that—*something* has already happened."

And something's *name is Godric.*

Eva smirked at Flynn's shocked expression. "Don't fret—look, he's winding down." She jerked her chin toward the fracas. It was true; Godric's fists were no longer connecting to Paul's body. There were two men on Godric's left arm—which was truly fearsome to behold, the bulging biceps ribboned with ropy blue veins and smeared with mud and blood—and a man holding onto every other limb: five men it took to hold him down.

Warmth pooled in her belly just looking at his pale, sculpted body, old wounds colored by new bruises and fresh blood. He was beautiful and fierce and deadly, like some Greek warrior of vengeance.

"What should we do with him, boss?" a man wheezed, his lip split and bleeding.

Eva glanced around at the narrow road and the trees that hung low over it, their branches sagging even lower with rain. There wasn't a spot on the ground that wasn't wet, but at least the base of the large chestnut wasn't muddy.

Eva pointed to the spot. "Put him over there. Keep an eye on them, Andrew," she called over her shoulder, her eyes on Flynn, who'd rushed toward Paul and dropped to his haunches.

"Good God!" he yelled, glaring up at Eva. "He'll be lucky if his jaw works again. And his nose is broken—hell, maybe in two places. His right eye is already—"

"I think what you're trying to say is: *he lost,*" Eva said, her tone one of heavy boredom, which she certainly wasn't feeling. "Are you going to abide by your word and let us all three go, or do I have to shoot you—and then maybe Paul, for good measure? It might be a mercy for your family to be shed of him after this." She cast a dismissive look at the man still bleeding in the mud.

Flynn's face was suffused with red and Eva thought he might suffer some sort of seizure. "What kind of lady *are* you? I've met dockside whores less bloodthirsty and callous."

Eva didn't think that was a question.

Flynn's lips twisted with disgust. "You're a bloody savage—just like him." He gestured rudely toward the spot where Godric was slumped against the tree. "Mad! You're both mad! Come on, lads, let's get Paul back to camp." The men who'd moved Godric were now helping to carry Paul's large, motionless body.

Flynn motioned for them to go first, and followed, backing into the thick underbrush, not taking his eyes off Eva, as if he were afraid she'd pursue him.

Eva waited until the last of the men disappeared and then heaved a sigh and uncocked the pistol before running to Godric. "Keep an eye on where they went into the trees," she told Andrew. "They might return."

Andrew nodded, his hands shaking, but his jaw firm. "I'll keep watch. You see to his lordship."

"His name is Mr. Fleming."

"But I thought—"

"I know what you thought," she snapped, dropping to her knees beside Godric, who was blinking owlishly and listing to one side, blood running from a dozen cuts on his body, one half of his face already swelling. "Godric? *Godric*," she repeated when he didn't answer. Eva chewed her lip, her mind panicking like a trapped fox. "You must get up, Godric—we cannot carry you. Can you stand?" When he didn't respond she took his face in both her hands and turned him toward her. "*Godric, please.*"

She saw a glimmer of recognition deep in his dilated pupils and his lips moved. "Go without me," he whispered.

Eva turned to Andrew. "He's not lucid," she lied. "And I don't think he can hear me."

Andrew sidled closer, gun still pointed at the foliage, his lopsided gaze flickering over Godric's body. "He took some terrible hits to the head before he went after the other man," he said. "I can't believe he is still standing." He frowned. "Or sitting—or even conscious."

Neither could Eva.

"What are we going to do?" she asked. "We can't carry him."

They stared at each other.

"You go fetch help," she said. "I'll stay here."

He glanced down at his sodden, heavy skirts. "I can't move quickly—you've got breeches and boots. You should go. I'll stay here and—"

The sound of horses came from the same direction where the post chaise had disappeared.

Eva ranged herself in front of Godric, shielding him, and grinned up at Andrew when he automatically took the same position. *He just might be a right one, after all.* They both pointed their guns toward the bend.

"Don't shoot until we see who it is," Andrew ordered, his arms shaking badly.

Eva scowled but didn't bother to answer. Whoever was coming, they were taking their sweet time about it.

Her arms were shaking too, by the time a huge Shire horse with a snow-white muzzle rounded the bend. It was pulling a battered farm wagon, and the old man holding the reins resembled his horse, his beard and hair white beneath a large battered hat.

"Do you think—"

Before Andrew could finish his question, Eva saw one of the postilions—she thought his name was Joe—sitting in the back of the small wagon.

A wave of relief strong enough to knock her off her feet flooded her. "Thank God!" She dropped her arm, allowing the tears she'd been holding back for what felt like years to mingle with the rain. "Thank God."

Chapter 13

"I thought you said you knew how to play?" a cranky, familiar voice snapped.

"I *do* know how to play." The second voice was male and affronted, and it took Godric a second to place it: the boy, Andrew.

"You didn't say you played like my old nurse."

"I'm sorry," Andrew snapped. "I didn't realize I was sitting down with a Captain Sharp."

"I didn't realize I was sitting down with somebody's old granny."

"If you're going to be nasty, I'm going to—"

"Oh hush, don't get your smalls in a twist."

A muffled gasp and then, "You're the most horrid female I've ever met."

"The *most* horrid?" Even in his groggy state Godric could hear the amusement in her voice. "Well, it's good to be the best at something, so I'll take that as a compliment."

"That's it. I'm—"

Godric opened his mouth to tell them to shut up, but all that came out was a grunt.

"You're awake!"

He winced at Eva's loud shriek, forced his eyes open, and squinted against the light, flinching at the sight of a looming, grinning face.

"Godric!"

"Quit making so much racket—you're going to—"

"Oh shut it, Andrew." Small warm hands took his face and he felt the bed move as a body came down next to him. "Godric?"

Godric grimaced. "Shh."

"See, I told you," Andrew said.

"Oh, hush, you. Godric? I'm sorry." Her whisper was almost as loud as her normal voice. "Does your head hurt? Mrs. Crosby said it would be—"

Godric raised a hand—a *shaky* hand. "Eva."

Blissful silence filled the room and he opened his eyes again.

This time he could make out her face, which was creased with concern. His head ached so badly that his eyes watered. Her full lips parted in shock.

"Head. Hurts." Forcing out the words hurt even more.

"Drink this." Andrew materialized behind Eva. "Mrs. Crosby said your head would hurt."

Godric frowned and looked at Eva, who made a face. "Laudanum."

Godric dropped his hand. "No."

Eva smiled, clearly approving. "Good—you don't need that. It just dulls your wits. How about food and some tea?"

He gave a slight nod, but even that hurt.

"Go fetch my husband some tea, bread, jam, and some of Mr. Norton's ham," she ordered without turning her head.

"First off," Andrew said, "I'm not your servant. Second, Mrs. Crosby said he should drink that tonic. She also said he was to have broth—gruel at the—"

"Mrs. Crosby is hardly an authority—she's not a doctor."

"She knows a sight more about it than—"

"No gruel."

The boy made a disgruntled sound at Godric's words and huffed. "Fine."

Eva smirked while Andrew turned and stomped out, at least not slamming the door.

"Who is Mrs. Crosby?"

Eva scowled. "The cook here. The woman thinks she knows everything—and she's bossy to boot."

Pot, meet kettle.

Naturally, Godric did not say that out loud.

"Do you want to sit up?" she asked.

It took a few moments of shifting, and he had to help her as she was far too small to lift him, but finally he was upright. After the initial rush of dizziness and nausea, he felt much better.

"How long have I slept?" he asked as she brought a chair closer to the bed and sat.

"We got here today at just after two and it's seven o'clock now."

He grimaced. *Five hours lost.*

"You hadn't slept much the prior two nights," she pointed out. "You needed it."

Godric lifted a hand to thrust his hair off his forehead, which was when he noticed he was wearing a nightshirt; he never wore nightshirts.

Eva must have seen his look and said, "It's Mr. Norton's son's."

"Who is Mr. Norton?"

"The innkeeper."

"Where are we?"

"At the Greedy Vicar Inn."

Godric's eyebrow shot up.

She laughed with obvious delight. "I know—what a lovely name for an inn, isn't it? It's only an inn, not a proper posting house, so there are just the two rooms available." She stumbled a bit on this last part, her cheeks flushing a charming pink, before hurrying on. "We're three miles from the village of Bellsley, but it's too small to have an inn or a constable or doctor or anything."

"Never heard of it," Godric said.

"Nobody has. This is the back of beyond, and we are dead in the middle of it. I didn't even know England had so many trees." She cut him a look of earnest disbelief. "Lots of woods about, which I suppose is how Flynn and his band can play Robin Hood so effectively."

Flynn.

"Tell me what happened . . . after," Godric said.

"The two postboys got free. Flynn wasn't lying when he said he didn't hurt them. One of them went to the nearest farmstead to get help while the other started walking back toward the main road—isn't that mad?" She cocked her head, her eyebrows arched high. "I mean, walking in *this* weather?"

Godric thought that was probably the wisest way to travel in such weather. "I daresay he's eager to report the loss to his employer. He'll be in a great deal of trouble when they learn a team and carriage were stolen under his watch."

She frowned. "But it's not his fault. Surely they should—"

"Could you finish the story before we begin our crusade, Eva?"

"Oh, yes. Of course. But you *will* help him, won't you? Both postboys, that is? Joe is still here; he's seems to have a case of the sniffles and is sleeping above the stable."

"I'll help them all I can," he assured her. "The rest of the story, please."

"So, er, we came back here and—" She gave him a sheepish smile. "Well, actually, that's about it. Oh, except that Mr. Norton is holding on to our guns." She scowled. "Andrew just handed them over."

Godric thought that was probably a fine thing, given how much the two young people argued. "Has anyone gone for a constable?"

"Mr. Norton said he'd send his son to the nearest town in the morning. It's just too dreadful out right now and he's worried the boy would be out well past dark."

They both turned toward the window. Godric could hear the insistent patter of rain against the panes; the light was weak and gray. "It doesn't seem any worse than it's been," he said.

"It's no longer bucketing, but it only stopped for about five minutes this evening and hasn't let up since. I fear we shall all be underwater soon," she told him with a sour twist to her mouth. "Mr. Norton said the banks of the river have overflowed and the roads in both directions are washed out. That's why we didn't send for the nearest doctor—he'd never make it here in his trap." She slanted him a look. "Do you think we should? Send for a doctor, that is?"

"No."

"Are you just saying that, or—"

"Eva, I am fine. I've boxed plenty of times." Although it was true he couldn't recall hurting so much before. "I just needed a bit of rest." Godric thought the lack of sleep these past few days had actually been more debilitating than the sore muscles and bruises from today's fight.

She heaved a big sigh and opened her mouth, but the door behind her opened. Eva shot to her feet, her expression instantly dark and thunderous. "Oh, Mrs. Crosby." She spoke with all the enthusiasm of a woman who has discovered a garden slug on a favorite bloom.

Godric's head ached with the sudden change of pressure in the room. *Good God. What now?*

The person who entered was not what Godric had expected when he'd heard the woman was a cook. This woman was almost as beautiful as his wife-to-be, but blond and green-eyed rather than dark, and a decade or so older. She was also taller and more generously proportioned. She would have been a stunner in any environment but was doubly so in the humble confines of an inn.

"You didn't need to bring it yourself, Mrs. Crosby." Eva glared at Andrew, who just shrugged helplessly.

Mrs. Crosby ignored Eva as if she'd never even spoken—not a wise decision, in Godric's opinion—and smiled at him brightly enough to singe his eyebrows. "Well, look who's awake. Good evening, Mr. Fleming."

"Good evening, ma'am. I understand you're the one who patched me up." He touched the bandage wrapped around his head and gave her a slight smile.

"I did that," Eva blurted before the other woman could even open her mouth. Her face immediately turned an ugly, mottled red.

The look Mrs. Crosby gave her was tolerant—but condescending: an older sister amused by her younger sister's antics.

Oh dear.

"It's true, Mr. Fleming. Your . . . wife, was very helpful." Godric was not mistaken in believing she was giving him a look of amused condescension and found he didn't care for it any more than Eva appeared to do, albeit for entirely different reasons. Why would this woman be suspicious of their marital status?

"I'm sorry you were accosted and robbed in what used to be a very pleasant neighborhood. It has become quite common now, as so many people in these parts have fallen on hard times." Her full, smiling lips sent one message but there was a hard glint in her eyes that said she was not without sympathy for the robbers' plight. Well, that was likely a common attitude not only here, but all over Britain, thanks to the government's disgraceful lack of action on behalf of the flood of injured, jobless soldiers.

"I'm afraid we were relieved of not only our possessions, but all our money."

"Mrs. Fleming informed me of that fact. Mr. Norton is pleased to extend you every courtesy, sir."

Well, that was something, at least.

Godric inclined his head. "Please extend my gratitude for his generosity. I wish I could say we'd not impose on him for long, but . . ." He gestured toward the window, and she nodded.

"I recommend you stay on for at least a few days, no matter the weather. That swelling on your right temple is a bit concerning and should be given a chance to heal. I told your . . . wife you should remain in bed and have gruel and broth for a few days. Just until you recoup your strength, which shouldn't take a man like yourself too terribly long." She allowed her wicked green eyes to roam his body in a way intended to get his blood all moving in one direction.

Eva was glaring at the other woman as if she were a venomous reptile that had slithered into their midst and then sunk its fangs into Godric's thigh. He couldn't help wondering if Mrs. Crosby understood the danger she was courting by teasing the volatile young woman. Part of him—the bigger part—believed she knew *exactly* what she was doing. Although why she would choose to taunt a stranger was beyond him. Perhaps it was merely the boredom of a too-attractive rural widow, provided she *was* a widow and not behaving like a mare in estrus even though she had a husband still in the picture.

"Thank you for your concern, Mrs. Crosby." He gave her a warm smile to demonstrate that two could play at the same game, and her brilliant eyes widened in surprise. "But I believe I'd like some tea, toast, eggs, and ham—my *wife* tells me Mr. Norton is quite a hand when it comes to curing. I'd also like a basin of hot water and the loan of a razor, if that can be arranged."

She nodded slowly, as if his words had pained her, and Godric felt a bit bad about putting her in her place, although it was better than letting Eva manage the matter.

"Will you take the draught I prepared for you, sir? It is one of my specialties and will get rid of any lingering ill effects." Usually when a woman looked at Godric with that much heat in her expression, neither of them was clothed.

"I actually feel quite well," he lied. "And I don't use laudanum." Not any longer, at least.

She bowed her head in a gesture of submission that was not entirely convincing. "Of course, sir." She took a step toward him. "If you would let me check your banda—"

Godric raised his hand as she reached for his head, his eyes flickering to Eva, who appeared to have swelled to three times her normal size, like some lethal tropical fish. "That's very kind of you, Mrs. Crosby, but I've already taken up too much of your time."

"I don't mind," she said, her lips twitching into a secretive little moue that said she was not easily deterred by mere wives.

How very odd—and interesting. And unwise.

"I'm sure you've got far better things to do than see to my minor cuts and scratches. My wife will tend to my needs. Is there any chance my clothes are—"

"I'm afraid I haven't had the time to see to them. But Mr. Norton has offered the use of a robe." She gestured to the clothes horse, where a plain woolen robe waited. "I know it is humble, but perhaps you might use that for the time being?"

Godric was not unaware of the work their sudden arrival would have caused her. "Thank you."

She gave him another of her meaningful smiles and then turned slightly so she could keep both Eva and Godric in her range of vision. "Your sweet young wife has been so worried about you."

Eva shoved past her, either carelessly—or purposely—jostling her. "Oh, please *do* excuse my clumsiness."

The women faced each other like two cats with arched backs, the air between them charged.

It felt as though the silence stretched, but Godric knew it was only the intensity of the two women's animosity.

The older woman, more wily by half, was the first to give way. "Of course, my dear," she said with a musical laugh as beautiful as her person. "I *do* envy your *childish* exuberance—so much like a playful kitten."

"Why, thank you for being so understanding, Mrs. Crosby. There's nothing I value more highly than praise from my elders," Eva whipped back.

Mrs. Crosby dropped a curtsy—a remarkably graceful one for a country cook—and took her leave.

Eva stalked after her and slammed the door, not caring that Andrew was still standing in the doorway and had to jump back to avoid having his nose mashed. She swung around, her eyes blazing.

Godric opened his eyes wide. "What?"

Her eyes and mouth screwed up. "Don't. Just—*don't.*"

Godric patted the bed where she'd been sitting before the cook interrupted. "Come sit."

She crossed her arms. "No."

Godric smiled, even though he knew he was playing with fire. "Are you jealous, darling?"

"Of *you?*" Disdain, loathing, and even a dash of amusement. She might be a kitten, but she wasn't without her defenses.

Godric chuckled, even though it hurt his head, and crooked his finger. "It's hurting my neck to keep it angled this way," he said, not telling her that his neck would hurt in any position.

"That's terrible," she said in a voice that indicated it was exactly what he deserved. Even so, she *did* come a few steps closer, stopping a little way from his bed. "Perhaps I should leave before she returns so that you will be free to flirt with that—that—"

Good God, she was adorable.

"You *are* jealous."

"No, merely nauseated. If you *must* insist on indulging in flirtation with every *crone*—"

He couldn't help snorting at the inapt description.

"*With every crone,*" she repeated through clenched teeth, "who slithers past, I hope you do so out of my sight and hearing at least."

Godric snatched up her hand before she could jump back. The small, cool fingers remained stiff in his grasp. For a moment he thought she might give him the slap he so roundly deserved for toying with her.

"If it bothers you, sweetheart, all you need do is ask me to stop. Nicely." He kissed the tips of her fingers and cut her a sly look from beneath lowered lashes.

Her jaw tightened, her lovely face flushed darkly, and she stared at him with eyes that blazed a hot blue-violet. "Oh, no, *darling.* I wouldn't interfere with your amusement for all the money in the *world*—I know the simple pleasures are all that remain once a man reaches your advanced age."

Godric threw back his head and roared. And then immediately regretted it. "Dammit!" he howled as a pain more brutal than the blade of a hatchet struck him through the temple.

"Oh dear," she cooed with mock concern. "Did you hurt yourself, *sweetheart?*"

His lips twitched with a pained smile. "You little shrew."

There was a sharp rap on the door and it opened without warning.

Mrs. Crosby stood in the opening, a large tray between her hands, her eyes as sharp as awls.

Good God, the woman must have *sprinted* downstairs and back.

Eva pulled away her hand and stepped back, her full lips tightened into a scowl.

"Here you are, sir." Mrs. Crosby set the footed tray over his lap, her hand *accidentally* brushing the most sensitive part of his body and causing him to jerk. "I beg your pardon," she said quietly, her eyes demurely cast down, her lips curled into a tiny smile.

Godric knew he was handsome, but he certainly wasn't *that* handsome. Just what the devil was the woman up to? Was she hoping to get him murdered in his sleep?

"I'm most grateful for your sedulous care," he murmured.

Her magnificent eyes flashed. "Is there anything else—" She left the question hanging, the implication clear.

"This is lovely, Mrs. . . . . er, Crosby. Thank you."

She nodded. "I shall send your water and razor up when you've rung for me to clear your tray."

Godric frowned. "Are you the only one working?"

"We weren't expecting any guests in this weather, so Mr. Norton gave the girls leave to go home before the water rose so high they *couldn't* go."

"Ah, I see. I'm terribly sorry to be putting you to such inconvenience."

Her lids turned heavy—*really, the woman was laying it on a bit thick.* "You could never be an inconvenience."

Behind her, Eva made an unsubtle retching sound.

Godric's face heated, but before he could formulate an answer, the cook curtsied and left the room with a seductive sway of her hips, brushing close enough to touch Andrew—who wore a fatuous smile— on her way out the door.

"Get in or get out. Either way, shut the door," Eva snapped when Andrew continued to stare in the other woman's direction.

Andrew flushed but stepped inside and closed the door.

"Why did you bring *her* with you?" Eva demanded.

"I didn't *bring* her, she brought herself. I could hardly stop her, short of wrestling her to the ground."

Godric doubted the slender, gentle-looking boy could have stopped the hellcat who'd just left, no matter how hard he wrestled.

Eva swung back to Godric. "I don't like her."

Andrew snorted. "Really? Because I never would have guessed."

Eva whirled on him, and Godric sighed. "Children."

They turned toward him, four pale cheeks flushed, two mouths compressed, four willful eyes flashing. Godric had the most powerful urge to pull the covers over his head and sleep until the rain stopped.

Instead he held his hand toward Eva. "Come here."

She flushed and chewed at the side of her mouth.

"Please? I apologize for being a wretch. Sit with me while I eat." He could see by her deepening flush, his invitation pleased her. It occurred to him, with no small alarm, that she was halfway infatuated with him and that teasing and playing with her would accelerate the process if he wasn't careful.

It won't matter a whit what you do, the snide voice said. *She is a young, impressionable girl who is eager to fall in love.*

Godric was not so sure that was true. Eva might be young, but her mind was as sharp as a razor, and he'd seen no indication during the Season that she was hanging out for a husband. Indeed, he believed her when she said she didn't want to marry. He was fairly certain her only problem with Mrs. Crosby's flirtation was that the woman would be so disrespectful in front of Eva.

Love and marriage are two different matters, my dear, deluded Godric.

"Did you see the way she rubbed against Andrew?" Eva asked.

You see, it's not me she loves, but Mrs. Crosby she despises, Godric told his smug inner voice.

"Did you?" she demanded.

Godric paused in the act of raising his loaded fork. "Er—"

"He *immediately* fell into her nasty snare and is madly in love with her." She tossed the fuming young man a look designed to annoy even the calmest of men, whose number young Andrew was certainly not among.

Her words acted like spurs. "That's not—"

Eva cut Godric a conspiring look. "*You* know she'd never even notice such a green sprig unless she was up to something devious."

"Green. Sprig." Andrew made a strangled noise of fury. "I most certainly am *not* in love with her."

"Oh, that's right." She snapped her fingers. "I forgot, you're in love with your blunderbuss."

"It's a—"

"Eva, Andrew." Godric used the tone he'd always employed on fractious soldiers, and it worked just as well on the two young people. Well, that was something, at least. Not much, but something.

"Can you refrain from bickering every five minutes? How about every five hours?"

The boy glared at Eva, his authority—such as it was—considerably diminished by his ludicrous eyewear and mismatched, borrowed clothing, which was not much better than his tattered dress. "It's *she* who always begins these things with one of her smart comments."

"Better than your *stupid* comments."

Godric cleared his throat before they could go at it again and said, "Please, take a seat, Andrew." Once he'd seated himself—as far from Eva as the small room allowed—Godric said, "I'd like to eat my meal without listening to an argument. Why don't you tell me, *Andrew*"—he cut a severe look at Eva, who assumed a martyred expression—"how you came to be on that stretch of road with an, er, arquebus." *Dressed in a blue gown.*

The boy pushed his glasses up his nose, momentarily distracted by the fact they were missing an arm and lens on one side.

"The short story is that my cousins beat me up, dressed me in one of my dead mother's gowns, and then dumped me off at the side of the road with the gun."

Godric paused with a forkful of—indeed delicious—ham halfway to his mouth. He set the fork down, food untouched. "Is this some sort of rite of passage in your family?"

Eva guffawed but quickly stifled it when he gave her a stern look.

Andrew squirmed, his slender body shifting beneath the borrowed clothing that Godric suspected must have come from the aforementioned son of Mr. Norton, a man whose nightshirt was big on Godric, who was not a small man. Andrew, not a great deal taller than Eva, swam in the huge, rustic trousers, which had been cinched around his narrow waist with twine, rather than a belt.

"My father—Stephen Lowell—died three months ago," he said, looking oddly dignified for all that he was dressed like a clown. "He was a scholar on the subject of ancient weaponry and had always lived modestly until this past year. It appears that he put money on the 'Change right after Boney got caught. Er, the first time. I did not discover the state of his affairs until after his death. I'm afraid his debts are quite onerous."

Godric didn't need to be a genius to see where this was going.

"So you went to your uncle for help?" he said, hopefully moving the story past the painful discovery that Andrew was destitute.

Andrew nodded, every emotion he was experiencing flitting across his sensitive features. "My uncle is an ironmonger—a very successful one—and wanted me to work for him." He must have seen Godric's amazement because he gave a weary smile. "No, not working forges or blast furnaces or anything dreadful like that. He wanted me to be his bookkeeper. But, er, well, I discovered some inconsistencies and when I went to ask him about them, he called me a liar and a thief and kicked me out." He cut Godric a nervous look. "He had two partners, you see."

"Ahh, and his partners weren't aware of the inconsistencies?"

Andrew nodded. "I know now I was naïve to go to him. But then?" He shrugged. "I didn't tell anyone anything—although I suppose I should have." Twin spots of embarrassment colored his narrow cheeks.

"Sometimes it is best to retreat and leave the fight for another day," Godric said kindly.

Andrew gave him a grateful look, his Adam's apple bobbing a few times before he continued. "I was packing my trunk when my three cousins—all ironworkers themselves—came to my room." His mouth twisted with self-disgust. "I think their immediate plan was just to thrash me. But when they opened my trunk, they found the dress—and of course they'd seen the gun when I arrived. I suppose the urge was impossible to resist." He cut Godric a remarkably dignified look. "The dress and gun are all I have left of my parents."

Godric was grateful for the distraction of shoveling food into his mouth. Eva, on the other hand, was staring at the boy with her jaw hanging.

Godric gritted his teeth, dreading what might come out of her mouth.

But then, to his stunned amazement, she leapt from her chair and flung her arms around Andrew, her shoulder knocking his already damaged spectacles off his nose. "That is a horrid story. Why didn't you tell me this before? I'm so sorry I was odious to you."

Andrew's horrified eyes met Godric's over her shaking shoulders.

Godric mimed patting her on the back and nodded and smiled his encouragement when the boy hastily complied. He sagged back against the pillow; well, perhaps they might have a bit of peace, after all.

Eva felt like the lowest form of snake as she watched Andrew carry Godric's empty tray from the room. Godric had asked him to do it so that Mrs. Crosby didn't need to put herself out—at least that was what he'd told Andrew. As soon as the door closed, she went back to Godric's bed but stopped when she realized how brazen that looked.

Godric yawned and then patted the bedding with one of his lovely hands, which now had swollen, torn, bloody knuckles. To her pleasant surprise he reached for her hand again when she sat.

"That was a nice thing you did for Andrew, offering him a place at your father's house."

She grimaced, holding his hand in her lap and studying it rather than look at his too-knowing eyes. "It was the least I could do after being *so* dreadful to him. I had no idea he'd had such a horrid time." Her lower lip quivered. "If I'd known all that—"

"Shh," he soothed, being so lovely to her it was making her feel even more anxious than when he was taunting and tormenting her. She risked a quick glance up, to find him regarding her with a strange, thoughtful look. She cocked her head. "What?"

He shook his head. "Nothing."

She thought it *was* something, but he was not the sort of man to be forced into making confidences—or forced into anything, really. And the way he'd responded to the few personal questions she had asked made her leery of asking any others. Especially of asking the question that was now branded into her brain: Godric had been married?

"Why do you look so pensive?" he asked.

Eva wanted to ask him why he had the right to pose such questions when she didn't, but she simply didn't have the energy for it right now. Instead she said, "I hate to admit it, but I now think that Mrs. Crosby was probably right."

His eyebrows shot up.

"About your staying in bed." The moment the words were out of her mouth, she realized how they could be construed. "I just meant that—"

He laid a big, warm hand over hers. "Shh." He once again made the shushing sound that reminded her of *that* night. "I know my own body and it's telling me I won't be able to sleep tonight if I don't get up at least for a few hours."

"Very well." She grimaced and then chewed the inside of her mouth, her cheeks flushed.

"What is it, Eva?"

"It's just that—well, Andrew was beside himself when we arrived and blurted out the name Lord Visel."

"Ahhh, I see. Well, that's not the biggest disaster of the day." His smile was crooked because his lip was split on one side, and his left eye was almost swollen shut. And then there were the bruises that covered his face, neck, and—she knew firsthand—magnificent torso, but he was still handsome.

"But it shall make it more difficult if we change our minds," she reminded him.

He frowned and then winced, raising a hand to the corner of his swollen eye. "Change our minds about what?" he asked absently as he pressed his fingertips lightly against the various injuries, as if testing to see how bad they were.

"Going to Scotland," she said in a hushed voice, before realizing how stupid that was since they were alone.

He smiled and once again took her hand with a casual confidence that made her breath catch. "I'm sorry, darling, but was there any doubt in your mind about our destination?"

The word *darling,* spoken in his deep, velvety voice, was distracting to say the least—deeply worrying at most.

"If we could have kept our doings quiet enough, we might have had a choice."

"Eva, I think you know we never had a choice, no matter how quiet we kept things."

He didn't say the words in a harsh or hurtful way, but his meaning was clear: when Eva had kidnapped him, she'd sealed his fate.

He smiled at her and brushed one of her cheeks with his hurt knuckles, the action making her want to crawl into his lap like a cat and just forget about everything: who she was, what she'd done, and how he was trapped with the results of her stupidity.

"I would have preferred to keep it quiet, to protect your reputation as much as possible, but I doubt having a few people know the truth—most of those, hiding from the law—will make a great deal of difference."

Eva leaned back until his hand dropped away from her face, as much as she wanted it to stay there. But she couldn't be touching him for what she was about to say. "I'm sorry."

"For what?"

She stared at him for a long moment, this man who—against all odds—she'd come to respect, and even like during their brief time together. Right now he was looking at her with sympathetic interest. Once she confessed what a dunce she often was, he would believe in her madness for certain.

You owe him.

Yes, she did owe him. So she took a deep breath and waved a hand.

"I'm sorry for this—all of it: hitting you on the head, tying you up, getting you beaten half to death, landing you *here*." Eva groaned and sprang to her feet. "I'm really not stupid, you know. Nor am I insensible to the fact my behavior is that of a fifteen-year-old boy rather than an adult woman most of the time."

Godric didn't think now was the time to smile at the very apt description. "I don't think you are stupid, Eva." That was most certainly the truth. No, she was far too clever and would run him a merry chase. "Nor do I think you behave like a fifteen-year-old boy." So that was a little fib, but she looked so agonized, he didn't think now was the time for jesting. "I think you were, quite admirably, trying to save the people you loved."

I would have done things just as mad, and madder, if I'd been given the chance to save Lucia and Carl or the rest of my bloody family, he could have said, but didn't.

Instead, he said, "Don't flog yourself over something that is over and done—there is no greater waste of one's precious time on this earth."

Listen to you, Godric. Perhaps you might listen to what you are preaching?

Yes, he *knew* he should, and there was no time like the present to begin.

She shook her head as she paced, her hands raking through her short curls and making them wild. "I wish my father would see it that way, but I dread seeing him. All my life he has cautioned me against my impulsiveness and thoughtlessness." She glanced over at him, her eyes shadowed with something he couldn't quite understand. "I suppose you will think this pathetic, but I've always worshipped my father and striven to please him and make him proud. But he is—" She flung up her hands. "Well, you must know something about him?"

Godric nodded. Indeed, all the *ton* knew of the icy peer; it was difficult to imagine the man was a father, but he knew the marquess had at least five children, and his wife was shortly going into the straw for a sixth.

"Well, you needn't worry about his punishing you, Eva. You will be my wife and he will no longer have that power."

She shook her head violently, setting her curls dancing. "No, he doesn't punish me—not in the way you're thinking. He will just *look* at me." She turned and did that *thing* she was so very good at doing: becoming another person entirely. Godric had to stare: Lord, it was as if the frosty Marquess of Exley had taken possession of his diminutive daughter's person.

He swallowed. "Yes, that is, er, quite the look," he admitted, actually feeling nervous under her frigid stare.

In a blink she was once again Eva, a surpassingly lovely, clever, and amusing young woman terrified of disappointing her demanding parent.

Godric felt for her. Even though his own father had been a proud and undemanding parent from the moment Godric could toddle, he'd had friends at school whose fathers had been brutal in their expectations. Seeing her in such a state of misery made him want to thrash the marquess, who sounded like a bit of a tyrant in addition to being cold.

A question occurred to him—something he'd been meaning to ask. "How did you learn about my foolish plans for your brother's wife?" he asked, his face heating at the memory of his horrid behavior this last Season.

"I knew you were up to something after you called off the duel with Gabriel, so I started to follow you." She gave him a sheepish look. "James helped me. It took only a few weeks before we learned what you were up to. But I knew nobody would believe me if I told them."

Unfortunately, Godric thought she was probably right about that. What sane person would have credited him with implementing such a disastrous, venal, cruel plan?

"I'm mortified by all the idiocy I've managed to perpetrate in such a short while," she muttered, kneading her hands as roughly as a lump of dough while pacing close by the bed on her next pass; close enough that Godric's hand caught hers and then yanked her down into his arms, wincing at the pain the action caused, but still not stopping.

He ignored the cacophony of inner voices that protested his actions, slid his hand around her delicate neck, pulled her close, and claimed her mouth with his.

This, my good man, is a dreadful mistake, a weary voice in his head told him.

Oh, don't I know it.

Godric knew he should put a stop to this, yet the way her body melted against his stoked the blaze inside him. And when she opened under his onslaught, he thrust his tongue into her mouth, desperate to taste her, even though the responsible part of him—the part above the waist—knew he was behaving disastrously.

The moment he slid inside her she opened wider, her body softening and her arms clasping around his neck as she all but crawled up his body, making soft, mewling noises he'd never have suspected from such a fierce little thing.

Godric plunged deeper, sucking her delicious tongue, and shamelessly pulling her closer. The pleasure of exploring her was worth gritting his teeth whenever she inadvertently kissed or kneed or grabbed a bruise or injury—which was most of the time as he was a bloody mass of pain.

But the pain was worth it.

He lazily penetrated her sweet, hot mouth, using every tactic at his disposal to lure her into his own.

Clever clogs that she was, it wasn't long before she was flicking her tongue daintily over his teeth and the sensitive skin between his lips and gums. When she was fully inside him, Godric took her tongue between his lips and sucked.

She made a delightful purring sound and rubbed her bottom against his aching rod, which felt bloody heavenly, but also brought him crashing to Earth: *Christ! He'd have her pinned to the bed if he did not back away from the siren call of her body.*

And would that really be so bad?

No, it would be delicious—for him—but Andrew or the Crosby woman could barge in at any moment. Godric swallowed his utterly inappropriate lust and pulled back, his cock aching just from a kiss.

She blinked in confusion, and he stared into eyes the color of hydrangeas, her body rising and falling with the rapid movements of his chest.

"I accept your apology, Eva," he said hoarsely, "even though I don't believe I deserve it."

She swallowed noisily, her pink, swollen lips parted. "Er, apology?"

Godric waited, giving her time to come back to herself.

"Oh, apology." She nodded several times, her eyes still lusthazed. "Wh-why don't you deserve it?"

Godric stared into her dilated pupils, wishing he'd not resumed this conversation. It was the last—no, the *second-to-last*—subject he wanted to discuss, but he felt like a heel to hear her apologizing for her behavior after everything *he'd* done.

"If I'd not behaved like an ass and a boor toward you and your family—especially your brother—" He swallowed hard. "Gabriel. Then you wouldn't have needed to protect him and his new wife from me, would you?"

She opened her mouth and then shut it.

"What?" he asked, dreading the can of worms he might be opening, but owing her at least that much. "Say what you need to say."

"Would you really have taken her? Drusilla?" she added, as if they both didn't know whom she meant.

It wasn't the question he'd been dreading—which was the source of his enmity toward Marlington to begin with—but it might actually be worse.

Godric pursed his lips and shook his head with genuine regret. "I don't know, Eva," he admitted, so ashamed of his behavior there should be a new English word invented to describe the feeling. "I feel as if I was in some sort of fugue before James called my name—it was as though he broke the spell, made me realize I was waiting in a rubbish alley to abduct another man's wife." Eva winced, but did not look away. "At that moment, I realized how madly I was behaving. But if James *hadn't* shown up just then?" He shrugged. "I don't know," he repeated. "So, one way or another, you really did save your friend and brother. The next time you think this is all your fault—or even mostly—think again."

He'd thought he would feel better when he'd got that part off his chest, but he just felt like an even bigger idiot as he looked into her eyes—so stormy and emotional a few moments before, but now cool, almost appraising.

He gave a dismissive flick of his hand, wanting to move on like the coward he obviously was. "I'd like to thank you for today—for taking care of me when I wasn't able to take care of myself."

Her lips curved slightly and he could see his words had pleased her. "You would have done no less," she said, apparently forgetting that *he* was supposed to be protecting *her*. "Besides,"—she grinned suddenly, the action making his heart stutter—"Andrew really did do his share, which wasn't easy wearing that dreadful dress."

Godric smiled, and then realized that she, too, was wearing new clothing. "Whose dress is that?" He knew it couldn't be Mrs. Crosby's, as her clothing would have drowned Eva's more delicate figure.

She grimaced and plucked at the skirt, as if just now remembering what she was wearing. "The maid—the girl who's not here—keeps clothes at the inn for the nights she stays over." She narrowed her eyes at him. "Judging by the horrified way Mrs. Crosby stared at my clothing, I'm guessing I'll never see it again."

Before Godric could answer, the door opened. Andrew came striding in and then stopped in his tracks when he saw them together on the bed, his cheeks coloring. "Oh, I say. I guess I should have knocked first—"

"Not at all, come in, Andrew." Godric released Eva's hand and she shot from the bed like a startled leveret.

That was just as well. Godric had clearly suffered mental damage during his brief fight this afternoon, a result of which was that he could no longer keep his hands and lips to himself.

"I brought you some shaving things." Andrew laid the items on the dressing table. "I'll just run down and fetch your hot water."

The door shut behind him and Eva made to follow. "I'll let you dress and shave."

Godric frowned. "Where are you going?"

"Down to the coffee parlor."

He didn't like the idea of her wandering about a strange inn. "Why don't you wait in your room—Andrew can accompany you when he comes back."

She gestured to the connecting door. "That's not my room. *This* is my room. Didn't you hear me earlier? They only have *two* rooms and Andrew has the other one."

Godric *had* heard that, but his brain had failed to process it. *Christ.* He realized she was waiting and gave her what he hoped was his normal smile. "Sorry, it seems my wits have gone begging."

"Mrs. Crosby said she would bring in a cot so that I didn't disturb your sleep by, er, well, sharing your bed." Her face was as red as a poppy.

He opened his mouth to say that he and the boy could share one room and give her the other, but they were supposed to be husband and wife.

So he nodded. "Well, then, that's how it shall be." He'd tell her later that *he'd* be the one occupying the cot.

She turned without speaking and left, closing the door quietly behind her.

Godric waited for the door to close before letting his head fall back against the headboard with a dull *thunk*. It was unfortunate that he'd not been beaten more badly today. Because having a broken arm or being unconscious was the only way he'd be able to sleep in the same room with her and keep his bloody hands—and other parts—to himself.

Chapter 14

For all that Mrs. Crosby looked like an angel and behaved like a courtesan, the woman cooked like a dream. As Godric had only a nightshirt and a robe, Mr. Norton—a large and exceedingly shy man—set the small coffee parlor aside for their private dining chamber, not that there was anyone occupying the bar parlor, where meals were usually served, in this weather.

When Godric tried to draw the man into conversation about his son's projected jaunt to fetch the constable, he'd blushed and hemmed and hawed in a way that made Godric suspect it would not be a healthy practice for a local business owner to set the law on Flynn's gang. Godric could hardly blame the man. Who'd want to go head-to-head with a band of violent thieves living right on one's doorstep?

Although he would much rather get Eva out of this backwater without calling in a magistrate, he worried about whether Flynn or his men would honor their agreement.

"Well," Andrew said with a somnolent, satisfied smile as he finished the last of his custard and sat back, his slender hands resting placidly on his belly, "that was delightful. I feel positively—"

"Stuffed like a Christmas goose?" Eva interjected. "You ate enough to feed three ostlers."

Andrew frowned and opened his mouth.

"I agree, Andrew," Godric said. "That was delightful. And this warm room is making me positively sluggish." He began to rise.

"You needn't stay and entertain me," Eva said, her expression telling him a different story. Godric would have felt flattered but was smart enough to realize it wasn't *his* company she wanted so much as not being left in Andrew's.

So he lowered himself back into his seat. "It's a bit too early for bed."

"We've got cards." She sat up in her chair, her expression eager.

"There are a few books if you prefer reading." Andrew gestured to the dozen or so titles held between bookends that appeared to have been made out of cannon shot. "But I'm afraid they're mostly drivel." He cut Eva a quick look. "Minerva Press, mainly."

Eva frowned. "Why did you look at me when you said that?"

"You're a female, and those are female books."

Eva's hackles rose.

"Actually," Godric cut in, before the fur started flying, "I've enjoyed quite a few of the Minerva titles."

Really, their expressions were priceless.

"You *have?*" Andrew asked, as though Godric had admitted to a penchant for going on the strut in Hyde Park wearing only a fur muff and bergère hat.

"He's lying." Eva's voice was flat and her expression was one of profound disgust, like a cat that had inadvertently gotten its feet wet.

Godric clutched at his heart. "I'm stung."

She crossed her arms, her standard battle stance. "All right then, name one of your favorite titles."

"Ah, you like them, too, do you?'

She flushed. "No, they're appalling, but Melissa consumes them like candies and they're positively littering the house."

"Hmm," he said, as though he had to think about the matter when, in reality, he did not. He didn't tell her that Minerva Press books had been the only ones available while he convalesced. Most were brought over by officers' wives and then donated to the hospital. Rather than slowly go insane from his own morbid thoughts, Godric had read them, dozens of them. "I suppose I like *The Castle of Wolfenbach* or *Count Roderic's Castle* best."

For the first time in his life Godric wished he had the gift of sketching. "Your expression is priceless, Eva."

"I must admit I'm surprised, sir," Andrew said.

"And why is that, pray?"

"Well, you being who you are." He glanced around, his eyes wide, and then whispered, "*A colonel.*"

"What? You think soldiers don't appreciate a bit of Gothic excitement while we are on campaign?"

Eva made another of those snorting sounds, like something from a miniature bull.

"I'll admit it had not occurred to me," Andrew answered, taking his question seriously.

"Well, you two might care to sit about, reading drivel, but I want to play cards. Go fetch them from Godric's room, Andrew."

Andrew's eyeballs bulged and Godric stood before they could commence brangling. "Actually, I forgot something up in the room, Eva. I'll fetch them."

"See?" she demanded, gesturing with a hand at Godric while staring at Andrew. "Now the man who saved us today is going up, all because you are a lazy, good-for-nothing, poor—"

Godric shut the door on their bickering. They'd behaved for hours; it was time they had a good go at one another. He'd not really wanted to go to the room, but he *had* wanted a word in private with Norton. He hadn't wished to pursue the subjects of Flynn and the magistrate in front of his young companions.

He passed the taproom and saw a lone customer at the bar. His back was to Godric, but his mode of dress proclaimed him to be a rustic, as he was not dressed in the dyed uniforms that Flynn's men had worn.

"Can I help you?"

"Good God!" His voice came out three registers higher than

usual, and he spun around to find Mrs. Crosby leaning against the door that probably led to the kitchen.

"I'm sorry I startled you," she said, not sounding it. "Were you looking for something?"

At least Godric now knew his heart was working well. "I wanted to have a word with Mr. Norton."

"He's not here. Perhaps I could help?" Her tone was a mixture of sin and velvet.

A bolt of lightning struck close enough to the inn to illuminate the dim taproom; the ensuing crack and roll of thunder was almost immediate.

Godric turned from the window to find Mrs. Crosby wearing another expression entirely. But it was gone so quickly he wondered if it was just a residual effect of the lightning.

"I hope he's not out in the elements," he said, becoming more curious about this woman—who was once again giving him come-hither looks—by the moment.

"So do I."

They stood in silence, their eyes locked. Godric felt a frisson of something, but it wasn't sexual excitement.

She reached out just as another bolt of lightning flickered, her fingers warm and rough on his temple. "Does it hurt?" Her touch was caressing. Utterly inappropriate.

Godric reached up and circled her wrist with one hand, gently but firmly removing her fingers from his skin. He was about to re-lease her arm when her other hand slid around his waist.

Godric laughed softly but didn't release her. "What is it that you want, Mrs. Crosby?"

She shrugged, her hand kneading the bruised muscles of his waist hard enough that he hissed in a breath, his hand tightening on her wrist until she made an echoing sound, her chest rising and falling more quickly now, her eyes hooded as her hand continued to hurt him.

Her full lips curved into a carnivorous smile. "What do I want? What do you—"

Godric saw the light from a door opening behind him and knew it could only be the coffee room.

Mrs. Crosby's smile shifted from aroused to amused and she dropped her hand. "Let me know if you want to take me up on that offer. Of help, I mean."

Godric knew who was behind him before he released the woman's wrist, and then watched as the cook disappeared into the kitchen before turning to face some familiar music.

Eva felt as if all she did these days was either sit in a carriage or pace a threadbare carpet in yet another cramped, filthy inn.

Although that wasn't really a fair assessment of the room she was in now; yes, it was small, but it was scrupulously clean and plenty large for a couple. Well, a man and wife who were currently speaking to one another.

Eva groaned, her mind's eye insistently playing the same image over and over again. Godric's broad back, female fingers gripping his narrow waist hard enough that the tendons stood out on the back of her hand, and Godric holding her other arm.

And then there was his face when he turned, sardonic and amused. "Sorry, darling, I stopped to talk to Mrs. Crosby. Were you concerned for my welfare? Or have you done away with poor Andrew and need help disposing of the body?"

"How droll," she'd snapped, infuriated by the way her voice shook. "But I'm actually headed up to go to bed. I seem to have developed a headache."

His smile said he knew that for the lie it was. He gestured toward the stairs. "After you."

"I hardly need an escort up the stairs."

He came close enough to lay his large, splayed hand over her lower back and leaned low to whisper, "I still need to fetch the cards, sweetheart." He kissed her temple.

He came up with her, fetched the cards, and then wished her goodnight before heading back downstairs.

And that, as they say, had been that.

Eva had heard Andrew moving about in his room some time ago, so Godric had been by himself—all alone—downstairs for at least an hour.

Or not.

"I don't care!" She forced the words through clenched jaws, her head filled with visions of him doing to Mrs. Crosby what he'd done to her.

Oh yes, you do.

She flung herself down on the bed, still fully clothed in the stupid borrowed dress and overlarge cloth slippers.

There was a tentative knock on the connecting door.

"What?" she called out, not getting up even when she heard the door open.

"What's going on in here?" Andrew's rather reedy voice sounded even higher than usual.

"Nothing."

"It sounded as if you were throwing furniture around—and marching in place."

Eva shoved herself up onto her elbows. "What did you do down there?"

Andrew blinked, which was when she noticed he'd taken off his laughable spectacles. "Where?"

"God, you ninny! In the coffee room. Where else were you?" His immediate frown told her calling him names probably wasn't the best way to get what she wanted. "I'm sorry," she said. "I didn't mean that. Did you play cards?"

Andrew's mild features were seized in an expression of indecision—likely about whether to slam the door in her face or not—but thankfully he was sunny natured and relaxed against the doorframe.

"We played for a while."

Probably until Godric was on the verge of ripping his hair out at Andrew's horrid bidding and pitiful trades. An hour playing cards with Andrew had likely left Godric curled in a fetal position on the hearth. She smirked at the image.

"And then we talked a bit," Andrew said, shattering that appealing vision.

"You *talked*? About what?"

He shrugged his shoulders with deliberate casualness and said, "Men's stuff. You wouldn't understand."

"Men's stuff."

His eyes narrowed into a nearsighted glare. "You needn't raise your voice at me."

Eva ground her teeth. Oh, but she *did* need. She desperately wanted to tell him he should be grateful she'd not leapt on top of him and wasn't currently thrashing the information out of him. Before she could lose all sense and do exactly that, he resumed his desultory story.

"Godric ordered a bottle of brandy and we just spoke generally. He's a fellow Etonian, you know." He paused, smiling proudly across at her.

She glared at his puffed-up countenance, her eyeballs hot.

Andrew, utterly unaware of the danger that faced him, continued, "Mainly we just talked about what I want to do—what sort of work. He said he'd help me find a secretary position."

Eva grunted. "Oh. What was he doing when you left?" Her face was as hot as a poker by the time the last word left her mouth. Luckily, Andrew seemed to find nothing amiss about a woman asking about her husband.

"He was reading."

"Reading?"

Andrew grinned. "He really *does* enjoy those Gothic novels, doesn't he?"

Eva didn't want to tell Andrew that he knew just as much—if not more—about her *husband* as she did.

"There is something odd going on here," she said, giving voice to a thought she really would have rather discussed with Godric if she didn't hate him so much at the moment. For all she knew, he would be *glad* that Mrs. Horrid Crosby had possession of their weapons.

"You mean with the Gothic novels?"

Eva rolled her eyes.

"What?" he demanded. "Why do you have to look at me like that?"

"You *make* me look at you like that." God, how she missed James. "Did you get the guns back from Mr. Norton?"

"No, I didn't. What's the hurry, anyhow?"

Eva wanted to hit him over the head with his bloody blunderbuss. "I told you to get them back half an hour after they *took* them. Why are you dragging your heels on this?"

"I don't understand why *I* have to get them. Why don't you tell Godric to ask for them?"

"Are you really asking me that? He just got beaten half to death." *And is in danger of being beaten the rest of the way tonight.* "Can't we do one thing without him? Besides, I'm not sure he's in his right mind with all the buffeting his head took."

Andrew's expression was one of genuine alarm. "Do you really believe his head is damaged that badly? Mrs. Crosby said—"

Eva leveled her index finger at him. "If you quote her *one* more time—or even mention her name—I'm going to make you very, very sorry."

He blinked, his lips parted, but no words came out.

"Now," she said when she was sure she had his attention. "Listen to me."

"I *am* listening. But what *you* want isn't listening—you want my agreement. You do realize we don't have any money to pay for all this, don't you? They don't know us from Adam and yet they've taken us in—three strangers without a bag or tuppence among us. They've given us shelter, clothing, and food. My guess is they took the guns to hold in payment."

Eva blinked at the thought.

"Yes," he said in an uncharacteristically snide voice. "I can see you don't think of *everything*."

For a moment he almost had her convinced.

"Don't you find their generosity a bit *odd*?"

He sputtered, "Are you demented? They are being *kind*. You *do* know that word? *Kindness*."

"Kindness would be offering aid without taking our guns."

"So, what are you saying? That this kind innkeeper and cook have taken our guns for nefarious purposes? That they are part of Flynn's vast underground criminal conspiracy?" He smirked at his weak jest, completely unaware of how much danger he was currently putting his blunderbuss in.

Eva could not believe he was so stupid. "What? You don't think everyone in the area is aware there is a notorious band of robbers and killers living on their doorstep?"

"We don't know they are killers."

"Look, I don't think either of them is part of Flynn's gang, but I daresay Mr. Norton gives Flynn whatever he wants, when and if he asks for something—just like everyone else who lives in such proximity to the gang."

Eva could tell by the way Andrew was chewing his lip that she was making headway into his thick, phlegmatic brain. For a university student, he was certainly torpid and credulous.

It wasn't that she didn't *like* him—even though he appeared to have no skills other than possessing a tediously expansive knowledge of outdated weaponry—but she was worried about his ability to assess a situation accurately. After all, he *was* the man who'd ended up penniless in a dress on the side of a remote cart road.

His finger moved to push up his spectacles before he recalled he wasn't wearing them. He frowned. "Let's say, just for the sake of argument, that you are right—not that the two of them have taken our guns for any nefarious purposes, but that they might be concerned about Flynn."

It wasn't what she wanted, but it was a start. "Thank you."

"I didn't *say* you were right; I *said*—"

"I *heard* what you said."

"Fine. So, that being the case, what is it you think is going to happen?"

Eva hated to admit it, but, "I don't know." He snorted and she couldn't blame him. "But I *do* know I want to have a gun handy when I find out."

"I still have my arquebus," he pointed out in all seriousness.

"I wonder if that is because everyone in the world knows the stupid thing would take half an hour to light and fire, even if it did have any *bullets* in it."

"It doesn't take bullets. How many times do I have to—" He stopped, swallowing his words at her undoubtedly murderous expression. "It just so happens I *can* use basic supplies to fashion what I need to make the arquebus useable."

"Oh, how comforting."

He ignored her taunt. "Besides, as I keep saying, they didn't *take* the guns, they just, er, didn't put them in our rooms after helping us carry Mr. Fleming into the inn."

Eva stared.

He threw up his hands. "Fine, they took them. Maybe Mr. Norton is oiling them?"

Eva could tell that even Andrew didn't buy that supposition.

He heaved a sigh. "I shall ask for them back."

"What if they don't give them to you? *Then* what will you do?"

He opened his mouth, but no words came out.

"After you've asked for them and they say no, it will put them in a difficult position. But if you *don't* ask, then . . ."

His expression was one of dawning amazement. "You want me to steal them, don't you." It wasn't a question.

"I want you to liberate them. If you want to be accurate, *they* stole them from us."

"Er, not really, because *we* stole them from Flynn—at least two of them."

She shook her head, utterly stupefied. "Are we really having this conversation?"

He raised his hands in a placating gesture. "Fine. *Our* guns."

"Good. So, what's your plan?"

"Plan? *Plan?*" He goggled at her. "This is *your* idea. What's *your* plan?"

With Godric indisposed, Eva was going to have to do everything. She could see that.

Yes, and we all know how well you handled the last matter of any importance.

All right, she could accept that kidnapping Godric might not have been the best way to resolve the problem he'd posed.

A loud crack of thunder made them both jump.

"Here's the plan: you go down there in the morning, when both of them are busy, and search their rooms."

"*What?*"

It took another fifteen minutes to convince him, and Eva's head was pounding by the time he stomped off and slammed the connecting door, but he'd given his word that he'd fetch the guns.

Of course now that all that was handled, she could go back to brooding and stewing about the idiot downstairs, and wondering what the devil he was doing, and whom he was doing it with.

Godric knew he'd not sleep a wink tonight. That was how it was with his blasted insomnia: sometimes even five or six hours were enough to get him up to fettle. And so he'd decided to leave Eva to cool her heels a bit. And then he'd proceeded to while away the longest hour and a half in recent memory playing piquet with Andrew. For a smart young man, he really seemed incapable of grasping even the rudiments of the game.

When Godric could suppress his screams of frustration no longer, he'd suggested they share a glass of brandy and have a comfortable coze.

After reassuring Andrew he'd assist in the delicate task of finding him a new position despite the fact that he possessed no letters of recommendation, the boy had yawned and then blushingly apologized. Godric had expressed his—dishonest—intention to read for a while and waved him off to bed.

Once the boy went up, Godric rang the bell, relieved that it was Norton—who appeared strangely nervous—rather than Mrs. Crosby who answered.

"Yes, my—er, Mr. Fleming?"

So, that answered the question as to whether the innkeeper had rumbled Godric's real identity. Oh well, it was past worrying about now.

"I wonder if you have a road book or map of the area?"

"Er, yes?"

Godric frowned. Why the hell was the man so nervous? Just because he knew Godric's identity and felt anxious about housing a duke's heir? He supposed that might be possible. After all, the Greedy Vicar was not the kind of inn set up to cater to the carriage trade. The stables were small and Andrew said there'd been a buckboard, an older cart horse, and stalls for a half dozen others.

"I should like to borrow it," Godric said when the big man— easily two inches taller than Godric's six feet, and at least four stone heavier—continued to stare.

"I'll fetch it, sir." Norton began to turn.

"Oh, and Mr. Norton?"

The innkeeper turned slowly back around.

"About the magistrate?"

"Ah, yes, Sir Bevil."

"My wife mentioned you'd planned to send your son?"

Norton nodded rapidly. "Yes, sir, first thing tomorrow, provided the weather clears some." As if managed by a theatrical crew, a crack of thunder shook the sturdy little building and Norton grimaced. "The thing is, sir, there's no telling if Anthony will even be able to get through. I went out myself earlier and saw the Nidd was lappin' at the Cutley Bridge. That were a good six hours ago. I reckon it'll be washed out by now."

Godric had vague recollections of coming over said bridge in the farmer's wagon. It had been not long after they'd left the dense section of woods.

He glanced up at the other man, whose expression was one of sheer terror. *Just what the bloody hell was bothering Norton and Crosby?*

"That wood to the south—Guisecliff?"

"Aye."

Godric knew about the name from the papers—the stories that had mentioned Flynn and his gang.

Something occurred to him. "You don't sound like a Yorkshireman, Mr. Norton." And Mrs. Crosby didn't sound like a Yorkshire-*woman.*

Norton shook his head, his expression increasingly miserable—and something else: Was that guilt?

"I've only owned the inn four years now. I'm from Dorking."

"Ah, what's a Surrey man doing in Yorkshire?" *And why do you look so very, very guilty?*

The door to the coffee room opened and Godric wasn't surprised to see Mrs. Crosby. Her expression, momentarily unguarded, was one of concern as her eyes flicked between Godric and Norton. "That leak in the cold room has gotten bigger, Mr. Norton."

Godric had believed the big man was frightened before; now his expression was one of sheer terror.

"I'd best see to that."

"Do send that map to me," Godric called after his scuttling form.

Mrs. Crosby leaned in the doorway, her arms crossed. "What map would that be . . . sir?"

"Mr. Norton said he would loan me his road book."

She nodded slowly, her eyes drifting over his person appraisingly. "I'll get it from him and send it up with your clothing in the morning—if that is soon enough? Or I could bring it up to your room tonight."

Godric smiled as he imagined Eva's response to seeing Mrs. Crosby again tonight. "Tomorrow will be soon enough." He thought she wanted to say something else, but she just nodded.

"Can I get you anything else before I retire for the evening?"

"No, thank you, I have everything I need."

Something flickered in her eyes, but he couldn't decipher it before she bowed her head. "I'll bid you a good night."

Once the door closed he glanced at the clock on the fireplace mantel: it was just before eleven. He grimaced; likely Eva was still awake and fuming.

So he plucked a book from the small selection without reading the spine, poured a little more brandy, and settled in, hoping to make himself sleepy by reading.

But *The Orphan of the Rhine*, for all its high, almost hysterical, drama could not hold his attention. Instead, he put the book in his lap and stared at the dwindling flames, the insistent pattering of the rain making him accept that they would likely be here at least one more day. And night.

It was better that Eva believed him to be up to dastardly deeds with Mrs. Crosby rather than know the true contents of his mind, which was filled with lustful thoughts of his delicious, maddening, amusing, enraging, intoxicating wife-to-be.

"Christ." He threw back the contents of his glass and shivered with pleasure as the rich liquid burned a smooth path down his throat.

He briefly debated the wisdom of having another before pouring it, resolving it would be his last. He didn't wish to be insensible while he lay in the darkness and stared at the ceiling tonight, but neither did he wish to be starkly sober.

The truth was that Eva had managed to worm her way under his skin. Not only her beautiful face and sweet little body, but the sheer volume of life that small package held. She'd been correct in her assessment of her behavior—she *did* behave immaturely at times. But if his behavior these past months was not immature, that was only because it veered into the area of dangerous stupidity. So, no, he didn't fault her for her impulsive actions. Indeed, he honored her for caring so much about her family.

But the sad, disastrous truth was that he had nothing more to offer her than the negligible protection of his name and some bed sport—granted, he suspected the bed sport would be rather spectacular. He liked and respected her, but he did not love her. And he knew what love felt like because his love for Lucia and Carl still owned his heart, utterly.

It wasn't conceit to say Eva was poised on the brink of giving her heart to him. She wouldn't have become so incensed by Mrs. Crosby's ridiculous behavior otherwise. Even if it was only infatuation brought on by their few kisses and his lamentable behavior beneath her skirts, it would leave her hurt when she realized he could not return her feelings.

It really was his hope they could live in relative amiability once they were married. He'd not been jesting about indulging her horse-breeding fantasy, which he truly believed was more than a childish whim for her—she knew an impressive amount about horseflesh.

He would spend his time in London and let her live her life. It would only rarely be important for her to leave Cross Hall. She'd need to be presented, of course, and they would move to the ducal seat when his grandfather died. But other than that, she could live the life she'd claimed to want: that of an unmarried woman, in all but name.

And you think that will make her happy? Living like a childless widow with her horses?

She wants children even less than I do.

Did she say that?

Godric paused, the glass halfway to his mouth, his brow furrowed as he tried to recall that uncomfortable conversation. *Had* she said she didn't want children? Or had he just assumed it? He shrugged and took a deep pull from the glass. It didn't matter—*he* didn't want them, which was enough reason for both of them.

If he wanted to be kind to her, he would not put an unwanted child inside her, he would ignore the incessant demands of his cock and stay away from her bed and stop kissing and touching her whenever the fancy seized him.

It wasn't that engaging in sexual acts with her would make her fall in love with him, but it *would* feed into her infatuation, which would mean pain for her when he finally went back to his own life.

It would be difficult for him to keep her at arm's length, but he would ultimately be doing her a kindness. And didn't he owe her that much, at least?

You're such a model of restraint, a veritable beacon of decency and self-control.

Oh, bugger off, he snapped, ignoring the mocking laughter that echoed in his head as he mounted the stairs to the small room he shared with his wife-to-be.

Eva's eyes were wide open and she was glaring at the ceiling when she heard footsteps outside the door: Godric's footsteps. She closed her eyes just as the door opened.

She didn't hear the sound of the door closing, and it was all she could do to keep from peeking to see what he was doing. The room was barely lit as she'd snuffed all but one stubby candle guttering on the far side of the chamber. She'd also pushed the furniture around a bit and then shoved the cot as far from the bed as possible—which wasn't very far—the foot end facing him. Eva wished she'd had the sense to turn on her side so he couldn't see her face, but it was too late for that now.

The wooden planks of the floor creaked softly and then came the distinctive sound of bone hitting wood, and an explosive, "*God-dammit!*"

Eva had to bite her lower lip hard to keep from laughing.

"So pleased to amuse you, my lady." When she kept her eyes closed, he added, "I know you're awake—unless you have some un-usual malady that makes you choke with laughter while you sleep."

She sighed and opened her eyes to find him rubbing his shin and glaring down at her. "Who the devil moved the bed?"

She shrugged.

He scowled, stood up, and came toward her. Eva hastily pushed herself up. "What are you doing?" She hated the fear she heard in her voice—but not as much as she hated the excitement.

He stopped abruptly. "What do you *think* I'm doing?"

She chewed her lip as they stared at each other in the gloom.

It was Godric who spoke first. "Go sleep in the bed. I'll take the cot."

Eva had to admit it was not what she'd been expecting. "I'm fine here."

"Eva." He used the tone that he'd not used on her recently—the commanding one—and she decided she disliked it more than she had before.

"Quit ordering me about; you're not my husband and certainly not the master of me. Indeed, I'm beginning to rethink this entire rush to the border." She paused and then blurted, "Why did you even come back here?" She wanted to howl the instant the humiliating question flew past her lips.

"What are you wittering on about?" He loomed over her, fisted hands on his hips, his thin, mobile lips twisted into a scowl. Eva saw the exact moment when he understood what she meant. Vile, odious, teasing, hateful creature that he was, he smirked. "Ah, so that's what's got you in a twist, is it? A visit from the green monster."

She flung back the blanket and surged to her feet, sick of looking up at him. "I'm sorry, *my lord*, I know men of your sort are accustomed to behaving like dogs in rut, but perhaps you could curtail your lust when I am trapped in the same building—nay, the same *room*—with you."

"What is my *sort*, exactly?"

Once again it was not the question she was expecting and Eva experienced such a welter of conflicting thoughts and emotions she thought the top of her head might pop off.

The only thought she could latch on to was one that was swimming inside her skull like a circling shark. "I hate you."

He grinned. "I don't think you do, darling."

"Don't call me that. And I don't care what you think."

"I think you're lying." His voice had dropped so low it was like the skitter of dry leaves across cobbles. Even in this light she could see his pupils flare.

She sucked in a noisy breath and crossed her arms tightly over her chest. "Well I'm *not.*"

Good Lord! Could I sound any more like a fatuous, nervous schoolroom chit?

He nodded his head with menacing slowness. "Yes. I believe I could very *easily* prove you wrong." The tips of his fingers ghosted over her jaw, which appeared to have a direct connection to her lungs and female parts. His touch also amplified the pounding of her heart, so that she could hear it in her ears, a distinct *thud, swish, thud, swish,* her blood being pumped throughout her body with an enthusiasm that left her dizzy. Rather than pull away, as her brain was directing, her traitorous body leaned closer.

"That's a good girl." His lips brushed over hers, far softer than the kisses they'd had earlier, and her body swayed toward him as her mind revolted at being called a *good girl.*

Oh, but he smelled of shaving soap and salty male skin and brandy and his scent overpowered her, just as his big body could overpower hers.

"Eva." He whispered the word with a caress of warm air that made her shiver. And then his warm lips settled on the thin skin below her ear and he trailed hot kisses down her throat, nuzzling his nose into the plain tucker she still wore around her neck.

She'd been too furious to undress and had just kicked off her shoes. Besides, it had been her plan to go sleep in the coffee parlor on the settee rather than share a room with him.

So much for that.

Her head fell back limply, like a flower on a stem too weak to support it. She felt a hot breath on her collarbone, and then a tug. She blinked her heavy eyelids to find him holding her fichu between smiling lips. He let it flutter to the floor and claimed her with his mouth.

Eva met him, standing on her toes, her hands sliding around his neck and tangling in his hair as their lips met, not violently or gently, but as if they belonged together.

He grunted softly, the sound one of approval. This kiss was even better than the one earlier today, and part of her mind wondered if it got better every time, an unimaginable idea.

His big hands slid around her waist and gently kneaded. When his mouth went wandering, she once again let her head fall back, drinking in the sensation of his skilled, hot touch on her skin.

Eva realized he'd unbuttoned her dress only when his calloused fingers pushed it from her shoulders, along with the loose chemise beneath.

"No stays, I approve." The words vibrated through her body as he spoke them directly over her heart, his clever hands divesting her of dress and chemise in one smooth shove past her hips. His hands ran up her naked sides and he shuddered violently. "My God, you feel good."

His words, more than anything he'd said or done to her thus far, rocked her to her core and she launched herself at him.

His entire body stiffened and he gasped in what sounded like pain, but then his hands slid beneath her bottom and he lifted her with a groan and carried her to the bed, laying her out across it.

His temples and brow were beaded with sweat, the swelling around his eye darkly bruised.

Eva throbbed as he studied her. She was fully aware how her legs and arms were sprawled before him but didn't care. "Did I hurt you?" she asked.

"Yes," he said, his hand pulling at his sash, his eyes roving over her with a hungry desperation that made her feel desirable and reckless.

"Good."

He chuckled and shrugged out of the robe with a hiss, his nightshirt obscenely tented. "You really are a little witch, aren't you?"

Eva didn't answer. Instead she moved a hand down her body, the action immediately drawing his eyes. *That* was the expression she wanted to see on his face at all times of the day: the expression that said she was the only woman in the world worth looking at. His breathing roughened as her hand moved over her belly, so she slid it lower, over the soft curve, and then into the thick, springy black hair that covered her mound.

"My God, Eva." He made a noise like a death rattle and Eva grinned. This, she realized, was power. No wonder Mia so often claimed that gently bred women had tools and means at their disposal that men—and their own mothers and grandmothers—often tried to keep them from using.

He'd caught his breath and was as motionless as a statue, as if waiting for her next move. Eva shivered when her damp palm grazed the small, slick bud pushing between her lips.

When he looked up at her, his expression was . . . well, she couldn't say *what* it was. But she liked it—she *adored* it.

And then he spoke, once again saying the unexpected. "Do you still hate me?"

"More than ever."

He gave a deep, sensual chuckle, his eyes dropping to her hand as if he could not look away for longer than a second.

There was only one thing she could do when he looked at her like that: use her second hand. She absently rubbed her belly, drinking in his raw desire and savoring it as if it were the most expensive wine in the world.

"You are a temptress," he muttered.

Eva's breathing became that of a laboring horse as she took in the long, dark shadow distorting the thin material of his nightshirt.

She heard another low laugh and looked up to find his gaze fastened on her other hand, which had moved from her belly to her breast, where she was stroking and pulling at her stiffened nipple. Well, who knew *that* would feel so good?

"I see you were not jesting about your experience, were you?"

Experience? she almost asked, only at the last minute recalling her boast from yesterday. *Was that only yesterday?*

Judging by the way he was smiling at her, he *liked* the idea that she had prior experience.

She shook her head, unable to trust her voice, her eyes dropping from his face to the far more interesting thing poking at his voluminous nightshirt.

He reached over his shoulder and pulled the garment over his head in one smooth motion, and Eva froze—her hands, her breathing, her eyes. She had seen one before, a penis—a cock and a prick and a rod, she'd heard the stable lads call it when she'd lurked and eavesdropped while they thought nobody else was listening. She'd seen them soft and floppy when the boys swam in the pond on her father's estate. And she'd seen *his* the other night. Still, it had been far away and the lighting dim. This time he was close enough to touch. The thick shaft was long and shiny, and something about it made her mouth water and her thighs clench.

He lowered himself swiftly over her, resting his weight on his elbows while kissing her with a vehemence that left her boneless. "You're so beautiful," he whispered in her ear, his teeth grazing her skin almost hard enough to hurt. "I want to eat you."

Just as suddenly as he'd dropped over her, he pushed up on his hands, his lips parted as he breathed heavily. "Are you sure you want this?"

Eva nodded without hesitation; she'd wanted this experience even before Mia told her how much pleasure it could bring—she'd wanted it ever since she'd been fourteen and watched one of the footmen mount a maid in a bedroom they'd believed was empty. She'd gone back every day, catching them at it over and over. Watching the young footman's powerful buttocks clenching and thrusting into the wide-spread maid had made her itch and squirm. Just as she was doing right now.

Godric didn't hesitate, and she instinctively knew it would be an entirely different story if he knew the truth—that she was a maiden. If he knew the truth, they'd likely wait until they were married, or perhaps he'd never do it? And they'd certainly talk and talk about it, until she'd want to bash him over the head rather than do *this* with him.

He knocked her already spread legs wider with one of his knees and slid his hands beneath her thighs, pulling her hips up high, until she was close enough to his pelvis to touch his erect organ. Without releasing her, he reached under one leg and took himself in hand, placing the fat, shiny head against her opening.

"God, Eva—you're so wet for me."

His words made her woozy.

"Tell me you want it," he ordered, pushing the alarmingly big head of his instrument against her entrance.

She gritted her teeth. "I want it."

The last word wasn't even out when he breached her with one powerful thrust.

Godric knew the truth the moment he plowed into her, violently and deep, employing all the care of a stallion mounting a mare. He'd never taken a virgin before, but it didn't take prior experience to know he had one now.

To give her credit, she didn't make a sound. But her already tight body—and by God, she was like a vise around his aching prick—stiffened until she felt like a warm, human plank in his hands. He lowered them both onto the bed, keeping himself buried, but not moving. Her hands had closed on his back like grappling hooks and her breathing was rapid and shallow.

"Oh, Eva."

"Shut up." The words came from between gritted teeth.

In spite of his mortification at how he'd just brutalized an innocent, he couldn't help being amused at her very Eva-like response.

"Why did you lie?" The words were harsher and more accusatory than he'd intended, but there was all-out war occurring in his body and it was the best he could manage. His mind reeled against the implications of taking an innocent so roughly, but his body required every ounce of restraint to keep it from pulling out and then slamming back in. Repeatedly.

"I lied because there would have been *this*. Must we talk and talk and talk *now*?" Fury and frustration and desire pulsed in her voice.

Godric gave a shaky sigh, and then—weak, worthless lout that he was—he began to pull out.

She gave a low groan and he froze.

"Does it hurt when I move?"

"No." It was more a grunt than a word, and he wasn't sure he believed it. But then she lifted her hips, retaking the part of him he'd just removed.

"Please," she whispered. "Don't stop."

Godric's body obeyed her order even before his sex-drugged mind had finished translating the words. He pulled almost all the way out, pulsing his head in the tight ring of muscle and making her whimper and squirm, before gliding all the way back in.

The noise she made was quite the most sensual sound he'd ever heard.

She was wet—soaking wet—and the sound of labored breathing and wet coupling filled the room, their mingled scent primal. Cognizant of her condition—in spite of whatever bravado she might show—he stroked into her slow and steady, working her gently until she began to soften and relax beneath him.

She made small noises with each thrust, her hands tightening on his shoulders each time he pulled out, as if to keep him inside. She might never have engaged in the act of coitus before, but her body knew what to do, and she clenched and released in rhythm with his strokes.

"Yes, Eva. That feels so good," he praised as he lowered himself to one elbow and slid a hand between them, his thrusts slowing but his cock penetrating her more deeply. "I want to feel your body when you reach your climax." She tightened at his words and he rewarded her with a deeper stroke, his thumb finding her hard peak and massaging the sensitive base, caressing her tiny organ until she began to shudder.

"Godric!" She thrashed and uttered nonsense words, her passage becoming even tighter as he worked her toward orgasm. And what a climax it was.

She contracted around him so hard it was painful. Godric grunted and grew still, his jaws clenched tightly as she came in seemingly endless waves, clinging to his shoulders with a grip that would leave bruises on his bruises. Her dark eyes were wide in the flickering light of the dying candle, her body jerking and inner muscles spasming in ever weaker contractions.

When her eyelids drifted closed and her taut body relaxed, he began to move.

Encouraged by her soft moan of pleasure, Godric worked her with deep, thorough thrusts, hilting himself each time. He gloried in the sheer masculine dominance of the action, filling and claiming her over and over, the erotic joining as old as humankind.

His eyes never left her beautiful, blissful face as his hips began pounding her with increasingly savage thrusts. When he reached the brink of control, he pulled from her body and pumped himself with his fist, spending in hot, lazy ropes on her belly.

He'd not even enjoyed the last spasm of pleasure when a voice in his head said, *Well, now you've done it.*

Chapter 15

Godric cleaned them both with a damp cloth and then lay down beside her, his big body causing the mattress to tip and roll her toward him.

When she scrabbled to hold on and stay on her side, a warm hand gripped her chin and tilted her face toward him. His expression was stern and she could see the questions lurking behind the haze of pleasure that still tinted his eyes.

Eva scowled, no matter how much she loved the feel of his hands on her body. "You are going to be tiresome and scold, aren't you?"

A small, surprised laugh slipped out of him. "You say that as if you overspent your pin money or recklessly crammed your hunter."

Eva shrugged.

"I might have *hurt* you—did that not occur to you?"

"You didn't."

"Yes, well, perhaps I might have liked to have some say in whether I deflowered an innocent—I suppose that didn't occur to you, either."

She felt as if he'd slapped her, and before she could restrain herself, she shoved him back with all her strength.

The surprising action, combined with his injuries—bruises so horrid and dark and pervasive she could see them even by low light—

sent him tumbling backward, and off the bed. He landed with a huge, dull thump that made the pictures on the wall clatter.

Eva flew out of bed and ran around to his side; he lay on his back, his eyes closed, motionless.

She dropped down beside him. "Godric? *Godric!*" She roughly shoved his shoulder and he opened his eyes. "Did you hurt your head? Are you stunned?"

His answer was to grab her waist and bodily lift her with an agonized groan. "Bloody hell," he muttered under his breath as he positioned her so that she was straddling his body. They were both naked, so the feeling was quite singular.

"Are you hurt?" she asked again, forcing her mind away from the spot where they were touching.

"Yes. I'm in agony."

She pursed her lips and was about to punch his shoulder when he caught her hand. "Ah-ah-ah, throwing me off the bed is quite enough abuse for tonight." Eva shifted a little and he sucked in a harsh breath. "Yes, that's much better."

Her face heated when he gently pulsed his hips, the friction delicious. It was ridiculous to blush and feel self-conscious, considering how wantonly she'd behaved only a few minutes earlier.

"Why did you hurl me off the bed?"

She shrugged and he pushed his hips up against her; it was her turn to gasp.

"Come, Eva. I think that is the least you owe me—some sort of explanation. What did I do, yet again, to make you so angry?"

It was just *so very* mortifying.

He pushed his hips up again and again, his expression teasing. "I'll torment you until you tell me."

"If this is your idea of torment, you will have to do it for a very long time."

He laughed. "Well, I'm afraid this is *all* I'll be capable of doing for some time—an hour at the least."

Eva suspected he was making a joke about something sexual, but she'd exposed her ignorance enough for one night.

"Speak," he ordered.

"I know you said you didn't want to do this." She gestured to them.

He stopped his distracting pulsing and his smile slid away. "I didn't want to do what?"

"You *said* you didn't want me—this way." Good God, was he going to force her to lay out the entire humiliating conversation?

"What? I would never have said that. Lord, how would such a thing have even come up in conversation?"

Eva ignored the elated leap in her stomach, and lower. "You said you'd not p-put a child in me."

He grimaced. "Ah, yes, that."

"Yes, *that*."

"Just because I don't want children doesn't mean I don't want this." He thrusted suggestively.

"You mean—"

"Very much so," he said before she had to explain. His hands slid around her wrists and held her, his thumbs stroking the soft underside. "You must be stark raving mad if—" He stopped, grimaced, and said, "Bloody hell. I didn't mean—"

"I know you didn't. It's just a turn of phrase, Godric. I'm not so stupid that I don't know that," she said irritably. "What were you saying? I must be stark raving mad if what?"

"If you ever believed I didn't want you *like this*," he said, his words a smiling echo of hers. "You are an extremely desirable woman, Eva. And sometimes, just occasionally, mind—when you are not throwing me off beds or pointing pistols at me—I find that I like you very well, indeed."

Eva was glad it was dark enough to hide what was surely an extremely red face. "Oh?"

He nodded and pulled her toward him, his hands like manacles around her wrists. "Yes, *oh*." Their lips met in a lazy, languorous kiss that lacked the intensity of earlier, but offered her far more opportunity for exploration.

He grunted and moaned approvingly as she learned the shape and feel of him, allowing her to explore all she wanted as his hands softly stroked her back, sides, and bottom.

When she finally came up for air, he was gazing up at her from beneath heavy lids, his lips slick and bruised and split on the one side. Which reminded her. "Aren't I hurting you—sitting on you like this?"

"Yes, but haven't you figured out yet that I like pain."

Eva met his teasing grin with a smile of her own. "I'm beginning to think there may be more than a few shingles loose," she admitted.

He laughed and Eva suddenly realized just how much she'd come to enjoy his company over the past few days. He was not at all as she'd believed him to be—stodgy and cruel and unpleasant. Instead he was amusing, surprising, and often kind. And he was also very, very good at *this*.

Unwonted, the memory of his hand on Mrs. Crosby and her hand on his waist came back like a bucket of cold water.

"Uh-oh," he said, reaching up to cup her face. "What is it now? I'm not letting you up until you tell me."

"You and Mrs. Crosby," she blurted.

"Ahhh." One of his eyebrows—the one over the unswollen eye—cocked in a particularly annoying fashion.

"Godric. You can't ask me questions about things that annoy or upset me and then mock me when I answer you."

His expression was instantly serious and he took her shoulders in his hands, holding her firmly. "You're quite right, Eva. So which one of the *things* is Mrs. Crosby—the kind of thing that upsets you, or the kind that annoys you?"

"Both," she retorted, pulling herself free and sitting up.

He sighed and then laced his hands behind his head, wincing slightly, reminding her they were still on the floor. "Do you want to get up on the bed?"

"In a moment. First let me put your suspicious mind at rest. I was *not* engaging in a clandestine amorous tussle with Mrs. Crosby. As much as I dislike telling tales regarding any woman, she approached me and put her hand on my face; when I removed it, she put her other on my side. That is when you arrived." He smiled at her and then shook his head, his eyes going vague. "I don't know what is wrong with her—or Norton, for that matter."

"Why, what do you mean?"

"Only that Norton is more nervous than a sack of cats and Mrs. Crosby won't stop flinging herself at me as if I were the most fascinating man in England."

"I thought you *were* the most fascinating man in England."

His eyes moved back to hers and his smile returned. "Oh, why, thank you, darling."

"I didn't say *I* thought that—but I thought you did."

"That's because I am," he admitted mildly.

"Well, then you should be accustomed to women *flinging themselves at you.*"

"I am, but not usually in the first ten minutes. Mrs. Crosby has been quite insistent since the moment I opened my eyes."

"Perhaps she is just bored? After all, there isn't much going on and Mr. Norton isn't exactly a stimulating conversationalist."

"True. But something still feels . . . off. Or perhaps I'm just imagining things."

"No," Eva said, weak with relief that he'd been entertaining similar suspicions to hers. "I've felt the same thing. Do you think Mr. Norton is nervous because he thinks Flynn will find out we are here?"

"The thought has crossed my mind."

"But Flynn let us go—surely he wouldn't be angry that we took shelter here. Indeed, what else could we do in such weather and with bridges down all over the place?" *And you unable to speak or move?*

"That is rational, my dear, but I'm not so sure Flynn is entirely rational."

Eva thought back to Flynn's maddened expression when he was hauling his battered brother-in-law away and had to agree.

"Well, I suppose the good news is that nobody knows what anyone is doing in this wretched weather."

He met her eyes, his own serious. "Yes, that's a very good point. Even so, I think we should keep our wits about us, and I want you to tell me if you see anything odd." He hesitated and then said, "It might be nothing, so don't mention it to Andrew, who doesn't look the sort to be capable of obfuscation. I'd hate for him to let anything slip to our hosts."

Eva worried her lip and then opened her mouth to tell him about Andrew and the promise she'd extracted earlier.

"What?" he asked.

She looked down into his battered face and saw how heavy and weary his one good eye looked. She shook her head. "Nothing." She'd told Andrew they should step up and take some responsibility, and so they should.

"Well," he said, sitting up, "I'm about to seize into a knot on this damp, cold floor."

Eva stood and then offered him a hand.

"It's a sign of my decrepitude that I'm seriously considering taking your hand." He grunted and groaned his way to his feet without her assistance. "But thank you for the offer." He seized her by the hips, his hands moving at a speed she wasn't expecting. He jerked her against him, their damp skin making a soft slapping sound.

"My parents always said I should be respectful and offer to help my elders," she gasped against him.

He grinned, a flash of white teeth the last thing she saw before the candle stub stuttered and gradually died. "I can already see you are going to be a great comfort to me in my dotage." He hoisted her up onto the bed.

"Godric, you really should use the bed, you're far too tall for the cot."

The bed shifted beside her. "Who said anything about either of us sleeping on the blasted cot? Besides," he said, his arm unerringly finding her waist in the dark and snaking around her, pulling her tight to his long, hard body, "I'm not tired. Hasn't anyone ever told you the aged require very little sleep?"

Eva smiled into the darkness, happier than she could recall being—*perhaps ever.* "It just so happens I'm not tired, either."

"Oh? The exuberance of youth." He molded her back so closely to his front she could feel the strong, insistent beat of his heart in her own body. "However shall we keep ourselves occupied, I wonder?"

She pressed her bottom against him and he purred.

"Ah, yes, *that.* Well, I might have mentioned I require a bit of recovery. So we have a good thirty minutes left to kill. Shall I light a candle and read you a bit of *The Orphan of the Rhine*?"

Eva chuckled. "Oh Lord no, is that really the title?"

"Mmm-hmm." He nuzzled her neck, his warm lips and the cool tip of his nose against her spine making her shiver.

"Did you really read Gothic novels when you were, er, ill?" Eva didn't want to bring up any subject that would disturb the delicate balance between them but feared she might already have done so when he sighed.

"I'm sorry, Eva. I really have made a dreadful muck of things—of course you can ask me questions about my life before. I might not answer them all—nor do I expect you to answer all of mine—but it is your right as my wife to ask them."

Eva clenched her teeth at the words *my wife.* Yes, she wanted to know about that—most desperately—but pushing too hard at first . . .

You coward.

So what? she whipped back. *What has my intrepid nature and impulsiveness done for me thus far?*

It got you here.

Well, Eva had to admit that was a direct hit.

"What are you thinking? I can feel your delicious body tightening up."

"I want to know what happened to your family."

Now it was his turn to tighten up. As the silence dragged and dragged and his arm loosened around her, she knew she'd made a mistake.

She'd opened her mouth to tell him not to bother when he said, "I know I owe you this, but the story is one I've never spoken aloud before."

The desolation in his voice drove a spike of fear through her chest. What kind of horrid story was this? Why had she asked? Why not leave well enough alone? "I'm sorry, I didn't—"

"Shh, you need to know. And what's more, I suspect I need to tell you."

Chapter 16

Godric had known the day would come. He'd been behaving like a child hiding behind a tree, believing others couldn't see him because he couldn't see them. And look where that had led him— led Eva?

"I know you heard what I said when I was fighting." He could tell by the way her body went still that she knew what he meant. "My wife died that day—the day I divided my regiment to go back to our encampment after a scout delivered information that it was under attack."

Godric took a moment to tuck the horror of that day back into its box. She needed to know about Lucia and his family, but no-body—man *or* woman—needed to know the gory details.

"I'm so sorry about your wife," she said quietly.

"Thank you." Godric could not tell her the rest, could not even speak Carl's name. What could one omission possibly hurt when he had so many other truths to tell her?

"The fighting was brutal and I was badly injured that day. An extended hospital stay was necessary. It was during that time that the Fontainebleau Treaty was signed and, as you likely know, many English people flocked to Europe. My family were among those. The

ship they were on encountered two corsair vessels. Rather than surrender, as a wise captain would have done, the captain of the *Valiant*
tried first to outrun the ships and then, when that failed, loaded his
six guns and fired. The only reason these details are known is because
there were three survivors."

She gasped. "Oh my God. The ships, were they—"

"Yes, both corsair ship captains swore allegiance to Sultan Assad
Hassan." Godric swallowed the hatred and bile he felt as he proceeded to lay out the faulty logic behind his idiocy. "I had plans to go
after the sultan and his cronies, but of course the British Navy took
care of that for me when they took Oran."

"So you came after the only member of the sultan's family you
could find, seeking vengeance."

"Yes. That is what I did," he admitted.

"But you know that Assad was the man my brother Gabriel was
fighting? He and Assad were sworn enemies."

"Yes." How could Godric explain that it hadn't mattered—that
the truth hadn't mattered? That he'd burned from the inside out for a
target—any target—for his pain and hatred.

"I understand—I do," she repeated, as if he'd said something.
"That doesn't mean I think what you did was right, but I have to
admit I could see myself doing the same thing in your situation. Will
you tell me who was on the ship?"

He drew in a shaky breath. "My parents, my two brothers, their
wives, my nephews—twelve and fourteen—and my sister, who was
nineteen."

Eva awkwardly turned herself in his arms, until they were chest
to chest. He was grateful she could not see the grief that gutted him.
"I'm so terribly sorry, Godric." She pressed her face against his, the
wetness on her cheeks mingling with his. "So terribly sorry."

He pulled her tight and held her, and for the first time in over a
year, he did not mourn his loss alone.

* * *

Eva had no idea what woke her. The room was dark and silent and, for a brief moment, her mind worked to sort out the singular sensation of having another body—naked—pressed against hers.

"Did you have a good sleep?"

Godric's deep, low voice rumbled through her body.

"How long have I slept?"

"Not long, perhaps an hour."

"And you?"

"I'm afraid not." She heard the tired smile in his voice.

"This insomnia you have, is there nothing you can do for it?"

His arm tightened and he said, "Sometimes exertion helps. When I am at home, I will hit the heavy sandbag I keep for that purpose. Or go riding at first light. Or any number of things that might help exhaust me."

Eva's body thrummed at the suggestion hovering just between his words. She swallowed to force down the lump that was obstructing her throat. "And is there not something we could do now?"

"There is."

Eva heard his grin. "Your body must ache," she said.

"I ache in more ways than one—and in some places more than others."

Eva laughed softly. "You think you are being sly and clever and charming, don't you?"

"Am I charming you?" he asked, nuzzling her temple and making all the hairs on her body jump to attention.

"Not yet."

It was his turn to laugh. "So, tell me of this much-vaunted experience you crowed about."

Eva groaned. "Can't we speak of something else?"

"Indulge me."

She heaved an exaggerated, put-upon sigh. "Well, you know that at least one of the claims I made was untrue."

"Yes," he mused, the hand that was resting on her hip absently stroking, his thumb repeatedly brushing the thin skin that stretched over her jutting hip bone. "But it cannot all be boasting as you seem remarkably unshocked by certain events."

"Oh, that."

"Yes, that." His thumb moved from her hip bone to her sensitive belly, which quivered beneath his touch.

"Er, well." Eva had to force herself to recall what they'd been discussing. Ah, yes, her lack of shock. "What do you know of my stepmamma?"

"Ah, the mysterious and beautiful Lady Exley. The rumors abound, but I know some of them must be true as there is six feet of evidence in the form of her oldest son."

"She was with the sultan for seventeen years—longer than she'd lived in England. Her approach to, well, just about *everything* is tempered by that time. It is her contention that women should know what to expect in the marriage bed." She chewed her lip and then added, "She also believes they should demand pleasure from their husbands as well as give it."

The silence around them seemed to echo with her disclosure, and his hand had gone still. Eva was beginning to wonder if she'd shocked or disgusted him when he said, "Ah, so she is wise as well as beautiful." He kissed her on the forehead. "I shall have to find some way to thank her."

Eva wasn't entirely surprised by his response, but she did find it unexpected. "You don't find me overbold and unladylike?"

He chuckled. "I do. But it appears that I *like* it."

Her body warmed under his words.

"Your w-wife was not like me?"

He grew still and she wished she could pull the thoughtless words back.

She heard him swallow in the darkness, and then he said, "No. L–Lucia had been raised in a convent."

Eva bit her lips between her teeth to stop pursuing a subject that was likely to bring both of them pain. But it was like poking at a heeling scab; it hurt, but was difficult to resist.

"Was she Italian?"

"Portuguese."

"How did you come to meet her?"

Again the pause was so long, she'd given up on hearing his answer when he said, "She was the daughter of a Portuguese officer. I saw her first at a dinner her father gave to honor us for liberating the area from French soldiers." His voice had taken on a pensive, dreamy quality. "She was the only woman at dinner, which made it difficult not to notice her. But there was more than that—"

He broke off and Eva stewed as long as she could bear it. "Was she very lovely?"

"Hmm? Oh—" He sounded as if she'd dragged him back from some more pleasant time, and Eva could only wonder at her stupidity. Why was she making him speak of a woman he'd obviously cared for? She'd gone beyond picking the scab; she'd ripped it off and was now rubbing salt in the wound.

"Beautiful? No, she would likely be considered average—perhaps handsome—but there was a serenity, a gentleness, in her eyes that was like a balm in the midst of such unrelenting violence."

"Did you marry right away?"

"Hmm? Marry? I did not see her again for a year. Her father had been killed and she'd been taken in by relatives. It was only by chance that we met again. But I knew then—" He stopped and seemed to shake himself. "We were married for five years before she died." His tone had gone from introspective to closed—he was done with confidences. But the little bit that he'd shared had made one point achingly clear: he had dearly loved his wife, and it appeared he still did.

Godric couldn't believe he'd just behaved like such an arse—speaking of one woman while sporting an erection for another. He was hot with shame at his boorish behavior and slid his fingers through her wiry curls—curls so different from Lucia's waist-length silky locks, but just as lovely. "It was a long time ago, Eva. I know you are curious, but it is part of a life I left behind," he lied, knowing all too well that Lucia haunted his dreams so frequently he was afraid to close his eyes some nights. "I don't want to keep that part of my life secret, but neither do I wish to dwell on it."

Liar, you'd rather dwell on it in secret, like a miser hoarding his gold.

Godric gritted his teeth against the infuriating thought and turned his attention on the living, breathing, enticing woman in front of him, rather than the increasingly dim shade in his memory.

He rolled onto his back, bringing her with him. "It is you I would like to dwell on," he whispered into the darkness. "Straddle me," he ordered, his need for her suddenly intense. Her instant compliance was gratifying and arousing and Godric slid his fingers between her spread thighs, both of them gasping as he stroked a finger through her wet heat. "God, I love the feel of you," he muttered, his thumb circling her stiff peak while he slid his middle finger into her passage.

She made a low whimper and her body arched to take him deeper.

"Are you sore? Too sore for this?" He pumped her gently to illustrate.

"A little," she admitted in a voice strained with want. "But not enough to make me want you to stop."

He chuckled at her open admission of need; he really did owe Lady Exley his gratitude. Because of her wisdom, the woman in bed with him was demanding and giving, rather than cringing away from his touches.

You never touched Lucia this way.

He flinched away from the words, his mind shying away from the treasonous thought as well as the image of his modest, shy wife that accompanied it.

Above him, Eva grunted and ground herself against him, so he increased the power of his thrusts and slid a second finger to join the first. Her hips were beginning to move, to take him deeper.

"That's right," he urged roughly, "ride my hand—take what you want from me, Eva. Use me for your pleasure."

His words were like the flick of a crop to a horse's flank and she began posting him in earnest. He pumped her with one hand, his other roaming up and down a thigh that could only have become so muscular from years of riding astride. The long, lean muscle flexed and lengthened as her lithe body hit its rhythm.

Around them the windows rattled from the gusts buffeting the house, and the rumble of thunder presaged a crack of lightning that burned the image of her into his brain: head thrown back, small hands covering her high, pert breasts, lips parted in silent ecstasy as she quickened her erotic gyrations.

She was as wild and fierce as the storm that held them all in its grip.

Godric growled and used his free hand to work her to climax, desperately wishing it was his cock, rather than his fingers, that were buried inside her when she came apart.

All too soon her body went limp and she lowered her hips to where Godric held himself at the ready. He met her on the down stroke, thrusting deeply into her heat and holding her hips still as the echoes of her orgasm massaged his swollen cock. And when her plea-sure had passed, he could still feel the pulse of her heart as she throbbed around him.

He slid from her with aching reluctance, the action causing every particle of his being to cry out. But the temporary punishment was worth it when she dropped her hands to his shoulders and slammed her hips to meet him on the upward thrust.

"Like that?" she gasped.

Godric gave a half-mad joyous laugh as she rode him as if she'd been doing it all her life. "Yes, Eva," he babbled drunkenly. "Just like that." He buried his fingers deep in the soft flesh of her hips as he pounded her with a savagery that would surely leave bruises, and Eva met him thrust for glorious thrust.

Godric recalled himself in the nick of time and withdrew from her body. It took only one stroke before his cock spasmed with violent, almost painful, contractions that wrung him out until he was as limp as a rag.

"Are you trying to kill me?" he asked with a last shudder of orgiastic pleasure.

She twisted and flopped down beside him, her breathing as ragged as his. "I can think of worse ways to die."

Godric laughed, unable to recall the last time he'd been so content. Or so happy.

Godric awoke to a sight he didn't immediately recognize: sunshine.

"Good morning, slugabed."

He looked over at the sound of Eva's voice. She was sitting by one of the room's two windows, reading.

"I hope you're not reading my book, since you were casting such aspersions," he said with a huge yawn, wincing at the pain in his split lip and swollen eye.

She snorted and put the book aside before coming to the side of the bed. "I believe you may have gotten some sleep." She looked at his face and winced. "Lord, you look ten times worse than you did yesterday. Your face is so colorful we could hang it up as holiday bunting."

He regarded her through slitted eyes. "You do know how to wake a man, darling. If my aged, decrepit memory serves, my hideous looks didn't deter you last night." Godric allowed his lips to curve at the memory of some of his more sleepless moments from the night before. Her cheeks darkened and he laughed.

"You are a wicked old man," she accused, making him laugh harder.

Godric pushed himself up with a low groan and bunched two pillows behind himself. When he was sitting upright he saw that her eyes were fastened on his groin.

"The cock is crowing," Godric said mildly, smoothing the covers over his hips and then making his rod dance for her.

She gasped, her face so red he feared for her health.

There was a knock on the door but before either of them could say anything, it opened. Godric yanked up the blankets.

"Ah, you are awake." Mrs. Crosby smiled at them, either unaware or uncaring of the look of death Eva was shooting her. "I thought I'd bring this up before I left." She lifted the breakfast tray.

"Left?" Godric asked rather stupidly as she placed the tray over the ridged blanket that covered his hips, her lips curved in that same, tiny smile.

"Yes, I'm going to take the wagon and see if I can make it into town. We are running desperately short on supplies." She gave the tray of food a significant look.

"But I thought the bridges were washed away?"

"They are, but the rain stopped sometime around three o'clock this morning, so I will try a cart track that leads to the bridge farther down."

Godric recalled the road she meant from the map last night. Indeed it had occurred to him to ask Norton when next he'd seen him why nobody had used the road. But then he'd not seen the man again. He turned to Eva. "Hungry?"

She shook her head, her eyes still riveted on the other woman. "I ate some time ago."

Godric took a sip of the strong dark coffee. "I'd meant to try that track today," he confessed. "Although I'd thought to do so on foot. I'll be glad to make the journey for you," he told Mrs. Crosby.

"Ah, that's very kind. But the truth is I'm looking forward to a chance to get out."

He could certainly understand that, as he was beginning to feel a bit stir-crazy himself. "Where is Norton?"

"He took the hack and set out for the magistrate at first light."

"Oh?" Godric paused in the act of cutting into a thick slab of honeyed ham. "What happened to his son going?"

"Anthony came down with a chill and I recommended he stay in bed." The look she gave him said at least *some* of her patients listened to her orders.

"I should like to go with you," Eva said.

Mrs. Crosby turned to her and blinked, as if only now noticing she was in the room. "Oh? But it is just an old wagon—not much room and the seat is a board."

Eva snorted. "I think I can manage." She plucked at her gown, an expression of discontent on her face. "I should like my own clothing."

Mrs. Crosby's eyebrows shot up. "To go into town?"

Eva began to puff up, digging in for a battle.

Godric hastily swallowed his ham and said, "I agree with my wife. It would be better, I think, Mrs. Crosby. A dress is a hindrance in such weather if something should happen to the cart."

She gave him a long look and then shrugged. "Very well. Your clothing is clean. I will bring it up when I come to collect the tray."

"And I shall go, too," Godric said.

Something very much like alarm flickered across her lovely features. "Oh, but there is no room for three."

"Well then, maybe *you* could stay behind," Eva suggested sweetly.

"I shall throw some hay in the back and ride like a reclining king," Godric said before the cook could reply.

Mrs. Crosby shrugged her shoulders. "Suit yourself." She abruptly reached out and snatched up his half-full cup of coffee. "This is dreadfully cold, I shall fetch another."

Before Godric could demur, she was out the door.

Eva heaved a sigh. "Well, that will be an enjoyable journey."

"You could always stay here and read," he suggested with a

smirk, slathering a chunk of bread with something that looked like plum and orange marmalade.

"Very droll." She pushed off the side of the bed. "I don't want her coming up here again. I'm going to fetch my clothing from her."

"Don't forget my coffee," he called after her retreating back. "I'm going to need all the fortification I can get, trapped in a wagon with you two," he muttered under his breath.

Eva dressed while Godric finished his breakfast. When she came out from behind the screen, it was to find him smiling beatifically at nothing in particular, his coffee cup clutched in loose fingers.

"Lord, you look as if you could sleep for a month, Godric."

He chuckled. "I had a rather vigorous evening."

She shook her head, her face, predictably, heating. "Are you sure you shouldn't stay and rest? I can handle the beast on my own," she added.

He gave a rather loud laugh, slurped the last of the coffee and set the cup down with a clatter. "I'll get dressed."

Eva wanted to argue with him because he looked like death warmed over, but she wanted him along on the journey.

"I'll go tell Andrew what we are doing."

Godric merely blinked owlishly and made a shooing gesture with one hand. "Give me ten minutes."

Eva wouldn't be surprised if he was asleep in ten minutes, but said nothing. Instead, she turned to the connecting door and knocked.

"Come in!" Andrew called.

He was crouched over the small table he'd converted into some kind of desk. Spread out across it were parts of—

"Good God, Andrew, are those our guns?" Eva demanded, shutting the door harder than necessary before striding across the small room.

His head whipped up and he frowned. "Yes, I got them as you said—this morning."

"Why have you torn them apart like that?"

"This is just one of them."

"What are you *doing*?"

"Cleaning it, if you must know," he retorted. "Neither of them is much to brag about, but they'll be worth even less if they don't fire correctly."

Eva supposed he had a point. She grunted. "Where did you find them?"

He carefully laid down the piece he was cleaning. "You know those two doors at the end of the hall?"

"The ones that look like doors to more rooms?"

"They *are* other rooms."

"Really? I wonder why Mr. Norton said they only had these two?"

"Well, likely it's because they are crammed full of stuff."

"What kind of stuff?"

He shrugged and turned back to his work. "All kinds of things: furniture, clothing, crates of brandy."

"Huh." She pushed the odd information from her mind and pointed at a tea saucer with a gritty black mess. "What's that?"

"Hmm?" He glanced up and saw where she was pointing. "Oh, that's something I devised so that I don't need the requisite three feet of smoldering saltpeter-soaked rope."

Eva stared.

He sighed. "Don't worry what it is. All you need to know is that the arquebus will fire as quickly as most other guns the way I've set it up."

Eva would believe that when she saw it, but in the interest of harmony she kept her opinion to herself. "Where is the other gun?"

"Under my pillow."

Eva fetched it and opened the breach. "Where are the bullets?"

Andrew looked up. "Why?"

"Because I *want* them, that's why."

"But why do you *want* them?" He had that look, the one that said he was prepared to argue until the bitter end. Eva knew the expression well: it was one her family dreaded seeing on *her* face. Now she knew how they felt.

"Godric and I are going into town and he'll want a pistol along," Eva said, not exactly lying. He'd not mentioned it, but surely he would want one.

Andrew perked up. "Oh. I want to go."

"You'll have to sit in the back of the wagon in the straw with Godric. There is only room for Mrs. Crosby and me on the seat."

His cheeks flushed at the mention of the other woman's name, and Eva rolled her eyes.

She tossed the gun onto the bed. "Load this so we can bring it along. And you've got ten minutes to put that gun together. Can you do it?"

He gave her a scornful look. "With my eyes closed."

"Do it standing on your head if you like—just do it quickly." She knocked on the connecting door. "Godric? Are you dressed?"

She heard something that sounded like laughter and opened the door to find him just where she'd left him on the bed. But now he was tipped onto his side, laughing.

She rushed to him and dropped down on her knees beside the bed. "Godric! Good Lord, what is wrong?"

"Numb."

She could barely hear him. "What? What's numb? What happened? Is it your head—that blow to your temple?" And was it her fault for making him spend such a delightful, but vigorous night?

"Tongue."

"It's your tongue?"

"Tongue. Tongue ith numb." His eyelids fluttered closed and drool oozed from the corner of his mouth.

"Godric!" She shook his shoulder vigorously, but that only served to dislodge him from his precarious perch on the bed. He slid slowly and bonelessly to the floor, far too heavy for her to stop.

"Andrew!" she yelled, unable to pull her eyes away from the prone figure on the floor. "Come quickly, it's Godric—something is wrong with him. I think—he's—" She heard motion behind her and turned, her jaw sagging at the sight in the doorway: Andrew with his hands in the air, Mrs. Crosby behind him, holding *their* pistol and wearing a very, very unpleasant smile.

"Been poisoned," Eva said weakly.

Chapter 17

"He'd better be all right," Eva said, her hands chafing against the too-tight rope Andrew had tied around her wrists—but only after the cook had made him remove his first, far looser, attempt.

"You do repeat yourself, don't you?" the older woman asked as she and Andrew dumped her unceremoniously into the straw in the back of the cart. "I already told you—at least four times—that it is nothing but a sleeping draught. Now"—she turned to Andrew—"tie that around her mouth."

Andrew looked from the neckcloth she thrust into his hands to Eva.

"Go on." Mrs. Crosby poked him with the point of the pistol.

Andrew mouthed the word *sorry* as he reached for her.

"You don't need to do this," Eva said calmly. "I give my word I shan't make any racket."

Mrs. Crosby just laughed.

Once Andrew was done, Mrs. Crosby gave the gag a tug to make sure it was tight enough and then poked Andrew again. "All right, well done. Come along now."

"Er, where are you taking me?" Andrew asked as they walked away. "Perhaps I might go with you and Eva—you could keep an eye on me that way. Wouldn't it—"

His voice faded away as they moved out of hearing range and Eva furiously worked at the ropes binding her wrists and ankles, but there was no give. She groaned in raw, infuriated frustration. She should have *known* the woman was a rotten piece of work. She should have loaded the bloody pistol herself and brought it into the room.

Should have, would have, could have.

She thought back to Godric's oddly vulnerable-looking form as he lay on the floor, his breathing shallow and a sheen of sweat on his gray-tinged skin. *Oh God. What if Crosby was lying? What if she'd really poisoned him?*

Why would she lie? You saw the look in her eyes. If she wanted him dead, he'd be dead.

That was true, and the thought cheered her. For all that the cook was clearly a bloodthirsty villain, she'd yet to prove herself a liar. Unless you counted the fact that she'd kept this maniacal facet of her personality a secret, of course.

The sound of heeled boots on cobbles heralded her return and Eva stopped squirming. The cook peered over the side of the wagon, the pale sun at her back, leaving her face in shadow.

"Now it's just you and me, *my lady*."

Something about her soft, almost gentle voice, made Eva's spine tingle.

Mrs. Crosby climbed onto the seat, and then snapped the reins, sending the big old draught horse into a grudging walk.

"I'm sorry you are suffering such discomfort," Mrs. Crosby said, not sounding in the least sorry, "but it won't be for long."

Well. *That* didn't sound ominous.

They rumbled along in silence after that and Eva tried to look for landmarks. But they must have been in an area bordered by fields because all she saw was the occasional hedge over the high sides of the wagon. They couldn't have ridden for more than ten or fifteen minutes when the surface of the road changed and Eva recognized the sound of wood on wood as they rolled over a bridge.

She gave a bitter laugh beneath the gag.

The cook turned slightly and said, "Yes, only *one* bridge was washed out, I'm afraid. The three of you were just so trusting. Of course Joe knew the truth, which is why he developed such a convenient chill and took to his bed."

Eva wanted to bang her head against the wood. She'd wondered at the postilion's heavy sleep, but hadn't thought to try to wake him the three times she'd checked on him, believing he deserved the opportunity to rest.

"Don't worry, my dear. Joe won't take any permanent harm."

The fact that the older woman could read her mind so easily was less than comforting.

They'd not gone much farther before a canopy of increasingly dense trees appeared overhead. Eva guessed this was the same wood they'd been in . . . *yesterday*? Could it have been only *yesterday*?

She'd not paid close attention during the ride from the woods to the Greedy Vicar, but it seemed as though it couldn't have been longer than thirty minutes. She felt the rickety wagon slide occasionally. The rain might have stopped but it would be a while before the roads—especially little cart tracks such as this one—cleared.

A few minutes into the woods she felt the surface beneath them change again, this time to something softer, grass or plants or perhaps a ground covering of fallen leaves. The trees were so thick in this part of the forest, it felt like dusk. Eva had a sick feeling that Crosby was taking her to Flynn's camp. When she recalled his infuriated look the day before—and her taunting—she knew things would not go well for her.

Perhaps five minutes later the wheels slowed and then stopped. Crosby hopped off the seat and then must have unhooked the horse because Eva heard the jangling of a harness and the sound of hooves moving away.

Crosby returned so silently that Eva yelped behind her gag.

"Sorry to startle you," she murmured, sounding subdued all of a sudden. Well, the deep, primeval sense of the trees bearing down on them was enough to subdue anyone.

"I'm going to cut your feet loose," Crosby said in a warning tone. "If you have any ideas of kicking me or running, I beg you will reconsider. Quite honestly, I wouldn't mind shooting you. I wouldn't need to kill you, just hobble you."

The flat, almost bored tone of the other woman's voice was more compelling than the threat.

Once Eva's feet were free, Crosby pulled her upright and Eva saw there was a tiny cottage with a shed off to one side. The horse was standing in the open stall, contentedly chewing hay.

"Come along." Crosby pulled her over the splintery wood, making her grateful she was wearing her buckskins or she'd have slivers lodged deeply in both cheeks.

There was smoke coming from the chimney, so Eva wasn't surprised to find the cottage inhabited. She *was* surprised to see the occupant who was slumped in the corner, his big frame overwhelming the small cot that had been shoved into the corner so that two walls might offer support for his battered body.

He shifted on the cushions that kept him upright and squinted through mostly swollen-shut eyes before his distorted jaw opened just enough to say something that sounded like, "Dora," and then wince at the pain speaking must have caused.

"Oh, hush, Paul. You shouldn't talk, you know that." She dragged Eva to the only other place to sit in the room, a heavy, rudely made wooden chair. "Sit." She shoved Eva down and then proceeded to tie her securely to the wooden back and legs. "There," she said with a satisfied huff, coming around to stand in front of Eva when she'd finished. "Now, you just sit here and wait while I go fetch an old friend."

Paul muttered something incomprehensible and Mrs. Crosby whirled on him. "You just hush, you hear? This is none of your concern. And if you keep talking, your jaw will never mend. Not exactly a tragedy in my opinion, but I'm sure you feel otherwise." She went to the small cupboard, where a basin and several pieces of crockery stood. "I'll clean this up when I return. But for now"—she poured something cloudy into a small glass and brought it to the reclining man—"you should drink this. It will help you sleep. And sleeping will help you mend." He stared hard at her for a long moment before grudgingly taking the small glass in his giant fingers.

Mrs. Crosby smiled. "Good," she said. "I'll be back in half an hour. You just rest for a while." She turned to Eva, and so missed the sight of Paul dumping the contents of the glass between the bed and the wall. "And you. Don't try anything stupid."

Eva glared, but the other woman chuckled and turned, taking the empty glass from Paul and setting it on the counter before tucking the pistol into the waistband of her skirt and marching out the open door. Eva heard the slide of metal, and then the sound of a lock turning, and shifted her gaze to her companion.

He shook his head, closed his eyes, and lowered his head back against the wall, breathing deeply. Eva thought he'd fallen asleep when he suddenly swung his long legs off the bed, groaning at the pain. He shuffled slower than any turtle she'd ever seen, lurching his way over to the counter, where he picked up a . . . knife.

Eva swallowed as he turned and began lurching toward *her*. She stared at his destroyed face as he hunched toward her. His jaw, for all that Mrs. Crosby had said it would heal, looked as crooked as a mule's hind leg. His eyes were two puffy slits and she could barely catch a glint of eye between the sore, purplish folds.

Eva closed her eyes and held her breath, realizing with blind clarity as she faced the end of her life that she loved Godric and he would never know.

A big, hot hand landed on her shoulder and she felt the cold kiss of steel run down her temple. The knife gave a sudden jerk and Eva screamed, the sound filling the room. Which was when she realized she wasn't dead at all and opened her eyes, squinting up at Paul's shaking form.

But he wasn't looking at her; he was studying the ropes that bound her arms. Time crawled with agonizing slowness as he sawed the rope with a blade that must be as dull as dirt, grunting with pain at every stroke.

When he'd freed her right hand, he gave her the knife and staggered away, collapsing on the bed so hard it was a wonder he didn't break it.

Eva's eyes darted between his prone form and the rope she was sawing so vigorously it chafed her wrist. He didn't move so much as a hairsbreadth, and Eva thought he might have lost consciousness. Once her other hand was free she worked on her ankles, her pulse pounding in her ears. A half hour, Crosby had said—how long had she been sawing on these ropes? How long had it taken Paul to make his snail-like trip across the small room? Ten minutes? Fifteen? Certainly not twenty. Her hand slipped and the dull point of the knife gouged her boot, poking a hole through the fine, soft leather and nicking her leg beneath.

"Blast and damn!" She caught her lower lip with her teeth and blinked away tears as she resumed her sawing, hoping to high heaven that she could still run. She cut the last of the ropes and quickly examined her leg through the hole. The wound wasn't deep, but it smarted.

She had almost reached the door when she recalled Paul; he'd helped her—she needed to check that he wasn't hurt. Well, hurt any more than he already had been. She approached him on tiptoe, the knife clutched in her right hand. He opened his eyes when she neared the cot.

There were tears streaming from his eyes, and she didn't think they were just from pain.

"Do you want some of the tonic?" she offered in a hushed voice, as if somebody were listening. "There is some left. You really should rest, you know."

Eva had never seen a man so big and strong cry, and it left her feeling helpless. "I'll fetch it for you, shall I?" Precious seconds ticked away while he stared, until finally his head moved in a slight affirmative motion.

Eva hurried to the counter, laid down the knife, and uncorked the solution. She had to help him sit up, and his big body was heavy and weak, so it was a task that took yet more precious minutes. By the time he was in a position to drink without choking, she was half mad with worry, her hands shaking as she carefully tilted the bottle into his mouth. Once he'd swallowed most of the contents, she set the bottle on the floor and covered him with the blanket he'd kicked from the bed. She turned to leave but his hand shot out and gripped her wrist.

Which was when Eva remembered the knife was still on the counter. But when she looked in his eyes, it was not a murderous look that met her. Instead, he gave a slight nod and said, "Key," although it sounded more like "shgree."

Eva recalled Crosby locking the door. Paul released her wrist and pointed generally in the direction of the cupboards.

She considered asking him to be more specific but knew that would be cruel.

The cupboards turned out to be shockingly empty and she found the key hanging from a nail at the back of one of them.

Her hands fumbled and slipped as she tried to jam the heavy skeleton key into the hole. *Was that a wagon? Voices? The sound of horses?*

She groaned, wrenched the key violently, pulled open the door, and came face-to-face, once again, with her own pistol.

Godric swam in warm, thick treacle, his limbs oddly light but non-responsive to his will.

Something unpleasant poked and prodded and worried at his arm and he groaned and slapped it away.

"Lord Visel, you must wake up. Please, Godric. We must go after Eva, sir. I can't—I can't do it without you."

The name *Eva* made him pause, but the swirling mist surrounded him before he could discover why that should be so.

"Oh, God. I hope you won't shoot me for this, but—"

Freezing water shocked him out of his warm cocoon. "Lord. Visel."

Godric's head snapped to one side with a loud *slap*, the grinding pain in his temple yanking him the rest of the way from his slumber.

"Please, Godric."

Once again his head snapped to one side, and this time the action made his eyes open.

"Stop. Hitting. Me."

"Thank *God!*" Hands landed on his shoulder and shook him until his teeth rattled. "Mrs. Crosby has kidnapped Eva and I believe she means to kill her."

The words were more shocking than ice water or slapping, and Godric gritted his jaws against the haze that threatened to claim him. "H-how long?" he asked in voice he didn't recognize.

"I don't know—perhaps four hours, maybe longer. She locked me in the still room. I screamed for hours before somebody came—it was Mr. Norton's son, Anthony. It turns out he's soft in the head, so Norton never could have sent him. He's a kind boy, but it took at least an hour to convince him to let me out and—Godric? Are you falling back to sleep?"

Godric's eyes fluttered open and he saw Andrew raise his hand for another slap. "No," he wheezed, gathering every speck of strength he could find and pushing himself upright. The room spun and he pitched forward and immediately lost his breakfast.

He continued to do so until nothing came up. Andrew, who'd been wisely standing some distance away, ventured closer. "Could I, er, get you anything?"

"Coffee." Godric pushed off the bed and swayed drunkenly, his eyes seeing four of everything as he scanned the room for his clothing.

"I don't think you should—"

"Go!"

The boy fled, and Godric dropped to his hands and knees and crawled toward his clothing, which Eva had laid out for him earlier.

My God, Eva. If any thought could fight its way through whatever Mrs. Crosby had given him—likely laudanum—it was the thought of Eva alone with her. Thanks to *his* idiocy.

By the time Andrew arrived, he'd managed to pull his shirt on, backward, and tangle his legs in his robe and nightshirt, which he'd pushed down rather than up.

The first cup of coffee immediately came back up, but Andrew had had the foresight to bring a pot, and only half of the second cup suffered a similar fate. By the time he had on his shirt, waistcoat, leathers, and boots, he was working on a third cup, his head still feeling as if it were stuffed with a huge wad of wool, but at least he wasn't drifting in and out of consciousness.

Andrew approached him with a cravat and Godric waved him away. "Tell me again," he ordered, pouring his own cup this time, his hands as weak as a babe's while he listened to the same recitation as twice before. But now he was much more lucid.

By the time Andrew had finished, Godric heaved himself to his feet. The room swam, but it settled quickly enough. He shrugged into his coat and snatched up his hat and gloves. When he opened the door, he ran smack into a huge, soft body.

"Good Lord!"

The boy—and that's what he was, for all that he was as big as a bloody house—scuttled back, shying away from Godric as if he didn't outweigh him by at least five stone.

"It's all right, Anthony. This is Godric—remember I told you about him?"

The boy hesitated before giving a frightened nod.

"He won't hurt you, will you, Godric?" Andrew gave him a pointed look.

"No, of course not. I beg your pardon, Anthony, thank you for freeing Andrew." The big, simple boy smiled tentatively. "We need two horses—do you know where we might find any nearby?"

He shook his head sadly.

"Goddammit," Godric cursed, making the boy jump. "Er, sorry about that, Anthony." He turned to Andrew. "You say she was going north?"

"Yes."

He glanced at Anthony. "Did your father go to get the magistrate?" he asked, not holding out much hope for a sensible answer.

But the boy nodded vigorously.

"I think his father told him to hide, didn't he, Andrew?"

Again the boy nodded.

Godric checked the pistol Andrew had handed him, peering through bleary eyes. "Well," he said, once he'd assured himself it was loaded. "It will be better to go on foot than sit here. Indeed, a walk shall help clear my head." He fixed Andrew with a speculative look. "You should go hide with Anthony and wait for Mr. Norton."

Andrew drew himself up in a manner very reminiscent of the battle stance he usually took with Eva. "I don't think I can do that, my lord."

Godric sighed; nothing could ever be easy, could it?

Chapter 18

Eva found herself back in familiar territory, sitting in the heavy chair with a gun in her face. Luckily, Mrs. Crosby and Flynn hadn't yet gotten around to tying her up or killing her or whatever it was they'd planned. Indeed, they'd been over in the corner arguing furiously while the woman kept the gun trained on her.

Mrs. Crosby was looking increasingly agitated, her hand shaking, which Eva felt could not be good for her health. It had taken her a good five minutes to convince the woman that she'd escaped without Paul's help. Lord knew what the unhinged cook would do if she learned she'd been betrayed by her own henchman.

Their voices suddenly went from a whisper to a shout.

Or at least Mrs. Crosby's did. "No!" She spun around, the gun now trained on Flynn. "I won't do it—I don't care what stupid promise you made. I want him *here*—I want him to watch while I kill somebody *he* loves."

"Dora, this is a turrible big mistake—this kind o' madness will bring the might o' the government down on us."

"I. Don't. Care!"

"Yours is not the only opinion that matters," Flynn bellowed back, finally losing his cool, spittle flying from his mouth. "Will you kill all o' us for your own revenge?"

Her entire body shook, and even holding the gun with two hands, she could not keep it straight.

"Put down the gun, Dora. Let the girl go."

Her arm began to sag and Eva had just begun to exhale the breath that was threatening to burst her lungs when Crosby's arm swung around in a blur. Flynn, for all his bulk, tackled her just as her finger squeezed the trigger. The report was deafening in the small confines of the solid stone cottage. Eva saw chips of stone fly from at least three places as the bullet ricocheted, pulverizing whatever it impacted but thankfully stopping before it reached Eva's skull.

Her head rang and she moved her jaw from side to side, as if that would clear her ears. Flynn was sitting on Crosby, who'd stopped fighting him, but was weeping so hard Eva could hear it despite her freshly traumatized ears.

Flynn looked over at Eva, his expression one of infinite sadness. Just then the door flew open and four or five men ran to their leader.

Eva could see that Flynn was shouting; clearly she wasn't the only one deafened by the shot.

He ordered them to take Mrs. Crosby back to their camp. Not until they'd carried the still weeping woman from the room did the big highwayman turn back to Eva.

"Her 'usband—Paul's brother—died that day. She's never been quite right since, destroyed by grief—like 'is lordship was, I've 'eard."

Eva wasn't about to discuss Godric with this man. He must have seen that on her face, because he sighed heavily and said, "Come. I'll take you back to the inn."

Eva jerked away from him. "I'm not going anywhere with you."

She couldn't hear him laugh, but she could see his tired smile. "You're a scrapper, aren't ye? I reckon you'd 'ave made a fine member of my merry band." He cut a glance at Paul's prone form and muttered something Eva couldn't hear. That was fine; she had no interest in listening to any more of his drivel.

"I want my gun," she said loudly.

His eyebrows shot up. "Why, so you can shoot me with it?"

"It's not loaded," she pointed out.

His lips curved. "But you'd shoot me if it was, wouldn't you?"

She shrugged, tired of the conversation, her head aching. "Possibly."

He laughed again but handed her the pistol, butt first.

When Eva snatched it away, he said, "It'll take you a few hours to walk back."

"Which way?" she yelled, shoving the gun into the back of her breeches and adjusting her clawhammer and overcoat to cover the bulge.

"Take the cart track to the muddy road and take a left. Keep goin' to the first road that bisects it and take a right. That'll bring ye right back to the Vicar."

Eva headed for the door, but Flynn's voice arrested her.

"Oy, girlie."

She turned.

"You won't tell—about Dora." The humorous lines of his face were suddenly grim—his expression that of an old man, rather than a fearless rogue. "They'll come for 'er for sure if they know she took a pot shot at an earl's wife."

Eva knew he spoke the truth. She also knew she would've done the same thing in Dora Crosby's position if she were to meet someone responsible for Godric's death.

"I won't tell," she said, turning away and shutting the door on any further conversation.

The trail through the woods was well marked, if narrow. She strode over the soft sphagnum and rotting leaves in the direction Flynn had given her. The forest was dense, but sunlight broke through in places, and it looked like diamonds glittering on the path ahead of her.

Everything else aside, it was a lovely day for a walk.

They'd turned away from town after crossing the—perfectly fine—bridge. Godric knew Mrs. Crosby wouldn't have taken her captive into town.

They'd trudged on in silence until they came to a muddy track that bisected the road.

"Did they go this way?" Andrew asked.

Godric glanced at the rutted mud, which looked as though something *might* have driven through it since the rain had stopped.

"Straight, or right?" Andrew prodded when Godric didn't answer. The boy was good for keeping him awake, but he did tend to maunder on and worry and wonder out loud. Incessantly. It made Godric appreciate Eva's company more and more. Say what you would about her impulsivity, the girl wasn't afraid of her shadow.

Godric pointed to the road that headed north, into the woods.

Andrew groaned. "Why did I know you were going to say that?"

"Perhaps because you know Flynn's band is more likely to hide in a forest than in the middle of a cow pasture?" Godric set off down the road, keeping to the grassy verge rather than the brown troughs that were a good five inches deep with mud.

"It's a good thing I brought my gun, since we're definitely headed into bandit territory," Andrew said after they'd marched a few moments in blessed silence.

"Yes, it's a good thing," Godric agreed. Not because he *actually* agreed, but because putting one foot in front of the other took all his attention. The truth was, Andrew was far more likely to slip and blow his own head off—or perhaps Godric's—than anything else. But he simply hadn't the strength to argue when Andrew had gone into excruciating detail regarding how he'd altered the big weapon so that it would fire without needing a live flame and twenty minutes to load it.

The day was still dry, although the clouds had begun to gather. Godric hoped Norton got back before it grew dark. If he brought the magistrate with him, they would find the note he'd left with Anthony and could at least *begin* looking for them.

"Why do you think Mrs. Crosby did it?" Andrew asked for the dozenth time.

"I couldn't say," Godric lied, for the dozenth time. In fact, he had a pretty good idea what was going on. She had some connection to Flynn or some member of his gang. And she must have thought bringing Eva to them would serve as a bargaining chip for something she wanted. What he *didn't* know was whether Flynn would take advantage of such a plum as a marquess's daughter, or whether he would live up to his promise.

He felt Andrew brush up beside him with his arquebus cradled in his arms, the business end pointing toward Godric's head.

"Er, Andrew, could you prop it over your shoulder as we discussed?"

"What? Oh! Yes, yes of course. So sorry." He slung the weapon over his opposite shoulder and cradled the butt with both hands. "It's quite heavy," he said a moment later.

Godric sighed. "Would you like me to carry it for a stretch?"

"Er, no, thank you. That is, perhaps in a little while."

Godric knew the boy had a deep attachment to the gun and didn't begrudge him his feelings, but he did wish he'd left the antique behind. If they had to move quickly, it would be less than useful to tote a heavy gun along while running.

"If you don't mind my asking, sir, how long have you been married?"

Godric glanced down at the boy, but Andrew's eyes were on the approaching woods and his lips were parted as he struggled to keep up with Godric's punishing pace. He had no agenda that Godric could see. "Not long," he finally said, and then, "Why?"

"I was just curious." He cut Godric a quick glance. "You should have seen your wife's face. If looks could have killed, Mrs. Crosby would be a smoking cinder." His voice was an interesting mixture of awe and amusement.

"Oh?"

"If it hadn't been for you—and her concern about what you'd been given—I think Eva would have jumped on Mrs. Crosby, loaded pistol or no." Andrew laughed in obvious admiration, but Godric felt queasy. That would have been a fine piece of work: him stupidly nonconscious and Eva getting shot on his behalf. The cold fist that closed around his heart made him stumble.

Andrew set a hand beneath Godric's elbow. "I say, sir, steady on. Do you wish to take minute?"

Godric couldn't breathe and worried he'd lose his footing if he took another step, so he stopped, spread his feet wide, propped his hands on his knees and bent low, his head hanging while he struggled for breath. How easily there could have been another dead body on his conscience this morning—another name he could add to the ever-growing litany. He was some sort of walking bloody curse, and anyone who spent too much time with him would pay the price.

"My lord?" The soft, tentative voice gradually penetrated the dense fog of fear in his head.

Take yourself in hand, Godric, you can wallow in self-pity later. The boy—he's counting on you. Perhaps you might get him killed, as well.

Godric thrust himself upright and Andrew jumped back. "I want you to go back to the inn," he said in a harsh voice he'd not even used on his soldiers.

Andrew's face fell. "But, who will help you if you encounter trouble?"

"If I encounter trouble I'll turn back," Godric assured him, rather than tell him the truth—that Andrew was far more likely to hinder than help.

"Respectfully, sir, you're in no condition to do this alone. I will go with you."

Opium, exhaustion, pain, and gnawing worry about Eva that verged on terror made him snap, "I wish you would not, Andrew. Quite frankly, I don't want to be responsible for you in addition to myself. You will only slow me down, get in the way, or likely blow my head off with that bloody gun," he said cruelly.

Twin spots of color on Andrew's cheeks were all the more noticeable for his tightly compressed lips and pinched, white nostrils. "Very well," he said, his voice stiff and dignified. "As you put it that way. I shall go back to the inn."

Godric let him go without saying anything or bidding him good-bye. Instead he trudged toward the woods, where the road disappeared as if into a dark maw.

He'd walked in eerie silence for perhaps fifteen minutes when he heard a soft scuffing sound. He whipped out the pistol and spun in a circle, only to find Andrew some ways behind him.

"Don't shoot!" He staggered backward and lost his footing, scrambling awkwardly to keep his feet while holding the big, ungainly weapon.

"Bloody hell," Godric muttered, and then waved the boy forward. Once he was within speaking distance, Godric shook his head. "What about *going back to the inn* didn't you understand?"

"Eva wouldn't have left you," Andrew said, as if that was explanation enough.

Godric didn't tell him that Eva likely wouldn't have required as much assistance as Andrew did, either. Instead he heaved a sigh, turned, and they walked in awkward silence.

Godric had just decided to have mercy on the boy and utter a few comforting words, when a mourning dove's plaintive—and remarkably close—cry shattered the silence.

Andrew shrieked and an explosion only slightly less deafening than cannon fire went off not far from Godric's right ear. A plume of sulfurous smoke surrounded them and he turned slowly to find the boy staring at him, one side of his face blackened with soot, his glasses sagging by their remaining arm.

"I'm so sorry!" Andrew shouted loudly enough to be heard back in London.

As deaf as she was, even Eva heard the explosion that must have come from just around the huge tree bordering the road. She also heard the sound of loud voices that followed. Moving quickly, and, she hoped, silently, she hid herself behind the first big tree and kept her eyes on the road.

Her mouth stretched into a grin when she saw the cause of the noise, and she barreled out of the trees without any thought for danger. The two men were obviously just as deaf as she was, and not until she was almost on top of Godric did he slip the pistol from beneath his coat and begin to turn.

"It's me!" Eva shouted.

"Eva!" Andrew yelled at the same moment.

What followed was a confusion of shouting and gesturing, until Godric hooked his arm through Eva's and pulled her along with him.

"Let's carry on this conversation while we get the hell away from here. We can talk as we walk."

It seemed they'd set out after her on foot and some animal had frightened Andrew into discharging his stupid gun.

Eva was just about to insult him, loudly, when Godric jerked her so hard, he almost took her off her feet. He turned to Andrew and put his finger crosswise over his lips and then mouthed *horses*.

They bolted for the trees, needing to split up, Andrew behind one tree, and Godric, holding Eva, pressed against the rough bark of another, his body hard and warm and comforting behind her.

The riders came around the same bend where Andrew had discharged the gun, and they must have heard it because both of them had weapons drawn. Eva's eyes widened as she took in the high-stepping gray.

"Papa!" she yelled, not realizing that tears were streaming down her face until she felt the wind on her face as she sprinted toward him.

Chapter 19

Eva noticed two things immediately: first, her normally exquisite, impeccable father was dusty and dirt-stained. Second, he appeared more coldly angry than she'd ever seen him in her life—which was saying something. He stared down at her with eyes like pale blue diamonds, tapping his crop against his very dirty top boot.

Eva gulped.

She'd believed Lord Visel's eyes were similar to her father's, but she'd been wrong. So very, very wrong. There was warmth in the gold rings around Godric's eyes; the Marquess of Exley's irises were the frigid gray of an alpine lake hidden beneath layer upon layer of ice.

She felt movement beside her just before the man who'd accompanied her father, Lord Thomas Byer, caught her up and lifted her off the ground, holding her so tightly she couldn't breathe.

"Evil," he said, using Gabriel's nickname for her. "What have you done?" His voice was hollow and so sad she almost didn't recognize it. She squirmed in his embrace until he released her, lowering her to the muddy road, but keeping his hands on her waist.

"What are you doing here, Tommy?" she demanded, staring up at him, shocked by the expression of misery on his face. Viscount Thomas Byer was well-known for his languid airs, his lack of concern for anyone or anything, and being the oldest student at Oxford. He was generally referred to as a Care-for-Nobody, although Eva knew that was not true. He was her brother's best friend—two outcasts who'd found each other Gabe's first year at university.

Before he could answer, her father said, "Perhaps we might return to the inn before we engage in such discussions?"

Eva turned to face him, shuddering at the leashed fury that burned beneath the blue.

"Of course, Father."

His eyes flickered to Godric, who'd come to stand beside her. "Shall I give her a hand up, sir?"

The marquess nodded abruptly and Godric's hands closed around her waist and lifted her up behind her father. The journey back to the inn was a silent one, which was probably just as well since Eva's ears had only just stopped ringing when the Greedy Vicar came in sight.

Godric strode beside them, his expression closed and unreadable. Tommy rode on her father's other side, his face set and grim. The only person who seemed the same as ever was Andrew, who couldn't stop gazing at his blunderbuss in wonder, no doubt surprised it had actually fired.

She was grateful to be seated behind her father, and not to have to meet his gaze. Never had Eva seen her impeccable father so dusty and mud-spattered; he looked a decade older than when she'd last seen him. Was it possible for a man's hair to go gray in so short a time? Because the Marquess of Exley's inky-black hair was indeed a striking and snowy white at his temples. His eyes were still more cutting than the sharpest blades, but the skin beneath them looked bruised.

When they cantered up to the Greedy Vicar's small stables Mr. Norton and his son Anthony came out of the inn.

"Welcome back, my l-lords," Mr. Norton stammered, his gaze flickering between the men and finally landing on Godric. "Er, I'm sorry, sir, but the magistrate is off on the circuit."

Godric nodded.

"That is just as well," the marquess said in his precise, diamond-sharp tone. "I don't wish for an audience."

Nobody said a word as the five of them trooped into Mr. Norton's small coffee room.

The marquess cut a cursory glance around the small but impeccably clean room. "Have you any other guests?" he asked.

"Uh, no, my lord."

"Then I will engage your entire inn for the evening."

"Er, Papa?"

He turned those cold eyes on her, and Eva swallowed. "There are only two rooms."

"As to that," Norton said, looking as if he couldn't believe his mouth had opened and he'd shoved words out of it, "I'll quickly make my two other rooms ready."

"I thought you had only the two rooms?" Godric demanded, and Eva realized Andrew hadn't told him about the others.

Norton winced. "No, I've got four."

Now Godric looked just as grim as the other two men.

Eva yawned; she wanted to crawl into bed and leave them all to it.

"I'm sorry, Mr. Fleming," Norton babbled. "It's just that, well, Mrs. Crosby kept the rooms locked, you know." He shifted from foot to foot.

"What's this about rooms? And who is Mrs. Crosby?" Tommy said, his gaze fixed on Eva in a way that made her squirm.

"The cook here," she answered. "It's a long story. But if the rooms are habitable?" she asked Norton, eager to get away from the penetrating stare of her father and equally disconcerting eyes of Tommy, a man she'd never seen serious for more than thirty seconds but who now looked as old and stern as the marquess.

"Aye, 'course." Norton all but sprinted toward the stairs.

Godric stepped up beside her. "I'll bunk with Andrew, sir. Eva may keep the room she is already in and you and Lord Byer can have the other two."

The marquess looked at Godric as if he were something he'd inadvertently carried in on his boot. Eva saw the earl's face redden, but he did not look away. She was proud of him. Meeting her father's gaze head-on was not for the faint of heart.

Godric turned to Eva and gave her a reassuring smile. "You go up, Eva. I'll pop in to collect my things in a few minutes."

Her father said to her, "Take an hour to put yourself to rights and then come to the coffee room."

Eva was at her bedroom door when she realized Tommy had followed her. "Could I talk to you a moment?"

Eva would have rather not talked to anyone—ever again—but nodded. When she went to close the door, he shook his head.

"It's not proper, Eva. Leave it open."

Eva stared at him; just who was this stodgy, bossy man? His stern expression suddenly infuriated her. "Why are you here?" she asked rudely.

"Gabe and Drusilla have their hands full, and I knew your father would come alone if I didn't force my company on him." Tommy closed the distance between them and took her chin in his warm, slightly roughened hand and tilted her face up. "Has Visel—" He stopped, his jaws clenching. "Has he—"

Why, the nerve! "That's none of your concern," she said icily.

He winced, but did not release her. "You're quite correct. It doesn't matter what has transpired. It was vulgar to mention such a matter in your presence. Don't worry, Eva. I will take care of you— and sort out this mess." His hand slid from her chin, over her jaw, and stopped behind her head. He swallowed hard and leaned closer, almost as if he were about to . . . *kiss* her.

Eva tried to jerk her head away, but he was *strong*.

"The truth is that I don't care what happened between you. You can marry me, Eva. You needn't sacrifice yourself to—"

"I hardly think what my betrothed has or has not done is any of your affair, Byer."

Eva gave a startled yelp and turned to find Godric leaning in the doorway, his arms across his chest, his posture lazy, his expression amused. But his eyes—

Tommy dropped his hand and the two men moved toward each other in an almost synchronized fashion. Neither stopped until they were only inches apart. She noticed they were almost the same height, although Tommy was leaner.

"You have no authority when it comes to her." The air in the room was charged, like the sky before a storm.

Godric's lips curled into an unpleasant sneer that Eva hadn't seen since the morning after she'd kidnapped him. "I'm going to have a word with Eva."

"Then I shall stay."

Both men seemed to swell to twice their size.

Eva went to Tommy and set a hand on his shoulder. "You should go, Tommy." When he failed to move, his gaze still pinned to Godric, Eva added, "I'll be fine, but you need to leave us."

For a moment she worried he'd argue, but he jerked out a nod and left without another word.

Godric's gaze was cool, polite, and distant. "I need to know what happened today before I speak with your father, Eva."

So, they were back to *that* relationship, were they? She crossed her arms. "I shall tell you under one condition."

A laugh slipped out of him. "I beg your pardon?"

"Give me your word you will *not* tell anyone what I tell you."

They locked eyes for a long moment.

"This is our business, Godric."

Her use of his name seemed to soften him. "Very well, you have my word."

Eva told him the story in as few words as possible. He was silent until the part about Dora Crosby taking a shot at her.

"Good God! The woman needs to be brought before a magistrate, Eva. She might have killed you."

"But she didn't."

"No, but she must—"

"You gave me your word," she reminded him. "Are you going to break it?"

He scowled. "Of course not, but—"

"Do you want the rest of the story, or not?"

He stared in slack-jawed wonder. "You really are a little termagant, aren't you? All right, go on, the rest of it."

Once she'd finished he asked, "And you don't believe she is coming back here?"

Eva thought back to the wreck of a woman she'd seen being hauled away. "I shouldn't think so. I think Flynn will take care of her—along with her brother-in-law." She gave him a hard look. "Who is considerably worse off than I'd expected."

Godric flushed under her accusing look. "Yes, yes, I was a brute. I *am* a brute. But we already knew that, didn't we?" He clearly didn't want an answer. "So Flynn really is as good as his word."

"I have to admit I was surprised, as well."

Godric's eyes narrowed and his lips curved into an odd smile.

"Why are you looking at me that way?"

His eyebrows jumped and he smirked in a way that made her legs weak. "What way is that?"

Eva gave an exaggerated sigh. "I'm not in the mood."

"I was just imagining you, holding your own against her, even when she had a gun on you." He grinned. "You really are quite something, aren't you? You didn't need me and poor Andrew to come rescue you at all."

Eva scowled and tried to ignore the warm rush of pleasure she felt at the admiring look in his eyes. "I can't believe you brought Andrew along with that wretched gun of his."

"He did his best. But I *am* going to make him put that gun back to its original state."

"I don't want my father to know about any of this," Eva bit out.
He blinked. "What?"

"You know what he will do if he hears about Flynn and what
happened."

"Yes, he will use his political clout to have them hunted down
like the deserter scum they are. And I shall help right along with him."

"Oh? In spite of the fact you just gave me your *word*?"

"Eva—"

"Aside from giving me your *word*, what do you think Flynn and
his gang will say when they are brought to book and some of them
decide to tell their stories? Will you let all this"—she waved a hand to
encompass everything—"become fodder for newspapermen?"

Eva could see she'd struck the mark.

Godric nodded his head, his expression reluctant. "You have a
point. All right," he said with a heavy sigh, "this shall stay between us."

"You need to tell Andrew that."

He nodded absently, his mind on something else. "You'd better
get cleaned up." He hesitated, his jaw flexing. "Your father asked to
speak to me. What is Byer doing here?" She could tell by the slight
flush over his cheekbones that he'd not wanted to ask the question.

"He came in Gabriel's stead," Eva said.

"Is that it? Or was there some agreement between you?"

Eva's eyes widened. "Agreement?"

He gave her a look of annoyance. "Yes, agreement—Eva—of a
romantic nature."

"With *Tommy*?"

"He wants to marry you," he pressed on, his jaw tight, his expression dogged.

"He's like a brother to me, Godric."

He snorted. "I hope Byer doesn't look at his sisters the way he
was looking at you."

"Tommy doesn't have any sisters," she said rather stupidly, too
stunned at the implications of his words to come up with anything
better.

Godric snorted and then turned away to gather his few things before opening the door to Andrew's room. "I shall see you down in
the parlor." He shut the door to her chambers and Eva collapsed into
the nearest chair.

Tommy in love with *her*?

No, that was impossible.

Wasn't it?

Fortunately, Lord Exley wasn't yet in the parlor when Godric
entered three-quarters of an hour later. Instead, it was occupied by
Norton along with two young girls, one dressed in a maid's mob cap,
the other clearly a scullery girl who must've been pressed into emer-
gency service.

"Where is Lord Exley?" he asked the innkeeper.

"In his room, er, sir. Along with the other gentleman. That is, *he*
is in *his* room, not his lordship's."

Godric would have laughed at the big man's terror of the marquess if the situation weren't so grim. Besides, Exley *did* tend to make
a rather menacing impression, even though the man was actually
quite slight of person.

"His lordship ordered a meal to be brought in, but Mrs. Crosby
ain't here. I can cook in a pinch, but"—Norton worried his lower
lip—"we ain't had no members of the aristocracy before—unless you
count Sir William Tavish, but he's a knight and don't—"

"Mr. Norton." Godric employed the tone he'd always employed
on skittish men while cannons exploded in their ears and death occurred all around them and they wanted to run and hide.

"Er, yes?"

Just then the door behind Godric opened and Norton's jaw fell
open.

Godric knew who was behind him without even turning to
look. "Mr. Norton?"

Norton's eyes grudgingly slewed in Godric's direction.

"Please bring something simple—bread, ale, perhaps some of that ham of yours and those delicious vegetable pickles?"

Norton nodded frantically. "Aye, we've got that."

"Good man," Godric said, clapping a hand on the big inn-keeper's shoulder and propelling him from the room.

"I shall ring when we are ready for you to bring in your repast, Mr. Norton." Exley's voice was so soft you had to strain to hear it, but it worked like a match to a fuse. Norton couldn't get out of the room fast enough.

As ragged and filthy as he'd appeared on the road, the marquess was now equally spotless, his trim figure impeccably coated and booted. His pale gaze was fastened on Godric in a way that made him feel as if he'd tied his grubby neckcloth too tightly.

Exley examined Godric in silence, an uncomfortable silence that went on so long Godric began wondering if the other man was de-ciding whether or not to bypass conversation entirely and simply take him out to a convenient field and shoot him.

"Have a seat, Visel."

Godric took one of the four chairs around the dining table and Exley sat across from him. Now that he could study the other man more closely, he saw signs of age other than the white hair at his tem-ples. Deep lines radiated from his startling blue eyes, and the thin skin beneath them was smudged purple from what had likely been an ex-hausting journey. Of course, the gray hair and lines might simply be the product of having such a daughter rather than riding halfway across England—

"I encountered my employee, James Brewster, not far south of Doncaster."

Godric nodded. He'd seen the young groom currying the mar-quess's horse out in the inn stables. To tell the truth, he'd been stunned that Exley had brought James along rather than discharging him on the spot for helping his daughter carry out such a caper. Per-haps the man wasn't as inhuman as he looked.

"James told me what happened. Everything," Exley added.

Godric heard the cool displeasure beneath the other man's words and knew instinctively it was not for him, but his daughter.

For the first time, Godric felt sympathy for the firebrand who'd captured both him and his future. What must it be like to have such a man for a father? Godric's own father had been a kind and gentle soul who loved his family, his tenants, and his book-filled library. The only person Edmund Fleming would have ever struck terror into was perhaps his steward—but because of his careless spending habits rather than any cruelty.

The Marquess of Exley was perhaps the coldest person Godric had ever met. Of course he knew the man's history—or at least the rumors: that he'd murdered his first two wives. He also knew Exley had killed at least three men in duels over his first wife. And then there were the tales—true, he believed—of his prowess at the gaming table and how he'd accumulated estate after estate from feckless gamblers over the years.

Yes, he could sympathize with Eva, now.

"I apologize for your predicament, Visel."

Godric's eyes widened at the marquess's words. "Er . . ."

Exley's lips curved up minutely at one corner. "You look surprised. Did you think I would hunt you down and call you out because my daughter kidnapped you?"

Godric flushed under the other man's cold amusement and Exley's smile became infinitesimally larger.

"Ah," he said, the single syllable making Godric feel like a boy of fifteen. "I can see you did."

"You needn't apologize for Eva's behavior, my lord. She's my betrothed and within a few days, weather willing, I'll be responsible for her actions."

Exley's remarkable eyes narrowed at Godric's tone. "My daughter wishes to marry you?"

He blinked at the bizarre question. "We've been alone together for days—and nights—and there have been multiple witnesses: post-boys, Norton, two other innkeepers, the boy—Andrew," *not to mention a passel of thieves and deserters.*

The marquess gave an elegant shrug. "People can develop such faulty memories when given the right incentive."

Godric snorted with disbelief. "Are you saying you'd bribe all those people?"

"*Bribe* is an ugly word."

Godric considered the fact that Flynn and all his band—not to mention Crosby—would also possess knowledge of his intimacy with Eva. Didn't he owe the other man that information?

He thought of Eva, and the promise he'd made; didn't he owe Eva his confidence?

"I think you should assume word has spread beyond that small number," Godric finally said. *There, that should cover Flynn and his band.* "Especially now that you've arrived and they know the Marquess of Exley is my putative wife's father."

Godric knew he'd scored a solid hit when an almost imperceptible mist of red swept over Exley's pale, razor-sharp cheekbones. Good, he *should* know that Godric had done a good job of concealing his daughter's identity before *he* came barging in.

"All the same," Exley said, his tone pure steel, "I will not sacrifice my daughter to any man just because there is a danger of scandal. Eva's happiness is more important to me than our family name or her reputation."

It was the first time Godric felt any liking for the human icicle across from him. "And you believe a union with me is anathema to her happiness?"

"Now that, my lord, I do not know. What do you think? Your recent actions would indicate you hold my family in some dislike. Such behavior does not seem propitious for a happy marriage." He paused, but Godric had nothing to add to his accurate, if painful, assessment. "I will not force her to marry you. I will not leave my daughter in your clutches if your intentions are to punish her."

As insults went, it was masterful.

Godric's impulse was to retaliate in kind, but the other man had more than enough reason to believe the worst of him.

"I'm deeply ashamed of my behavior toward your family." He hesitated and then said something he'd hoped to keep between him and Eva. "Your daughter probably saved my life by kidnapping me from the Duke of Richland's party."

Exley's eyebrows rose slightly, making Godric wonder irrationally just what it took to get a *real* reaction out of the man. "Please explain."

"I went to Richland's party planning to abduct your daughter-in-law."

"James Brewster advised me of that, Visel, but not your motivation for such an odious action. Perhaps you might indulge me with it, now."

The only time Godric could recall feeling so imperiled before was on a battlefield.

"I have no explanation, sir." He shook his head, his thoughts jumbled as he tried to recall his thought process during the months leading up to that night. The rage that had driven him to increasingly reckless actions. "I wish I could say I would have come to my senses, but I have no certainty of that. If Eva had not acted, I would have made the worst mistake of my life."

A muscle in Exley's jaw flexed "Are you aware your cousin continued with your plans, Visel?"

"Good God! You mean he took Mrs. Marlington?"

"No. I mean he took Mr. Marlington's *child* and held him for ransom."

Godric had heard of people's hearts seizing, but he'd never believed it was true. He surged to his feet. "Bloody hell! Is the child—"

Exley held up one slender white hand, his gaudy ruby signet ring winking dully. "The boy is safe."

Godric slumped into his chair, his heart resuming its work, now pounding so hard he could feel it knocking against his ribs.

Exley continued. "Gabriel and Drusilla put a stop to his plans." Exley's gaze became even colder—which Godric wouldn't have believed possible. "Your cousin's plans were of a fatal nature."

Godric squeezed his eyes shut as if that would block out the other man's words. "Did—is—was anyone hurt?" he finally forced out, unable to look.

"Rowland died in the ensuing struggle, as did one of his cohorts. But Gabriel, Drusilla, the child, and Lord Byer were unharmed."

That *did* make him open his eyes. "Byer was there?"

"Yes."

No wonder the man hated him. Godric had to swallow several times to force down a lump of shame, relief, and fury—at *himself.* "I was not aware of his plans regarding the child. But I *did* instigate the matter with Mrs. Marlington, so I am not without blame."

Exley just stared.

Godric had no idea what either of them would say next when the door opened and Eva stood in the doorway, her magnificent eyes flickering worriedly from her father to Godric as both men stood.

"I didn't mean to interrupt."

Godric hardly recognized this tame, spiritless version of the woman who'd kidnapped him and brandished weapons at highwaymen. He had to admit he did not care for it.

"Come in and sit, Eva," Exley said in the same level, dead tone he said everything. He looked at Godric. "I believe we are finished here, are we not, Lord Visel? I'd like to have a private word with my daughter." It was not a request.

Godric turned to Eva. He could hardly ask if she wished to be left alone with her own father, but he could see that she knew what he was silently asking, and she nodded slightly.

As he looked at her, it occurred to him that this might be the last time he'd see her. The marquess, he knew, would act swiftly once he'd made his decision. Although Godric had believed they were as good as married, he could not stand in Eva's way if she chose to leave here with her father.

What he hadn't expected was how such an admission would make him feel: hollow and cold and hopeless.

Chapter 20

Eva's fear deserted her somewhere between her room and the parlor. For the first time in her life, she was not afraid of the disappointment she would see on her father's face. But just because she wasn't afraid didn't mean that sitting without squirming beneath his icy stare was easy.

As they locked eyes with one another Eva wished, as she'd done a thousand times before, that she understood him—that he would show some part of himself, no matter how tiny, to anyone other than his beloved wife. Only with Mia did Adam de Courtney appear even remotely human. It was as if he had only enough of himself to spare for one person.

He wasn't cruel to Eva and she *knew* he cared for her—as he did all his children—but the man himself was forever remote, a hazy promontory in the distance that she would never, ever reach, no matter how hard she strove for it.

Her sisters had stopped trying to know him years ago—around the time when Mia had come into their lives and provided so many of those things they'd been missing: like joy and affection. It wasn't as if her aunt and grandmother—who'd raised them—hadn't loved them, but both women had been as emotionally frozen as her father.

When it appeared that her father would be content to stare at her for the next eon, Eva asked the question that burned in her. "Has Mia entered her confinement? Has she—"

"Not yet."

Although he would never say as much, she knew he was worried about Mia and anxious for her. Her stepmamma was not a young woman, and childbirth was not easy even for women half her age. Shame washed over Eva as she realized she'd taken away the person Mia loved most, her husband, in her time of need.

"Are Gabe and Dru—"

"They are well."

Eva wanted to ask about Gabe's son, Samir, but she didn't know whether her brother had told their parents about the little boy yet, or not.

"Gabriel's son, Samir, is also fine."

Eva sagged with relief.

"I would like to talk about *you*, Eva."

"Yes, Father."

"Has Visel treated you well?"

The question surprised her. "Er—" An image of Godric kneeling between her thighs, his lips slick and—

A throat cleared, and Eva's head whipped up. The marquess appeared. Eva squinted. *Could that be embarrassment in his eyes?*

No, impossible.

"Yes, he has treated me well," she said.

"And do you wish to marry him?"

Eva gaped. "I've been with him for days, I—I understand that I must do the proper thing, that there is no other choice."

"There are always other choices." Her father's voice was dry. "And this choice is yours, Eva, not Visel's and not mine. If you do not wish to marry him, you shall leave here with me."

"But . . . I don't understand."

"Answer the question, Eva. Do you wish to leave here as Visel's wife? If so—" He reached into his pocket and handed her a neatly folded paper.

Eva unfolded it and stared. It was a special license with both her and Godric's names on it.

"If you do not want him, you will leave with me and the matter will be forgotten." His expression was cool and dispassionate.

At first Eva thought the snapping sound she heard happened in the room, but then she realized it was only inside her own head. Something had broken—some bond or barrier—and years' worth of anger came forth in a torrent.

Eva jumped to her feet. "Don't," she said in a voice that was so like his—so quiet and cold—that she momentarily shocked herself. "Don't talk to me like that—like I'm nothing more than a problem to be solved and then filed away."

If anything, his eyes became colder. "And how *should* I talk to you? Should I congratulate you for bringing me tearing across the country on such a matter?"

"No," she whipped back. "Of course not. But you don't have to treat me like a recalcitrant child."

He gave a laugh that was utterly mirthless. "A child? You kidnapped a man. Not only that, but you did so with the assistance of a *servant*, a commoner who could be transported if Visel saw fit to bring charges against him for such a crime."

The truth of his words was like a club and she shuddered at the danger she'd exposed her very best friend to. "I did it for Gabriel," she retorted, barely able to force the words out. "I just wanted to help him, Papa. I didn't—"

God. What if they'd been caught? What if Godric hadn't been who he was, but a petty individual disposed to punish those weaker than himself? What if James had gone to jail?

Eva squeezed her eyes shut, but the tears flowed anyway.

And then the impossible happened: strong arms closed around her, the unprecedented action robbing her of all the strength she'd husbanded for this confrontation. She gave in to her emotions and sagged against her father's lean, spare body, her own shaking with the force of her weeping. The events of the past weeks and months were a jumble in her mind—those of the last few days even more confusing. But somehow he managed to keep it all at bay, by holding her tight with one arm and stroking her hair with his free hand.

"Shhh, Eva," he murmured, his breath hot on her scalp. "I'm sorry," he said, his voice strained. "You are right, Daughter. I should speak to you as a woman, not a girl."

His apology—and the admission that followed—was so surprising that her convulsive sobs stopped as abruptly as they'd started.

Her father had apologized to her.

She felt his body shake and realized he was chuckling—the Marquess of Exley was actually laughing. Eva was glad he was holding her upright or she might have fainted from the shock of it.

"If I'd known those words would quiet you so quickly, I might have used them years ago." The gentle amusement in his voice made her heart expand with all the love she felt for him; all the love he didn't want from her.

His hand continued its soothing stroking, his low voice rumbling through her. "I wish your stepmamma were here, Eva. She'd know what to say. Mia always knows what to say." He sighed. "I've not been much of a father to you, I know." She made a demurring noise. "No, don't deny it," he said, his voice heavy with regret as he released her, holding her at arm's length until they could meet each other's eyes. Eva could only gaze in wonder. When had her father ever worn this expression before? Self-doubt, shame, and a host of other emotions mingled on his usually expressionless visage.

He released her and she wanted to pull him back, but he left her only long enough to bring his chair closer to hers. "Sit," he said, taking her hand when she did so, his fingers warm and strong. "It doesn't matter what happened between you and Visel these past few days, or who knows about it." She knew what he meant: consummation. "I

will not let you go to a man who will not value and respect you." He
hesitated, his pale face flushed, and he gave a smile that almost looked
shy. "I love you too much to do that, Eva." She blinked and he
laughed. "She will be insufferable." At her confused look he said,
"Mia has told me for years that I should tell my children how I feel."
An expression of pain spasmed across his face. "I would give my life
for you, Eva, and I want only happiness for you."

Eva's eyes began to tighten and his lips curved into a smile that
actually showed a flash of slightly crooked teeth. Had she ever *seen*
her father's teeth before?

"Please don't cry again, Eva; it turns me into a puling coward."

Eva gave a watery laugh at his ridiculous claim.

"I wish you had time to make this decision, but there is none.
Not only is the situation volatile, but I must get back." He didn't
have to say why, and she certainly agreed with him. "If you decide
you wish to leave with me, rest assured I will see that no word of
these past few days gets out." His expression hardened and Eva shivered at the cold determination she saw; the man was implacable.

"You should know that Byer has expressed a desire to marry you.
When he learned that you were with Visel, well, he expressed his
feelings for you most vocally. I'll be the first to admit I'd not expected such depths from the man," he said musingly, and then
shrugged. "He told me he loves you." An hour ago that news would
have stunned her, but she'd seen the truth of her father's claim in
Tommy's eyes. "You needn't accept Byer *or* Visel, Eva. You can
come home to Exham. Mia and I were planning to tell you this summer that you needn't return to London. The only reason we insisted
on one Season was to give you an opportunity to experience something other than school or life at Exham. It wasn't meant to be a punishment."

He looked so remorseful that Eva felt bad about the way she'd
behaved for months on end. "It wasn't all a punishment, Papa. I enjoyed being with Gabe and Drusilla. But I do not want to have another Season—especially without them."

"So that is settled, then. If you decide to come back, we can find something else for you to do." His lips twitched up on one side. "I know you've got a fine eye for cattle and I wouldn't be opposed to giving in to Brewster's incessant nagging to buy more bloodstock. We've certainly got the room for you to try your hand at breeding—on a *small* scale," he added when Eva squeezed his hand hard enough to make him wince.

"Oh, Papa! Really?"

He was definitely smiling now. "Oh, Eva, *really.*"

She warmed under his teasing more than his actual offer, although the offer was the culmination of all her dreams. She could return to Exham and actually raise horses? It had been all she'd wanted since the time she'd cajoled Brewster to allow her to attend her first foaling.

It sounded too good to be true. Eva met his questioning, curious stare. "You really mean I could choose my own stock, have a hand in actual daily operations and not just watch from a *ladylike* distance?"

He raised his hands in a gesture of surrender. "Yes, yes, yes. You will be your own mistress in this matter—short of bringing your cattle into the castle or moving yourself into the stables, of course." He hesitated and then said, "For some time Mia has argued you have talents that are not being utilized. I agree—you are a superlative horse-woman. She's also argued you should be allowed to develop your talents without certain, er, how did she put it—ignorant male hindrance."

Eva laughed. Yes, that sounded like Mia.

He gestured to her clothing. "I agree that gowns in the foaling or breeding sheds are dangerous." Eva began to grin and he lifted an admonishing finger. "You will be allowed such liberties on *my property only*, Eva. The first time I catch you riding astride in town and scandalizing villagers—"

"Of course, Papa." She bit down on her smile. It was like a dream come true; it was the only thing she'd ever wanted.

Godric's face, red, smiling, and sweaty, flashed through her mind's eye. *Not the only thing you've ever wanted.*

She lifted her hands to her hot cheeks and shook her head. *No.*

It is true. You've had him for these few nights and you want more. You want more of him and the things he can do to you, for you . . .

Her father squeezed her hand, the action piercing her erotic imaginings. "The decision is up to you, Eva."

He released her hand and stood. "I will leave you for a little while to think on it. I am taking Bounder into town. I left James in charge of securing a decent team for our chaise."

"James is here?" The marquess winced at her screech. "Sorry, Father, but—I'm just surprised he is with you."

"It seemed a prudential decision for several reasons." He frowned at her. "He was quite stricken to have left you, Eva."

She nodded miserably.

"I know you are not insensible to the wrongs you have done him, or the difficult position you put him in," he said, reading her expression accurately. "I assured him that he mended the situation as well as he could have after his *initial* mistake."

"It was all my fault, Papa. James didn't want to come along. I know he just came to keep me safe."

"I know it was your fault. But perhaps in the future he will know to talk some sense into you or find somebody else who will talk some sense into you, before giving in to your every demand."

"Thank you for not punishing him, Papa."

One dark brow arched. "It is not for *me* to punish him. I will leave that in Brewster's capable hands."

Eva winced; James's father was as terrifying as her own.

"Yes, just so," the marquess said, once again interpreting her correctly. "Now, if there is nothing else?"

Eva shook her head as she looked up into her father's blue eyes—eyes clouded with concern now rather than disappointment—and thought of Godric's, and how she'd believed they were similar.

Other than being blue, they were nothing alike, she saw now. Oh, her father and Godric were both strong, powerful men—they shared that characteristic. She respected her father a great deal and saw many of his qualities in Godric—for all that Godric had behaved like a madman these past months.

But he'd not acted like a madman these past few days. He'd apologized for how he'd behaved and appeared genuinely ashamed of his actions. If there was one thing Eva could sympathize with, it was being ashamed of one's actions.

As the door closed behind the marquess, she sagged back in her chair.

She could lie to herself all day long, but the truth was that she *did* want Godric.

He'll never love you. He doesn't even want to marry you—and he certainly *doesn't want to have a child or family with you.*

I'm not looking for love—I'm not even looking for marriage, and certainly not with a man like Godric Fleming.

Oh, Eva.

The voice was so sad it actually made her stop and think; *was* she looking for love?

She growled at the foolish thought. *You don't know the first thing about what I want,* she foolishly accused her own mind.

If your father's offer is indeed your only dream, then why is there any question about your decision at all?

Eva gritted her teeth against the infallible logic. *Godric made a similar offer—he even mentioned having an aunt who'd bred horses. So the decision isn't between having my dream* or *abandoning Godric. I can have horses and Godric.*

Yes, but Godric made that offer when he thought the two of you would be forced *to marry. What do you think he would say now, Eva—now that he might not be doomed to a future chained to a woman whose children he never wants to have? Or perhaps you think the marquess gave Godric the same choice to shab off as he's given you?*

Eva knew her father wouldn't have given Godric that choice. She held both their futures in her hands.

The relentless voice in her head had one last question: *So, what do you think Godric would do if he held both your futures in his hands?*

Eva closed her eyes, but that offered no reprieve from the truth: if Godric had been given the same choice as she, Eva would already be rolling away in a carriage with her father.

The door to the parlor opened and Eva's head jerked up.

Tommy strode in and shut the door with a decisive click. "I need to speak to you," he said, his voice almost harsh. In the five years she'd known Thomas Byer, she'd never heard anything but flippancy, amusement, and mockery from him. The man looking down at her with dark, unsmiling eyes bore no resemblance to the Tommy she knew.

"Of course, Tommy. Please, have a seat."

Unlike her father, he'd not bathed or changed since his arrival, and his face was taut, dusty, and tired as he dropped into the chair the marquess had just vacated. That was another thing she'd never seen before: Thomas Byer looking anything less than immaculate. The man was almost prettier than she was, and he *certainly* took more pains when it came to grooming his magnificent body and handsome face. He was, in other words, a dandy. But not today.

"You cannot throw away your life like this, Eva."

"I'm not—"

He lifted a hand in an imperious gesture. "I know you can be the most stubborn creature on earth, but now is not the time to allow your willful nature free rein."

Eva scowled. "Why do—"

"I realize saying something like that is the best way to get your hackles up, but you know I am speaking sense. Come away with your father and me. I'll take care of you." He hesitated. "It would be my *honor* to take care of you. You don't need to marry Visel just to avoid scandal. In fact—" His cheeks flushed. "In fact, I forbid it."

All the confusion she'd been feeling at his words coalesced into anger, like a boiling pot converting water to steam. Here was yet *another* man who thought he knew what was best for her.

"It may surprise you to hear this, *Lord Byer*, but I don't *want* to be taken care of. Indeed, it may surprise you to know I'm *tired* of being treated like a slobbering infant." He opened his mouth but she raised her hand. "And it particularly might surprise you to know that I am capable of making my own decisions." Her eyes narrowed at the open skepticism that flashed across his face before he could hide it.

Of all the arrogant, conceited, obnoxious—

"I am *not* saying you are incapable of making your own decisions, Eva. I am saying you are dreadfully outmatched when it comes to pitting your wits against Visel. This is the same man who goaded Gabe to violence." He paused, his patient, long-suffering expression only making her more furious. "This is the same man who mocked you—your *incipient madness*—at every opportunity these past few months. You are not thinking clearly, Eva."

"When did you become so knowledgeable about what I think, Tommy?" He flinched at the heat in her tone. "The only thing you know about me is what you see or what I've told you. You like my exterior well enough—just as a great number of other men do." His sudden flush told her that was a home truth. "As to anything beyond that, the only things I've ever told you about myself are superficial— my love of horses, my hatred of balls and fussy gowns. The truth is, you know *nothing* about me and yet you are prepared to make one of the most important decisions of my life—*for me*. Your arrogance is simply breathtaking. I would *never* presume to do the same thing to you—"

"That is because I'm a *man* and you are a young girl barely out of the schoolroom—"

"A *girl*, Tommy? Is that what you are thinking when you look at me? Is that how you would treat me if I were to accept your offer to take care of me? Like a *girl*?"

His already flushed face turned a dull red as he absorbed the unmistakable tenor of her words.

"Very well," he said, "I *do* want you as a man wants a woman and have done for quite some time." The flash of heat she saw in his eyes was unmistakable to her, now that she'd seen a similar look in Godric's. Tommy wanted her—wanted to do the same things Godric had done to her. Yet the knowledge gave her no joy. Not like thinking about Godric.

Tommy laid a hand on her shoulder. "But that is a different point, Eva. As to the situation that you are in right now? Well, when it comes to worldly matters, you should defer to those with more— nay, with *any*—experience of the world outside of nineteen years in the country and one Season in town."

She jerked away from him. "You have *no* right to—"

"Will he give you children, Eva? Will he give you a family?" he asked harshly. "You needn't speak. I know he won't—I can see the answer on your face. He is afraid of the very blood that flows through your veins."

The words were like the blow from a club. And they were all the more painful because she knew they were true. "How *dare* you?"

"I dare a great deal because I *love* you, Eva, and I have done almost from the first time I met you." The air rang with his startling declaration. His face—handsome, familiar, belonging to a person she'd thought she knew—was that of an impassioned stranger. For the briefest moment, she thrust her angry indignation aside and ached for him, for the love she saw reflected in his eyes. She ached because she knew she could never return it.

A week ago she might have thought she could love him—but that was before these few days with Godric. Before Godric, she hadn't even known the depth of emotion she was capable of feeling for a man. After all, other than a brief period of time when she'd mooned over one of her father's grooms—a stout, scrubby-looking man who'd been as glorious as a centaur on horseback—she'd never felt the slightest twinge of interest for a man.

But now? Now she knew she could never return Tommy's affection.

Eva struggled with the anger that still threatened to overtake her at his arrogance, instead considering the man before her. Tommy was her dear friend and deserved her kindness right now.

He leaned toward her, his gaze dark and intense. "Come with me, Eva. Let me take care of you. Let me cherish you as you deserve."

"But, Tommy, I don't *love* you."

Rather than stop him, her words made him smile. "You like me well enough, don't you?"

"Of course I do, but that's—"

"Love will come in time, Eva. I know it. Besides, you don't love him either, so that doesn't—" He stopped, his handsome eyes widening as they fixed on her face, all the color that had built in his cheeks slowly draining away. "My God, Eva. Tell me you aren't so foolish as to believe you love him?" He gave a derisive snort. "Whatever you feel for him is infatuation, Eva, nothing more. This marriage would be a tragedy for you, can't you see? He fears the strain of madness he believes runs through your veins. You are tainted to him. He despises not only your family, but who and *what* you are. Even if you *do* love him, he would never, ever love *you* and would—"

"That is quite *enough*, my lord." Eva's entire body shook with rage at a lifetime's worth of having to listen to others tell her how she felt, or how she *should* feel. "As foolish as my feelings may or may not be, they are none of your concern. You've made your point—and your feelings—clear. Trust me when I say both are *greatly* unwanted. Now, I beg you will take your advice, your *love*, and your person out of my sight."

"Eva, I didn't mean—"

She turned her back on him.

There was a long moment of silence, and then she heard his booted feet and the opening and closing of the door.

Eva commenced furious pacing. *How dare he? How dare he presume to say such things to me? To—*

To what? To tell you the truth? That Visel never wanted you as a wife? Do you really need somebody else to tell you that?

It's not the truth! It's not!

Eva knew she was behaving like a child. There was only one person who could tell her whether it was the truth or not.

One way or another, Eva would get an answer out of him.

Chapter 21

Godric wasn't surprised to find Byer waiting for him in the room he shared with Andrew.

He gestured to the small table with two chairs. "Please make yourself at home," he said sarcastically, carrying the bottle of brandy and two glasses that he'd fetched from Norton and setting them on the table crowded with various arquebus parts.

Thankfully, the boy had gone into town with the marquess. Godric had been looking forward to an hour or two of peace before Andrew got back to their crowded little room. But here was Byer.

"I want a minute in private with you, Visel," Byer snapped behind him.

Godric turned and held out a glass, amused by the other man's expression of surprise. "I had surmised as much, Byer." When the other man reached for the glass, Godric pulled it back and gave him a look of mock confusion. "I'm sorry—did you want a drink, as well? Or did you mean you wanted a moment in private with me at twenty paces first thing tomorrow morning?"

Byer scowled at Godric's laughter and snatched the glass from his hand. "You really are an ass, aren't you?"

"Probably," Godric said, taking a sip of liquor and savoring the burn before lowering himself into the room's only comfortable chair.

"Do you even have the capacity to feel shame at what you've done?"

Godric sighed. "Is that what you came to talk about? My defective character? You'll need more than a minute for that."

"Everything's a joke to you, isn't it?" Byer slammed the untouched glass down on the nearest table. His expression of pure dislike should have looked foolish on his tired, dust-smudged face, but his filthy, wrinkled appearance somehow made his loathing all the more potent.

Godric found the sight of Byer's dishevelment interesting. The man was a notorious dandy who'd always paid more attention to his wardrobe than most women did. Also, Byer was famous for his torpid temperament. Indeed, it had been difficult most of the time to believe Byer had a pulse. And yet here he was, positively deranged with jealousy. He'd been smitten by his best friend's sister, who apparently viewed him as nothing more than a brother—if her reaction to him earlier was anything to go by. Lord, how that must sting.

Godric felt a pang of sympathy for the other man, although he doubted Byer would appreciate his voicing that sentiment.

"Do you really need to ruin her life? Just let her go." Byer's tone was rough and rude, but Godric could hear the pleading tone beneath the command. "You don't really want her—her blood would sully the great house of Tyndale. And you've never done anything but insult her, so I know you can't actually *like*—not to mention love—her. You wanted to *kill* her brother and abduct her dearest friend. All of that adds up to your being a disaster of a husband for her. And I've not even begun to take into consideration the disaster that is *you*. Your outrageous behavior this past Season was that of a dangerous wastrel, and your infamous whoring—particularly with other men's wives—and the low, wretched company you keep, all point toward a life that will end in violence sooner rather than later. You don't want a wife, Visel, and you wouldn't know how to do right by one if you *had* one. So let her marry a man who will love and protect her. A man she might actually come to love."

"Who would that be?" Godric teased with a mocking grin. "You, I suppose? Indeed, she likely loves you already—how could she not as you are such a self-proclaimed paragon of masculine perfection."

Byer's pale, sharp cheeks tinted and he gritted his jaws so hard Godric was amazed that steam didn't come out of his ears. He knew he should stop teasing the man, but the truth was he found Byer's insistence on knowing what was best for Eva insulting and irritating.

So, your pride has been stepped on, rather than any feelings you might have for her?

Godric ignored the annoying inner voice, a skill born of decades of practice. Instead, he fixed his gaze on the man across from him, who appeared to be on the verge of flying apart. He tossed back the remains of his drink and set it down on the table before standing, the action bringing them to within a foot of each other.

"Tell me, Byer, aside from your wardrobe and unreciprocated love, just what *do* you have to offer her?"

"She might not love me—*yet*—but at least I would give her children and a family." Byer sneered. "Will you? Answer me honestly. Are you even capable of having feelings for someone other than yourself? I'm not saying that you were always like this, but I think we both know you are not the same man you were before the war. You are useless for anything other than killing and war. You're an empty husk of a man with nothing but revenge fantasies to keep you waking up each morning."

Godric's jaw had sagged slightly at the other man's audacity. He was about to tell him what he could do with his interfering ways when a slight movement caught his eye: the connecting door to Eva's room had been eased opened. It was so small a crack that he wouldn't have noticed it if he'd not actually been looking in that direction. Godric doubted the person on the other side could actually see him or Byer, but they'd be able to hear every word. There was only one person he could think of who would be listening.

Now is your chance to do one good thing for her. Byer might be a puffed up fop, but he is right about one thing: any other man in the country would be better for her than you will be. It might cause a moment of pain, but you could ensure she makes the correct choice with only one small utterance. Say it, Godric.

For once, the voice was not mocking.

"She told me she didn't wish for children," Godric blurted, ignoring the sound mental advice he'd just received.

Byer gave an ugly laugh. "Well, she would, wouldn't she? After all, you've made it plain all Season—to all of London—what you think of her bloodline. She's hardly going to tell you the truth."

Godric felt his face get hot, all the more so because the other man was right. He'd behaved like a pig and had no defense for it. And what Byer didn't know was that he'd *continued* to let her believe the same lie even while engaging in bed sport with her these past few days.

Godric opened his mouth to dispute the ridiculous claims, as he should have done days ago.

But then Byer said, "Even if mistakes were made or you actually condescended to give her children, you would never love them, would you?"

Carl's face rose up in his mind as it had looked the last time Godric had seen it: cold, pale, and lifeless. He expected to feel the familiar, gut-wrenching pain, but instead, he felt nothing: he was as dead inside as the son he'd left buried a continent away.

"Don't you have anything to say for yourself? Or will you just wantonly ruin her life as you tried to do to her brother and friend? Or perhaps she was next on your list for revenge?"

Godric met the other man's furious eyes. Behind Byer's rage, there was fear and hurt: he loved Eva with all his heart and he was fighting for her.

He was fighting as Godric should be fighting—if he loved Eva.

If you loved her.

Godric swallowed the bile that almost choked him and summoned the hard, cold, supercilious smile that had been his mask every day of this past Season. "You've uttered a home truth, Byer: I don't want children." His gaze flickered across the cracked door, and then he took another breath and said the only thing he deserved to say, "And even if I did wish for children, I'd not want mad ones."

Godric could have ducked Byer's fist, or guarded against the hit, but he stood still and let the man knock him on his ass.

His head rang as he lay on his back and smiled bitterly at the ancient beams holding up the ceiling, waiting for more punishment—*hoping* for it.

But the other man was looking down on him with disgust, as if he'd not even soil his boot by kicking him.

Godric didn't blame him. He wiped the blood from the corner of his mouth. "If you believe she will have you, Byer, then I will gladly step aside. If she wishes to wed you, I shall shower you with rose petals and do my part to make sure this entire incident never sees the light of day. How's that for an offer, Byer?"

Byer's face was a mask of loathing. "You are a pitiful excuse for a man, Visel," he said, flexing the pain out of his right hand. "And you are certainly not worth a sore hand."

Godric could not agree more.

"Was there anything else?" he asked in a bored, insulting tone that would have guaranteed a dawn meeting in most situations.

Byer's handsome face flushed a dark red and his nostrils flared. "No."

"So why don't you get the hell out of my room and get on with your happy new life."

Byer pivoted on one foot, not giving him another look before striding toward the door and slamming it behind him.

Godric's entire body was hot and his pulse was pounding in his temples—and not just from the punch to his face.

Even the voice in his head sounded amazed and disgusted. *You did it, didn't you? You were scared she'd go with Byer so you just made sure she'd have no choice, didn't you?*

Get fucked. Godric pushed himself off the floor, deliberately keeping his back to the connecting door.

You coward; you're too much of a coward even to admire your handi-work.

Godric's gorge rose as he forced himself to turn and look at the connecting door: it was closed.

Well, good, then, that is done.

He dragged his aching body over to the window. The day was beautiful—just like a painting: cerulean blue skies with white puffs of clouds. The only sign it had been raining for the past three days was the unusual number of puddles, which sparkled like diamonds under the late day sun.

He'd done the right thing by her, no matter how much his words must have hurt her.

Bringing home a wife—even one as amusing as the woman only one thin door away—wouldn't assuage his pain for long. She was vibrant and loving and would want and deserve an entire man, not a walking shell. She would come to hate him once the novelty wore off; bed sport would only hold a woman like that for so long.

She would need love, and as much as he might want to give it to her, he was no longer capable of the emotion. He knew what it was and could see it around him, but he was like a deaf man who'd once known music. What he knew now was only the echo.

In any event, the deed had been done; after what she'd just heard, she'd never want to look at him again, and he couldn't blame her.

It was all for the best. Even if he'd not lost the ability to love, only an idiot would believe that loving yet another person was a cure for losing everyone he'd ever loved.

No. Loving another person just meant you had one more person to lose.

Chapter 22

Exham Castle, Devon
Eight Weeks Later

"*Here* you are. Why am I not surprised?"

Eva glanced up from the new mare their teaser stallion, Liberty, was currently courting, to Tommy, who was dressed as impeccably as usual. His coat sported no fewer than a dozen capes, his cravat was a white froth with some gemstone winking in its folds, and his high-crowned beaver tilted at just the right angle on his glossy brown locks.

Eva was exhausted just looking at him; it must have taken him two hours to reach such perfection.

"Hallo, Tommy, I'll be just a minute."

"How is she?" he asked, gesturing toward her newest acquisition.

"Just grand, isn't she, James?"

"Aye, my lord. She's a right 'un."

Tommy's eyes narrowed when he looked at the big groom, whom he'd not warmed to—a feeling he made no effort to hide.

Eva bit back the flare of irritation Tommy's treatment of her best friend always sparked and turned to James, who was holding the mare's lead. "Give me a moment."

"Yes, my lady." He bowed his head and humbly pulled his forelock, his lips pulled into a slight smirk that made Eva want to kick

him. He'd been behaving like a groveling servant ever since Tommy
had raked him over a few weeks earlier, reminding him—most insuf-
ferably—who was mistress and who was servant.

James had taken the bollocking in stride, as a good servant does.
But Eva and Tommy had had their first major row; the outcome of
which—five days of silence—demonstrated that both parties were
equally stubborn.

Although James hadn't said as much, Eva was left in no doubt of
his feelings toward her betrothed of only two weeks.

Speaking of her betrothed . . . Eva met Tommy at the paddock
gate and let him kiss her cheek.

"Eva, darling?"

"Hmmm?" She blinked up at him, her mind on the maiden mare
James had just led away, rather than the six feet of male loveliness in
front of her.

"I'm off to town to do some shopping for your stepmamma."
Eva could well imagine what was on that list: all items for the up-
coming wedding. Mia didn't care that the wedding was taking place
in the castle chapel with only family and a handful of friends attending. After Catherine's even smaller gathering earlier this year, Mia
seemed determined to make the most of this opportunity. Eva would
have thought her stepmamma's recent delivery of a healthy son a few
weeks earlier would have slowed the older woman down. But, no,
Mia was a bundle of irrepressible energy and had focused her attention on making the most of this wedding.

Eva smiled up at Tommy. "Well, that's good, then. I hope you
have a fine time," she finished lamely. She hoped she was successful
at hiding her relief that he was spending his day elsewhere. The way
he hovered around her was . . . suffocating, so a day free of said hovering would be a pleasant relief.

His perfect mask stayed in place, but she saw a glint of something
not so placid behind the surface. "Are you sure you won't join us—
Melissa and me?"

Eva perked up. "Melissa is going with you? That's good." Eva

needed to thank her sister for taking on so much of what she was beginning to think of as "the Tommy Burden." She'd hoped he would
be less demanding of her time when she'd accepted his third offer of
marriage, but he seemed to become worse with each passing day.

"There's room for one more," he said with a cajoling smile.

"I can't. But the two of you enjoy yourselves."

He frowned. "I've gone in just about every day this past week—
and Mel always accompanies me. You haven't joined me one time,
Eva. Don't you think people will think it odd that you cannot accompany your betrothed on a shopping excursion meant for your
own wedding?"

She felt a familiar flare of irritation. "I don't care if it appears odd,
Tommy. That's another thing you seem to have conveniently forgotten about me since we've become engaged: my lack of interest in
what other people think of me."

"I didn't mean it that way." He was beginning to look a bit
strained around the eyes, so Eva curbed her temper. "You know I
had to use every bit of persuasion with Sir Walter to let me have
Clancy here, rather than bring the mares to him. So—" She trailed
off, hoping he would put the pieces together.

"But I thought that was a few days off?"

"We want to clear the book before he gets here. You know how
busy this time of year is. We've not only got four maidens to manage,
but all of Papa's stock, as well. James will need me as he'll be teaching the other lads to work with Liberty so they'll be able to take over
teasing in the future."

Liberty was their only teaser stallion—a horse who would spend
time with each mare daily to determine when the mare came into estrus. Once the time was right, the breeding stallion would then be
brought in to cover the mare. Proper teasing could not be rushed and
it was labor-intensive, requiring expert handling of both teaser and
mare.

Eva took off her hat and whacked it with her hand. "What I'd
really like are *two* teasers, but of course we are nowhere near justify-

ing such an expense. My father always allows his tenants to bring in mares around now, so we've got a whole list of those, too." She mashed her hat back down on her head. "This is the end of breeding season, Tommy, and we are at our busiest."

His full lips were compressed in a scowl. "And it's necessary for you to be part of the activities?"

"Activities? You mean in the breeding shed?"

"Yes, Eva, that is what I meant. Will you, along with a handful of men, be present when a stallion mounts and covers mares?"

Eva had a genuine laugh at his prudery. "Lord, Tommy, how else did you think I proposed to breed horses?"

"I certainly did not expect you to be part of every aspect, no matter how low or vulgar."

"You cannot be in earnest." But his stern expression told her otherwise. Eva sighed. "You *know* this is the time of year that horses engage in their, er, low, vulgar activities. James and I have been run ragged managing the construction of the new breeding shed these past few weeks, as well as renting a stud, purchasing mares, and a dozen other things. To be honest, I would rather not have begun our operations here only to have to remove them to Byer Court, but—" She broke off, sure he didn't need *that* decision explained to him. "In any event, the mares are here and it's already late in the season. I can't wait until after I arrive at my new home."

He held up a hand. "Very well, you needn't get worked up about it."

"Oh? *Needn't* I? Because I feel as though we've discussed this subject repeatedly over the past two weeks since we agreed to marry. I began all this"—she waved to the area around them, to encompass her new breeding operation—"before I accepted your proposal, so it should come as no surprise to you what I am doing. And before I accepted your proposal, I made it very clear what my plans were and you made no demur. But every day you take issue more and more with what I am doing."

The muscles in his jaws flexed, his elegant nostrils flaring. "Yes, you are quite correct. I suppose I just thought your interest in the matter would be more, er, well, at a remove." He grimaced. "Blast it, Eva, you know what I'm saying. How many women do you think spend time not only selecting their own bloodstock but then participating in shoeing, training, and *breeding* them?"

She crossed her arms and tilted her head as she stared up at him. "I don't know, Tommy. I've not taken a survey on the subject. How many?"

He pulled off his hat and shoved his hand through his hair, mussing the perfection. "For the life of me I cannot think what possessed your father to grant you such liberties. I'm sure that when Gabe arrives, he will agree with what I'm saying and—"

"First of all, I am guessing you would be very, very off in your estimation if you think Gabe would be anything but supportive. And second, I don't care *what* his—or anyone else's—opinion is."

"Not even mine?"

Eva ignored his question and asked one of her own. "Tell me, Tommy," she asked in a low, silky tone. "Is it your intention to curtail my unseemly activities once I am your chattel under the law?"

"That is unkind, Eva. You know I would do no such thing."

"I don't know anything of the sort. And this conversation has brought my ignorance home to me. You are *ashamed* of what I am doing. You are worried how it shall look to your tenants, your relations, your friends—whomever else you consider important."

"Someone needs to be concerned. You show no interest in anyone's opinions other than your bloody stable boy's."

"You can*not* be jealous of James."

"Don't be foolish," he snapped. "Just because I find your behavior inappropriate does *not* mean I am jealous of a *stable lad*."

"Well. I'm relieved to hear it. By the by, James is not a stable lad. He's been a groom for several years already and he is now the manager of my small operation—an operation which employs four people at this point and I hope will have five times that number in a few years." Eva took a step toward him, angrier than she'd been since that

day at the Greedy Vicar Inn—the day when Tommy had gone to
Godric and forced him into a conversation that he'd had no right to
initiate.

*A conversation that you weren't supposed to hear, but one that certainly
set you straight, didn't it?*

Eva ignored the dig and focused on the matter at hand. "If you
have an issue with my behavior, now is a very good time to bring it
up, Tommy. The wedding is still days away," she reminded him.
"There is plenty of time to change our minds."

Tommy's face softened as he looked down at her, and then he
cupped her jaw with one large, kid-sheathed hand. It was all Eva
could do not to yank herself away. "I'm sorry, Eva. You are correct.
I'm behaving like a fool. It's just—well, it seems you have more interest in spending time in the stables than you do with me."

That was true, but it was hardly politic to admit it. Instead she
brought up another matter she wanted to keep at the forefront of his
mind. "You promised me that you had no expectations, Tommy.
You promised me we would enter this marriage as friends."

He swallowed hard enough for her to hear it. "I know I did. And
you are right to bring me up short for my behavior. I'm afraid I can't
stop myself from wanting more of you, and yet you will hardly let me
touch you—even to kiss you."

Which was exactly what she was afraid of. It was also *exactly* what
her stepmamma—the only one other than Eva and Tommy who
knew the truth—had warned her.

"You just kissed me a moment ago," Eva said, although she
knew what he meant.

"I want you properly," he murmured in a low, hungry voice. He
lowered his mouth slowly enough over hers that she could have easily moved away. But she didn't. Not because she wanted him, but
because it would soon be her duty to submit to kisses and more.

His mouth was soft and warm, his lips fuller than Godric's. The
sensation of his body pressing gently against hers was not unpleasant.
When it appeared he would not open his mouth, she flicked her

tongue between his lips. His body momentarily stiffened, but he didn't push her away. Instead, he pulled her closer.

His hand slid around her head and his fingers bunched in her hair as he took control of the kiss. The sensation was pleasant and he was most certainly skilled at making love with his mouth. Eva softened against him, allowing him to take her in his arms, his body big and hard and warm against hers, his arms taut with the barely leashed passion she evidently ignited in him.

The cool mental observation made her release his broad shoulders, which she'd grasped without realizing, and squirm in his grasp.

He let go and stepped back, his pupils huge, his pale cheeks flushed with arousal rather than irritation for a change. He stroked his thumb over her chin, his lids heavy and desire rolling off him in waves.

"By God, you are—" He stopped and shook his head, his expression a complex blend of lust, frustration, and more besides.

Eva slid her hand around his wrist—elegantly sheathed in buttersoft leather—and gave him a squeeze before setting his hand aside.

"There, we've kissed, Tommy. And when we are man and wife, I will give you all of myself that I have to give—my body and my friendship, but not, I hope you know, my love. I am not insensible to the sacrifice you are making—no," she said when he opened his mouth to demur, "it *is* a sacrifice, and I am grateful. But I will not lie to you about the way I feel. Nor will I give up this." She waved her hand to encompass everything around them. "If you do not want a horse breeding operation at Byer Court, you should tell me now."

His lips curved and he suddenly resembled the old Tommy—the one before this fiasco with Godric—her brother's amusing friend whom she'd enjoyed teasing about his rotten taste in cattle and impeccable taste in clothing. "Don't be silly, Eva—I can hardly wait to see the stables restored to their prior glory, and it will be a perfect place to house all the horses even you can accumulate." He raised her hands to his mouth and lowered his head to kiss her fingers, and then stopped. "Lord! What happened here?"

She glanced at the crushed fingernail he was eying with horror; it was torn and there was a purple bruise blooming beneath the nail.

"I was helping shoe Hedge Bird and my hand got in the way."

Tommy grimaced—whether at her confession, or the name of her mare, she wasn't sure. Once again a glimmer of irritation showed. "You'd better wear gloves or you'll have hands like hooves, darling." He smiled while he chided her, but Eva knew he was appalled. "And I really wish you'd let the lads handle jobs of that sort. If James isn't sufficient you can always—"

"James is more than sufficient." She tugged her hands away.

He opened his mouth, as if he might argue, but then smiled and said, "Come, walk me to my chariot."

A snug little curricle waited in the courtyard, her sister already ensconced on the richly padded seat. The chestnuts were fine high-steppers that had more looks than wind: her husband-to-be was not, lamentably, much of a judge of horseflesh.

"Hallo, Mel."

"Hallo, Eva." Her younger sister smiled, her gaze questioning as it flickered across Eva's person, lingering on her face and then moving to Tommy's. A frown marred her smooth forehead and Eva wondered if her lips looked as recently kissed as Tommy's. While not censorious, Mel's glance was still not approving. Mel had never been so judgmental before, but ever since Eva had come back from her *adventure*, she'd felt as if there was a gulf separating her and her sister.

"Thank you for going with Tommy to take care of the things that *I* should be handling," she said.

Mel's golden, freckled cheeks—so much a bane to her sister—darkened slightly. "I'm happy to do it."

"And she is excellent company and keeps me from choosing the wrong color ribbon and endangering my life with the marchioness," Tommy added with a valiant smile. "Oh, I say—did I remember the list, Mel?"

Her sister's rather serious expression lighted and Eva was momentarily stunned by her sudden . . . *animation*.

Mel held up a piece of paper filled with writing. "You took it as far as the great hall, where you proceeded to leave it on one of the side tables. Fortunately for you, I am not such a scatterbrain."

He laid a hand over his heart. "What would I do without you? Likely be skewered on a spit by your delightful stepmamma."

Mel giggled and Tommy put a boot that was as highly polished as glass on the footboard and gracefully swung himself up. He smiled down at Eva, a perfect London dandy. "Can I bring you anything from town?"

She glanced back at Mel, who was still glowing from the brief exchange, her eyes riveted to Tommy. "Er, surprise me," Eva said, stepping back from the carriage.

He touched the brim of his high-crowned hat and then nodded. "Let 'em go, Boothe."

Mel shrieked with delight and seized her bonnet as the elegant curricle leapt away. Eva watched until the carriage disappeared beyond a stand of elms, and then she turned and slowly walked toward the sprawling stables, her brain awhirl. But the sight that met her when she entered the spacious breeding shed put all other thoughts from her mind.

James, Willy, Scott, and Michael, her four employees, as well as Mr. Brewster, were ready and waiting. But that wasn't all. To her immense surprise, her father and stepmamma were standing just outside the big enclosure.

Eva stared. "What are you doing here?"

Mia grinned. "We come bearing gifts." She gestured to a rude, squat table that stood at a safe distance. On it were a bottle of champagne and several glasses. "We've come to toast the new endeavor in the time-honored fashion: with champagne."

"Oh," Eva said, flushing with pleasure. "Why, thank you. But we've not got Clancy yet, so it'll only be old Liberty and two nurse mares. Besides," Eva added, "I thought champagne was for ships?"

Mia shrugged. "Ships? Horses? Champagne is perfect for all occasions."

"Well, as long as you don't try breaking the bottle over Liberty's hindquarters."

There was laughter all around as her father opened the bottle with a loud pop and then poured pale golden liquid into each glass. It was Mia who handed the glasses around.

"To a fruitful breeding season, the first of many to come," the marquess said, raising his glass.

"To a fruitful season," they all echoed, followed by the clinking of glasses.

Once they'd each had their drink, James and Willy went off to fetch the horses, and the other two lads readied the room for its first inhabitants, not that everything wasn't already prepared.

"You've done a good job here," the marquess said, his look encompassing both Eva and Mr. Brewster.

Brewster nodded. "Aye, Master, but 'tis her ladyship and James what did it all."

Mia squeezed Eva's shoulder and pulled her aside as her father spoke with his stable master. "I'm so happy for you, Eva. This is what you've always wanted, isn't it?"

She met Mia's huge green eyes and saw the reservations hidden there.

"Yes, Mamma, this is exactly what I wanted."

"Exactly? I hope so, Eva. I want all three of you girls to be happy."

Eva looked away from her too-knowing eyes, and then remembered the pair of brown eyes she'd just left in the courtyard. "Mel is certainly getting into the spirit of the preparations—I almost feel bad this ceremony will be so small and unimpressive."

Mia smiled, but it was not her normal, joyous expression. "Yes, she is enjoying going on these jaunts, for now, at least."

Eva frowned. "What do you mean? For now?"

"Are you ready, my dear?" the marquess asked, coming up alongside his wife.

"I am, darling."

"Oh, are you two leaving?" Eva asked, unable to keep the disappointment from her voice. "I thought you might stay?"

Mia grinned. "Oh, the last thing I want is to give your father any more ideas about breeding."

Eva's jaw dropped.

The marquess sighed heavily and shook his head. "I can see I shall have to start muzzling you before I let you leave the house."

Naturally, Mia laughed and the two wandered off, her stepmother leaning her head against her husband's shoulder, the marquess holding her tight with one arm, as if he would never let her go. Eva had to swallow several times as she watched them depart. What must it be like to be so obviously in love, even after many years?

Somehow, she suspected she would never know the answer to that question.

Godric had been staring at the same letter for some time. So he turned it over and picked up the next, continuing the farce that he was actually doing work. Not that anyone was watching or cared *what* he was doing. Hell, not even *he* cared that he was sitting in the vast cavern of a library going over correspondence. Alone.

Oh, stop or you shall make me weep.

Godric felt nauseated by his self-pity—an emotion he was generally able to restrain until the wee hours of the morning. But tonight not even Andrew was here, and he was having difficulty keeping the feeling in check. He'd become accustomed to the younger man's presence at meals and in the evening, the times of the day when solitude was least desirable.

You didn't have to be here alone, the annoying resident in his skull pointed out.

That was true. He'd been invited to the same dinner party as Andrew—the one at Lord Ingram's, the second largest landowner in the area after Godric. When he'd been a younger man, Godric had often got up to mischief with Baron Ingram's sons, all of whom were long married with families of their own.

Godric was the area's most eligible bachelor—albeit long in the tooth—and his neighbor, Lady Ingram, seemed to labor under some compulsion to throw young females at him. The last dinner party he'd attended, three weeks earlier, had been horrifying. At least for Godric.

Andrew, however, had enjoyed himself thoroughly, even though, as a penniless young male, he was not particularly marketable. Still, that didn't seem to matter to the younger man as he appeared to have no eye to marriage.

But just because Andrew did not wish to marry did not mean he didn't wish to socialize.

So Godric was alone tonight. How pitiful had he become, sighing heavily over the loss of his nineteen-year-old dinner companion?

He put aside the letter in his hand—a bill for candles—and picked up the familiar spidery handwriting of his grandfather.

The letter was not long, and a cursory reading of it was sufficient to communicate the thrust of its content: When was Godric coming to the ducal seat?

This was the third letter in six weeks, and Godric had responded to the prior two with vague references to repairs, obligations, et cetera. But he would have to go soon; it was cruel to keep the old man waiting. He set down the letter and went to pour himself another brandy—the third, and final—for the evening.

When he'd first come home to Cross Hall, he'd waited until Andrew went to bed each night to drink himself into unconsciousness.

After two weeks of that, Andrew had come to him, his sensitive face frightened and concerned. "You look ill, my lord. *Very* ill. I feel it would be remiss of me not to recommend a physician."

"Your recommendation is duly noted. Consider yourself relieved of any responsibility," he'd said, and then continued on his path of self-destruction for another week.

Once again Andrew had come to him, but this time he'd come to Godric's bedchamber with a quack in tow.

Godric had placidly submitted to the requisite poking, prodding, and inevitable bleeding, after which he'd informed the physician—privately—that it would be worth his life if he said anything to Andrew other than the words, "His lordship is as healthy as a horse."

Rather than return to his downward spiral, Godric had taken the opportunity to examine himself and his future. If he wanted to put a period to his existence, surely he could do so more efficiently and expeditiously than drinking himself to death?

After a visit to his weapons room, which Andrew had explored a mere thirty minutes after arriving at Cross Hall, Godric decided he did not quite wish to shoot himself yet, no matter that he now had a bewildering array of options. The boy had organized and repaired every one of a remarkable number of antique weapons there.

And so Godric had gotten on with the business of living, albeit without any joy. But then, he'd given up expecting any joy in his life a year and a half ago, hadn't he?

As receptive as several local widows and more than a few tavern wenches had been to his attentions, Godric had lost the energy to carouse—in any form or fashion. The extent of his gaming was the occasional hand of cards with Andrew, which was generally enough to exterminate all interest in gambling of any sort.

He slept as poorly as ever, although when he closed his eyes now, he increasingly saw a different face from those that had haunted him for so long. The expression he saw on Eva's face was one he'd only ever seen in his mind's eye: that of a young woman who'd been thoroughly crushed by what Godric had cruelly and knowingly—but not truthfully—said within her hearing.

It was for the best.

That was a refrain he told himself often. For most of the day it either was not necessary to repeat in his head, or if he *did* need to remind himself, the five words functioned quite well as a thought suppressant. But at night, when he was sitting in his large, empty house, alone, the five words were less than compelling.

He took a sip of brandy and allowed himself to revel in his pain, like a dog rolling in its own excrement. He hadn't seen Eva again after delivering his killing words. She'd dined in her room and then left the following morning with her father and Byer.

It was for the best.

After all, what had he wanted? A last glimpse of her angry or tearstained face? Or had he wanted her to do what she seemed so very good at: to fight for those she cared about—the way she'd fought for her brother and his wife?

But that's assuming that she ever cared about you, isn't it, Godric?

Godric laughed softly; as if he'd done anything to earn her respect, friendship, or even affection.

They might have been approaching something nearing friendship, but he'd killed that as thoroughly as one squashed a wasp.

He couldn't stop seeing her just as she'd looked when he and Andrew had encountered her on that road. She'd strolled away from near death—rejecting the offer of a ride, incidentally—and a nest of bandits, with nothing more than an empty pistol. Surely there could not be another woman in England like her?

But just as surely there were things even her fearless soul chose not to confront; or at least there were things she deemed not worth confronting, and Godric was one of them.

He took another miserly sip from his glass, put on the spectacles he needed for reading—smiling at the thought of how Eva would taunt his decrepitude if she saw him, and just as quickly banishing the thought from his mind—and then turned back to the pile of correspondence and picked up another letter.

He was halfway through the first paragraph when it occurred to him to look at the salutation: it wasn't to him, it was to Andrew.

Andrew sorted and opened the mail and laid it out for him. Obviously he'd put this private letter in the wrong pile.

Godric was about to place it aside, no matter how intriguing the contents of that first paragraph might have looked, when he caught sight of the cramped signature at the bottom of the page.

What the devil? His hand tightened and the crinkling sound of paper brought him back to himself.

You are an honorable man; honorable men do not read other men's letters.

That was true.

Godric stared at the page he'd turned facedown and was about to release. How could he not read a letter from this person?

Very easily. You put it aside and move on to the next.

So he did that. And then commenced to read half a page of the new letter without seeing it before tossing it aside and again snatching up Andrew's personal correspondence.

Oh, Godric.

Godric slammed the door on the chiding voice. And then he read Andrew's letter.

Chapter 23

"That's a good girl," Eva crooned into Meadow's twitching ears as she waited for James to return with Liberty.

Meadow was the last of the mares Mr. Brewster had brought in. They'd placed her one-year-old in the nearest stall as the proximity of stablemates kept mares—even experienced, older mares like Meadow—calmer.

Their operation appeared to be off to an excellent start and her staff of three were doing excellent work, but Eva was rather anxious about tomorrow.

The stud she was bringing in, Clancy, was both wildly expensive and young. He'd be servicing four maidens—young mares who'd never been covered—and Eva suspected the procedure would be far different from that of the past few days.

Liberty, her father's stud, was a stallion the marquess had won many years ago, along with the rest of some bankrupted lord's stables. Her father had ridden Liberty quite regularly until the stallion had strained a tendon and never really been one hundred percent afterward.

A few years ago the marquess had spoken of selling Liberty, and Eva had exerted all her efforts to keep the old boy. He was a remarkably placid stallion who always seemed to have an expression of amusement.

Her father had given in but had wanted to geld him. Again she'd begged. And when James's father had weighed in—arguing Liberty could earn back his fodder and more as a stud—the old stallion had been left intact. His offspring littered the area and were a fine infusion into the rural bloodlines.

Indeed, her father had kept several of Liberty's foals, such as one by Meadow, which now pulled the gig Mel liked to use.

Thinking of Mel made Eva recall her sister's odd behavior these past few weeks. Eva might be oblivious when it came to other people's emotions, but she would wager a pony that her sister was sweet on Tommy.

Eva wasn't sure what to think about that. On the one hand, it was probably normal—after all, Mel knew so few handsome young men. Although she was seventeen, she'd not gone away to school as Eva and Catherine had.

While it was true that Mel was active in their small neighborhood, her sister had been exposed to few men—certainly none with Tommy's fine looks and polish. Unlike Eva, who hated social functions, Mel enjoyed attending the local assemblies, but she was so very, very shy that she rarely danced or—

"Here then, my lady. You awake?"

Eva's head whipped up at the sound of James's voice, and she recalled that she was hanging on to poor Meadow, who likely was wondering what was wrong with her.

"I'm awake, James. Go ahead and bring him in." Eva didn't bother with a twitch for the older mare. Instead she'd clipped a lead to her halter and stood off to one side as James brought Liberty closer.

They watched as Liberty and Meadow got reacquainted. The old stallion was a gentleman and didn't rush broodmares, even ones he knew as well as Meadow.

"Are you sure you don't want one of the lads here to help?" James asked with a huge yawn as Liberty politely sniffed Meadow's raised tail.

Predictably, Eva yawned, too. "I'd rather not pull them away from their tasks, but what do you think?"

James eyed the two older horses, who seemed to be having a quiet conversation like friendly old acquaintances. "We shouldn't make a habit of it, but I think we can let the lads be."

She cut him a wry look. "That wouldn't be because you have something you want to say to me, would it?"

James gave her an innocent look, but she wasn't persuaded.

"I saw you hovering around earlier when Lord Byer came to the office." By *office* she meant the stall where they kept the papers that had already started to add up, even though they'd only acquired the four mares. But they'd also managed Liberty this season, and she'd kept notes for all his mares, too. Organization was not her strong suit, but she was trying her hardest. "Tell me, how much of my conversation with his lordship did you hear?"

"I'd *never* Evasdrop."

Meadow's tail began to twitch and James gave Liberty more slack to allow the stallion to nuzzle the mare's hindquarters.

Eva had to smirk at his use of Gabe's term for her habit of lurking. "I *saw* you, James."

James opened his mouth to answer, but then Meadow squatted and leaned back into the stallion, her position eager and receptive. Even a smallish stallion like Liberty could be dangerous to humans while covering a mare, so Eva didn't distract James.

Liberty was experienced at his job and Meadow remained stationary, so the entire procedure took less than a minute.

Once the stallion uncoupled, James walked him back and forth in the large area to cool down while Eva guided Meadow into the adjacent stall, where her colt was eagerly awaiting her.

At first, she'd been unhappy that her father and Brewster had cautioned against taking on more than four broodmares this year, but now she was grateful. It would be hectic enough to move this many animals, especially when she wasn't quite sure what the facilities at her new husband's house would be like.

Husband.

Eva swallowed hard and latched the stall gate, leaving mother and child together and coming around to where James was stroking Liberty's neck and crooning calming words.

"Hopefully that calmed him some for tomorrow."

"Oh, aye," James said in his silly *horse* voice. "Liberty's a lad, ain'tcha?" he asked the stallion, who indeed appeared to nod his head. "And you're kind to all the lasses, hmmm?" Again the horse seemed to know what he was asking.

"So, back to the question I asked you earlier," Eva said. "What did you hear today and why were you frowning?"

James gave her a lofty look. "It ain't for a groom to tell his mistress such things, my lady."

"It ain't for a groom to abandon his mistress on the Great North Road, either," she reminded him. "But that didn't stop you."

A red stain crept up his neck and colored his face. "You're never going to forget that, are you?"

"No." Eva didn't tell him *why* she wouldn't forget it—that it had been the best five days of her life. That was all he needed, to think he'd actually *helped* her have a fine adventure. "But you know I forgive you," she added, even though she'd already told him that.

He glanced at her. "Was he cruel to you?" Eva heard the raw concern in his voice.

Although she'd been back for weeks, she'd never spoken of Visel—even to James. Instead, they'd gone back to their pre-kidnapping relationship as if the whole affair had never happened.

"No, he wasn't cruel."

They led Liberty back to his stall.

"You know when we were at that inn—the, er, Greedy Vicar?"

As if Eva would ever forget. "Yes?"

"I met that lad who was with Lord Visel—the one with the blunderbuss—Andrew. He was a nice bloke," James added awkwardly as he removed the stallion's halter and scratched behind his ears.

Eva grinned as she imagined Andrew's reaction to James's misidentification of his precious firearm. "Andrew is nice. What did he have to say?"

James cut her an odd sideways look and shrugged. "Oh, not much. Just that Visel wasn't such a bad sort."

"No, it turned out he wasn't," she admitted.

James nodded and patted Liberty on the hindquarters, his mind obviously elsewhere. The stallion nickered softly and moved eagerly toward Scott, who was waiting with the curry brush and oats.

They didn't speak as they walked back to their office/stall; Eva wondered what it was that James was trying—and failing—to say

"The more I think on it, the more I think we should save Moon-spinner for last," she said, the thought popping into her head suddenly. "I'd like to get her in with Liberty at least one more time, preferably two." She dropped into a rickety cast-off chair and recorded Meadow's information in the book.

When James didn't answer she looked up to find him leaning against the wall.

"Have you seen his lordship's house—what's it called?" James asked the question without looking at her, and she could hear the worry in his voice.

"Byer Park. And, no, I've never seen it, but his lordship says the stables are almost as big as these, just in need of repair." She shrugged. "I daresay we'll have our work cut out for us, but that won't be so bad, will it?"

Still he didn't look at her.

"What is it?" she asked tiredly.

"I don't think you should marry him."

Eva wasn't surprised by James's words. They'd been getting into each other's business since the first time she'd sneaked into the stables and met him shoveling out a stall. For years they'd gone on nighttime journeys that would have turned their parents' hair white if they'd known.

Eva had gotten drunk her first time with James, although he'd done so far earlier without her; she'd seen her first horse race and mill with him; and they'd sneaked off to the traveling fair that came through each year, visiting a tent that had given Eva demonstrations of the sorts of things Mia had told her about.

James knew secrets about her that even Gabriel didn't know. And Eva knew things about him that could put his life in jeopardy.

So, no, James's words weren't surprising. What *was* surprising was that it had taken him so long to say anything.

"Are you saying this just because you heard us argue? You know I argue with everyone, James."

He nodded rather too quickly.

"We're just finding our way with each other. I'm sure we'll disagree less after we are married."

"Hmmph." James looked about as convinced as he sounded.

Eva chewed her lip; what else could she tell him? That she didn't think she should marry Tommy, either? That he was her only choice when it came to a husband? That there was no time to find another? That it wouldn't matter if there was time, because whoever it was still wouldn't be the *right* person?

She wanted to scream and smash things, but she simply had no will left to struggle.

This wasn't about her or Tommy, this was about the child. Bringing a fatherless child into the world was condemning it to a life of slights and ignominy. She had no choice.

"You just got off wrong-footed with Tommy, James. He thinks you should have stopped me from kidnapping, er, *him*." Eva couldn't even say his name.

James snorted. "That just shows how little he knows you, don't it, my lady?"

"He won't always be so stiff around you. Things will get better."

"It's not me I'm worried about, my lady. It's the way he is with *you*."

"What? He loves me and says he has done for years. He's the one getting the short end of the bargain." James had no idea just how true her words were.

"I think—I think … ah, bugger!" He grimaced. "Sorry, my lady."

"If you apologize to me again for using stable language in a stable, I'm going to hit you, James Brewster. Now, just what do you think? I wouldn't ask if I didn't want to hear it. Besides, I've got nobody else to talk to. The only person who understands me even half as well as you is the marchioness, and she's got her own concerns." Besides, this was one problem there was no solution for. Godric didn't want children, especially with her, and Eva was pregnant with his child. End of story—at least with *him*.

Tommy, on the other hand, had been almost delighted to accept another man's child if it meant she would marry him. When she'd asked whether he could *love* another man's child—especially *that* man's child—he'd been hurt.

"I will love him or her as my very own." He'd given her his familiar wry grin. "You must have heard that I'm not my father's blood son, so I cannot—nor do I—set any store in such things. A child is a child. And yours will be mine and we shall raise him or her together—with the rest of our children."

That had given her pause, but she'd kept her mouth shut—plenty of time to consider having more children later. What mattered was that she'd believed him; he *would* love her child as if it were his own. But the days since their engagement had brought out some other parts of his character she'd not expected. She believed Tommy hadn't expected those reactions, either.

"I think you shouldn't rush into things, my lady. That's all," James said, his words breaking into her thoughts.

"For pity's sake, James, I can't wait—I don't have the time."

There, she'd said it. Well, it had been simmering for days. Besides, she'd pretty much told James about every other important event in her life. Why would this be any different?

"You've got nothin' but time. His lordship has set you up right pretty here, and by next year we—"

"I *must* marry now."

He frowned, his forehead furrowing. "You ain't sayin'—"

"Yes."

He dropped his head back against the wall with a loud *thunk*, his big hands covering his face. "Does the marquess—"

"I haven't told him."

He dropped his hands. "Aye, I suppose he'd likely have Lord Byer out at dawn somewhere."

She pulled a face at him. "Don't be such a dimwit, James. It's not his."

His jaw sagged and he sputtered, "*What?*"

"Why are you acting so stunned?"

"I ain't acting!"

Eva sighed.

"If it ain't the tulip's, er, that is, his lordship's," he corrected when Eva glared, "then why are you marrying *him*? Lord." His eyes became even rounder. "Does Byer even *know*?"

"Of course he knows! What kind of villain do you think I am?"

He raised his hands. "All right, all right. That was a dumb question."

"You're full of them."

He didn't argue. Instead he said, "What about Lord Visel?"

The name clanged in the small room. Eva gave him a grim look. "What about him?"

James's face was practically glowing. "Does *he* know? Well, I mean, he's the da, right?"

Eva put her hands on her hips. "So?"

James made a choked, gurgling sound. "It's just, er, he *said* he wanted to marry you—I mean, I can't believe he would shab off. He seemed like an honorable man."

"Oh, he's honorable, all right."

"Well then, what in the name of Pete is the trouble?"

"He never said he *wanted* to marry me, you dunce."

James scratched his head, opened his mouth, and then closed it. "Out with it."

"Er, well, wouldn't he *have* to marry you now? I mean, given the circumstances?"

She gave a bitter laugh. "Oh, I'm sure he'd willingly fall on his sword."

"I don't understand."

"It's not complicated: Visel would be forced to marry me, while Tommy *wants* to marry me."

"Um, er, but—" He looked as though he was in actual pain.

"*What?*"

"Well, aren't *you* being forced to marry Lord Byer?"

Eva blinked, trying to recall whether those were the words she had used. "Perhaps I phrased it incorrectly."

"Can I just ask one more question without you punchin' me or yelling?"

"Have I punched you or yelled at you, yet?"

"No, that's why I asked. I figure it's past time as you rarely restrain yourself this long."

She rolled her eyes. "Ask."

"Who do *you* want to marry, my lady?"

It was Eva's turn to stare with her mouth open.

"It's just—well, you must have *liked* him? Lord Visel, that is," James said after a long moment.

"What makes you think that?"

He gave her an openly confused look. "Well—you wouldn't have—" He jerked his head toward the stalls they'd just left.

"I wouldn't have—what? What is wrong with you? Have you developed some sort of palsy? What are you trying to say? For God's sake, just *say* it."

He gave an agonized groan. "I'm tryin' to say you wouldn't have done *that*—you know, like Liberty and Meadow just did—if you'd not liked him. Er, at least a little. Maybe?" Whatever he saw on her face was making him look slightly hysterical.

"I can't believe you just compared me to a broodmare."

He threw his hands in the air. "Well, I'm sorry, my lady, but all of this just makes no sense."

"It makes perfect sense when you know that he didn't want me—and he *especially* did not want a child with me, a *mad* child."

"No! He never said such a thing?" James, who generally looked like a harmless, oversized stuffed bear, suddenly resembled the real animal, terrifying and fierce.

"He did." Her wretched voice broke on the last word and he took a step toward her, his expression one of horror.

"Oh, here then, my lady, I didn't mean to make you cry."

She reached up and felt her wet cheeks. "Oh, bollocks. Now look what you've done."

Eva flung herself at him and he awkwardly patted her shoulder. "Here now, my lady. It'll be all right, then." He sounded just as he had crooning to Liberty, and she laughed.

He held her out at arm's length and stared down at her with terrorized confusion. "What?"

"You're talking to me the same way you did to Liberty." She gave another watery chuckle, followed by a big sniff as she wiped off her face.

But James wasn't to be distracted by humor. "This just ain't right, my lady. It ain't."

"I know," she said softly. "It's awful. But there is nothing I can do about it, is there?"

James stared at her for a long, unhappy moment, and then said, "No, my lady, it seems there is not."

Chapter 24

It was a few days after Eva's argument with Tommy and her discussion with James that Eva discovered the reason behind Melissa's censorious looks. But by that time, the house was too full and hectic to talk privately.

The guests had all arrived in a cluster earlier in the afternoon.

First her sister Catherine and her silent, wheelchair-bound husband, Douglas, along with his five year-old son, Philip.

Next came Gabriel, Dru, and Samir.

And finally, filling two large coaches, were Baron Ramsay and his ever increasing family.

The only close relatives who wouldn't be coming were Eva's uncle Cian and her grandfather, the Duke of Carlisle, both of whom were traveling on the Continent.

While Eva was only marginally acquainted with Lord and Lady Ramsay, she knew their pestersome twin sons, Lucien and Richard, all too well from family visits over the past five or six years.

The boys were two years her junior and had attached themselves to Eva and Gabe like limpets every summer. Eva had been jealous of Gabe's time and didn't like sharing her brother's company during his all-too-short visits. As a result, she'd considered the twins interlopers and treated them dreadfully. Not that they'd ever appeared to notice or mind.

She'd not seen them since last summer and was stunned when they'd hopped out of one of the coaches earlier. Gone were the scruffy, irritating children she remembered, and in their place were two identical, tall, gorgeous young gentleman. The transformation was miraculous.

As for Gabe? Well, this was the first time she'd ever avoided his company. From the brief look she'd had of him when he'd arrived, he was eager to corner and grill her about her marriage to his best friend—not a subject she cared to discuss with anyone these days.

Dinner was a lively affair as everyone—with the exception of Eva, and Catherine's husband, Salford—noisily reacquainted themselves as if they'd not seen each other in years, rather than just weeks.

Her family knew how busy she'd been with her new venture, so they seemed unconcerned by her unusual silence. As for Baron Salford, well, the man perpetually dwelled in the doldrums, so nobody took notice of his behavior, either.

Eva was not skilled when it came to reading other people's emotions, but even an impervious lump like herself could see all the looks Mel gave Tommy when she believed nobody else was watching. Eva was disgusted with herself for not noticing before.

For his part, Tommy's eyes drifted all too often to Eva, although the expression in them was not that of a man in love.

More and more Eva saw hints of concern when he looked at her. Oh, he still *wanted* her, but she was beginning to doubt whether what he felt for her was love or just a need to possess her. Eva had seen that look before. Although she'd been slighted by men like Visel and his cronies during her Season, she'd had her share of—unwanted—admirers.

There'd been a wealthy, widowed viscount in his forties who'd gazed at Eva with a rapt expression during the few dances she'd been unable to avoid him. He'd examined her the way a collector might look at a painting or the way Eva looked at a perfectly matched pair of grays: with covetousness. There'd been a darker component to his stare that left her uneasy. She now knew that what she'd felt was his physical interest in her. Specifically, his interest in breeding her. The revulsion she'd felt at the time had caused her to be even ruder than usual, and the rejected lord had joined in taunting her the next time she saw him.

Other, less repellant suitors had shown themselves, every last one of them either interested in the money she would bring to the marriage, or her person.

Tommy's expression, she realized with lamentable tardiness, was not unlike that viscount's look, although he did not make her recoil at the thought of his touch. But neither did she look forward to her wedding night, or all the nights after.

Later, after dinner, when everyone was absorbed in a deafening game of charades in one of the sitting rooms, Eva slipped away unnoticed, hoping to get some much-needed sleep.

But she spent the night staring at the ceiling, her mind a whirling, endless jumble.

She rose before dawn and headed to the stables, excitement for the day pushing aside her worries about Mel and Tommy.

"Good morning, my lady." James was bright-eyed and bushy-tailed, his grin telling her he was as excited as she to get on with business.

"How is he?" she asked, even though she could guess the answer.

"Fit as a fiddle and as fine as a fivepence."

Eva snorted.

Eva had chosen Clancy as stud for two reasons: one, she knew Sir Walter would accommodate her in a way that most other stud owners would not and allow her to bring Clancy to her mares, rather than the other way around.

The second, far more important reason was that Clancy's bloodlines could be traced back to the three royal progenitors of all thoroughbreds. He'd raced three seasons, and though he'd never been a champion, he possessed impressive speed on the flat and a winning track record.

In any event, she was very happy to have Clancy for five days, and had every intention of using him each day, regardless of how much the foolish wedding preparations threatened to interfere.

Mr. Brewster believed three covers, one a day for three days, was as good as you could expect before the mare went past the peak of her breeding cycle. After that you not only risked diminishing returns, but also injury to the stud from an unreceptive mare.

It took four of them to handle Clancy, especially when it came to Eva's newest mare, Moonspinner, who was a skittish maiden. Although she'd been teased twice daily for a week, she clearly found Clancy a different kettle of fish from sweet old Liberty.

They'd just finished having Liberty jump her, wearing a shield to keep him from actually servicing her, when Gabriel joined them.

Eva raised her eyebrows. "My, you're up early."

He grinned, his white teeth flashing in his tanned, handsome face. "I wanted to get a look at your operation. Besides, Mother said you only had four working for you, so I thought you might appreciate an extra hand."

"Especially an experienced one."

Gabe had helped with the breeding of his father's horses in Oran and knew what he was about when it came to cattle. He quickly stripped off his coat and rolled up his sleeves as James brought in Clancy.

"Good morning, James. I'm here to offer an extra set of hands," Gabe said.

"It's good to have you, sir. Want to take charge of the assist?" James offered with a cocky smile.

Gabriel laughed. "No, I'll leave that in younger hands."

By *assist* James meant the person responsible for adjusting Clancy's breeding organ if the stud required assistance entering the mare. Eva wondered with amusement if she should tell Tommy that *she'd* assisted today.

Gabe caught her eye and gestured toward Scott, who looked nervous about holding the twitch and had gripped poor Moonspinner's lip rather awkwardly.

"Let Mr. Marlington take that, Scott, and watch how he uses it—he's got a light touch."

Scott nodded, clearly eager to pass the burden.

Not only would Eva never want to have horses injure each other during a covering, but she really did not want to abuse Sir Walter's trust in her, so she'd taken extra precautions with each of the mares and Clancy.

Moonspinner's back feet were bagged in thick felt booties on the off chance she kicked back at Clancy. James had strapped a thick blanket to her neck, back, and withers, in case Clancy became overly amorous.

Horse breeding, as Eva knew from years of loitering around the stables—and particularly after the last few busy days—could sometimes be a violent event. The actual time the stud spent servicing the mare was brief and generally trouble-free. It was the few seconds before and after the mount that were the most critical, and everyone worked in silence.

Luckily, Clancy was skilled at his job and finished with a minimum of thrashing and, remarkably, after he'd dismounted, there were no visible signs on either horse that hundreds of pounds of living flesh had just come together.

Eva didn't realize she'd broken a sweat—she'd been holding Moonspinner's front leg—until Gabriel tossed her a clean cloth.

"Thank you," she said, wiping her brow. "It was good to have you here," she added, meaning it.

"She's a lovely mare," Gabriel said, stroking the quivering flesh of the mare's arched neck. "You chose well, Evil."

She grinned at him as the lads led both horses off.

"Are you done here—at least for the time being?" Gabe asked. "Did you eat breakfast?"

"No, I had to get down here."

"Of course you did." He snatched off her hat and ruffled her hair. "Perhaps we might go find a bite to eat."

Eva grabbed back her hat. "Just let me record Moonspinner's information and I'll go with you." She hesitated and looked down at herself. She was wearing her usual outfit—buckskins, boots, and coat—and most of her family members were accustomed to it by now. But there were guests. "Unless you think I should go clean up first?"

Gabriel laughed. "Who is this woman and what has she done with my sister?"

She smacked his shoulder as they walked to the small office.

Eva pulled off her gloves—which she'd actually remembered this morning—and entered the information with comments and observations about both horses and the manner and duration of the covering. With any luck, Clancy had done the trick and Moonspinner would produce her first foal in eleven months.

When she'd finished, they left the stables side by side.

"So, what did you think?" Eva asked, even though she didn't want to seem as if she *needed* his approval.

"I'm impressed, but not surprised. I believe you have an aptitude for horses in general. I think you will do well." Coming from Gabe, whose father had owned *thousands* of horses, that was a compliment, indeed.

"You might want to tell that to Tommy," she said. He frowned and Eva flicked a dismissive hand. "Forget I said that. Instead, why don't you tell me what it is you've come to say to me? And whose message are you delivering?"

Gabe smiled. "That obvious, am I?"

"You wouldn't be awake and about this early without a reason. I just don't know what your reason's name is."

He sighed. "Nobody said anything, but I can see how it is between you and Tommy."

Eva groaned.

"What?" he asked, opening the door for her before following her into the cool dimness of the castle. "Are you two fighting?"

"Not exactly."

He took her by the arm and stopped her, turning her toward him. "What were you thinking, accepting him, Eva?"

She jerked her arm away. "Lord, Gabe, don't beat around the bush."

"I won't, because it seems everyone else is. Have you all gone mad? Even Mother has nothing to say on the matter."

She began walking. "There is nothing to say."

"You don't love him."

She cut him a sneering look. "Look who is suddenly the expert on love."

"Don't try to start a fight—I won't be distracted."

This time it was Eva who stopped, shoved Gabe into an alcove and whispered, "I've discovered something dreadful."

His eyes widened. "Good Lord, what, Eva?"

She swallowed and bought herself a few more seconds while she made sure she wanted to say the words out loud. "I think Mel may be developing a, er, tendre for Tommy."

Gabriel's face shifted into an expression of disbelief, and then he laughed.

"What is *wrong* with you?" Eva demanded. "That's not funny. It's—it's, well, I don't know quite what it is, but if it is true, it certainly isn't good."

"Mel has been wild over Tommy for years, Eva. Trust *you* to only notice it now."

It was her turn to stare wide-eyed. "You're jesting."

"Ask anyone."

"Does Tommy know?"

"Lord, I don't know. I should think he does—he's not oblivious, like some people." Eva smacked him. "Besides, it's not as if Mel has taken pains to hide her infatuation—well, other than from you."

Eva ignored the dig. "How did I not see this?"

He cocked an eyebrow at her.

"Fine, never mind, I know. I'm Evablivious." Yet another word Gabe had invented for her. "I never really believed it until this moment," she said, "but it's true—I really am oblivious."

He chuckled and grabbed her in a huge hug that lifted her off her feet. "You are, but we love you anyway."

"Put me down, you savage," she muttered. "I've always believed Mel and I were close. Why didn't she say anything to me?"

He lowered her feet to the ground but did not release her, resting his hands on her shoulders and staring down at her.

"I daresay she didn't want to embarrass herself, Eva."

"I don't understand—how?"

"Well, Tommy made his admiration for you obvious—disgustingly so, in my opinion, as did every other single male under fifty who wandered within your radius—while Mel is—" He chewed the inside of his cheek.

"Mel is *what*? Why can none of you ever finish a thought without prodding?"

Gabe ignored her question. "Mel possesses neither your beauty nor your rather magnetic personality."

"I'll give you beauty, because I can't avoid it in the mirror—but *magnetic personality*? Ha! You were with me all Season. The only thing I seem to *magnetically* attract is taunting and abuse."

He shook his head. "You are, indeed, oblivious. But that is a topic for another day—or eon. Right now I want to know more about your discovery of Mel's feelings for Tommy. Is that the reason for your distant behavior toward him?"

"Well, that's part of it," she said, not completely untruthfully. "How can I marry a man my own sister is in love with?"

Gabriel grimaced with distaste. "When you put it that way . . ."

"What other way is there?"

"I don't know. You should talk to Mother about such things— you know she revels in opportunities to spout wisdom."

She punched his arm. "Show more respect."

"Ow." He rubbed his arm, his eyes speculative. "I know what you mean about Mel, but, Eva, you can't make Tommy fall out of love with you and *into* love with her. People simply love whom they love; there is nothing you can do to change it."

She wanted to tell him she understood that all too well. Instead, she said, "I realize that, Gabe. But I also don't have to marry the man my sister has been mad about for what—five?—" Gabe nodded and she groaned. "Ugh, five years of unrequited love? How horrid. If I were Mel, I would have stabbed *me* while I slept years ago."

Gabe laughed. "Well, I suppose we should all be grateful you've never fallen in unrequited love. I'll advise everyone to lock their doors, just in case."

Eva forced herself to laugh, rather than throwing her arms around him and wailing out the truth.

"If it makes you feel any better, Eva, Tommy has felt the same way about *you* for almost as long. So although you might be dashing one person's hopes, you're fulfilling another's."

She cut him a dark look. "Why didn't you tell me this before?"

"Because I didn't want to." He dodged Eva's fist this time. "Honestly? I wasn't quite sure of his feelings for you until you were out of the schoolroom—likely because he knew I would hurt him if he showed any overt intention of taking you as his child bride." He opened the door to the breakfast room and Eva stopped in the open doorway to stare at the assemblage.

"Look who I brought to join us two-legged creatures," Gabriel announced to a smattering of laughter.

Eva glanced at her father, who was looking at her apparel—scuffed top boots, scarred leather breeches, and dusty coats—with a pained expression.

Her stepmother laid her hand over the marquess's and he sighed and turned back to his plate. Mia grinned and winked, and Eva mouthed the words, *thank you.*

When Eva risked a look at Tommy, she saw he seemed just as displeased as her father.

She also saw that Mel sat beside him, immaculately coiffed and dressed, her adoring gaze riveted on the man who was aiming his own—censorious—gaze at Eva.

Eva stumbled and Gabe had to steady her. "All right, Evil?" he whispered, his expression worried.

Eva couldn't answer. All she could do was look at the other two sides of this ridiculous triangle she was in. Lord, what a bloody farce. How was it that she, who had always avoided romantic or emotional imbroglios, now seemed to be enmeshed in one?

That hardly matters now, does it?

No, she realized quite suddenly—it didn't. What mattered was that she figure out a way to extricate herself. And soon.

Chapter 25

With less than two days until the wedding, Eva knew she did not have time to devise the perfect speech—not that she would have been capable of doing so had she been given a hundred years. She knew that the longer she dragged her heels, the worse it would be. Still, she simply could not seem to make herself pull Tommy aside and have *The Discussion*.

Even she—as oblivious as she was—was not insensible to the embarrassing mess she had created for her family. In forty-eight hours many of her relatives and some of their closest friends would be sitting in the family chapel expecting a wedding; a wedding she simply could not go through with.

Of course, not going through with it meant there was only one choice for her: She would have to confess the truth to her father, and then go away somewhere to have her child. And afterward she would have to turn the baby over to some family to raise—people who would be well paid to treat the child decently, although they might not ever learn to love it. The notion left her feeling empty and ill.

"Bugger and blast and bloody damn," she hissed under her breath as she strode toward Mia's apartments. Her stepmother had sent a message down to the stables, and the tenor of it had been such that Eva knew she could not ignore it. So she'd handed over the rest

of the day's duties—not much was left—to James and then went to
her room and submitted to her new maid's attentions.

The poor woman barely spoke as she untangled Eva's unruly
mop, her pensive gaze settling on Eva's unfashionably sunburnt face—
the result of always forgetting a hat—and moving on to her battered
and scuffed hands.

Based on the woman's—Philpot's—horrified reaction, she wouldn't
be with Eva long.

Eva was now dressed in one of her least vomitous morning
gowns and hurrying to arrive at the appointed time, cursing herself all
the way that she'd not made the time to speak to Tommy. So now
she would have to don the gown Mia would want her to try on,
rather than tell her the truth.

Ugh.

She rapped on the door and then entered Mia's lair.

"Ah! There you are."

Mia grinned up at her from a settee, where she was reclining
with her son, David, and watching her youngest daughter play.

"Eva!" Julia jumped up and thundered across the room with a
clumsiness she could not have inherited from either parent, but must
have somehow gotten from Eva.

Eva caught her up and spun her around, inadvertently clipping a
bronze statue and sending it clattering on the wood flooring. She grimaced and set her half-sister down before turning to face the music.

But Mia was smiling. Of course she was. Eva had never seen her
stepmamma angry, and never wanted to.

"And how is young Master David?" Eva asked, peering at her
newest sibling, who was snoring softly.

"He's far better behaved than Jibril was at this age," Mia said,
nodding to the nursemaid who was sitting in the window seat with
her mending. "Can you take him to bed, Mary. I'm afraid we have
some serious wedding-gown business to attend to."

Once the maid was gone Mia turned to her daughter and smiled.

"Julia asked to be here when you tried on your bridal gown, didn't you, darling?"

Julia nodded her reddish-brown head vigorously and Eva grinned and squeezed her hand. "All right, I guess I'd better get about it."

Mia's maid helped her into the gown, which even she had to admit was lovely. It was an unusual shade of blue and she couldn't help noticing it made her eyes appear larger and more violet.

Knowing Eva's hatred of lace and ribbons and furbelows, the gown had a simple, snug, low-cut satin bodice with a narrow skirt that had a single thin petticoat. The only adornment was a wide blue velvet ribbon that ran beneath her bosom. The effect was to accentuate her figure, which she knew was a much admired hourglass. For all that she generally found her overlarge breasts an inconvenience, they looked rather nice sitting within the tight bodice, the tops of them creamy swells.

When she came out into Mia's sitting room, both her step-mamma's and Julia's mouths formed comical O's.

Eva glanced down and saw a flush spreading across her prominently displayed breasts.

"Mamma, Eva looks like a princess."

Eva's face was scorching.

Mia nodded. "Yes, darling, she does." To Eva she said, "I know your father has a necklace that belonged to your mother. It is a pretty thing—a thin silver chain with a beautifully wrought, lacy cross. I will have him send it to your room. Whether you wear it on your wedding day or not, I think you should have it."

Eva nodded, unable to speak for fear of blubbering. Trust her stepmamma to think of her predecessor, a scorned woman who'd been dead for almost a decade and a half and whom nobody mourned. She swallowed convulsively and turned so abruptly she stepped on her hem and heard a familiar ripping sound. She stopped and shook her head, disgusted and disheartened and simply tired of being her.

She heard a rustle behind her and the soft click of a door before

Mia came up and took her into an embrace. They were almost the same size, but her stepmother always felt so much more substantial.

"It is only a small tear, Eva, and easily fixed."

Eva nodded. "Thank you for thinking about my mother." She swallowed yet again, but could not stop the tears from trickling down her cheeks. Lord, but she'd been a watering pot these past weeks.

"I know she would have been very proud of you—of all three of you. Any mother would."

"Do you think I am like her? Will I *become* like her?" The words were so soft, Eva could barely hear them.

Mia's arms tightened. "I think you are like Eva—and there is nobody else in the world quite like you. I cannot speak for your mother—other than looks, and you are indeed as she was, one of the great beauties of your age. But I can speak for your father. You are not him, Eva. While you have some of his characteristics—your loyalty, your intense need for privacy, and your keen, ready wit—there are many parts of you that are your own. This *life* you are living is your own—not your mother's or your father's. For years Adam hid from his life. And your mother, Veronica? She was driven to end hers by demons none of us can ever know."

Mia turned Eva around, which was when Eva realized there were tears in her brilliant green eyes. Her stepmamma was truly lovely, but her face bore evidence of a life that had not always been easy. Strands of white mingled with her vibrant copper hair. And the lines around her eyes were deep—laughter and sadness combined—the signs of a life thoroughly lived.

"I hope you live your life to the fullest, Eva. I believe your mother would have had the same hope for you." And then she took Eva in her arms and let her cry. Great wracking sobs for the woman she had never known.

"I beg your pardon, Eva, but have you gone quite *mad*?"

Eva cocked an eyebrow at Tommy's question, aware of the exact instant when he realized what he'd just said.

"Ah, *Christ!*" He scrubbed a bare, pale, exquisitely manicured hand over his face, pressing his fingers against his eyelids. "I didn't mean that, Eva."

"I know you didn't." Lord, but she was exhausted. She'd wanted to go back to bed after speaking with Mia, but she owed Tommy— and everyone else—better.

So, here she was, engaging in a second emotional episode before dinnertime.

She grabbed Tommy's wrist and pulled his punishing fingers off their delicate targets. "What has happened to us? We never used to spend every moment together arguing."

He sighed and leaned back against the bookshelf.

He'd been in the library with Mel when she'd gone looking for him. The two had been sitting at a respectable distance across from each other, on their own settees, each cradling an open book in their lap. The atmosphere in the room had been . . . Well, Eva didn't know what it had been—charged perhaps. When Eva apologized for interrupting and had asked Tommy for a moment, Mel had almost fled from the room.

"Is aught amiss with Mel?" she asked now, as they both strove to recover from what she'd just told him: that she would not marry him.

"Hmm?" His eyes were on the monstrous fireplace, which even at this time of year needed to be kept burning to banish the chill from a room made entirely of stone.

"Mel—she looked, well, I don't know, but not the way she usually does."

Tommy gave a dismissive shrug. "There is nothing wrong that I've noticed."

Eva was beginning to think Tommy was about as observant as she was.

"Is there no way I can change your mind about this, Eva?"

"No." Eva felt a pang about her bald rejection, but his reaction was not as bad as she'd thought. As she looked at him, she thought he did not appear entirely surprised or disappointed. Surely he, too, must have noticed they were not the people they'd once been. Although he would not admit it, Eva thought he might actually be relieved. He'd gotten the *thing* he'd spent years longing for—her—and it had proved quite different in reality. Eva's old nurse used to frighten them all with the adage, "Be careful what you wish for, or you might get it."

"I shall come with you to tell your parents," he said, standing straight, his hands automatically moving to check his cravat, his coat.

"I appreciate the offer, Tommy. But I'd rather speak to them by myself. I shall tell them you stand ready if they want you."

"Are you quite sure?" he asked yet again.

"Yes." This time she could see his relief. She stood on her toes and kissed his cheek. "Sorry about all this, old man."

He nodded, obviously still poleaxed.

Eva left the library and leaned against the door for a moment. Well, there was that, done. Only another dozen or so people to go.

"Eva?"

She saw Dru headed her way and grinned. "I received your message, by the way."

Dru flushed. "I'm sorry I sent Gabe to do my dirty work, but I knew he couldn't stay away from the stables, so I thought he'd be the advance force." Dru slid her arms around Eva and gave her a firm embrace before releasing her.

Gabriel's wife was tall, a good six inches taller than Eva, and she possessed a voluptuous body she'd always disliked. But since marrying Eva's brother, Dru now wore more flattering—and more revealing—gowns. She was blooming and clearly a woman in love.

"Do you have a moment?" Dru asked.

Did she? Well, what was the rush? She could upset the apple cart at any time. "Of course, for you—always."

"Shall we pop into the library?"

Eva grimaced. "Er, perhaps not. Why don't you come with me to my chambers? I need to get out of this"—she pulled at her skirt—"and go to the stables *one last time today*." She put emphasis on those words so she'd not have to argue yet again. But she should have known Dru would not nag her. At least not in her current love-softened state.

On the way up to her rooms Dru talked about Samir, Gabe's young son, who'd only this year come to England from Oran. "He is a wonderful little boy, Eva, and your brother is so good with him."

"That doesn't surprise me," Eva said, opening the door to her bedchamber and ushering Dru inside. "He's always been excellent with young children."

Dru flushed with pleasure—a compliment for her spouse clearly touched her heart. Well, in that, at least, they were of the same mind.

As Eva stripped off her clothing Dru wandered the room, her motions self-consciously casual, and Eva knew what she was waiting for.

"I just ended the betrothal," Eva said.

Dru whirled around. "Oh, did you? I'm so glad!" Eva laughed and Dru flushed. "I'm sorry, that sounded terrible. You know that Gabe and I would love nothing more than for our best friends to marry. But not if—"

"Not if they aren't in love," Eva finished for her.

Dru nodded and flopped down into a chair. "Well, thank heaven that is over. Now I can quit avoiding you and enjoy my time here."

"Drusilla!"

"What?"

"How can you enjoy yourself at a broken betrothal?"

Dru shrugged. "Well, it's better than a broken marriage."

Eva supposed that was true. "Do you know how miserable it is going to be, breaking this news to everyone? Especially my parents?"

"Oh, pooh. You and Tommy were the only two who didn't seem to understand what was happening. I've been here less than a day, and the two of you are so nervous around each other it is enough to make a person jump out of their skin."

Well, Eva couldn't disagree with that.

Dru pushed herself out of the chair. "I can't wait to tell Gabriel."

Eva rolled her eyes. "Please, don't let me keep you from your enjoyment."

Dru laughed. "Lady Exley has planned a picnic down by the folly—will you come?"

"Is that *now*? I thought it was tomorrow."

"Yes, *Eva*. It is now—the time of day when people generally have picnics."

"Yes," she said absently, wondering if her parents had already gone down to the lake. "I'll be down after a while."

"See that you are," Dru scolded. "If I know you, you're likely to hide in the stables all day."

Eva blushed at her friend's accurate prediction. "I'll be there," she promised again.

After Dru left, Eva headed to her father's study. Mia was likely already marshalling the troops, but her father was not as enthusiastically social, so she wasn't surprised when she found him seated at his desk, his head bent as he studied something closely.

"Father?"

He glanced up, his powerful gaze hidden by the glint from the spectacles he wore to read. Eva thought it was odd how adding that covering to his gaze somehow made him appear almost vulnerable.

Unfortunately, he removed the spectacles and set them on the desk. "Come in and sit."

Eva clasped her hands in front of her. "Actually, Papa, what I have to say won't take long."

"You've ended your betrothal to Byer."

Eva stomped her foot before she could stop herself, the action drawing her father's gaze to her filthy top boots. "How is it that everyone knows?"

"Does *everyone* know?"

"Well, Dru suspected, and I don't think Tommy was surprised, either."

The marquess made that low humming sound that always made Eva think of a big jungle cat, not that she'd ever seen a real one.

"I suppose I should make some sort of announcement?"

"Oh?"

Eva sighed heavily. "Unless you would rather do it."

"Rather?" he repeated.

"Would you please make some sort of announcement, Father?"

He nodded slowly, picked up his glasses, and put them back on. "Was that all?"

Eva would never be able to predict what the man would do if she lived to be a thousand years old. "Yes, Father."

He turned back to studying whatever it was that so engrossed him, and Eva fled.

It seemed she was not destined to get far, however, as Mel appeared to be hovering near the grand staircase, with Lord Ramsay's twin sons standing on either side of her like matching bookends. Matching *gorgeous* bookends. Good God! Could they be only seventeen?

Her sister, perhaps a year older than the young men, was looking exceedingly pretty and flushed.

Well, this was interesting.

"Oh, Dru said you were talking to Papa," Mel said.

"Hallo, Eva," the twin not wearing spectacles—Lucien—said, his confident smirk telling her that he was already aware of his effect on the opposite sex.

"Lucien." She turned to his twin, an almost mirror image but for his glasses and less-than-impeccable clothing. "Richard, good to see you both."

"Eva," Richard said with a slight nod.

"We couldn't miss seeing you get leg-shackled, could we, Rich?"

Lucien's silent brother merely regarded Eva thoughtfully through his ridiculously thick lenses.

Eva knew Lucien had been infatuated with her two summers

earlier, because he'd followed her around like a faithful puppy, eventually asking her if she'd wait until he was older to marry him.

Richard had not suffered a similar infatuation. Indeed, Eva had always found Richard's aloof, level gaze a bit off-putting and far too mature for his years. As much as Lucien liked to believe he was a polished Corinthian, he still smacked of callow youth.

And Richard? Well, Eva wasn't sure what he smacked of. Although he was slenderer and less eye-catching—for lack of a better word—than his more gregarious brother, he possessed a quiet appeal that was all his own.

"Did you need me for something?" Eva asked her sister, ignoring Lucien's amused smirk and Richard's cool regard.

Mel visibly wrenched her eyes from Lucien's tall, blond, godlike figure. "Er, need something?"

Eva was stunned; how could her sister lurch from one infatuation with a pretty face to another in a span of hours? Was that all it took for Mel to fall in love?

Besides, for her money, Richard, with his dark-horse ways, was the far more attractive brother.

Eva blinked—why was she even thinking about any of this? She snapped her fingers in front of Mel's face to wake her from her trance.

Mel scowled. "What?"

"I'm going down to the stables and then heading over to the picnic." She turned and headed down the stairs.

"We'll go with you," Lucien declared.

Eva stopped abruptly and Lucien and Mel, who were right behind her, almost piled on top of her.

Richard, she couldn't help noticing, hadn't followed. Instead, he was leaning against the wall, watching them all with a superior smirk.

Mel was gazing at Lucien, and Lucien was gazing at Eva.

It was preposterous! Her sister had already begun to form an attachment to a person of the male sex who could not stop looking at Eva. Was it some conscious choice that put Mel in that position?

Eva didn't have the time or energy to think about it. "I'd rather meet you both at the lake."

Lucien went from looking like an arrogant pink of the *ton* to a kicked puppy in a heartbeat, Mel looked confused, but Richard looked even more sardonic.

Eva rolled her eyes and all but sprinted toward the stables, leaving the three to get on with whatever it was they were up to.

The truth was that nothing critical awaited her, but she simply needed to be somewhere quiet to think. James had taken Clancy back to the squire's, and Eva felt as if a weight were lifted from her now that the expensive stud was back with his owner.

The stables were blessedly quiet and Eva slumped into the old chair she had liberated from the piles of moldy furniture that were stored in the east wing of the castle.

She tipped her head back and closed her eyes, waiting for the familiar sounds and smells of the stables to soothe the chaos in her head. She was weak and exhausted just now, but she'd made the correct decision.

Whether Mel actually did love Tommy—or whether she was now in love with Lucien—Eva had still done the right thing.

The question of the child she was carrying—and how she would manage—would not be an easy one to resolve. But then, Eva didn't have to make every difficult decision all on one day.

If you'd told your father, he would have made your decision for you.

Eva knew that was true. If she'd told her father she was carrying Godric's child, he would have felt duty bound to tell the earl—and then perhaps shoot or stab him.

She knew her father had meant what he'd said at the inn—the decision *was* hers. But she also knew the marquess would want her to think very, very carefully before closing off what he would see as the best decision for the child.

And he was right. All along, Eva had been thinking only of the best choice for *her*. All she'd done was think about the humiliation of marrying a man who didn't want her child. But that was selfish; she knew she would need to give a great deal of thought to the matter before ruling out Godric.

Yes, it would be a humiliating marriage and one devoid of even the little friendship they'd had before she'd become pregnant. She could marry him to give her child a home, but she could not forgive him. And she would need to spend her life guarding her child against his dislike and fear.

"Ah, Lady Eva—there you are."

Her head whipped up. "James—what are you doing here? I thought I told you to take the day off after returning Clancy."

"Well, I was going to," James said, twisting his hat in his hands, "but then I met a gentleman at Sir Walter's who'd come to talk to the squire about a stud he had to sell."

Eva perked up. "Oh?"

"Yes, quite remarkable, really, from the Godolphin line and an overall fifth."

Eva just as quickly unperked. "Lord, James, such a stud is far beyond our touch. Far beyond Sir Walter's, as well."

James nodded vigorously. "I know, I know, but the gent who owned him is proper dipped and in need of quick funds."

"How much are we talking about?"

The figure James mentioned made her jaw drop.

"There must be something wrong with him?"

"Sir Walter seems to think he's solid."

"Huh. Well, I hope you got his name and direction so we can—"

"He's *here*," James whispered noisily, as if the man were outside the stall.

"In the stables?"

"No, he's waitin' in his traveling coach. I told him you might wish to know more." He shrugged.

"Well, what are you waiting for?" Eva stood. "I'll go change into proper clothing and you can—What?" she said, when James shook his head.

"He's got a problem and can't easily leave his carriage—not without some help."

"Goodness. Injured like Salford, you mean?"

James hesitated and then said, "Er, yes, my lady, he's not so different in some ways."

"Ah, well, if you don't think this would offend his sensibilities?" She gestured toward her clothing.

"Oh no, my lady. He seems the sort to understand."

Eva somehow doubted that, but her desire to talk to the man overrode her already limited patience. "Let's go meet him—if he is expecting me, that is?"

"I believe he'd like to see you, my lady."

Out in the courtyard stood a magnificent traveling coach, certainly not that of a man strapped for money. But who knew? Some men believed they had to puff off their wealth in order to attract more.

"Let's see what he has to offer before we start asking questions," Eva whispered as they crossed the courtyard. "I'd like to take my measure of him."

"I think that's a brilliant idea," James said with almost giddy enthusiasm.

She grinned up at him as they approached the carriage, which had heavily draped windows. "I think you're more excited about this than I am."

"I think it's safe to say that's true," James muttered as a slight servant in handsome navy and silver livery hopped off the back and came forward to open the door.

Just then Eva realized she'd never asked the gentleman's name. She turned to James to ask him just as he lurched down and seized her around the waist. "Up you go, my lady."

"James! What—"

"Hush," he advised in the same voice he used to soothe horses. "It'll be just fine. I hope."

Too stunned to struggle, Eva found herself being lowered gently onto a plush seat in the darkened interior, the door snapping shut a second later, and the carriage lurching forward.

"James!" she shouted, but the well-sprung coach was barreling down the drive.

Eva scrabbled at the heavy drapes that covered the window and ripped them open, exposing the interior of the carriage to the light.

She turned to the other occupant and gasped. *"You!"*

Chapter 26

Godric thought it was touch and go as to whether she would decide to remove the gag on his mouth.

Her eyes were like midnight-blue marbles and her fine, slender nostrils flared just like the beasts she so adored.

"You!"

Godric couldn't help grinning around the gag, even though he suspected it was a gruesome—and likely provoking—sight.

She used her fist to pound on the roof of the carriage. "James! *James!* You'd better turn this carriage around or you shall be very, very sorry." Nothing but the sound of carriage wheels and wind answered her threat and she turned back to Godric.

"This was your idea, wasn't it? Some sort of perverse punishment."

Godric waited for her anger to settle down. And also for her to remove the bloody gag.

She opened her mouth—no doubt to scold—and then seemed to notice his appearance.

"What's going on?" she asked, her dark blue gaze flickering over his wrinkled coat, flattened, stained cravat, and the rope tied around his boots at the ankles.

When her gaze made the journey back up again, he saw her delicious lips were parted in shock. Godric raised both his eyebrows, the only form of communication left to him.

She closed her mouth and swallowed, her eyebrows lowering as if she were faced with a particularly sticky and unappealing problem.

Finally—*finally*, she huffed out an irritated sigh and leaned forward, her hands going to the thick cotton cloth they'd tied behind his head. The position brought them close, intimately close, but she refused to meet his gaze while her hands worked blind behind him.

Godric thought she'd lost weight, the lovely bones of her face more pronounced, making her look like a tragedienne. She pulled off the gag and tossed it to the floor.

"Thank you," he said, his voice hoarse from the yelling he'd done—the first day.

"Turn sideways and I'll untie your wrists."

He obliged.

"Lord. Who tied these?" she asked in a tone of respect mingled with horror.

Godric snorted. "Andrew."

"No! Really? Why, they are—"

"Works of art?" he suggested, not bothering to keep the irony out of his voice.

"Yes, actually. Move over, I'll need to sit behind you. This might take a while."

Godric scooted to the far edge of the seat and she lowered herself behind him, her clothing allowing her to move swiftly and easily in the confines of the coach.

Oh yes, he'd noticed her clothing—first thing, actually. He was tired and hungry and sore, but he wasn't blind. Or dead.

"Who would have guessed Andrew possessed such a skill?" she said.

"Certainly not I—at least not until I woke to find myself tied this way."

"Oh. He took you in your sleep?"

"Not sleep," he said shortly.

"Ah." Her fingers tugged and pushed and nudged and he felt perhaps the slightest loosening. "So, Andrew and James."

"Yes."

"Do you think they are the masterminds of the plot, or is there a ringleader?"

"Lord," Godric said, "I hadn't considered that. Who the devil would come up with the idea if not them?"

"I can think of one or two people," she said grimly.

"Please, enlighten me."

"How long have you been in this carriage?" she asked, ignoring his question.

"Since they took me from Cross Hall—three days by my count."

"Hmm, they made good time."

"Ha! It certainly didn't feel like it from where I sit."

She snickered.

"How did they get *you* in here?"

"What? You mean other than James manhandling me?" she sighed. "He told me there was a man in the carriage in desperate need of money who was looking for a buyer for his stud."

Godric laughed.

"I'm glad you think that is amusing."

"It's like luring a baby with sweets."

"Perhaps you would prefer to spend the duration of your time in this carriage with your hands bound?"

"Oh, God, Eva—have mercy. My arms feel about ready to fall off."

"Hmph." But her fingers resumed their labor.

"What do you think is the aim of this abduction?" she asked after a few moments of silent work.

"I should think that was obvious."

Her fingers stopped. "You don't think they are going to try to take us all the way to the border?"

"I have no idea." He hesitated and then said, "I *do* know that your James wrote Andrew to tell him you were engaged to marry—

in a few days, if I recall correctly." *As if the date isn't emblazoned on your brain, Godric.*

"You read Andrew's mail?" she asked in horror.

"Not on purpose." He grimaced. "Hell, that's a lie. He left it in my pile of correspondence and I'd read a quarter of it before I realized it wasn't for me."

"So then you read the rest of it."

"Have your laugh; I'm sure *you've* never invaded anyone's privacy." Again her hands stopped. "Are you actually getting anywhere back there?" he asked.

"Perhaps you wish to untie it yourself," she snapped, falling for his diversionary tactics just like a baby rabbit wandering into a snare. "And what did you mean with your snide reference to invasions of privacy?"

So, not a baby rabbit, after all.

Godric sighed. *Why keep lying? Being in this carriage with her is a bloody gift—even if it feels like ripping a bandage off a still raw wound.*

"I know you were listening at the door in the inn that day."

This time her hands disappeared entirely, as did the warmth of her body. Godric turned to find her back on her seat, her face flaming before she grabbed the drapes and yanked them shut, plunging the carriage back into near darkness.

"Why are you telling me this now?"

"Because I regretted saying the words I said as soon as they left my mouth that day."

"Then why didn't you come to me and apologize?"

He ground his teeth. "Because I thought I was doing the best thing for you—giving you a gift by getting you away from me."

Bitter laugher filled the darkened space. "You have an odd sense of what constitutes a gift, Godric."

"I was a bloody fool, and when I read about your marriage to Byer—well, I behaved like an even bigger fool."

"Explain."

He was grateful for the darkness, because his face must look like a flaming torch. "I did not do well after I returned to Cross Hall. Andrew was concerned for me. He brought in a doctor—"

"Were you ill?"

Was that concern he heard? A glimmer?

"Godric, please don't make me drag this out of you piecemeal."

"I was drinking so that I could sleep; I was drinking so I could forget. I wanted to forget you, Eva."

Small hands landed on his chest and shoved him back against the seat. "Why are you telling me this now? Do you think I'm so stupid as to believe you've had a miraculous turnabout? Who told you, Godric? Is that why you're here? Is this all some elaborate prank?"

Godric inhaled her scent deeply into his lungs. "Told me?" he repeated stupidly.

She shoved him hard enough to make his head smack against the wood above the squabs.

"Ow! Dammit, Eva."

"Who told you?"

"Told me what?"

"Who told you about the child? I will not be lied to and manipulated. You can answer me honestly, or I will open the door and shove you out of the carriage, I give you my word on it."

His heartbeat thundered in his ears and his entire body broke out into a sweat. "Eva, darling, I don't doubt you for an instant, but—"

"Don't call me that," she snapped.

"I'm sorry," he said quickly. "Don't go, Eva," he begged when she began to pull away. "Please, don't go." Braving a broken nose, he leaned toward the dim outline of her face. "Are you pregnant, Eva? With my child?"

She pushed him away in an instant. "This is *my* child, and if this entire farce was concocted to—"

"Eva." To his surprise, she stopped. "I knew *nothing* about any child. You have my word."

"It makes no sense," she said after a long moment, her voice thick. "Why would you say you regret what you did? If you didn't know about the baby, why would you say—"

"Because I love you, Eva. I love you, and I'm a liar. I lied to you that last day and I lied to you on those few, oh-so-precious days we were together." Godric stared into the darkness, desperately wishing she could see him, even though it would expose his shame to her eyes. "Pull back the curtains, Eva."

A moment passed before one of the curtains opened halfway. Her face was tear-streaked and agonized. "I don't understand you," she said, her voice pulsing with pain. "Why would you say such a thing if it wasn't true? I have never, ever felt the way I did for—"

"I said it because I was a coward."

She slumped back against the bench, clearly—and justifiably—overwhelmed by his insane reasoning.

"I told you I had a wife, but I also had a child."

Her eyes opened slowly.

"He died along with his mother. I was too late to save either of them that day. You accused me weeks ago of having the war hysteria. I believe you were right—but not just from years on campaign. I think I became mad from the losses that came so fast, so relentlessly." He cleared his throat and stared up at the roof of the carriage, blinking rapidly. "You would think losing two people at once would cause a single pain, but it doesn't: it's not all of a piece, it is two overwhelmingly huge pains that buffet you ceaselessly. I became lost in my agony and received an injury thanks to my inability to focus. And because I was in the hospital, my family came to see me. And because my family came to see me—"

She crawled onto his lap, straddling him, and wrapped her arms around his body.

"And then it wasn't two deaths I mourned, but nine, Eva."

Nine. Eva tried to imagine losing nine people she loved. That would be everyone; Godric had lost everyone.

He pressed his face against her hair. "I hoped I would die, but I couldn't kill myself—why not die in the cause. But then I made it through the worst battle in the war without a scratch." He gave a hollow, humorless laugh. "And as time passed, the inconceivable happened, I began to get better. What kind of heartless, soulless beast could not only survive such destruction, but begin to thrive?"

Eva had no answer and was bitterly relieved when he did not expect one.

"So I thought I could avenge my family. When that was done, my life would be over, one way or another. But of course you came along and, thank God, foiled my plans." He dug his chin into her shoulder as if to pull her closer, reminding her that the poor man was still bound hand and foot.

"You are like some magnificent, formidable force of nature, Eva, like a comet or a shooting star in human form. I saw what was happening to me as if I were an observer in my own body, watching myself become captivated by your fire."

Eva swallowed with a noisy gulp, her arms tightening until they hurt.

He kissed her jaw, cheek, ear—anything he could reach. "Oh, my love. I thought I could not live through all of it again, Eva. I thought I could not bear having one more person to love. How could I ever want one more person whom I could lose? But when you were gone, I realized that living without you—most especially because of my own idiocy and cowardice—was far worse than the fear of one day losing you."

Eva squeezed him tight, her eyes streaming. "You are no coward, Godric. You are the bravest man I know. And you are the only man I've ever loved." She pulled away just enough to capture his mouth with hers.

He groaned as she assaulted and invaded, tongues and teeth clashing, the taste of copper mixing with salty tears.

Meanwhile . . .
Andrew turned to James as the postilions slowed their teams to a trot. "Give it another listen, will you?"

"It's only been a quarter of an hour," James said.

"Yes, but you said things were sounding, er, rather violent. Perhaps it would be wise to check."

James shifted his considerable bulk and angled his body so he could look around the side of the carriage.

"They've closed the curtains again."

"Is that good, do you think?" Andrew grimaced. "Or did she close them to hide the body?"

James laughed as he sat back.

"I'm pleased you find it amusing, but it is *my* fault he's in there with her."

"It's *my* fault *she's* in there with him," James countered.

"Yes, but she is not in any danger."

James nodded. "Aye, reckon you've got a point there."

"Listen again," Andrew ordered.

"Why don't you?"

Andrew narrowed his eyes and James laughed again, a deep, infectious sound that made Andrew feel inexplicably happy, regardless of their current situation.

"All right, all right," James said, "I won't make you release your grip on the guard. I don't know how you sat up here for so long," he mused as he shifted once again so that he could lay his ear against the roof of the chaise.

"I felt too guilty sitting inside," Andrew admitted, and then lapsed into an anxious silence as he waited for the other man's verdict.

Andrew didn't want to say anything against James's mistress—he liked Lady Eva, after all—but he feared for his employer's health. He'd not even needed to lay his head against the glossy coach to hear her yelling earlier.

She was an exceptionally small woman, but she was fierce—the way some small animals could be ferocious and frightening well beyond their size. Like a weasel. He suspected she wouldn't like that comparison. But still, it was apt.

Andrew believed that he would never forget, if he lived to a hundred, the way she'd taunted Flynn the day of the fight. She'd glared up at the huge highwayman—easily twice her size—and not backed down. If the robber had even twitched a hair, Andrew was certain she wouldn't have hesitated to shoot him. Of course, that day her anger and fury had been used to *protect* Lord Visel, who'd been in no shape to protect himself. Today that anger was likely being used *against* the poor man. And although the earl was conscious this time, he was also bound hand and foot, which left him rather vulnerable, to say the least.

"Well?" he prodded James, unable to bear the suspense.

James cut him a sideways glance and then pulled away and sat back, shrugging his massive shoulders, the action rubbing against Andrew's livery-clad body. "Nothin'. It's quiet in there—well, except . . ."

"Except what? *What?*" Andrew pictured poor Lord Visel writhing on the floor at the spitfire's booted feet.

James scratched his head. "I think I might have heard . . . laughin', maybe?"

"Laughter? That could be good. Couldn't it? I mean, depending on the laugh. Was it, er, happy laughter?" He swallowed. "Or was it of the maniacal variety?"

James shook his head. "I dunno. And it might not have been laughin'. Something, but not yellin'. That's good, right?"

Andrew caught his lower lip in his teeth and worried it, his eyes locked with James's.

"She wouldn't hurt him too much? Not in a permanent way?" he finally asked.

James tilted his head and grimaced. "Permanently? No, likely not permanently."

Andrew groaned.

James shifted on the bench which was clearly too small for his big frame.

"I don't know how you managed to do this all the time," Andrew said, shifting his own arse—much smaller and bonier—on the padded but narrow bench.

"Nah, not all the time. Not even much—just on that trip up north, mainly when I didn't want to ride inside with the two of them." He jerked his thumb back.

Andrew could certainly understand that.

"But you're right," James said, shifting. "I wouldn't want to be a footman."

"Me neither."

James grinned down at him. "I reckon you'd be the smallest footman I've ever seen."

"Very droll."

"Where'd you get such small livery, anyhow? And it looks a bit, er, odd," he added.

"I found it in one of the attics at Cross Hall."

James leaned down and sniffed. "Ah, thought I smelled camphor."

Andrew lifted up a velvet sleeve peppered with bare spots. "It has the look of the Baroque era about it."

"Oh? And when would that be?"

"Late sixteen hundreds."

"Ah, quite an old place, then? How are the stables?"

Andrew shrugged. "I don't know. They're, er, stables."

James clucked his tongue. "Now you see, that's the sort of answer that would get you in trouble with your new mistress."

"*If* I still have a position after this. And if the two of them do what we hope they are going to do." Andrew allowed all his worry to show as he looked up at James. "Were we mad to put them together like this??"

James's mouth pulled up into that crooked smile Andrew found so comforting. "You mean like two ferrets in a sack?"

Andrew gave another moan.

"What time is it?" James asked.

Andrew pulled out the serviceable pocket watch he'd had to purchase after his uncle took his father's watch. "We've still got another hour," he said, returning the watch to its pocket and looking up.

"An hour," James said, his gaze speculative.

"An hour," Andrew agreed, and he turned in the uncomfortable seat, and they watched the countryside pass by in silence.

Chapter 27

It was Godric who drew back from their marathon kiss first. Of course he was also the one in pain—two kinds of pain, now. "Darling?"

"Mmmm?" She kissed his chin, his cheeks, his nose.

He shifted his hips and whimpered. "Pull the curtains shut," he said in a hoarse voice.

She froze.

"Do it, Eva," he repeated, using *that* voice—the one that had always commanded instant obedience from his men. Naturally Eva hesitated just long enough to make him worry it wasn't nearly as effective on women. At least on one woman.

"I'll make you glad you did," he promised.

Honey, it seemed, really was more effective than vinegar, and she quickly reached for the partially opened side drapes and pulled them shut.

"Close that gap in the front ones, too, sweetheart."

He felt her slender body jolt, but she complied.

"Good," he said. "Now take off your breeches—but not your boots," he added swiftly.

"But—"

"Hush, just do it."

"This won't be easy," she complained, but she moved to the back-facing seat and he heard sounds of compliance.

"Nothing worthwhile is easy, darling. Take you, for example."

"Ha! You are quite brave for a man tied hand and foot."

Godric laughed, waiting patiently as he listened to the sounds of struggling, grunting, and the occasional muttered complaint.

"There," she said, her voice rather breathless. "I've got them off."

Godric groaned at the image. "Tell me what you are wearing," he ordered gruffly.

"You really are a naughty old man."

"I know," he agreed. "Tell me."

He heard a heavy sigh and then, "I've got on my coats, but no breeches or, er, smallclothes."

He had to swallow repeatedly to clear his flooded mouth. He *was* a filthy old man.

"And your boots," he rasped.

"Yes, my boots."

"Oh God." He let his head fall back with a painful *thunk*. "I wish I could see you."

"I could open the curtains."

His head whipped up. "Don't you *dare*."

A low, sultry laugh filled the darkened coach.

"Now, untie my ankles."

"You give a lot of orders for a man bound hand and foot."

"Be a good girl, and I'll let you unbutton my breeches when you are done."

He grinned at the sound of boots scrambling on the chaise floor.

"This would have been a lot more comfortable if I'd done it *before* taking off my breeches."

"Mmmm, but I like imagining you just the way you are."

She gave an unladylike snort of derision, but Godric noticed her fingers worked with remarkable swiftness to loosen the knots.

"There," she said.

He shifted on the bench seat and spread his feet, flexing his cramped leg muscles before positioning his arse in the middle of the narrow bench seat.

"My fall, Eva, straddle my thighs and unbutton it."

She had no smart retort for that.

When she lowered herself onto his spread thighs he just about lost consciousness imagining what she looked like. Her hands shook and she fumbled with the buttons.

"I don't want to waste time untying my hands, darling, so you'll have to do all the heavy lifting."

She made a gulping sound, her fingers froze for an instant, and then she resumed her labors. "So," she said in a tone of strangled bravado, "that's how this marriage is going to be?"

Godric laughed; his Eva.

He stopped laughing when she pushed open the flaps of his breeches.

"Push them down a bit, just a—oh, yes, that's good. Now, take—*urgh*." A small, warm hand wrapped around him and he had to bite down on his lower lip to keep from shouting something vulgar.

"You just hush, now," she murmured in a voice that shook, which made her audacity all the more impressive. "I'll take care of the heavy lifting."

Eva marveled at the size and heat and feel of him. She also marveled at the things she could make him say—the way she could make him sound with just the smallest—

"Good God!" he shouted as she squeezed him just the slightest bit.

Eva grinned.

"Now, darling," he said, and it was his turn to have a shaky voice, "if you don't want to humiliate your betrothed . . ."

Eva knew what he wanted—she'd spent the last week watching horses mate, for pity's sake—but it would be something of a trick with his hands still restrained. Still, where there was a will, and all that.

She sat up high on her knees, one hand clutching his shoulder, the other holding him between her legs as she lowered herself slowly over him. Which was when she realized how easy—and rewarding—it was to make him beg.

"Please, Eva." His breath was hot against her chest as his head rested against her.

"Please what, my lord?"

He gave a breathy, demented laugh. "Have mercy, darling. Please, take me inside your body."

His words rocked her to her core and she lowered herself onto him, taking his thick length all in one, long slide.

The noises they made filled the carriage while he filled her, his size momentarily shocking her, the pain of the stretch a familiar, lovely, surprise.

"All right?" he gasped against her throat, and then he laved the exposed skin, humming his pleasure. "Salty."

She swallowed convulsively at the raw desire in his voice, her sheath contracting around him and making them both shudder.

"Ride me, Eva, hard. I want you to use me and—"

His words broke off with a guttural moan as she lifted almost all the way off, and then lowered again, grimacing slightly as he touched some exquisite place deep in her womb, where their child was growing. She tightened at the thought, the pleasure causing his rod to jerk inside her.

Once again he begged. "Please."

Eva responded to his ragged whisper, and she began to post. On the third or fourth stroke she discovered something magical. If she tilted her hips just so, she could rub her—"Oh, Godric!"

After that it was a blur of exquisite friction, raw gasping, and deep, glorious penetration. When Eva began to lose control of her hips, Godric took over, lifting them both off the bench with the force of his thrusts, mashing her head against the roof of the carriage as he drove into her with a savagery that detonated an explosion of pleasure, sending shock waves through her body.

Still he did not stop, pounding her ruthlessly until, "Eva," he hissed against her shuddering body. "I'm going to—"

He grunted and hilted himself, his hips still raised off the bench as he spasmed and jerked and emptied himself deep inside her body.

"Are you asleep?"

"No. Are you?" She shifted slightly, the movement jostling his sensitive, softening prick, which was still inside her.

He kissed and nuzzled the damp, hot skin of her throat. "Darling?"

"Hmm?"

"Are you ever going to untie me?"

Eva laughed. "Perhaps."

Godric grinned, in spite of himself. He lifted his hips suggestively. "Didn't I just earn my freedom?"

"Oh, no. That was all my work, if I recall correctly."

"If you were to release me, I might be able to settle my debt."

"Ohh, that sounds promising. But I think I'd like to hear you beg. Again."

He felt her smiling lips as she nuzzled the sensitive skin beneath his ear.

"Please, my darling, my only love?"

She shivered. "I love hearing you call me that." The humor had gone from her voice, replaced by a fierceness that wrapped around him like a fist.

"I love you," he whispered, and then added, "If you untie me, I can show you how much."

She laughed and slid off him, both of them making interesting noises when they uncoupled.

"All right, you are most persuasive. But first I am putting on my clothing."

"That is an excellent idea," he said. He felt a lingering concern at the back of his mind that the carriage could stop anytime, the door could open, and—

"Where do you think they are taking us?" she asked as the sounds of boots sliding and scuffing filled the coach.

Godric closed his eyes and imagined what she would look like. "I haven't the faintest idea, nor do I care." And then something occurred to him. "But do you need to go back? I know the letter I read"—his face flamed at the admission—"said you were hiring a stud. I know it's the tail end of breeding season. Do you need to get back?"

There was a long pause before she said. "Thank you."

Godric squinted into the darkness, as if squinting would improve comprehension. "Sorry, darling, but what are you thanking me for?"

"For caring about my business."

"Oh. Well, of course I care. I know how much you wanted it."

"And you don't find my interest in breeding and training horses, er, unfeminine?"

Godric grinned. "Believe me, sweetheart, I heartily approve of your interest in breeding of any sort."

Something hit him in the shoulder. "Did you just throw something at me?"

"Yes, my hat. Now, scoot to the other side and turn."

Godric complied and she went back to work on the Byzantine knot.

He recalled something she'd said earlier. "You said you thought the two boys wouldn't have come up with this on their own?"

She snorted. "No. I smell the work of my stepmamma."

Godric's eyebrows shot up. "Really? But I thought she hated me."

"But she *loves* me and wants me to be happy."

"And *I* make you happy?"

"Funny how you can still fish with both hands tied behind your back."

He laughed. "What a shrew you are."

Eva didn't dispute the accusation. "I have to admit," she said, her finger now able to fit between one of the top strands, the one cutting into his forearm, "that I wouldn't be surprised if they were taking us—" Both her words and fingers paused as the carriage began to

slow, the sound of the wheels changing with the change in road surface.

Godric cocked his head; that sounded like cobbles, not road.

"You wouldn't be surprised if what, Eva?" he asked as the carriage rolled to a stop and then dipped with the weight of somebody
jumping off the back.

"I wouldn't be surprised if they were taking us right back to
where we started," she said.

The door opened and her young henchman stood in the opening, his face wearing an amusing expression of terror. "We're home,
my lady."

"Well, look at that," Godric said, smiling at Eva, "you're right
yet again, darling."

Her groom gave him a sheepish grin. "Aye. Reckon you'd better
get used to that, my lord."

Godric threw back his head and laughed.

Epilogue

Later . . .

Adam sat on the thick blanket, Mia leaning against his side, both of them staring out at the last revelers enjoying the remnants of the lawn party.

Gabriel and Drusilla had rounded up Gabriel's son, two of Ramsay's children, and Lord Salford's little boy—a quiet, sad child who seemed to have taken on the aspect of his moody parent—and were attempting to teach the unruly group that croquet mallets could be used for something other than weapons.

Lord and Lady Ramsay had disappeared into the small spinney on the far side of the lake, no doubt happy to enjoy some time to themselves while their children were being entertained.

Lady Ramsay's twin sons—remarkably similar not only in looks but in posture—were standing on either side of Mel, who was basking in the glow of so much undivided male attention.

The sight made Adam look for Lord Byer. The viscount was leaning against the ravaged banquet table, his arms crossed over his chest as he regarded Melissa and her coterie with a slight, perplexed frown on his handsome face.

Eva and her new swain were seated on one of the benches inside the folly, looking out over the lake as the sun dipped low. They were not touching, but their heads were close together and they appeared to be engaged in a conversation that required copious hand gestures from both parties. Adam's mouth twitched at the sight. Visel had better like arguments, heated and otherwise.

"Adam?"

"Hmm?"

"Are you angry at me?"

His lips curved into a genuine smile as he contemplated how she was going to weasel her way out of this. "And why would I be angry with you? Because you kept Eva's condition from me? Or because you conspired with another man's servant and one of my own grooms to abduct our daughter? Or because you organized a wedding, knowing full well it was not going to occur? Or because—"

Her hand, which had been lying beside his, crept closer, until she'd laced their fingers together. "Well, when you put it like that . . ."

Adam couldn't hold in his snort of disbelieving laughter, which of course told her that she'd won. Yet again.

"But you're not entirely correct, Adam."

He laced their hands tighter. "Oh?"

"There *is* going to be a wedding." She sat up and turned to him, looking up at him through those catlike green eyes that could still stop his heart. "You were so wise not to have disposed of that license you took up north with you."

He narrowed his eyes at the love of his life. "I suppose it helped that I couldn't seem to locate the license to dispose of it."

Her wicked lips curved into a smile that made him shockingly hard. "Yes, well, you know how careless I can be with my correspondence, leaving it on your desk, my desk—"

"In locked drawers to which only I have the key," he finished for her. "Or to which only I *should* have the key, I suppose I should say."

She brandished her dimples at him, and that, as they say, was the end of that.

"Well," he said in a voice that was mortifyingly gruff with desire. "I suppose it all worked out for the best." He glanced at Byer, who'd switched his brooding gaze to Eva and Visel now that Mel and the twins had wandered down to the lake and were messing about with the rowboats. "I suppose not the best for everyone," he amended.

"Oh, I don't know," Mia mused, following his gaze. "I think Tommy only believed himself to be in love. I think the reality of Eva frightened him. You saw how much they argued once they became betrothed."

Adam gestured to Eva and Visel. Eva was now standing, one hand on her hip, shaking her forefinger at her betrothed.

Mia dismissed the bickering not-yet-newlyweds with an airy wave. "Oh, well that's different."

Adam snorted.

"I'm serious, Adam. It is obvious Lord Visel adores her spirit and he, himself, is not overly concerned with appearances or the opinions of others. Tommy, on the other hand . . . Well, I think he was drawn to Eva's independence, but he really craves a more steady, conservative woman."

Adam watched with horror as his wife's eyes slid down to the lake. One of the twins was in a boat with Mel, the other in his own boat, and the three young people were slapping the water with oars and soaking each other while trying to tip the other boat over.

"I wonder," Mia mused. "Young Richard is too serious, but Lucien might just—"

"If you even *consider* meddling with Ramsay's family, I will beat you and then lock you in the dungeon."

She gave him a melting look. "Oh, Adam, you say the sweetest things." She lifted their joined hands and stared up at him with hot eyes as she gave him a lingering kiss that employed both lips and tongue, the gesture more erotic than another woman stripping down to the skin.

Adam shook his head at her and she grinned.

And then, inexorably, her eyes moved toward the gloomy viscount and then back to the activity on the water, her expression that of a general surveying his troops.

Adam gave a weak laugh of surrender and fell back onto the

blanket. Well, at least it wasn't *him* she was turning her formidable mind toward.

Still, he thought as he sighed, closed his eyes, and listened to the sound of his family and friends talking, laughing, and, yes, arguing— he couldn't help pitying the four young people who had inadvertently captured his devious wife's attention.

Adam's lips curled into a grin. Those poor children had no clue what was in store for them.

Author's Note

In order to maintain timelines between the first two books in the Rebels of the *Ton* series, I've taken liberties with dates for the thoroughbred breeding season.

The natural season for horses to conceive is roughly April to August. However, the growth of thoroughbred racing has had a tremendous impact on horse breeding cycles and the breeding season has been artificially manipulated to ensure that horses foal as close to January 1st as possible.

In the interest of historical veracity, I've chosen to portray the public's perception of mental illness closer to what it would have been in 1816, rather than what it is today.

Keep in mind that Western society used extreme procedures such as lobotomies—the majority of which were performed on female patients—to treat some forms of mental illness as late as the 1970s and '80s.

Not until the later part of the twentieth century has society begun to approach mental illness with a degree of humanity.

Please read on for an excerpt from *Infamous*,
the next Rebels of the *Ton* novel by Minerva Spencer.

Chapter 1

"Quit yanking on your cravat, Richard—you look as though you've been mauled by those rats you're so bloody fond of," Lucien said under his breath.

Richard laughed. "Thank you, Luce, I can always count on you to give me the words with the bark still on them."

Lucien's cheeks darkened. "Sorry."

Richard couldn't help noticing that his twin's eyes were in constant motion as he searched the swelling crowds for something. Or someone.

And Richard could guess who.

"I don't mean to be an arse, Rich," Lucien said. "It's just—"

"I know, I know. It's a burden to have a barnacle like me stuck to your side." Richard patted his brother's shoulder.

Lucien snorted. "Idiot."

"Fool."

They both grinned.

Richard squinted around at the multitude of people packing the receiving area of the Duke of Stanford's town house. "Remind me why I'm here again," he asked his far better dressed, more attractive, and more gregarious identical twin.

Well, identical in theory.

In addition to the spectacles Richard wore and his brother did not, Richard was a good stone and a half lighter than Lucien, who'd filled out in the chest and shoulders in a way Richard hadn't quite managed yet.

And then there were the spots that had plagued them both from age fourteen. Lucien's had magically disappeared when he'd turned seventeen, but Richard's had only gone away this past year.

So, identical, but different. Richard smirked at the thought.

"You're here for the girls," Lucien reminded him, somehow able to speak while smiling, a new skill and something that must have been on the curriculum at Eton his last year—the year Richard had skipped, instead going straight to university.

Richard snorted. "Yes, because all the girls were so impressed by the way I trod upon—" he made a frustrated *tsk*ing sound. "The devil! I can't even recall the poor girl's name."

"Nobody remembers that incident except you," Lucien said. "Well, and likely her. I don't recall her name, either. You need to stop thinking that nobody likes you, Rich. If you just put yourself out a bit, you'd see."

He could not believe his twin could be so oblivious of the insults, mocking names, and even an ode, that had circulated about Richard this Season. He could only think that Lucien was so insensible because he was falling deeper in love by the day and could see nothing other than one spectacularly beautiful face. Whether she was in the room or not.

"And," Lucien added, "if a roomful of pretty women isn't enough reason to be here, remember your promise to Mama."

Oh, that was hitting below the belt.

Unfortunately, it was true. If Richard hadn't—in an extremely weak moment—promised their mother to stick it out for one Season, he could have been tramping the Fenlands and adding to his already considerable beetle collection.

But their mother, Baroness Ramsay, had approached him just after he and Lucien had returned from a year of unfettered hedonism on the Continent, and he had foolishly capitulated.

So, here he was. Thank God it was getting near the end of the
Season because he wasn't sure how much more tomfoolery he could
bear. In Richard's opinion, a London Season was remarkably like a
term at Eton, but with girls to join in the mockery.

Richard sighed and scanned the crowd. And then immediately
wished he hadn't. Because, dead ahead, was the Duke of Dowden,
Richard's worst tormentor from Eton.

"Good Lord," he muttered beneath his breath, turning so that
Dowden wouldn't spot him.

The duke hadn't changed a whit in the almost three years since
Richard had last seen him. He was still the physical embodiment of
male perfection, tall, broad shouldered, and handsome. And he still
had the same punishing wit and barbed tongue.

It didn't matter what Richard did or said; Dowden would abuse
him. And only the two of them knew the reason why.

The names, digs, and even a snide ode some wit had composed
about him, didn't bother Richard any more now than they had at
school. However, it *was* a damned shame that Dowden had so much
influence over the ladies.

Especially over one girl in particular: Miss Celia Trent.

Just thinking Miss Trent's name gave Richard a heavy feeling in
his groin—a situation with the potential to embarrass him right here
in the middle of the Duchess of Stanford's ballroom if Richard wasn't
careful.

He wasn't the only bloke who suffered such a physical reaction
to the woman's sensual, almost overripe beauty, but he *was* the only
man in the room whose twin was madly in love with her.

Richard felt like a dirty dog about the way his body reacted to
the woman his brother hoped to marry, but he was a human animal
in his prime breeding years, and he could hardly control his body's
reaction to such stimulus.

Could he?

But he *could* control how he behaved. And so he strictly main-
tained a respectful reserve toward the object of his lust and his brother's
love.

Not that his behavior mattered a whit to Miss Trent, who seemed to have taken an aversion to Richard from the first time they met.

Well, after she married his brother, they would have years to become accustomed to each other.

Lucien leaned close to him and said, "I'm going to speak to Celia's father tomorrow."

"Why do you feel you have to marry her, Luce?" Richard demanded. "Just because you kissed her?"

Lucien hissed. "Would you keep your bloody voice down?" He glanced around, as if anyone else cared about their conversation. "You know I've been thinking about it for weeks now. Long before the kiss."

"Yes, but you only started mentioning *marriage* since that irritating lawn party a few days ago—which was also the same day—"

"Yes, yes, you already announced that, thank you very much. It so happens that that particular . . . issue is what has made the matter, er, pressing."

"Why?"

Lucien rolled his eyes. "You know why."

"I don't, actually. It's not as if you ruined her." Richard snorted at that phrase. "*Ruined her*," he repeated. "How stupid and dramatic that sounds. Have you ever given any thought to that phrase and what it means? As if she were some sort of object, like a plate you dropped and *ruined* because it is now broken. It's not as if kissing or sexual intercourse can only happen one time, so how can you ruin a woman by having sex with her? I have sex with delightful regularity. And yet nobody says that *I* am ruined."

Lucien was staring at him in a familiar way. Richard could almost predict what his brother would say: *What is wrong with you?*

"What?" he asked when Luce only stared.

"Mother must have dropped you on your head. That is all I can think of to account for it."

"Besides," Richard said, ignoring the tired insult, "I saw her after you kissed her. I can tell you without equivocation that she most certainly did not appear *ruined*. Perhaps you should think on it a few days."

"I don't want to. There have to be dozens of men soliciting her father for her hand."

Richard wanted to ask why they'd do so if she was so clearly *ruined*, but kept that unhelpful question to himself.

Instead, he said, "Maybe some of them have also—"

One dangerous look from his twin's narrowed eyes froze the rest of the words in his throat.

Instead, Richard soothed his brother. "Even if there are a hundred men, none of them can be more eligible than you. Indeed, you possess the only thing Trent is looking for in a son-in-law: lots and lots of brass. Even I, as woefully ignorant of *ton* gossip as I am, know the man is below the hatches. If Miss Trent knocks you back, her father would probably marry you himself."

"Very droll."

Richard could see his brother wasn't listening. "Are you sure about this, Luce? You've hardly had a chance to live life or explore the world. We had a smashing time on our trip, didn't we?"

"Yes."

"Well, don't you think—"

"I love her." Lucien's voice was low and firm.

Love. Richard rolled his eyes and heaved a sigh at the ridiculous word. It was his contention that human beings were not designed for monogamy. He strongly suspected what his brother was feeling was actually lust and attraction.

How could a person possibly fall in love with somebody when you were allowed no more than a few minutes to chat with them a couple times a week?

Richard considered trying to tell his brother that it was his breeding imperative that was driving him to distraction and sending him to Miss Trent's father's house tomorrow, hat in hand.

But those were both subjects on which his mother had told him he must be circumspect.

"People don't care to be compared to ducks or beetles or horses, Richard. You must reserve your observations on man's biology for those who can appreciate and understand them."

Lucien was not one of those people.

There was no point in arguing. Besides, Richard could understand his brother's fascination—if not love—for Miss Celia Trent.

Before meeting Miss Trent, Richard had believed that all healthy, attractive, unattached females under the age of forty were largely the same. Which was to say desirable. He'd never felt his brother's brand of madness for one woman in particular.

But one look at Miss Trent's gorgeous face, voluptuous body, and lively blue eyes had turned him into a gaping fool just like every other man—married *or* single.

Connect with Us

Visit us online at
KensingtonBooks.com
to read more from your favorite authors, see books
by series, view reading group guides, and more.

Join us on social media
for sneak peeks, chances to win books and prize packs,
and to share your thoughts with other readers.

facebook.com/kensingtonpublishing
twitter.com/kensingtonbooks

Tell us what you think!

To share your thoughts, submit a review,
or sign up for our eNewsletters, please visit:
KensingtonBooks.com/TellUs.